ELLIE'S MINOTAUR

Ellie's Minotaur

Flynn Alexander

Facing Goliath Publishing

First published in the United States by Facing Goliath Publishing LLC.

www.FacingGoliathPublishing.com

ISBN: 979-8-9888085-2-7 (paperback)
IBSN: 979-8-9888085-1-0 (e-book)

First Edition: 2023

To my amazing daughter, who inspired me to pick up writing again and gave me the courage to publish this novel, something I had given up back in my youth.

One

Cold pressed against her cheek, hands, and forearms. Her consciousness aroused but she refused to let her eyes open. Other senses came back, one by one, whether she liked it or not. A musty, stale odor filled the air, the smell of *old* and the smell of *forgotten*. She felt the cold on her body; she heard a thundering silence; she tasted a dryness in her mouth that felt like a lump, as if she had stuffed a handful of cotton balls between her teeth.

Finally she relented, and let her eyes flutter open, just a crack, then more.

Her vision was blurred and it took several seconds to focus. The room was in fading light and she was lying on the floor. Her eyes adjusted to the darkness as she took in her surroundings.

She wanted to squeeze them shut again. The room was empty, dirty, and old. A window lay on the wall in front of her. Bars split the fading daylight that was filtering through, and the brick around the window was chipped and crumbling. She forced herself to slowly sit up, pushing herself up on her hip and propping up her arm.

Pain shot through her right side and her head felt like it was splitting in two. Even the dim light from outside seemed bright, causing her to squint.

She must have had quite a night partying. She couldn't remember any of it, however.

Am I hung over? Why am I here?

She couldn't remember coming here or ever being here before. She didn't remember drinking, though her dry mouth and splitting headache seemed to be telling her, and quite forcefully, that she had. Or something else.

Do I drink?

The realization that she didn't know shocked her. In fact, she didn't know anything - not how she got here, not why she was on the floor, not even her own name.

She shook her groggy head, light exploding in front of her eyes like fireworks, causing her gasp. The sound seemed loud in the empty room, like the rest of the world was silently on hold. She took a deep breath and tried to compose herself. The fog was lifting, albeit slowly.

She attempted to stand, a slow, deliberate process as her body ached and felt unsteady. The room gently spun as she pushed to her knees, accelerated as she brought her knee up and planted her foot. She pushed to her feet and everything began to lurch violently, almost pulsing in front of her eyes and swirling like a circus pinwheel in a funhouse. She stumbled forward toward the window and fell back to her knees, vomiting a stream against the wall below the window.

She panted on her knees, clenching her eyes shut and tried to wait for the vertigo to pass. After several minutes of deep breathing, the world steadied and she once again tried to stand. The room settled this time and she was able to slowly move the last couple feet to the window, her rubbery legs wobbling like a newborn fawn trying to stand.

She looked out and saw fading green grass, on the verge of discoloring to brown leading to a spattering of large trees with few leaves left hanging on. She realized she was in a building that was several stories high, and estimated she was on the third or fourth floor. Down below she saw an empty and slightly overgrown circle drive, with leaves blowing under the trees. Looking off to her right out the window she saw a road that stretched away from the circle drive and to an empty intersection in the distance. The naked trees allowed her to see through them to the intersection, and beyond to a faded yellow building that looked like a house sitting on the corner.

The cloud in her head swirled as if being ushered by a stiff breeze as the house seemed to stir something in her memory, though it remained just beyond her grasp. She felt a familiarity with it, but could not quite get a grip on what or why. She scanned her view, but even with the leaves mostly fallen, too many trees prevented the view of anything else.

She pulled at the bars on the window, but they were solid and cold, marking her prison cell and splitting the fading light to mark her with a pinstripe jumpsuit. She pressed her hands to the glass, which was beginning to frost with condensation as the sun was setting over the building behind her. She gathered that it was getting toward late fall, and she was facing east, making the yellow house to the southeast. The house was already becoming a beacon for her, an anchor that she could cling to as she tried to jog her memory.

The building dropped down to a single floor off to her left and she could see an entry way as that section jutted out to the north. It seemed out of place. This beautiful architecture extended north to south with high windows, and a sudden flat fixture out front that looked like an old 1960's era school building, very drab government and bureaucratically lacking in character.

As she stared, a faded outline seemed to materialize around and over the flat structure, almost like a pencil drawing held over top of the window, shone by the light coming in but allowing the outside to pass through the paper. The outline slid in and out of focus, floating like a dream. It rose as high as the surrounding architecture with four stories, three of large windows and the fourth reaching into the roof with a single tower in the middle stretching to the sky like it was out of a fairytale. At its peak was a spire extending toward the clouds and cutting through wisps of fog, the full moon shining down from beyond it. The fading sunlight had darkened and the purple glow of night wrapped the spire. The glow gave the entrance a majestic quality, a strength, giving the structure an aura of power.

She blinked, and just like that it was gone. The flat structure remained with the moon just beginning to peek its face out as the sky darkened toward twilight. She felt a let down, disappointed at the disappearance of the regal structure.

Shaking her head, with smaller firecrackers erupting this time, she turned back to the room she found herself in. She scanned the chamber again. At her feet was a rag, the size of a small dish towel. She picked it up, and it had a strong odor, causing her head to swoon at the smell. She dropped it away before the odor took her consciousness again. The rest of the room was dirty and in ruin. The walls had marks and holes in them, and the room carried a musty odor to her nose. Black dirt and mold filled the corners, the chunks of plaster a faded and colorless gray.

Sucking in another deep breath, she still failed to understand how she came to be here. She turned around to make her way to the portion of the building with the entryway. Flat or majestic, it appeared to be a front door and way out of this run down dump.

Time to get out of here, she thought.

Walking to the doorway, she hit the lightswitch by to the right of the frame.

Nothing happened. She flicked it up and down, frowning. With an overwhelming sense of trepidation, she leaned out into the hallway. The apprehension felt heavy on her, though she didn't understand why. Sure the atmosphere was creepy, but with no memory of how she got here, she shouldn't feel almost paralyzed with fear, should she?

Regardless, all she saw was the dark swirl of purples and

black off to her right and left. Letting her eyes adjust, she realized there was another door with the last rays of daylight bleeding through off to her left. Of course, this was the opposite way she wanted to go, away from that front exit she saw out the window.

The hairs on the back of her neck rose. She could hear her heart thundering in her chest, her head pounding in rhythm with the pulsating. She could make out items in the hall on the floor that appeared to be garbage, and graffiti littered the decrepit and broken walls.

There must be a stairwell off to the right, she thought. *It has to lead down to that entrance lobby area, and my exit.*

She again glanced into the darkness, then back toward the light in the room down the hall. The light flickered into the hallway, as if riding a gentle wind, making it appear to be more than just the last rays of the sun coming through the windows. She began taking steps toward the light, flashing and darting its meager glow out into the hallway, feeling lead involuntarily. Her feet barely cleared the ground and made a scraping sound as they dragged her forward. Her heart thundered as the door loomed in front of her, light dancing, acting as a siren drawing her in, pulling her toward it. The thought of mosquitos being pulled to bug zapper flashed across her mind.

It doesn't end well for the skeeters.

A voice in her mind told her to stop, to turn around and run the other way, to curl up in the corner, to go back to the room and close her eyes, to do anything, anything but keep moving forward. She tried to relay this message to her feet but somewhere along the way it wasn't making it through and her feet kept scraping the floor forward. The doorway started to come into view.

She slowly rounded the corner into the threshold, moving tentatively, with her eyes squeezed to slits, ready to clamp them shut to keep out anything bad.

This is not me anymore.

The thought startled her into opening her eyes, and before she could wonder why she would think such a thing, the contents of the room came into view and shook her.

The flickering in the room was emitted from a series of candles assembled on the floor of the room. A pentagram was drawn with a candle at each point. The candles had been burning for a bit as the wax pooled at their base. Scanning the room, words were written all over the wall in red.

Inflamed words such as *DIE BITCH!* and *RUN WHORE RUN!* Were strewn all over the walls. More unsettling were *YOU CAN'T HIDE* head high by the window, *BURN IN HELL* underneath it, and *TRY TO RUN EL* scrawled at an angle up the wall. Others began but she couldn't make out the message as they deteriorated into frantic and angry scribbles of paint.

Ellie felt her heart slamming against her rib cage, her chest shaking and shuddering. She could feel her breaths coming in ragged gasps, her chest too tight to allow her lungs to fill fully.

Get a hold of yourself El.

She tried to take deep breaths and get control of herself. She wanted to sink to her knees and clench her eyes until the nightmare was over like a small child that pulls the blankets over her head until the bogeyman is gone, but she forced herself to look around once again.

OK. I'm OK.

She realized that she was calling herself Ellie, as in Eleanor, as in El. For a moment, she felt a triumph, a piece of herself coming back and a bit of control. Directly following that, however, was the realization that all these crude and violent messages on the walls were directed *at her*.

I'M COMING FOR YOU

Two

Tears were rolling down her cheeks and she felt herself shaking. Her knees felt weak, the weight of her body too much to keep upright. The silence in the room was deafening and the room was spinning in circles, every word sprayed over the wall seemed to be pulsating and whirling around. The crimson color - that of death.

After a few moments of ragged, rapid breaths the room began to slow. Ellie began to get a hold of herself, bit by bit. She willed the strength to return to her, *demanded it* from herself. She focused her eyes on the words across the room, a derogatory slang that was unflattering. She stared at it, focusing on it so hard that everything else in the room faded.

When it stopped and everything stabilized, she took a

deep breath in, all the way to the bottom of her lungs, feeling it all the way to her belly, held it for a couple of moments, and then let it out with a thundering *WHOOSH!* that echoed off the walls of the room. It was so violent that the candles at her feet flickered and threatened to go out. It was just how Anna had told her to do it.

Back in control, she felt a surge of anger.

You are in some deep shit here, she thought.

Wait, who's Anna? Her confusion returning, she felt on the tip of her brain more of her memory floating, just out of reach, an apparition taunting her.

She shook her head and focused on what was in front of her. The walls were similarly chipped, cracked, and failing as in the other room. Plaster coating was falling away to reveal yellow brick underneath. The window was barred and there was a dark room off to the right. There was fallen plaster and chunks of brick all over the room, and an old tarp covered in dust in the corner. The tarp was faded and seemed to exude despair, as if to say that she wasn't getting out of here and she would end up in the corner just like it was.

The pentagram had a skull in the middle of it, what looked like that of a small steer with the horns splaying out to the side. The horns had been painted crimson as well, drips had pooled and partially dried off each. At least she told herself it was paint. It seemed to sneer at her, finding wicked amusement in her fear.

As she continued to scan the room, she saw nothing more of interest. The writings covered the walls with various attacks directed at her and what was going to happen to her.

They were written in blood, or something intended to look like blood. They were not important and she let them fade into the background, no longer seeing them.

She peered into the dark room and saw a silhouette staring back at her. She took a step backwards and her heart stopped cold.

The shape moved in unison. She squinted and then reached down, grabbing one of the candles off the pentagram. Using it, she slowly approached the dark room.

As she made it to the threshold, she realized that it was a bathroom off the main room. She slowly crossed into the room, illuminating the mirror above the sink and saw her reflection. The surface did not appear to be a traditional mirror, but something more like some kind of metal, making her reflection a bit distorted, adding to the haunting picture staring back at her. Her face was pale and her eyes sunken, the normal amber radiance dull of its glow. Her dark brown hair, normally down to her shoulders in the back and framing her face, was tousled and erratic. She had a dark bruise above her left eye that caused her eyebrow to cover part of her eye and there was dried blood around her mouth. As she raised her hand to her eye, pain shot through her head. A brief but scattered memory of a man grabbing her, spinning her around and hitting her, full fist, her falling into a wood desk. She remembered a room, someone screaming. She remembered hands around her neck, and squeezing.

She moved the collar of her shirt and sure enough, dark bruises, some shaped like fingers, covered the pale skin around her throat. Her earlier sense of dread made sense now, a foreboding raised by her subconscious. Further details refused to return to her.

She reached down to turn on the sink. She hesitated and held her breath, not sure if she could take the disappointment if no water flowed. The building appeared abandoned, the water likely shut off. She turned the knob, air rushed out, water sputtered then began to flow. She slurped the water down her scratchy throat, feeling the cotton mouth feeling starting to dissipate. She splashed cold water on her face, over and over, then drank more. She ran her wet fingers through her hair and straightened it back down. Despite its coppery flavor, she had never tasted anything better. It was refreshing as a dunk in the bay or standing in the rush of a stream.

Ellie took another deep breath, all the way down to the bottom of her lungs and let it erupt out of her.

A cleansing breath. Reset, start fresh, push forward.

She looked in the mirror again at herself. Color had already begun restoring her face. She stared deep into her own eyes, trying to find more of herself.

The eyes are the window to the soul, she thought.

She felt that fuzzy feeling again, as if that part of her was just out of reach. She took account of what she did remember.

My name is Eleanor, I go by Ellie.

I was attacked in a room with a desk. A friend was there and was screaming. Who was she? She couldn't remember. She shook her head again, trying to free the haze. It was as if the wisps of fog that floated around the spire she imagined earlier were still floating inside her head.

I woke up here, on the floor. I had cotton-mouth, and there was the foul smelling rag. Drugged perhaps, like in the movies, with a rag to knock me out?

But why drug her and leave her here? Where was she?

If she was drugged, that likely explained her foggy head and the strange vision she saw out the window earlier - a hallucinatory side effect.

She knew it was autumn, probably getting late with the chill in the air. She rubbed her arms for warmth, as there was no heat in the building. The sun was almost set at this point and the start of the moon was peaking out. She could feel the temperature dropping with night's darkness closing in.

She scanned her body head to toe, feeling her legs, abdomen, and her back for any other signs of attack or injury. Her back was stiff, and her head was still pounding, she found a sensitive area on her rib cage, and it was indeed discolored with bruising. She had been put through the ringer. As she pressed on the wound, a flash of a foot slamming into her ribs, knocking the breath out of her flashed in her mind.

Some of it started to come back.

*   *   *

I was in the office, with a big desk and file cabinets on the back wall. To the right was a doorway that led to the back. I was smiling and talking with her friends. The small, strong girl was Anna, and the plump older lady was Virginia, Ginny for short. Wait, no not Anna. Who is Anna? The girl there was Kayleigh. She was short and plain, the kind of person that was just there, just kind of taking up space and existing. Ginny was there though. She was a jolly lady, all smiles with her curly gray hair bouncing as she laughed. We were all laughing about something, I was putting books back on the shelf to the left of the door. I had just said something funny, and everyone was laughing.

I remember feeling safe, I remember feeling loved, and I remember that I hadn't felt that in a long time, if ever. It was just after lunch, I remember the clock on the wall showing just after one o'clock.

Then the door flung open and a dark figure rushed in. It's just a silhouette rushing forward, as if made of black smoke, without a concrete structure. The shape struck me with a forearm across my upper chest. I was flung up against the bookcase, the books raining down on me. The fist came rushing toward me and hit me in the face. I fell backwards, spinning and hit the desk with my head.

Ginny and Kayleigh were screaming. The room spun as I looked up, Ginny stepping back with a look of horror on her face, Kayleigh running toward the assailant, either to get to the door or to try to fight him. She tried to get by him and he grabbed her. She struck him and tried to get around him, but then he hit back, and she went down. He reached down and covered her face with a rag, and she stopped struggling. He let go and she sank to the floor.

As she fell he turned back and kicked his foot out at me. It struck me in the ribs as I was trying to get up, to help, to join the fight. I rolled away as my ribs erupted in pain. I scrambled to my feet and rushed him blind with rage.

But he was ready. He sidestepped and I tripped on a book, falling right into the strong arms, the rag quickly clamped over my face. I tried to hold my breath and claw at it, I tried to turn my head and get a look at his face, I tried to free myself. His face was a mist, a darkness, nothing, a vacant black that went on forever. I was slammed to the floor and a hand wrapped around my neck, pressing into the floor. The fingers dug in and the rag was pressed harder against my face. As I finally couldn't hold anymore and breathed in, the fumes from the rags filled my lungs and my head.

The darkness rose from his face, wrapped itself around my head, and I began falling away, the view from my eyes getting further, and further. I fell into the abyss and the distant light blinked out of sight.

And there was nothing but darkness.

*   *   *

Ellie remained staring into the mirror, willing more to come back. She was still unsure of much of who she was, but the cover had started to peel. She felt more was closer.

Who were those friends she remembered? Why did she feel so loved, and why did that feel so foreign? What was the dark shape that accosted her? Why was she here? Why was she left here?

Is she alone here?

She thought back to all the writings on the wall and turned

around, candle in hand, stepping out of the bathroom. The stretched candle light flickered against the wall, illuminating the words.

I'M COMING FOR YOU

Three

The young girl of ten limped home. She had taken herself to school for the last time. After relentless bullying from other kids about her clothes' state of disarray, she had been beaten by Anita Sanchez, a hefty, relentless seventh grader. She didn't even know why - Anita had hit her from behind as soon as they passed the basketball courts heading away from school. Kids surrounded them and cheered her on while she hit, kicked, stomped, and belittled Ellie.

Ellie didn't fight back - she never did. The beatings were normal, old bruises became new bruises. The overcrowded and underfunded Ariad Oaks MIddle School never noticed, bringing in new, young teachers and administrators ready to change the world only to have them leave shortly after burned out and beaten down, their ideologies and hope crushed under the weight of a dilapidated school system and a community that didn't care.

For once, she didn't even try to hide as one of the Drug Cars passed by, it's bass rattling its frame and Ellie's eardrums. She just didn't care anymore - the release of being an accidental victim in the crossfire that erupted through the neighborhoods might be better than what was next. It happened all the time. It had happened last fall and her favorite teacher at the school, a young man named Seth Johnson who hadn't been disillusioned yet, had been gunned down. Mr. Johnson had been at the school for just over a year and managed to maintain his exuberance. He had stopped a fight Ellie had been involved in the year before. Well, it wasn't a fight, more like a public beating, but he had stepped in. He had taken a lot of time helping her get her reading caught up and told her that she could go anywhere, be anyone, in a good book.

The car continued by with its purple lights underneath and smoke billowing from tinted and slightly cracked windows.

Remembering Mr. Johnson made her feel worse, if that was possible. She had already endured a difficult day, and based on how she left the "house" this morning, the night was only beginning.

Another man was at the apartment, a filthy public housing project where she had an old mattress she had found laying in the laundry room (it wasn't used for anything else). As she was leaving, the man had left and her mother had another score she was heating up to take. El wasn't sure what it was but it didn't matter. Her mother had only three states: angry, high, and passed out. In El's experience, passed out was the best, angry was the worst. Angry was when she blamed El for all her problems, which usually escalated in some form of beating.

Angry was last night.

Everything was Ellie's fault - every time she didn't have a hit, or money, or an easy life. To emphasize the point, her mother would hit her with anything near. A woman of only twenty-nine, she looked much older. Her body dilapidated and malnourished, ravaged by drugs, scarred from beating she herself had undertaken from her many suitors that called to trade drugs for her body. She could have been a beautiful woman with her jet black hair, dark brown eyes, high cheekbones, slender but strong physique - or what once was.

Ellie almost remembered what it had been like. She knew her mother had been pregnant young and the man had left her behind. She was pretty sure that her mom had given it a try, working and trying to take care of Ellie. Elizabeth Sloan had lived in cheap housing and worked whenever she could, scraping by for a while.

By the time Ellie was four though, the toll had beaten her into submission. Ellie didn't know much about her grandparents, but she had heard, usually in a drunken rage or on the other side of a high, that her grandpa had beaten her mom and her grandma. He had been a factory worker, working third shift and spending the rest of his time on his two hobbies: drinking and fighting. Either at the bar or at home, he would drink until he had to hit something.

When Ellie's mother had become pregnant, he had thrown her out. He wasn't going to feed another mouth. Her mother was just as angry, a surly woman who hated her husband but didn't have the means to do anything about it.

Ellie's mother made it at the start by claiming government assistance, living in section eight housing, and stealing when she could from her own parents. That well dried up when her mother had had enough of her father and blasted him with a twelve gauge while he sat in the decrepit lazy boy in front of the television after beating her mom for the last time. When someone finally complained about the smell, the police found him in the chair and her in the bathtub. A murder-suicide they called it.

That ended the little bit of help that Elizabeth did receive in helping raise her child. By this time, she had masked her pain and failures in plenty of alcohol, and was graduating on the spectrum. When Ellie was five, that's when the prostituting herself had started for Elizabeth, and not long after the heroin had started, when she could get it.

The years rolled by and the steady decline had wreaked havoc on Elizabeth's personality, mind, and body. She had managed to get Ellie to school when she had been partially lucid, but that was years ago and Ellie only went now because she wanted to.

The latest beating and the still painful loss of Mr. Johnson, who actually seemed to care for Ellie, was just too much. She didn't think she would even go back. Of course, the alternative at her "home" wasn't much better. This was the cycle that she went through: bad morning at home, she sought release at school, bad day at school and she vowed to never go back on her way home, bad night at home until she hid and went to sleep.

She wasn't sure she could take another night like last night at home either. Thankfully, Elizabeth was typically too weak to inflict much damage on El and she could just ride it out until she tired herself out. Last night, though, she was on a roll. She hadn't had a fix in several days and was losing control. She tried to offer herself and when that was refused, she tried to offer Ellie. Ellie had overheard and shrunk away, slipping up to her safe space up in the attic of the project housing. This clever find had been her escape for years. Though not exactly comfortable, it had so far protected her from any abuse at the hands of her mother's suitors.

When she had come back down, hoping to find her mother asleep or gone, she was waiting. Obviously, she had not ended up with a fix so instead she summoned extra strength and attacked Ellie with an old broom handle, moving to her fists when it broke.

The bruises had barely formed when Ellie was forced to take the beating from Anita. Now Ellie had to head home and see what state the apartment was in. She hoped that her mother had had enough "stuff" to have her knocked out.

Ellie rounded the last corner stepping over trash blowing in the wind. It was warm for late winter and the sun was still shining its last few rays before calling it a night. She walked along a chain link fence in disarray, keeping her eyes away from the group of men huddled at the end of the vacant lot. She ignored the unintelligible shouts from the old man sleeping in trash on the doorstep of one of the project buildings. She turned up the steps to the last one in the row and walked through the open door, looking pathetic hanging on one bent hinge. Even the graffiti on the walls seemed sad, old, and listless.

She climbed the lonely steps to the third floor, passing a

young man sleeping (or so she told herself), half on the steps, half on the landing. His face was deathly pale and his eyes appeared open to a narrow slit. Saliva hung from his partially open mouth and sores ran up and down his forearms.

Ellie arrived at the door and pushed it open, stepping inside. The apartment was essentially bare except for what might have been a couch in a previous life and a small table. There was a TV on the floor by the wall that had never worked. The rest of the floor was covered in garbage, everything from old cans of food to needles and condom wrappers. The rotting smell and the scattering of cock roaches didn't phase her. She simply wanted to hide in her "room" where she had some control.

Her mother was passed out on the couch as she carefully crept past, trying not to step in anything too disgusting. She had just found these shoes in a trash can a few miles away a couple days ago and she didn't want them covered in any of the nastiness. It was amazing what people threw out. She had found some incredible items in the garbage, as long as you knew where to look. Plus, it gave her a reason to stay out of the apartment.

She circled the couch to put a blanket over her mother. Regardless of the hostility and hate from her mother, she was still her mother and she had a sense of duty.

Upon coming around the couch she found Elizabeth Sloan's eyes wide open, lifeless and vacant, her body covered in her own vomit, traces of blood scattered throughout. Her body was contorted in pain and her mouth twisted in terror. The smells emanating off the couch revolted El and her stomach flipped in circles. She turned and threw up her lunch - a carton of milk she slipped in the cafeteria at school earlier that day.

It could easily be argued that Ellie had always had to take care of herself. However, this day was the day that her adulthood officially started. She was on her own at ten years old.

She simply turned and left the apartment, walked back down the steps, passed the man lying on the landing, now convulsing violently, turned left out on the street and began walking.

She didn't weep, didn't shed a tear. She had always been alone, a burden, a dingy adrift in the violent seas of the projects - *unwanted.*

Eleanor Sloan walked as the sun set, kept walking through the night, never once looking back. Never once knowing where she was going, but knowing this - she didn't want to be here and no one was going to come look for her.

*   *   *

Ellie remembered that day, flooding back to her. The lovelessness, the loneliness, the isolation, and the fear.

Unwanted.

This all flashed through her head in an instant as the flickering light jumped, illuminating the hideous insults briefly before they passed back into the shadows. This went through her head while the deafening roar erupted through-out the building, freezing the blood in her veins, rendering her immobile.

She suddenly became that scared ten year old again, and wanted to just curl up, close her eyes, pull the covers over her head, and wait for all the scary to pass. But it didn't pass then, and it won't pass now.

I keep moving. When it's bad, I get moving and keep moving, she thought.

All of this in the three seconds the roar rattled the building.

She moved quickly to the door, willing her heart to stop thundering so hard so she could hear. What she heard chilled her to the core. There was a snorting, an animal-like panting, echoing down the hall. It seemed to be all around her and she couldn't get a sense of the direction it was coming from.

I guess the question of whether I am alone has been answered at least, she thought. *And it's a pretty emphatic NO.*

She peaked her head around the doorframe, quickly scan-ning one way, then the other. She pulled back to process what she saw, which was -

Nothing.

The hallway appeared completely empty in both direc-tions. She still heard the snorting. Puzzled, she stole another glance. Still nothing.

She had to get out of the room. There was only one way out, leaving her cornered if she stayed put. She stepped out into the hall, leaving the room and the bathroom behind. The light from the candle didn't make it very far in the hall. She held it up high to get as much distance. Coupling this with the last few rays of daylight sprinkling through doorways into the hall, she saw -

Nothing. Still nothing.

"Fuck" she muttered to herself, and started trotting back the way she had come, hoping to find the staircase at the end of the hall to lead her to her original destination upon waking. Ellie focused on the first floor entry she had seen from the window. She hugged the wall, as if that would provide her with protection, and scurried down the corridor. Almost tip-toeing in her run, she tried to make as little noise as possible.

She was half way there when the thudding of a door crossbar echoed down the hall in front of her and the entry to the stairwell swung open. What happened next was in slow motion.

Light erupted from the stairwell, illuminating a figure as it stepped across the threshold. The snorting increased in intensity and volume. The figure entering the hallway had black leather boots, black pants leading up to a black jacket. Its hands were just black blobs, with what appeared to be no discernible shape. The figure stood well over six feet tall, and on its shoulders was an inhuman, grotesque face.

Ellie took all this in while she put on the breaks of her trot, her feet skidding forward and causing her to topple backwards on her backside, still sliding forward toward that *thing's* jaws. Her eyes could not break away from the creatures blazing eyes, crimson red and glowing. She saw horns reaching away and toward the ceiling.

She skidded to a stop, still clutching the candle, flickering but holding strong from the fall. There was a staring contest for what seemed to be an eternity but was no more than a split second.

"*ELLLLLLLLIIIIEEEEEEE*" hissed through the air, floating towards her. She remained paralyzed, until the things hand came away from its body. Previously hidden in the shadows was a large item in its paw. It had a long stem leading up to a head of two large oval shapes.

Ellie could see a substance drip off the head of the double bladed ax and drop to the floor. This, along with another ear shattering roar, broke her paralysis. It didn't take a lot of imagination to determine what that substance was…

She spun around, sprang to her feet, and ran, legs pinwheeling on the floor like a cartoon. Traction caught and she bolted forward.

Her legs pumped, pushing her back in the other direction, past the room with the pentagram and the steer skull, and onward into the darkness, the candle, by the grace of God, stayed lit as she sprinted. She could hear the animal behind her, snorting, its large feet (hooves maybe?) slamming onto the floor of the hallway. She could hear the snorting turning to a deep, throbbing laughter as it pursued her.

Ellie reached the end of the hall and tried to take a sharp right. She slipped on fallen drywall pieces and went down, slamming into the wall. She picked herself up and pushed on, the candle gone for good. As she continued forward, losing her sense of direction, there was a split to her left, or the hallway continued forward. She felt the options as much as saw them in the gray gloom. She paused for a second, trying to decide, unable to make out detail in either direction.

She continued straight ahead for another twenty feet before slamming into a wall. Her hands broke some of the collision but her body followed through into the plaster. She saw stars in her head and heard the sound of the plaster pieces cascading to the floor, the sound incredibly loud in her ears.

A dead end, she thought, and almost chuckled out loud.

She turned around peering into the darkness, trying to find her pursuer. *Maybe it thought I went left.* She began feeling her way along the wall. The only light came from where she had come, through the little alcove and a room across that had the final fading daylight leaking through. Her hand struck something metal. She paused slowly, feeling along it.

A door. She felt along the frame until she located the handle. She began to slowly depress it, trying to be as quiet as she could, her heart thundering so loudly, she swore it could be heard down on the street and half way across town.

Then it was there. Out of the darkness emerged the *thing.* It stood before her and roared, five feet away. Ellie instinctively bolted to her left. With impossible speed for a *Thing* so large, it reached out and grabbed her by the hair with one massive hand. She felt herself yanked back, and thrown up against the wall. It held her there, and she could feel leather around her throat as the *Thing's* fingers tightened.

It let out a deep snarl as its crimson eyes bore into her and its foul breath enveloped her. It took a step backwards, pulling her away from the wall, and then slammed her back into it. Dazed, she stood up against the wall as it shifted the giant double headed ax from its left hand to both hands. It raised it to its shoulders, roared again and swung it violently toward her.

Ellie broke her haze just as the monster began to swing and she simply dropped. She hit the floor and bounced with her feet, lunging back to her right as the ax slammed into the wall above her. She sprinted back to the door. The monster lunged after her. She hit the door handle and yanked the door open. Diving through, she stumbled forward into more darkness. She could hear the snarls behind her, feel its breath on the back of her neck.

The floor disappeared from under her in the dark and she fell forward. She threw her hands out and was able to absorb most of the impact on the steps, turning her shoulder she rolled down the last few steps onto the landing and hit the far wall. She scooted along the floor away from where she fell until she was in the corner of the landing.

She peered back up the stairs and saw nothing but blackness. She sat in the dark, listening for her pursuer. Her whole body screamed from the abuse and the fall. Trying to convince herself to unwrap her arms from around her knees and head further down the stairwell to increase the distance from the creature, she found she was frozen in place. Rocking back and forth, a gentle sob drifted from her pursed lips, and tears pushed themselves past her clenched eyes.

Then she heard the gentle click of the door at the top of the stairs closing, and there was nothing else. She let the darkness completely envelope her as she curled up there, trying to quiet her panting and get control over herself.

And to process all that had happened.

Four

Without knowing how much time had passed, Ellie raised her head from her knees, still surrounded by darkness. Convinced (*please God please God*) that whatever had pursued her had retreated, she knew it was time to move. It didn't make sense, but then nothing about this did.

She reached out gingerly along the floor, terrified of what would await her in the darkness, until she found the lip of the first step. Crawling forward, highly aware of the noise of dragging herself across the concrete landing, she swung her legs over the edge and placed her feet on the second step. Reaching up like a blind man, she waved her arms until her hand struck the railing. It rattled as she grabbed it, the sound echoing down the stairwell. She yanked her hand back as if struck. The hand rail shook as it hung onto the crumbling wall by a thread.

After a moment of intent listening that yielded only the thundering of heartbeat in her ears, she decided nothing was coming after her and pulled to standing.

Slowly making her way down in the darkness she thought, *there must be a way out of here on the first floor.*

Her ribs burned as she raised her arm from falling down the steps, and she could feel the trickle of blood under her shirt. She focused on the beacon, that flat front (*spire to the clouds*) that she saw out the window.

She tried to prevent her gasping from making noise, but it seemed to echo off the walls of the stairwell. She didn't have her wind back yet from the fall, and all she could muster was short, ragged breaths. Each drove a burning pain through her chest like a hot fire poker behind her sternum and in her throat.

She just needed to make her way down these stairs.

The concrete leveled out and she was at the landing. She felt her way around the wall, the cool metal touch of the stairway door, on past it until she hit the corner. Tentatively, she lowered her hands along the wall, trying to locate the railing to continue down the steps.

The silence thundered around her, anxiety rising. The darkness seemed to be a tangible thing, wrapping itself like a boa constrictor. The purple and black tendrils weaving themselves around her head and torso, squeezing in on her. The weight of it pressed against her chest and ribs, preventing her from filling her lungs. She fought to keep the thoughts out and focus on the task at hand.

Why is this happening to me?

The victim-thoughts pressed in - these led to despair, inaction, and passiveness.

Keep it simple. Stairwell, first floor, exit.

The railing wasn't where it should be. She felt holes in the crumbling wall where it once held on.

Of course, it always has to be the hardest it can be, she whined to herself.

She fought those thoughts, but felt the grip slip. She heard a meek whimper and realized it had escaped her tightly pursed lips.

As she gingerly reached forward with her foot, she struck … something. It was a large chunk of smooth concrete. Why was it sitting on the floor? She moved her foot left and right, raised it up, and reached with her hands. She felt nothing in the darkness.

She probed with her foot, not striking anything. The concrete chunk sliding forward made a scraping noise on the landing, until it abruptly didn't. Moving her foot to the ground, her foot found nothing but open air, just at the same time as she registered an echo of the concrete chunk hitting the ground below. The recognition caused her to twist her body back, but her weight was off balance, and she tumbled forward. She threw her body backwards onto the ground as her foot went over the edge. Shin scraping jagged concrete, she managed to get her weight forward enough where her knees struck the top step. Scrambling, she quickly pulled herself up by pushing with her knees. Feeling a wave of adrenaline flow over her, she realized how close she had come to going over the edge. She crawled back to the edge and felt along the jagged concrete. The stairwell was just — gone. It seems it had collapsed, probably piled up on the first floor below.

Finally, the despair took over and she sank down the wall back to the floor.

Always to the floor.

As she felt the cold floor under her and sobbed in her chest, trying to limit the noise, she thought about the floor. Unwanted, cast aside, on the floor…

Five

Thirteen is a strange age, strange for any young woman entering adolescence, even worse for Ellie. She was in her second "home" since she had been picked up off the streets, this a youth living center known as the Sanctuary Home for Youths, though most of the kids called it the Sanctuary Home for Youth Teens, or just Shyt House. Ellie had no idea where it came from; she wasn't sure anyone knew, it had just been dubbed Shyt House at some point, the name stuck (and was well earned), and it had just been passed down.

Shyt House had been open in some form or another for twenty-three years. It had changed hands a few times, but ultimately, had been a forgotten dropping point for youths. A sort of sadistic spin on graduation rates, the criminal rate of the girls in the Shyt House for prostitution, drugs, or violence was astronomical. It was more like a pit that these forgotten souls were thrown into and if they survived to be sent on their way, they were damaged beyond repair. It was basically a tax right off for those involved, rampant with fraud, and only the bare minimum resources actually impacted the residents.

She had been placed here four months ago after a couple years at a similar place. Both places were in some ways the same place - overburdened and under caring. In other ways, this was a whole new world - or hell. The first home had been coed, with boys initially tormenting her and beating on her, but as she was one of the older kids; they simply weren't able to do too much damage. Besides, if she kept her eye contact away and looked down, they lost interest. The two and a half years were just lonely. Shyt House was a girl's home, and the girls were relentless. Instead of losing interest, it was blood in the water, and they were sharks. So while Ellie was adjusting to strange new emotions and adjusting to being a teenager, she also had to contend with relentless bullying. Anita Sanchez was but a house cat compared to the lions in this jungle.

After walking out of the projects in Baltimore, she had ended up at the bus station. Tailgating with a small family through the barriers and then stowing on a crowded bus while the driver was distracted, she had ridden up I-95 to Philadelphia. She had to get off the bus and had been caught at the bus depot, but had run off into the darkness of the night.

It hadn't taken long for her on her own to end up being caught by a police officer and placed in the first home after no one could figure out where she came from and she didn't offer them anything. Another lost soul on the streets, resources overburdened, a place had been found for her - case closed.

The other girls weren't the only issue at Shyt House - the head of the house, Elizabeth Bath, was a sadist. She was a wiry woman with a constant purse of her lips and furrow of her brow. Rumor had it that she had been a nurse until multiple allegations of abuse of children surfaced after two patients died within months of each other. She had been banished to the Siberia of Philadelphia - the Shyt House.

Ellie didn't miss the sadistic poetry that was her life trading one abusive Elizabeth for another.

And she took it out on the girls in her care. Ellie didn't have it the worst (that was saved for Shayna, a big-for-her-age and just big-all-around girl who constantly reeked of B.O.), but she was in the sights for sure. That's what happened to the timid, weak mouse that did her best to stay out of the light lest be seen.

And shit rolls downhill - Shayna liked to use Ellie as her personal punching bag.

"The hell yo think yo doin?"

She was sitting on the concrete ledge on the side of the two story Shyt House. Its dark brown planks rose away from her to an upstairs window, one of the rooms that fit two girls but housed five on the second floor. The house was in shambles, filled with shag carpet marked with cigarette burns, yellowed linoleum, and dingy, warped walls. The inside always seemed to smell like cigarette smoke and hate, if that had a smell. Ellie usually hid on the side of the house if the weather was decent; the front porch was warped and missing boards. Plus, one side had rotted out, causing it to list to one side.

Ellie closed her eyes from the book she had found, realizing her hiding was ineffective today. Reading was one of the few things she found joy in - an escape to a different world where the heroes always win. The stories and the possibilities, to go anywhere to be anyone, the courage to stand up and to *win.*

She was sitting outside in the cool not-quite-spring air, on the side of Shyt House where most of the time she could be alone and hidden.

She was not out-of-sight-out-of-mind today.

"Bitch, I am talkin to you" and El was yanked to her feet.

Her book was snatched from her hands and Shayna laughed, which sounded more like a chortle by a pig in heat. She let go of El and looked at the cover.

"The cat-ker… and the ree-yie? What the fuck is dis shit?"

"The Catcher and the rye" El mumbles, keeping her eyes cast down at her feet. Her escape into books was a love that she had kept from her time with Mr. Johnson. They allowed her to dream into better worlds that were way out of the reach of her reality.

"Bitch, you sayin' I keen't read? You callin me dumb?" Spittle came off her enormous lips as she leaned into El's face. Ellie could feel the heat coming off her body and see the sweat stains in the rolls under her arms and boobs. Her posse pulled in close around her, encircling Ellie and trapping her. The claustrophobic feeling welled up in her chest, pressing hard against her rib cage.

Shayna pushed her hard into the side of the house, causing her to bounce off it. She stepped back and looked Ellie right in the eye, raised an eyebrow and the corner of her mouth, pushing her lips out. She held the book up over her shoulder and ripped it two right down the binding. She then proceeded to start tearing pages out of one side and throwing them.

Ellie's eyes welled up in tears as she stood, her one escape from the pains of reality floating away on the gentle breeze, landing in the variety of April puddles. The side of the house was mostly gravel and trash, with a few weeds trying to poke through. The hard ground was littered with puddles in the various depressions. Her breath became ragged and short, sticking in her throat.

"Bitch is crying. Cry baby bitch cry!" Shayna laughed. Then her face went serious and her brow furrowed, looking like one big eyebrow across both her eyes, which were now wide. Her mouth taut and tight she hissed through her teeth in her best Ms. Bath impression. "Maybe Baby Bitch needs something to cry about."

Her jet black skin seemed to pull all the light from the world, everything outside of Shayna blurred and became gray.

Ellie was already hurting; the beating to come wouldn't hurt as much as losing the book. These were hard to come by. She had come across this a few blocks away at the middle school, slipping in with some students and swiping it from a table in the library. There were stacks of them on a cart, and she didn't think anyone would notice one missing. She had planned on returning it when she was through.

She went numb, closed off her mind, and tried to go somewhere else. She did what she always did and started to slide down the wall to the floor. Always on the floor, underneath everyone else, hiding down low, staying below the smoke.

Before the beating could start, a voice rang out.

"Leave her alone."

Shayna turned in surprise, and even El raised her eyes to see her savior. It was the new girl, Cheryl, one of the few white girls at the home of fourteen girls other than El. Cheryl was tall, well built, but not big. She was several years older than Ellie.

El's heart leapt. Someone was standing up for her. She was important enough for someone to fight for her. Energy began to flow through her and her hands curled to fists. The darkness that enveloped the world faded and sun rays through the clouds became clear, seeming to illuminate the new girl.

"You know what you doin bitch?" Shayna said, incredulous that someone was standing up to the Shyt House Bully. "You sure you know wha' bout to happun to you?"

"Yes, I am going to improve that Pillsbury face with my fists." Cheryl's delivery was cool and confident, her words carried over with sharpness yet a complete lack of emotion.

Shayna was startled, and started to look worried.

"I gunna fuck you up" she stammered, but didn't take a step forward.

Cheryl strode over smoothly, gliding over the ground without touching it, gracefully closing the distance in the blink of an eye, but unrushed.

"Bitch you best back -" Shayna never finished, because her teeth were jammed back into her mouth with a violent jab. The palm of Chery's hand drove Shayna's head back and before it could rebound she hit her again, and again.

A barrage of strikes with such fluidity that all El could do was stare in awe. Shayna tried to crumple her frame to the ground, but Cheryl's two sidekicks grabbed her to hold her upright, and Cheryl kept pummeling her.

Then it was over. Shayna's massive round body was on the ground, her head at an awkward angle and the lights out. Her breathing was labored and she snorted, her nose and mouth ruined. Blood drained off her face like a waterfall and mixed with the leftover puddles from the overnight April rain.

And it was silent.

"Thank you" was all Ellie could muster, a confused smile on her face. Her eyes were wide and alive, a radiance in them that served as reverence for her protector.

Cheryl took one look at her.

"Give me your coat."

Ellie's brow furrowed with confusion, and her smile slowly began to fade.

"I said now."

Her smile was gone and the light left her eyes like a candle in a stiff wind, extinguished and left to charred black. Cheryl hadn't been helping her; it was just prison warfare, the new girl establishing herself by taking on the biggest bully in the yard in a furious flurry and violence of action.

Ellie started to shrug off her coat, one arm then the other. The April air felt ice cold in her t-shirt, but the cold came from the soul crushing realization that one bully was traded for another.

She gently held it out, knowing from experience that there was no point in even the smallest glimmer of hope.

Cheryl took the coat and put it on. It had been a bit too big for Ellie and was a bit small for The New Shyt House Bully.

With such speed and grace that Ellie couldn't even brace herself, Cheryl grabbed the front of her shirt, throwing her down into a puddle. Water splashed over her head and shoulders, and before she couldn't even breath, a foot pressed her head down into the water.

Fear and panic took over her as she struggled. Suffocating cold water and darkness.

No no no no, her mind raced but could only think of the word.

And then the foot let up and she pulled her head up, gasping. The girls all around were laughing at her, giggling at her in the mud puddle while Ellie was overcome with fear that she would drown in an inch of water in a depression on the side of the Shyt House.

Except they weren't really laughing at her, they were just glad it wasn't them. And Cheryl wasn't laughing - with a languid expression on her face she squatted down and grabbed Ellie's chin. She waited for her to stop blinking the filthy water out of her eyes.

"Don't ever make me repeat myself."

Then she rose and left, striding away with the same grace as before, as if nothing had happened.

Ellie shivered. The brief moment of trust and companionship, that brief feeling of meaning something - being someone worth fighting for - left a wound deeper than if she had just been beaten by Shayna.

She lay there next to the puddle. On the ground, the bits of gravel digging into her arms and side. All alone.

Like always. Some things never changed.

*　　　　*　　　　*

Some things never change, always on the ground. Weeping in the stairwell, alone and frightened. Again, just like twelve years ago at the Shyt House.

She remembered Shayna just lay out there for hours, just as she did. Eventually, Ellie just rose and left. Ms. Bath came out and found Shayna when she didn't show up for dinner (regardless of how bad the food is, the girl did not miss a meal). Ms. Bath didn't panic, called an ambulance, and they took her away. All the girls were asked what happened and no one said a word. It wasn't spoken about after that and Shayna never came back.

Twelve years ago, she thought. *I am about twenty-five then. Another piece of me coming back.*

This realization gave her a burst of energy, like the jolt from a shot of espresso on a groggy morning.

An espresso sounds good, she thought. She could almost hear the hiss of a machine. Was that another part of her coming back?

Ellie exhaled in a rush and pulled herself up from the

floor. She ran her hands back to the door and gently pulled it open. Musty air met her in the face like the opening of an ancient tomb.

Apt thought, marching into my tomb, she thought, shuddering as she recalled the creature chasing her.

She stepped across the threshold and onto the second floor. The very last of the dim glow of twilight seeped through the air, not enabling her to see clearly, but causing the dancing shadows to grow darker with the passing seconds.

She scooted forward as the remnants of her memories of Shyt House hung in her brain like a light fog - the beatings from the other kids, the lonely lock ups in the room under the stairs without food, the sharp edged voice of Ms. Bath cutting into her. Ellie was slowly beginning to feel herself coming back, but now she wondered if perhaps it was best left in the darkness of the forgotten.

She cringed as her steps crunched on chunks of plaster and fallen brick on the floor, the sound reverberating throughout the empty halls. Creeping across the open expanse at the top of the stairwell, she realized that this was a larger section of the building with wings reaching out to either side. The largest section had appeared to be the middle as she had looked out the window and found the entrance below.

One more floor down and I can get out.

She stepped to her left off the stairwell, creeping along the wall until it dropped off into a hallway. Squinting in the darkness, she saw -

Nothing.

The darkness enveloped the hall, the entirety of it

swallowed up and leaving a thick, black expanse. The edges of the walls seemed to melt away and all the blackness devoured all sound, light, and movement.

Blackness, like the room under the stairs at the Shyt House.

Blackness, like death.

Her pulse quickened again and she began to feel any of her newly found energy and confidence melt away. She was frozen like a terrified rabbit cornered by a predator, no way out.

She resisted the urge to just sink back to the floor and close her eyes, to lie on the floor and wait for it to pass as she had so many times before. The blackness seemed to reach for her, tendrils reaching to pull her in. She felt it swirling around her, enveloping her and drawing her toward it.

She back pedaled, tripping over debris and falling down. Scooting in a crabwalk, she pushed herself across to the far wall, panting, trying to calm herself.

You damn child, she scolded herself. *Afraid of the dark like a baby.*

Self-deprecation did not have the effect she hoped for as she felt herself shaking. Pushing along the wall, she found herself back directly across from the stairwell. The twilight was back, a very subtle flickering light, like a gift of life driving away the swirling darkness. She glided toward it, around the corner and away from the dark, away from her goal of the entrance from the window.

As she slowly came around the corner, drawn to the flickering light, she realized it was not the dying twilight, but a series of burning candles every thirty feet or so staggered on either side of the hall. Her puzzlement stopped her, and she scanned the hall.

Debris littered the floor, the dust covering a tiled floor that ran down with doors on each side, staggered. An old radiator sat off the wall halfway down and graffiti littered the walls. Paint had peeled off and large sections of the plaster were missing, exposing yellow brick underneath. Two thirds of the way down the hall she could see an archway that led off to the right, some abandoned shelves partially standing. Rusted piping ran near the ceiling, causing the shadows to dance from the flickering light. The shadows appeared as ghastly apparitions mocking her as she stood at the opening, the dark lurking behind her. She half expected eerie organ music to begin playing like some scary Halloween story.

Am I in one of those horror movies? she thought. This seemed to shake something as well. She liked movies, she used to go with –

The last of the memory refused to solidify in her foggy head. Frustrated, she shook herself, returning her gaze to the stretch of hallway, pulsing with malignant shadows and dancing demons.

She struggled to find the inner strength she desperately wanted to be there. After a few moments, ghastly demons won over the tendrils of darkness and she began forward down the hall.

She felt small, just like back in the Shyt House. Hours upon hours in the darkness in the room under the stairs, silent and alone. She had learned quickly from the first time when she had screamed and cried, afraid in the dark as the door had opened and the beating ensued. She never made a peep after that.

Ms. Bath had known how to make someone feel small and unimportant. Ellie had been in the room under the stairs when she had had her first period. She was terrified and had no idea what was going on, no mother or older sister to help her. She had sat there, terrified both at what was happening to her as well as the repercussions for countless hours. When the door had opened, Ms. Bath paraded her in front of everyone and made them laugh at her. Then she had beaten her with the belt for being indecent.

Ellie had learned one thing from those experiences at the Shyt House - how to be small and invisible. It was self-preservation really, just like the time when Madelyn had been blamed for tracks in the house. About a year into her stay, a stray dog had wandered in, leaving mud in the hallway. Ms. Bath blamed Madelyn and beat her for it. She insisted that she hadn't done it, and pleaded to Ellie for help.

"Well, what do you have to say," Ms. Bath said to Ellie. The fire in her eyes daring her to say otherwise.

Ellie knew that it was in fact, Ms. Bath who had left the door open - she and Madelyn had been in the yard when they had watched it happen. They all knew it - Ms. Bath included. That sadistic monster's eyes glowed red with rage, daring Ellie to say it as a long piece of ash fell from the cigarette from her lips.

"Are you going to tell me I'm wrong?" she hissed through pencil thin lips. Ellie swore she could see horns on her head sprouting out of her steel tight bun.

Madelyn's eyes pleaded with Ellie, causing her to look away.

Ellie shook her head and averted her eyes. Even that wasn't enough for Ms. Bath, not only did she have to break each girl but she had to drive them against each other.

"Say it!" she had screamed at Ellie, hitting her with the belt. "Say who did it!"

"Madelyn did it."

"Yes, I thought so," she had tittered, and then laughing had started in on the poor girl.

Madelyn screamed as Bath put her cigarette out on her arm. Then she dragged Madelyn down the stairs, by the arm, the sound "no, no, no" blubbering over and over. And the belt rained down. Ellie had felt ashamed as she heard the muffled screams, but more so felt relief that she was out of the cross-hairs. In the end, it hadn't even mattered. She felt the belt and was thrown into the darkness anyway.

Self-preservation.

That is what drove her forward now - not bravery or courage, but the fear of what was behind her more than the fear of what was in front.

But that would change shortly.

Six

Ellie stood at the entrance to the hallway, following the candles down the hall. The walls were peeling, abandoned, and gray. The white plaster faded and soiled, black mold crawled up from ornate air vents with a diamond shaped grate inside a square with loops in the corners that resembled horseshoes except the tips came most of the way together. Chunks of yellow brick ran along the wall, some places growing to a pile of rubble where the walls had crumbled. The candles were on ancient fixtures on the walls between the rooms, staggered.

Ellie stood looking at the vent, dented and damaged. As she thought of what the vent must have looked like, the broken pieces suddenly filled back in. Bending back into place where they were bent, reaching across gaps that were missing like vines stretching to connect to each other. The black mold suddenly crawled backward down the vent until it compressed to a single dot on the vent, and then disappeared entirely.

The bricks lying in the hall crawled back against the wall and the plaster rolled over it, as if a massive invisible paint roller came sliding down the wall. The hardwood floor, covered in dust and grime, suddenly began to shine and be without a blemish in a large sweeping action as if a ghost driven Zamboni came parading down the hallway. A carpet began to slither down from the far end, and even materialize under her feet, the two pieces meeting in the middle, coming together like long lost lovers reaching tenderly.

Rocking chairs materialized out of nowhere and began to line the hallway. As she blinked, the walls were full of art pieces and decor, vases of flowers appeared and light fixtures lined the walls where the candles were a moment ago. It was no longer dark or gray, light flooded into the hallway from the doorways up and down. An invisible hand stenciled on the far wall *"Veni Vidi Vici"* and piano sat on the wall next to it. A man was there, playing a gentle and soothing tune. He had a black suit with a black vest over a collared shirt closed tight against his throat. A narrow tie fed down his vest. He had dark hair combed to the side and a dark bushy mustache and eyebrows.

As Ellie stood there, listening to the tune and frozen where she stood, the man finished playing and stood. He strode down the hall toward Ellie and she was worried that he would scold her. He came right to her, but showed no notice of her standing there. As he was about to walk into her he raised his head.

"Mildred, you look lovely today. And tired, you must have worked hard." the man said, startling Ellie into stepping backward. She certainly wasn't Mildred and the man appeared to not even see her a moment before.

"Yessir, Dr. Sudd-sudder-lin," came a voice from behind her. She turned to see a middle-aged woman, sweaty and disheveled. She had frizzy brown hair down her face, and her eyes darted to-and-fro. "Yessir, I did. I picked apples and cherries and I unly ated three." She smiled a large smile that caused her whole face to turn to the right and her eyes to push to the corners to look.

"Yes, Dr. Sutherland, she had a great day today, out in the sunshine. She is feeling very well," a woman in a white outfit with a frock said. She guided Mildred by the elbow, gently but firmly.

"Very well, Nurse Murphy." Dr. Sutherland continued, "The beautiful sunshine, the crisp fall air, and the majesty of the trees in the orchard. The beauty of nature, and the bounty of a good day's work. Excellent Mildred, truly excellent." Dr. Sutherland gave her a warm and genuine smile as Nurse Murphy continued to guide her down the hall telling her "Let's get you cleaned up for supper."

His dark mustache danced with his smile and his eyes sparkled with a genuine joy in Mildred's chaotic happiness. He turned to the room directly on Ellie's left and entered. Ellie, feeling a warmth that she had not since waking on the floor, followed.

"Hullo Helen. The trees in the arboretum are beautiful this time of year. Which is your favorite?" Dr. Sutherland asked.

An older woman, perhaps in her early to mid-forties, stood by the seven foot high window in a simple white frock. She had wild graying hair, curly and wavy. It would have been beautiful if not for the snarled chaos. She turned and looked at Dr. Sutherland as he entered, her face showing the first signs of wrinkles, crows feet spreading away from her eyes. Her curly gray hair swung as she turned her head and revealed sharp green eyes, radiating an intensity. The left side of her face didn't quite follow the right side as she smiled. Her lopsided grin pulled her face to the right and her eyes tilted slightly to look at the doctor. She had a white, jagged scar that fed through the right side of her face and into her hairline up above her ear.

"Welllll hullloooo doctor." She said, and laughed, a cackling sound that came out *hee-hee*. Ellie couldn't help but think of an over the top stereotype of a Halloween witch.

Her pale skin came down to both a pointed nose and chin. Spittle flew off her lips as she laughed. She raised a long bony finger away from her hand, trying to point but the digit shook a bit. "That one there, there is my favorite." The word was drawn out *fav-o-righttt.*

"Ah yes, the Horse Chestnut. Beautiful tree with its white blooms. Dr. Munson brought in many of these beautiful trees from all over the world. The Horse Chestnut is from Pindus Mountains in southeast Europe. The beautiful white flowers with the yellow tips just bloomed, but in the autumn when the leaves fall, the bare branches will be shaped like a horseshoe."

Dr. Sutherland said this as a matter-of-fact, though it was obvious that Helen did not track on the information nor care. He continued to glance from his notes to her face.

The nurse setting the bed did not even acknowledge him, as if she had heard all this before, while Helen nodded up and down, not so much with her head as with her upper back, her entire shoulders dipping and raising. Her eyes twinkled and her smile stayed lopsided.

"Any visitors today, Helen?" the doctor asked. His face, still warm and gentle but also serious now, searched her face.

"Uh no doctor. No visitors."

"Good, good. You are doing well, I heard you were back out on the farm yesterday."

"Yessir, I helped with the cows. We gots a new-un!" Helen grew very excited.

"I heard about that. Great job, you helped bring new life to the farm. That must feel very good."

"Yessir, I helped. I wanna name-er Colantha."

"That's a pretty name. Is it a family name?"

Helen's face was lit up bright, but at the question, her brow furrowed. She struggled hard, but was frustrated and confused.

"I dunno - I.. I ... dun't 'member."

Dr. Sutherland moved on smoothly before it might escalate. "Great job, Helen. Let me go see what's going on with that calf." He smiled and left the room, motioning subtly for the nurse to follow.

Ellie, standing at the doorway, watched them step outside and could overhear their conversation.

"How is she doing today?"

"She's doing well doctor, upbeat, really perked up after being out on the farm yesterday and helping with that calf."

"Excellent news. Nothing lately about the young lady or the voices? Nothing about the monster?"

"No, not recently. Not since the episode last December. She seems to be adjusting to the new wing and enjoying the additional responsibility."

"Good, good. Beauty is therapy, work is therapy."

"Yes, doctor, it certainly is helping her spirits."

They drifted away and Ellie turned her attention back to the woman in the room. Helen was looking straight at her. Ellie was startled and visibly jumped. No one else in this strange vision (*dream?*) appeared to see her but Helen focused on her with her intense, radiant green eyes.

"Is they gone?" Helen hissed. Ellie glanced out into the hallway, seeing Dr. Sutherland and the nurse moving away.

"Are you talking to me?" Ellie asked.

"Why who else would I be a-jabberin' to?" Helen asked, waving her hand in the air. "I gots here in the middle wing now, so I can't be seen talkin' wid ya again. I gots in a lotta trouble for being in that tunnel. Didja find it?"

Ellie looked at her confused.

"I don't understand, where am I?"

"You know dat. We's call it the Farm. It's a-hopsital. For people with bad brains." She pointed to her head for emphasis. "We been through dis."

The words struck Ellie at her core and she felt herself go cold.

"Am. Am I a patient?"

"You, a patient?" Helen looked at her like she was crazy, which Ellie thought was ironic, and then burst out laughing. She cackled her *hee-hee-hee* laugh, throwing her head back as she stood by the large window, the sunlight reflecting off her silver hair, causing it to sparkle as her head flew back and forward.

She laughed so hard her chest heaved, spittle flew from her lips and her eyes cinched shut. She doubled over at the waist and had to put her hands on her knees. Ellie shrank back, feeling small and unsure.

Wake up, wake up. She wasn't sure which nightmare she preferred.

"Oh sorry hunny, just a minute, sorry" Helen said, gasping for air. Her cackling subsided and she drew in a big breath.

"Sorry hunny, I dun't mean to laugh. *I'm* a patient here, not you."

Ellie was confused, her brows furrowing together.

"I don't understand."

"You, hunny, you ain't a patient," she cackled. "You a ghost."

Seven

T he word ghost hung in the air, seeming to echo off the walls, bouncing around and reverberating in her head, down her spine, and into her heart. She just stood in the room unmoving, *unable* to move. As the word resonated through the walls, sending a chill to her soul, the chamber began throbbing in time to the word's echo. The walls and the floor, even Helen herself, pulsating to and fro, in and out. The throbbing stopped and the environment began to melt away, like a wet painting running down off a wall, until the gray, dark, decrepit version of the building remained. The echo of the word ghost slowed and drew out, like an old tape player running out of batteries.

The pretty flowers, the spring sunlight, the furniture, and the color had bled away - the broken plaster remnants of the building was all that remained.

Ellie stuck her head out into the hall. It was empty, devoid of a piano, art on the walls, or the stenciled latin words on the far wall *Veni Vidi Vici* - I came, I saw, I conquered.

She shivered and tried to collect herself. Those words on the wall seemed to call out to her, to mean something to her. Still, it stayed just beyond her grasp.

Am I dead? Am I a ghost that is haunting this place? Is this some other afterlife plane of existence that I am stuck in for all of eternity?

She thought about it again. She didn't believe this was the afterlife - she was a Christian and believed in God, Jesus Christ, and heaven.

I do?

She dug deep to remember, but all she could remember was the Shyt House.

Is Helen real and I am haunting her? And what in the hell was she talking about, getting her in trouble? Can I not remember her either?

So many questions ran through her brain like a busy intersection. She couldn't seem to get a grasp on any one. It seemed that regardless of her digging, her brain was stubborn - it was going to bring things back chronologically and she was going to have to walk the path if she wanted to move further down the line. No skipping ahead, no cutting in line, no shortcuts.

She sighed, and let her adolescent hell known as Shyt House come back, and pushed into getting out. *I came, I saw, I conquered.*

Ellie had made it out of the Shyt House, haunted by over three years under Ms. Bath, cigarette burn scars to remind her of her time, internal scars to haunt her every time she closed her eyes. But, as she left in the middle of her seventeenth year, she had thoughts that things would be better - similar to those thoughts as she began down the candle-lit hallway.

*   *   *

She lived on the streets of Philadelphia for six months, from early spring to fall, finding scraps and moving in and out of homes, working to stay safe and fed. Quite simply, she didn't know what else to do. Scavenging for food and staying away from danger filled most of her day. The looming winter didn't even begin to worry her as she had never thought that far ahead.

She strolled down the street in mid-September, a gentle breeze flowing on the beautiful and warm fall day. Her luck had turned as she had found a discarded pile of clothes, mostly in her size, and now felt brand new. She had cleaned herself up at Penn Treaty park, down on the Delaware river. As she had strolled down and enjoyed the sun in her face, she stumbled across a wallet under a picnic table. She had found sixty dollars in it - a treasure in her world. She had liberated the cash and put the wallet back.

Now she strolled down Market after finishing a lavish lunch at a pizza place that sold by the slice. Her belly full, she headed toward her favorite place, the one place she felt truly safe and could get lost in contentment - the Walnut Street West Library. She could spend hours in there reading a book and as long as she tucked herself in the back corner, leaving before closing, no one would bother her. One librarian, a portly lady right out of a sitcom with her large fluffy hair and bubbly demeanor, looking like she belonged more with a tray of fresh baked cookies, even talked with her each time she came in. Her motherly instinct tried to pry into her life, an awareness that she was on her own, but Ellie relented. She was always nobody to everyone and staying invisible managed to keep her safe on the streets.

As she walked on Market heading toward 40th street, she noticed a coffee shop that she had never even seen before. Her eyes passed over elements like this, not a part of her world, but with a fresh wad of cash in her pocket, maybe could afford to duck into that world, just for a moment. She smiled, picturing herself sitting at a table, sipping on an espresso or macchiato or some other sophisticated drink that she couldn't pronounce and didn't really even know what it was. She imagined the flavor as divine, and saw herself as somebody for a few moments.

She stood on the sidewalk, outside for a few moments, her lack of confidence beginning to overwhelm her. *What would I order? I can't even pronounce these things. Everyone will laugh at me and know that I am a nothing - a vagrant.*

Her smile faded, and she felt the tightness in her chest. Her shoulders dropped and she knew she didn't belong there. It was time to go to the library where she could read about the person she wished she was - she could become a sophisticated character sipping a ristretto, whatever that was.

She took a step forward to move on when she heard a voice.

"Ellie?"

She turned around and saw Madelyn, from the Shyt House. Madelyn was a year and a half older than Ellie. She had left shortly after the incident with the dog, but not before she had cornered Ellie behind the house. She had grabbed Ellie, in a firm but gentle manner, and looked her directly in the eyes. Ellie had tried to look away in shame, but a strong gaze from Madelyn prevented her from being able to.

Madelyn had simply stated "I don't blame you, it's not your fault it's hers. That woman is the Devil himself. Just survive and get the hell out."

With that she had walked away, and that night, had walked away for good. Once you get to that age, they don't bother looking for you. And if the money kept rolling in for each kid, Ms. Bath didn't care too much, she just took it out on whoever was left.

To see her now caused a rush of panic. She *said* it wasn't her fault, but it was hard to believe. How could she not blame her?

She tried to move away down the street, longing for the sanctity of the library, the park by the river, or even up under the bridge she slept at sometimes, deep in the shadows from some of the other homeless who talked to themselves as if they were having a conversation with someone who wasn't there.

Anything but facing this.

"Ellie, wait, please don't go."

Weaving among the thrum of people, like slipping into a river of blue shirts and red blouses, black suits and brown jackets, she wove effortlessly among those rushing to their shops, classes, or homes.

Madelyn, however, was cut from the same mold, and even more experienced than her - disappearing from her through the crowds on the street wasn't as easy. Ellie was caught within ten steps, Madelyn grabbing her arm in her way - firmly, but gently.

"Ellie, please stop."

Ellie tried to pull away but caught a look at Madelyn's face, a pleading gentleness. "Stop."

Ellie stopped, facing Madelyn but turning her body at an angle, closing off and ready to move away. She looked down at her feet and folded her arms to protect herself, unwilling to meet Madelyn's gaze.

"Hey, it's okay," she said. She rubbed Ellie's upper arm, and ducked her head down to meet Ellie's eyes.

Ellie raised her gaze to meet hers, seeing a warmth in Madelyn's blue eyes, her golden hair glowing like an angel in the sunlight.

She didn't bother to ask how Ellie was; she knew better.

"So, you got out of that hell hole." It was a statement, not a question. "I've seen you a few times, or at least I thought it was you. In a mass of people, I thought maybe I was seeing things, but hey, now I know."

Her face became serious.

"You aren't using, are you?"

Ellie's eyes shot up in a defensive squint. Growing up with the mother she had, she wouldn't even entertain anything like that. This was the one gift that Elizabeth Sloan did give her.

Madelyn smiled and softened her face, continuing.

"Come in, let's get a cup of coffee and catch up." She didn't give Ellie a chance to protest as she hooked her arm and pulled her back toward the coffee shop. She pulled open the door and ushered Ellie inside.

"Joe, I need to take a bit for an old friend here. Someone from before."

An older gentleman with a big, white mustache looked up from behind the counter, giving a big warm smile, his eyes twinkling underneath a head of bushy white hair. His rosy cheeks exuded warmth, his large figure like that of a teddy bear. He raised his hand in the air in reply.

"Take all the time you need, unless we get a line up here," his deep voice mumbled. It was soft, but floated across the room regardless.

That was when Ellie noticed that Madelyn had on an apron with the words *Facing Goliath Coffee* printed across it. She looked around, realizing that Madelyn worked at the coffee shop.

She smiled at her again, her eyes radiating light, the freckles across her nose scrunching. Again, Ellie thought of an angel. Madelyn leaned forward.

"I am so glad you are out of there. What are you doing? Where are you staying?"

Ellie pulled back a bit and diverted her gaze.

Madelyn just leaned forward further, lowering her voice she asked "Or at the urban campsite?"

Ellie looked up enough to affirm the suspicion. Madelyn just nodded and sat back.

Joe showed up with coffee and as he was putting it down, Madelyn continued.

"You look pretty nicely done up, are you working?"

The words cut through Ellie and pulled back again, starting to shut down.

She doesn't believe me, she thinks I'm a liar. She thinks I am a low life, sad and pathetic charity case. She is still mad about that day at the Shyt House. She pulled me in here to humiliate me.

All the words ran through her head and her eyes started dancing around the room, looking for an escape. *I knew I should have ran. Why didn't I listen to myself? I am so stupid!*

Entire scenarios began to play out in her head, Madelyn yelling at her, everyone laughing, her trying to run and falling over the tables, unable to get to the door which just kept getting farther away and smaller...

As she began to panic and her breaths started shortening, she felt a hand on hers. She tried to pull away, but the grip was Madelyn's - gentle but firm.

"Calm down. It's okay. I know you. I was you. You ran from that hell hole, you escaped. You're a survivor but now you're barely keeping it together. You are scrounging to keep yourself fed, safe and warm."

Ellie stopped pulling away and looked at her. *Close enough, though I haven't even thought about warm yet.* Her shoulders slumped in resignation. *I have no idea what I am doing.* Her eyes began to well up with tears.

"Hey, hey. It's okay. I've said that and I mean it. It's okay because I'm going to help. *We're* going to help," she said as she gestured to Joe, who was still standing next to the table.

She raised her eyes up to his. He smiled, gave a simple curt nod, patted her on the shoulder and turned his heel back toward the counter.

"I'm sorry, I have to go, I don't belong here," Ellie began.

"Relax, hear me out," Madelyn said. "I was you, until Joe helped me." She spread her arms about her and continued "This is Facing Goliath Coffee. It is a small chain of coffee shops to share wonderful coffee, but - more importantly, especially to you and me - to help people realize they matter. And Joe runs this one, and he makes sure we know that we matter."

She smiled again, pulling Ellie's arms toward her.

"After I left the Shyt House I had nowhere to go," she began. "I was even younger than you, but after that day, I was done taking the abuse. I marched right out. I actually spent the first night hiding in a church a few blocks away, St. Agatha. It was Sunday, and I was drawn to the beautiful music from their organ." She smiled at the thought, remembering the intoxicating sounds drawing her in like a siren. Her eyes twinkled as she recalled and Ellie realized how much she had changed. The color in her face, the life in her eyes, and energy emanating off of her.

"I took in the service and returned later, found a nice place to hide. I returned there each evening and ended up in circling coffee shops for most of the day. After a few days, a nun found me. Well, actually she apparently knew I was there. She told me about a place for girls, and I broke. I basically verbal-vomited my whole story. I wasn't quite eighteen yet, but she understood. I stayed there until the next service, when she introduced me to Joe. As you have already seen, he is quite possibly the nicest man you could meet and he gave me a job. He helped me save enough up and get a small apartment a few blocks from here."

She took a breath and watched Ellie's face, which was still somewhat stoic and uncomprehending. Madelyn opened her arms, a gesture asking "there it is, what do you think?"

Ellie sat unblinking, not sure of what to say next.

Madelyn sat there a moment longer, and then her brow furrowed. She once again leaned forward across the table. A sadness filled her eyes as she surveyed Ellie. In her excitement to give back, to help extend the grace she had been given, she had not realized just how broken Ellie was. As she surveyed her friend across the table, the tenseness in her shoulders, the folded arms closing off, the tight pursed lips, and the legs planted, facing toward the door poised to escape, a profound sadness came over Madelyn.

"Oh Ellie, it's okay. I understand, I've been there, I've been you. The feeling of being broken down, of being nothing. It's a lie. You aren't nothing, no matter what that psycho bitch at the Shyt House made you feel like or told you. You live on the streets, trying to stay fed and warm and safe, no one seeing you, you melt into the madness and chaos of the city.

You believe it yourself, that you aren't worth a damn and you have nothing to offer. But it's a lie, it's all a lie. You have something right here, a starting line, a new point of origin, chapter one of your new story. All that stuff before was just the prologue - it's not that it didn't happen, but it is the origin story of your strength, and you will write the rest of the story starting from here."

Ellie looked up finally, feeling the connection of what Madelyn was laying down. *But why would you do that for me?*

"Why not?" Madelyn said. Ellie hadn't even realized she mumbled it outloud. "We all deserve a little help. You can't make it through on your own, this world is hard enough with family and friends. That's what we will be - your family starting right here in this coffee shop. I am not saying it will be easy; you'll work hard. But you'll be a part of the family, you'll get your feet underneath you, and you'll find your path. Then, one day, you'll turn around and help someone else, the same way Joe helped me, and I can help you."

She gestured to Ellie's coffee.

"Drink that up, then we are going to get you going. You'll work here with me and Joe, and you'll stay with me. It's not much, but we'll make it work."

Finally, Ellie met her eyes and smiled. Not much of one, but a curl at the corners of her mouth. That infected Madelyn and her radiance returned, eyes twinkling and her grin spread from ear to ear.

As if out of nowhere, like an apparition suddenly materializing out of the ether, Joe was there, apron and uniform in hand. He extended them to Ellie, and she felt her hand close around them as she accepted them. Her smile grew larger.

And then her smile overtook the rest of her body and she began to cry, tears of joy. And then she began to laugh. And as Madelyn slid over to her side of the table and wrapped her in her arms, her whole body trembled.

It was a new start.

Someone wanted her.

*   *   *

She smiled in spite of her current situation, standing in a dimly lit hallway of some decrepit building. *The asylum.* Bits and pieces still swirled in her mind, the remnants of a head-ache clouding her thoughts.

The more she strained to remember, the more the head-ache came on. It seemed she would have to let it come back organically, like a seed growing into a flower, allowing nature to take its course while being patient and nurturing. However, with her situation, that seemed like it also might be dangerous. There seemed to be important details that could help her in the here and now that, if not acted upon, would come back to bite her. Literally, if that strange monster found her again. And who was this Helen? Dr. Sutherland? It seemed like a movie that she was in, another version of the building she was in.

And then there was the monster. It had chased her, and sent her down a flight of stairs, swung that big ax at her. Grunted, growled, and snarled at her.

Was that real? She rubbed the lump on her arm and felt the pain of a deep breath to remind her of the fall down the stairwell. *These definitely are. Do ghosts get bruises, feel pain?*

And my situation... What is my situation? I am in a strange building that is falling apart, there were those vile messages on the wall, and there is some monster roaming about. This can't even be real. Those things don't exist.

However, she heard that doctor and that nurse in the Other-Version, and they had mentioned Helen talking to a young woman and something about a monster.

The more she thought about it the more she determined she must be either in a bad dream or perhaps she is already burning in hell. If she was burning in hell, she would still be tormented by pain. And standing monsters with horns don't exist in the real world.

Don't misunderstand - monsters exist. They inflict pain for the sake of pain, they dominate for the sake of their own power and ego, and they seeth with evil. Evil monsters definitely exist, Ellie knew that better than most, but they were not eight feet tall with horns on their head, running upright while snorting like an enraged, possessed animal. *Well at least that's what I thought.*

Instead, they have the pale pursed lips of Ms. Bath, a cigarette with an inch of ash hanging from her lips. Her wiry frame with stretched, almost translucent skin, an amazing amount of strength swinging the belt for her skin-and-bones body. Her long, thin fingers, like talons pointing and reaching for you.

Ellie shuddered at the memory of the gray and brown bun, wrapped so tight it pulled her eyebrows up onto her forehead.

Evil looked like the people she used to see on the streets trading drugs, the transactions all too often devolving into violence, while she melted into the background.

And of course evil looked like Zach Weston.

She shuddered as yet another wave of memories came back. The goodness of the coffee shop, leading her down the path to her encounter with another evil, the biggest evil she had faced yet. A wolf in sheep's clothing, charming all the while pulling her in to devour her, like the siren's song.

Zach Weston.

Again, she lost herself in herself, memories flooding back like a tsunami, steps closer to knowing herself and her current predicament. She flew back to the coffee shop, the apartment, Joe and Madelyn, espressos and macchiatos and cappuccinos. The smell of beans and steam, the sound of the grinder, the smell of fresh flowers and the thrill of gifts. Then the devolution of those gifts into the trap of abuse.

Zach Weston.

Eight

The door dinged and in walked another stream of customers, filing in to stay warm on the cool October day. Halloween was approaching and the air had turned crisp. The smell of pumpkin spice and apples permeated everything, a floating autumn aroma that brought warmth regardless of whether you were sipping on a pumpkin latte or not.

Students wore a path through the door in their scarves and coats, coasting in from UPenn or Drexel, even from across the river at Temple. The cool air followed the patrons in, but was quickly met with the warmth of the coffee shop atmosphere. The sound of the milk steamer, the laughter of groups of people surrounding small round tables, and the gentle conversation filled the shop with an air of comfort and homeliness.

Facing Goliath Coffee was a popular spot to feel such warmth on the cool autumn days as the season pressed on toward winter. The conversations ranged from the upcoming holiday season to the progression of fall classes to the current state of the country and the world. The warm, gentle lighting caused a glow of decor with sayings such as *"Not Before my Coffee"*, *"Don't Ask, Just Pour"*, and *"The Powers of Man's Mind are Directly Proportional to the Amount of Coffee He Drinks."*

Ellie was working behind the counter, as she had for the past seven weeks, making all sorts of drinks, mixtures, and glorified ice cream masquerading as coffee. She had a roof over her head (well, it was Madelyn's one bedroom apartment, with an air mattress but still better than what she knew most of her life), a steady income from the coffee shop, and an ever growing (albeit slowly) self-confidence.

She had the makings of a family, though up to this point, it was decidedly one-sided. Joe and Madelyn shared with her, invited her to dinners, to the movies, and of course to church. Sometimes she accepted, but sometimes not. The sometimes-yes increased, but her demeanor was still closed off. She did not open up, did not strike up any conversations, and answered with the shortest response possible. She had not had a family, had not meant anything to anyone for so long, she struggled accepting that she mattered to them, regardless of their continued pursuit - and pursue they did, gentle but firm.

Joe Lockwood's demeanor was like that of a loving grandpa

mixed with a patient counselor. The coffee shop existed as an extension of Joe, his relentless work ethic ensuring the shop was humming along regardless of whether it was bursting at the seams as it was on this day, or if it was the doldrum period of an early weekday afternoon. A rotund man with his big mustache and bushy eyebrows that seemed to cover the upper half of his face and eyes, he glided across the shop with such grace that it barely seemed he was moving.

He did not say much, but he didn't have to. His very presence drove you to push for your best. The essence of love he exuded came with no expectations, and though Ellie was not opening up much, she felt it inside. Her heart was filling and Joe had the patience and understanding to let her open up in her own time, like a flower finally opening in the spring. She had weathered a long and damaging winter that had lasted most of her life, it was going to take time for even the strong loving rays of the sunshine to melt the drifts piled on her.

The slow process continued through the grinding of beans and the sound of pressurized water pushing through grounds. She put the three shots of espresso into the cup along with two scoops of Ghirardelli Dark Hot Cocoa, stirring it together. She poured the steamed milk on top, finishing with a foam layer and quickly shaping it into a jack-o-lantern for the season. She had found a hidden talent for the latte art, and threw a hat on top, gave it menacing eyes, jagged teeth, and facial lines to add to the Halloween scare.

She slid it down the counter to Madelyn who called out the name.

"Zach! Mocha up"

That moment would be the defining moment for the next

six years of her life, the moment that altered her upward trajectory. All that started with a...

"Woa, this is slick. I need to meet the person that did this masterpiece. Was that you?"

Ellie raised her head and saw a tall man in an overcoat with perfectly styled hair behind a movie star smile of sparkling white teeth. His strong jawline led down to a shirt with a loose tie and the top button undone. He wore what appeared to be an expensive suit (not that Ellie had a frame of reference) casually over broad shoulders and long arms. He seemed big as life with a six foot two inch frame, was a presence of power, and yet with this slightly shifted posture was not intimidating.

He commanded a presence as he stood, weight shifted to one leg and head cocked slightly to the side, the corners of his mouth curled up as he gazed at ... Madelyn.

"Oh no, my artistry consists of tapping the buttons on the register here and stacking twenties facing the same direction. The artistry comes from my friend hiding behind the counter there, that's where the magic happens."

The man turned his face and met Ellie's eyes. Her stomach fluttered a bit and she looked away. As much as she was drawn to him, or, as she would later think, to the idea that someone was taken by something *she did*, she couldn't handle the attention.

"This is fantastic. Unfortunately, I am going to have to have you make me another one, as I don't think I can ruin this. Can you make me another one?" he said with a smile. "And then, maybe we can enjoy them together."

Ellie smiled in spite of her discomfort, and kept working.

"What do you say?" he smiled. "Ten minutes with a cup of coffee for a poor soul like me, the chance to sit in the presence of true artistry."

He was handsome, flashing his winning smile, arms out and open. His skin still clinging to a summer tan, and blue eyes radiating, she struggled to look away.

She relented, however, despite the encouraging looks of Madelyn. She was just beginning to take care of herself, and she wasn't ready to complicate life further. Besides, she was still struggling to open up to Joe and Madelyn, there was no way she would be able to handle this. It was just someone else to let her down.

The man, however, would not give up easily. As she would later learn, he was driven by what he couldn't have, and he would do whatever it took to get it, or take it. Hindsight, had she sat down with him that first day, he likely would have lost interest and moved on. By turning him down, it became a competition for him, and he returned constantly over a period of several weeks, eventually bribing her with flowers on a slow day, and so she sat with him for a coffee.

Part of it may have been the Christmas season, the love, lights, and decorations bringing on a roller coaster of emotions. The move from pumpkin spice to everything peppermint had taken its hold and Ellie felt elation for the season followed by a sadness of a Christmas not like what everyone else seemed to experience. Shoppers entered with their prizes and families shared holiday joy in the coffee shop that she never had known. She found solace in the church, with its beautiful displays celebrating the birth of Christ, poinsettias lining the altar.

She had just returned from St. Agatha's and donned the apron, ready to peppermint-all-the-things when he entered again. She knew by now his name was Zach. He had a Christmas bouquet consisting of red carnations, mini white carnations, noble fir and white pine. It *was* all the things that exemplified the Christmas season and was as big as his head.

"No strings attached, just a happy holidays to you." He flashed his winning smile. "Oh on a completely unrelated note, how about a cup of coffee? Right over there." He pointed to the table under the frosted window looking out on the street, her favorite table as she sipped her coffee and watched all the happy families trundle by.

She smiled to herself again. In her head, it was sweet that he seemed to know that was her favorite spot. She would sit there and watch as people streamed by, in her head writing their individual stories as they hurried past the window. Each received a story just like the many out of the books she lost heraself in. Often, she would lose track of time and be at the window long after her shift was over.

It seemed sweet that he picked that table, later it would occur to her that she was being manipulated. He was a master salesman, noticing the little things not because he cared, but to use as leverage. This was to manipulate her mood, coerce her into spending the time with him.

"Okay, well I'll take my peppermint work of art and sit at that table. You'll know it by the gigantic, beautiful Christmas bouquet that is sitting on top of it and the lonely, pleading guy just waiting for a beautiful barista to sit with him."

She couldn't help but laugh. And she couldn't help but give in this time. He just had a way about him.

For the next hour, Ellie heard all about Zach. His high school football days, his college days, his fraternity, and his job as a financial broker at the big firm Bauschor and Allen downtown. Later (much later) she would realize that this should have been a clue on the narcissistic tendencies, but at the time she was overwhelmed by the attention.

To her credit, he wasn't all bad - he made her laugh, made her feel special, and most of all, gave her attention as if she mattered and had always mattered. This was the gift of his charisma. She not only felt like she mattered, but felt like he had always known her and she had always mattered. There may have been signs, but it wasn't like he hit her (that came later) or yelled at her (that came first). He may have been talking about himself to himself, holding up the mirror to admire the most precious person in his life, but his gift to make her feel *there* pulled her in.

He also enabled her perfect role - quiet and listening, not having to put herself out there. She deferred and what she saw as attention, was really blood in the water. Once she submitted to him, he lusted to control.

It started with him stopping in a couple times a week, usually with a gift, sweet words, and a flashy white toothed smile. Then he took her to dinner. That could have been the first sign, if she had just listened.

Nine

She crunched over the debris in the hallway as she crept along. The peeling paint, the flicker of the lights, and the dancing shadows seemed to be somewhere else. Almost in a trance, leaning into the memories as they came back, she was somewhere else, some-*when* else. Her footsteps kicked up dust that hung in a low cloud above the checkered tile of the hallway. The dust-mist added to the eeriness hanging in the corridor. It was a stillness in time, a rift somewhere between time, hovering and not moving forward. The mist seemed to linger in the air longer than possible

I should have ran right away. The signs were there, Madelyn told me to. But I didn't listen. Dammit, he wasn't even charming but

I was caught up in it. No one ever paid attention to me and so I just went along, I felt I had to.

Ellie sighed audibly, the sound echoing off the walls.

No, that's not even true. Nora wouldn't have let me say that, she mused, though she realized she wasn't sure who Nora even was. Something was there, on the tip of her brain, she could almost feel it, like a shape in the fog where she could just see a silhouette, but could not make out the detail. *She would have told me to stop lying to myself. I didn't WANT it to end, the thought of being alone and nobody again seemed worse than the yelling, the degradation, and the hitting. I played right into the role and let him control me. All those years wasted.*

Nora, Helen, these people were slowly melting back into her but she could not quite get a coherent picture around them.

The self-justification, the realization that she was a frog in water, the temperature being slowly turned up. Each degree that passed without her standing up was an affirmation that it was okay, that she was going to take it. And it started right then, that first dinner date, she jumped in the water. It was warm but not boiling. Warm enough to be comfortable, and that comfort was the attention. Ellie spent her whole life in the background and on the floor, trying to stay out of the way, out of sight, out of the line of fire. From her mother, a drug addict and prostitute, she had been a mouth to feed. *Well, at least at first.*

Over the years, Ellie had gathered little about her coming into the world, and the little she did know she wasn't sure was even real or something she had made up to at least have a story. Even a bad story that fit her circumstances was better than her life just being a blank page, at least with a bad story she was *something*.

Her mother came from a broken home, her father abusive to both her and her mother. Her mother, Ellie's grandmother worked hard to provide but was bitter and hateful. Between her dour outlook and constant movement from job to job, no one gave Ellie's mother much attention. Unless, that was, her father was beating on her or abusing her with his friends.

The cycle continues, Ellie thought. *My mother was beat on, and then I walked right into Zach Weston.*

She liked to think that if the water was boiling instead of a comfortable warm, if she had been hit or pummeled on that first date, controlled, told to leave the coffee shop and her friends, she would have jumped right back out. She wasn't so sure - she was so broken and low, on the floor, that even the bad attention was better than *no attention.*

Furthermore, it was the perfect role for her. She wasn't alone, but also didn't have to put herself out there. She didn't have to say much or make decisions, she didn't get to.

It's amazing what you can convince yourself of, she thought. *It's your fault, you deserve it, it's not so bad - all the lies you tell yourself.*

And that's what they were - lies. She remembered someone telling her that, but not who. She remembered that things were bad, and she knew that she had told herself lies, but she wasn't sure what had happened?

Why am I HERE?

She was becoming frustrated with herself. She put her

hands on her head and gritted her teeth. *C'mon and remember!* she shouted at herself in her head, as if willing more to come back would make the veil of fog lift and tell her all the secrets her heart desired. *Did I leave? Am I still there? Is this a dream? Did he finally kill me and this is my hell, a ghost in this shit hole building?*

She screamed, this time out loud and hit the wall with her palm, knocking the plaster right off the crumbling and decrepit hallway wall, exposing the brick. The brick stung her hand and the pain brought back a bit of clarity as she saw that first night, and she remembered when Madelyn had…

*   *   *

… helped her buy a new outfit from that store in the mall that wasn't really fancy, but tried to be fancy. She even taught her how to keep the tags on it and tucked in so that she could return it after "just in case." That didn't feel right to Ellie but she acquiesced, just planned on pulling the tags later.

She felt special, taking the time to get ready - something she had never done - and spending the time with Madelyn. She did her hair and make-up, and as she looked in the mirror she grinned like a fool. She almost didn't look like the same person. No, that wasn't right, she just looked like she *should*.

She looked like she didn't have the history, that the streets were out of her, and she was *sophisticated.*

He picked her up in his Audi, right at the coffee shop. She had changed at the end of her shift in the back, and Madelyn had helped her with her right in the back of the shop.

As he approached, he held his arms out, smiling and leaning back.

"Check this out, whaddaya think of this?"

Ellie looked a bit puzzled, but nodded with a short smile.

"My suit. Custom, Armani." When she just nodded again, he shook his head. "Armani, wicked expensive, custom made for me. Need it at the firm."

"It's very nice," she said.

His face clouded a bit and his brow furrowed. "It's not *nice*, it's a fuckin' Armani." He shook his head.

"Riiiight, ease up there big fella" Madelyn said. "How about her? A compliment maybe? Hair, outfit, beauty, smile. Something, anything." She shook her head, falling right into her protector mode.

Zach shot a look toward Madelyn, eyes sharp with anger, the wry smile still frozen on his face. The eyes betrayed what was beneath the smile, a burning rage lurking just beneath the surface.

Madelyn met the gaze, not one to be intimidated and the air was still for a moment, a buzz to it like one of those calm, electric summer evenings right before a big storm. It seemed to Ellie that the world slowed down all around her and she felt her breath catch. For a moment, things teetered on the cliff of chaos, threatening to fall into the abyss.

"Yeah of course. You look good" Zach said and flashed a winning smile. "Let's get outta here."

He slid back around the car to the driver's side and pulled open the door.

"She's a beaut huh?" as he slid into the Audi A7 he was leasing.

Madelyn again shook her head and opened the door for Ellie, who then slid into the seat. Zach sped away from the curb before Ellie could even buckle her seatbelt. He jumped into traffic, pulling in front of a pickup that blared their horn. His finger flew out the window as he told her all about the car.

"This bad boy has a turbocharged 335-hp V-6, rides smooth as silk, zero to sixty in four-point-seven." Zach continued on about the car, weaving in and out of traffic.

She looked out the window ahead and saw their destination - Prime Oceana. The large brick building dominated the corner of 15th St. and Daniels Rd. It rose high two stories, its brown brick glowing in the light of the street lamps. Dark awnings hung over the windows and a valet stood out front.

He sped across the lanes with the tires squealing, another horn blaring from an oncoming car. He pulled at an awkward angle up to the curb and lept out. A quick glance around and he nodded to the attendant, tossed him the keys and headed off toward the restaurant entrance. A carpet was rolled out and it was lined with stanchions and red velour rope.

Ellie was unsure of what to do until the valet sat in the driver's seat and passed her an awkward look. He turned his head and saw Zach heading up the carpet. When he turned back to her, his face had softened into a sympathetic sadness.

Ellie threw open the door and followed. She entered the restaurant and looked around. The entrance was raised above the rest of the restaurant. She looked down on a series of fancily decorated round and square tables spread through the middle of the bullpen, and long rectangular tables on the sides. On the right side were some private rooms closed with fancy curtains with a balcony with more tables above them. The room had lights running up the left side wall, and at the far wall was a long bar that glowed with a dull red. Behind the bar, stacks of bottles were shelved on glass shelves with a mirror behind all the way to the ceiling, which glowed with a golden hue.

Ellie was completely overwhelmed. In the time she took to take all this in, the hostess and Zach had already moved away. Her heart began to flutter and then race as she looked around in panic.

She looked around, scanned up and down the staircase on her right, and then her left.

Nothing.

She felt her breath quicken and become short. She didn't belong here, she wasn't fancy enough for this. She looked for safety in the only familiarity she had in Zach, already feeling a dependence setting in.

Scanning to the right, she finally found him descending the stairs with the hostess. She had passed right over them the first time as Zach wasn't being led by the hostess, he was beside her with his hand on the small of her back as they stepped off the bottom step.

She hurried after them. She caught up to them at the table, the two of them laughing, she with her hand on his shoulder. She looked at Ellie and her smile quickly faded and she hurried away.

Ellie just looked down at her feet, and slid into one of the chairs.

"This place is impossible to get into. I got a table - I know the guy that owns this place."

"Really?" Ellie replied, trying to raise her eyes.

"Yeah, well, I know a guy who knows the owner. Anyway it doesn't matter, I got in here. What can I say, it's good to know me." He smiled at his own comment. "I am moving on up at the firm, working with Tom Sauer, you know Tom?"

Ellie shook her head, but he wasn't really looking at her.

"Yeah, I work with Tom. He was just on the news the other day talking about the markets. He sees stuff ahead and just knows what's coming and I work with him. We manage a hedge fund of about $1.2 billion. I do most of it now really, Tom is kind of like the face. That's why I have that Audi, and can get in here. If you're not somebody, you're fucking nobody, you know what I mean."

He smiled at her, though maybe more to himself.

"I guess I've just always been that way. Starting quarterback, king of the frat house. I once pranked a pledge by supergluing his ass cheeks together after he passed out. It was hilarious. I was legend there, and now the same thing at the firm. Just the way I am, I always win, something gets in my way - well, you mess with the bull you get the horns, you know what I mean?"

Unsure of what to say, Ellie was thankful the waiter interrupted.

"Good evening, the special of today is the sea bass, on a

bed of linguine in white wine sauce, served with a lobster bisque. We recommend pairing this with the 2005 Trimbach Pinot Gris Sélection de Grains Nobles, a wine with a perfect balance of structure and acidity."

"Yes, that sounds perfect."

Ellie was shell-shocked at the prices and could barely read the menu. She was relieved that he ordered for both of them without asking her or even glancing in her direction. It avoided the inevitable embarrassment. She could just follow his lead and let him take care of things.

She felt out of place and uncomfortable as she looked around the restaurant. Other patrons were in suits and ties or extravagant gowns. The light was a dim glow akin to a setting sun behind the trees and a low dinner music that seemed to magically drown out activity from other tables without being overbearing, creating a sense of intimacy at the table.

Men looked sophisticated, a presence around the room. The women, beautiful, composed, and strong - confident. Candles flickered on the tables atop fancy tablecloths and surrounded by heavy, comfortable chairs. A large chandelier hung from the middle of the room, adding to the ambiance. She slid down in her seat, trying to sink into it further, to hide - she didn't belong here. Zach continued on about his job, his college days, and his car. It helped that her only participation was to nod here and there. He was impressive, at twenty-two, four years older than her, graduated from college at UPenn with a Bachelor's in Finance and a big time job right out of school at the firm.

She was an imposter, her new nice clothes that paled in price compared to the strong women in the room, and she reverted to her ways to cope - silence on the floor. She continued to slink down in the chair, cast her eyes to the table in front of her, and melt into the environment. Her silence was perfect for Zach to continue, and she was thankful for it, helping ensure she was able to hide from any spotlight.

The food was incredible, and so was the wine. No one asked her age so she sipped the sweet, acidic taste of the wine. She felt its warmth down her throat and into her belly, letting it calm her a bit. She added very little to the conversation so she just let Zach continue on about himself.

The meal finished up and the bottle of wine got lighter until they could see the bottom, Zach putting the last couple drops in his glass. The bill came and was paid and they rose to leave. He led her out of the restaurant and the car (*not just a car, an Audi A7, 335 horsepower V-6!*) was pulled up by the valet.

Zach tipped the valet and stumbled a bit into the car. The valet smiled and opened the passenger side door for Ellie and she lowered herself in.

Ellie was light headed as the tires squealed and the Audi raced away from the curb. She held on as he weaved in and out, rubbing his eyes and blinking from the effects of the wine. She held her breath as he crossed lanes several times.

She gasped as he scraped the curb.

"What the fuck!" he yelled. He turned to her, anger seething on his face. "You wanna fuckin' drive?"

His face contorted and eyes unfocused, he turned back to the road in time to realize he was in the left turn lane and jerked the wheel back.

Ellie closed her eyes and tilted her down, facing her feet and the floor.

A car next to them beeped the horn as they passed by. Zach slammed on his breaks and rode right next to them. He was drifting back and forth, in the lane. He raised his middle finger across the seat, catching Ellie's chin with his hand in doing so.

He then gunned the engine and cut the opposing vehicle off, barely clearing the front end and causing the driver to swerve and hit the curb. The car spun out as it overcorrected behind Zach.

"Whoo-ey! Fuckin'-a right bitches." He turned to Ellie, his eyes maniacal. "Mess with the bull and get the horns mother fuckers."

He sped off and blew two more lights en route. Eventually, the car came to a halt and she opened her eyes, dizzy and sick to her stomach. They were waiting to turn into the parking garage under a building full of condos. They managed to make it into the garage and park across a couple of spots at an awkward angle. She was a bit confused, but afraid to ask what they were doing here and why she wasn't being dropped off at the coffee shop or Madelyn's apartment. Zach got out of the car so she did the same. He came around and led her toward the doors.

"C'mon" he said. His voice was slurred but not malevolent, contrasting the yelling outburst on the drive.

Zach's condo was right downtown at the Shelby Towers, known as a well to do place for high class society to have as a downtown pad for during the work week before retreating to high end environments in the suburbs. Another badge of success Zach wore, he swiped his badge on the elevator and the doors slid open. With his hand gently but firmly on Ellie's upper arm, he led her in.

She was swaying before the elevator started moving, but Zach was leaning heavily on the wall of the elevator. The doors reopened as she looked at him, obviously struggling from the volume of wine. He shook his head and punched the button for the fourth floor.

The elevator ride was smooth and short. Ellie wasn't used to elevators, let alone with carpet and a fruited water jug. The door slid open and Zach walked out. Ellie walked behind him, heart thumping, feeling alone and unsure of what was coming.

She went along though, not confident in doing anything else. Clinging to Zach as the only element of her environment that wasn't completely unfamiliar, she felt like being led by a siren's song, not wanting to continue but drawn, her feet not listening to her brain. Continuing, one foot in front of the other, doing what she was told. She knew how following the siren's song ended from her many days spent in the library, and she felt she was walking into the same fate.

Zach pulled over in front of his door and fumbled with his keys, dropping them to the floor. Grunting, he bent over to pick them up, balancing himself with the crown of his head to the door. The number 418 listed on the door.

Zach finally got the door open, pushing it wide and turning around. His eyes were half closed and he smiled at her. It wasn't a friendly smile, but a knowing smile, the smile of someone who is used to getting what he wants and knows he's going to get it again.

Ellie shrank back a bit, causing his brow to furrow and then his eyes to go dark.

"Wha-the-hell ur you doing?" his words slurring.

He took a step toward her, standing up straighter. He seemed to grow taller right in front of her, towering over her. The lights seemed to dim in the hallway and the dark, gaping hole of the door expanded. It was a blackhole, pulling at her.

"You think I paid all tha, you jus' go home. No, you got dinner now, now it's you turn." His voice raised. Ellie felt herself sinking, down to the floor. She was small, the blackhole was so large.

What am I supposed to do? She had no idea. Did she have to go in? If she didn't, what would happen to her?

Scared, alone, unsure, she did what she always did - she diverted her eyes to the floor, did as she was told, and hoped she wouldn't hurt.

She walked into the blackhole.

*　　　　　　*　　　　　　*

As she stood in the hallway, she knew it was all wrong, that very first night. She didn't have to go in, there was no implicit contract that she said she did because she had dinner and had been graced with his presence. However, that was what *he* thought of himself. She hadn't known any better, didn't know what was normal or *right*, and never had anyone to tell her. Everything had turned in a matter of moments. Within all the chaos, she had clung to Zach, dependent upon him right from the start. Comfortable being controlled so she didn't have to do it, even if it was all just abuse.

Well, that's another lie to myself, she thought. *I had Uncle Joe and Madelyn.*

She remembered the two of them, the coffee shop, how quiet Uncle Joe had a presence about him, a softness under that big white mustache and bushy eyebrows. Picturing his round face and rotund belly jiggling as he laughed his bellowing chortle, she smiled in spite of her current situation. His deep voice, used rarely, was always full of wisdom regardless of how short his statements were.

She had them, and they had both warned her. Madelyn had shown concern immediately following the shortened and selectively edited version of that first night that Ellie had told her, Uncle Joe had after he started coming into the coffee shop and making demands of her.

He told her how he couldn't talk to her that way and that she wasn't to be treated like his property. Madelyn's choice of words was much more colorful and escalated over the time period after that first night.

Things weren't all bad in the months that followed. Zach wore a mask, projecting confidence and charisma. This was how he manipulated people. Maybe he learned this at the firm, or maybe that's why he did well there. Either way, beneath the mask was vastly different. It came out when Zach was drunk and his anger, resentment, and insecurity showed its ugly face.

The two of them would walk down by the water, or have dinner, take in a show, even attend a Flyers game and had box seats for Phillies opening day. As time passed, the mask peeled away. It started with demeaning words here and there, and shots to blame her if things went wrong, or a few comments to make sure she knew that she was less than him. He would laugh at her, let her know what she said was silly. She learned not to say anything, just stay in her place. She was less than him, lower. She was on the floor, and he slowly groomed her to be walked on.

As he became bolder, the controlling became more direct. Instead of manipulating her emotions and lack of confidence to control her, Zach began directing what she could and could not do. He told her who she could see, when she could go to the library, and began to even tell her when she could go to work.

This last item is what took it over the edge. Just shy of the nine month mark, it culminated in a confrontation in the coffee shop when he came in one evening as the crowd just finished dying down.

"Ellie, grab you're shit, you have to go."

She remembered standing there, confused, eyes cast down to the sink full of mugs in front of her. By this time, the lukewarm water had started to grow warmer, inching toward boiling but not there yet.

"I have to close up"

"Too bad. Let's go now."

"I can't leave."

"I didn't ask, come here."

Zach had stepped forward and suddenly Uncle Joe was there. He was a big man but soft like Santa Claus. That softness was gone and in its place was a towering man with clenched fists.

"Talk to her like that again…" he trailed off, leaving the rest of the threat unsaid. It floated there like an anvil ready to drop on the three of them. The tone was so hushed and soft, but it carried to every corner of the shop, like a light but frigid breeze. It stopped Zach in his tracks and his eyes flashed with a bit of fear. He tried to recover.

"Kiss my ass old man. She is leaving now." HIs voice trembled just a bit as he turned his shoulders in a defensive posture and backed away. He had put a table between himself and Joe.

"You sound a bit scared there Zach. What's wrong? Not used to someone bigger than you standing up to your bull-shit," Madelyn called as she came around the register.

Ellie had continued to look down, the soap suds drifting down her forearms and back into the sink.

Zach backed up a few more steps.

"C'mon, come with me now or to hell with you." His eyes darted over to Joe as he finished his sentence, beginning to sound meek as he stepped further away from Joe. He took a step forward toward Ellie behind the counter and Joe took a quick sidestep to get in his path again, causing him to flinch.

Ellie moved around the counter. Her eyes on the floor, she felt like she was floating above the ground. She was unable to meet Uncle Joe's eyes as she passed and mumbled a weak and barely intelligible "I'm sorry."

She moved to the door as Zach cautiously walked sideways to keep an eye on Joe. Once they were safely by the door and out of Joe's reach, Zach turned forward and grabbed her roughly by the arms, pushing her forwards. This time he did open the passenger door - and shoved her in the car. He hustled around the front of the car, jumped in and peeled out.

"You're done there. You're not going back that fucking place, you understand me?" Zach yelled as he sped off. Visibly shaken, he moved to full over compensation mode. "Fuck them, those assholes just want you to slave away. That old bastard thinks he can talk to me that way? I will fuck him up and burn that shitbox to the ground. Mess with the bull and get the fuckin' horns. I see him on the street and I will fuckin' end him." He hit the steering wheel and screamed, a primal rage bursting from him.

When the screaming had finally stopped, there was silence in the car. They had pulled under his building "You're staying at my place from now on," he had said. "Don't even think of setting foot in that place again."

She remembered how emasculated he had been, his facade of toughness shattered by a few quiet words from Joe. She remembered the crack in his front that had exposed his weakness and self doubt beneath.

She also remembered that after a few drinks that night that he had recovered. Johnnie Walker Black Label, she learned, was his violent drink, together he and Johnnie felt strong enough to beat on her, put her in her place, and inflate his ego by inflicting pain. She remembered what came after - that was the first night he had hit her. He had been rough before, grabbing her and leaving bruises, or pinching her and laughing. But that was the first night that he struck her. It wasn't the last.

Ironically, that September day was her nineteenth birthday. By that time, he hadn't cared enough to remember. Instead of balloon and candles, ice cream and cake, it ended with her doubled over on the floor after being pushed into a wall and punched in the stomach.

Now in the hallway, she felt her own rage take hold of her, feeling a small flame inside her flicker that she hadn't known was there. Suddenly, as she looked around the hallway, the dark open doors gaping at staggered intervals down the hall, she didn't feel fear, but anger. Fueling inside of her, she felt the rising energy in her like the start of tidal wave building and pushing toward shore ready to unleash power and destruction.

Her eyes suddenly felt laser focused and she began to notice details in a new way. Instead of the shadows dancing and laughing at her, they appeared to be shrinking away from her. She felt a new control wash over her, and with that anger and rage, a strange sort of calmness. She realized that the energy she felt wasn't out of control, but focused. That calmness was a sense of purpose. Escaping whatever this was, hell, a sick joke, a predicament she had gotten herself into - she still wasn't sure what it was, but it was time for it to be over. She didn't know where these feelings came from - the version of herself that she recalled as of now didn't fit with this.

Her posture had changed and she stood tall, her stride moved from timid creeping forward to purposeful strides ahead, charging to the task at hand. She inhaled a deep breath and felt in control.

Control not anger. She had to be calm and collected, thinking it through.

Anger is the enemy. Who told her that?

She shook her head; she couldn't remember.

But she felt ready. She took another deep breath. She was in control.

That is, until she heard the sound.

Ten

She remembered back at Shyt House when the kids had laughed. It was usually those who were older, having endured Ms. Bath's relentless abuse, breaking any spirit they might have had, who completed the cycle of abuse on the younger kids. They would be out and about, perhaps at the basketball courts down the street, or hanging in the decrepit park on the other side. If there weren't dealers pushing their poison, the kids would at least escape there for a respite from Shyt House.

The older kids, especially if they had recently been a target, would bully … someone. Cheryl would lead the way more often than not, but if she wasn't there, another would dutifully fill in. Ellie had been the target enough, but it was others as well. It usually ended with being on the ground, trying to be small, and hoping it was just bruises. Some of the kids ended up seriously hurt, and there was Tabitha, who was beaten so badly, physically and emotionally, that she found a different way out of Shyt House after with a dirty razor blade found in a dumpster and the bathtub behind a closed bathroom door.

What Ellie remembered most was not the toes of the boots that might strike her, or the fingers yanking her hair, or even the insults thrown. It was the *laughter*. The laughter while she was teased, the laughter while she was hit, thrown to the ground, and kicked. It wasn't the blows that rained down; she had learned a long time before to ignore it and go to another place. No matter how far away she went though, the laughter cut through like a loudspeaker following her. When she was beaten down, lying on the ground, laughter. If she was just there or nearby out of the range of the hate from Cheryl or whoever was delivering the abuse, she heard it. It cut through her even if it was directed at Tabby or anyone else.

The sound she heard now in the decaying hallway was laughter. It came in low, sounding soft and muffled. And it grew. Laughter, but not like laughter she would have had with Nora, or Anna. Not a musical and infectious laughter like Madelyn's in the coffee shop, or the jolly chortle from Uncle Joe. Not even the slightly-maniacal-but-not-threatening cackling for the Helen apparition (*she is the ghost, not me!*)

No, it was a diabolical laugh, menacing. It was the laughter that was generated from a perverse joy in someone else's pain. The sadistic sound of someone destroying happiness and pulling a soul full of light into the darkness of misery.

A chill ran down Ellie's spine and she shivered, suddenly aware that the hallway had become much colder, her breath misting in front of her in a small cloud. The candles began to flicker harder, the dancing shadows suddenly appearing angry, a cold breeze pushing down the corridor and the flames leaning away from it. She was half way down the corridor, her stomach tightening in a knot. Rotating her whole body, she peered back down the passageway with a clenched jaw. Her teeth ground together, the confidence gone, the internal flicker extinguished as she stood with heavy legs.

The laughter echoed through the hall, bouncing off the walls and coming back to her. It grew louder. And then footsteps.

Not footsteps, she thought.

Heavy, thudding noises followed the laughter.

Hooves.

Mixed in with the laughter was now an animal sound, sounding like snorting. The sounds echoed off the walls, floating from where Ellie had come from. Shaking the concrete from her lower body, she didn't waste time squinting into the darkness, but flew down the hallway.

Time to go.

She ran down the hall as the sounds came closer. As she reached the end of the hallway, she looked behind her. The sounds were increasing, deafening in her ears, rivaled only by her pounding heart.

The hallway behind her remained empty as far as she could see.

Using a turned over, rusted out cart and a hole in the

drywall, she scaled up the wall and reached for one of the burning candles. She stretched, reaching with her fingers. She brushed the base of the candle with her outstretched fingers. As she shot a glance down the hallway, she felt the cart shift under her. She grasped the candle's mount to steady herself, swearing she was starting to see shadows of the approaching beast.

C'mon, she thought to herself, stretching as far as she could.

She stretched a bit further and wrapped her fingers around the base of the candle, lifting it just clear of the base with her finger tips.

The plaster crumbled under her, forcing the rest of her weight on the cart, which then followed suit, toppling her over. She tried to leap off the cart as it fell apart, holding her breath. Her eyes never left the flame of the candle and it managed to stay lit as she stumbled forward.

Covering the front of the flame with her hand, she once again stole a glance backwards - still empty, dancing and mocking shadows her only company. The sounds continued to increase in amplitude - laughter, growling, and snarling.

She hurried the rest of the way down the hallway. She ran past decrepit and empty rooms, looming dark. She imagined some beast or demon jumping out of the darkness and grabbing her, pulling her in. She scurried along, trying to keep the candle lit, and trying to outrun her fear and thundering heart.

She felt the wave of anxiety wash over her, a cold chill as sweat ran down, and realized she wasn't even breathing. As she approached the end of the hallway, there was - nothing.

The wall just met at the corner and there was nowhere to

go. She turned in a full circle, once again holding her breath. Nothing but rooms up and down.

She heard a whimpering. It took her a moment to realize it was *her* - the sound was escaping her lips and her chest was shuddering. The sound of the creature was still echoing down the hall. There was nowhere to go, nowhere to run. The ceiling reached further away, receding as she began to sink down, sliding with her back against the wall.

Calm down and think, she scolded herself.

An elderly woman in a wheelchair flashed into her mind, her frizzy white hair up. She was fragile yet tough as leather, a lined and cracked face with sharp, fierce eyes.

Fight. Never back down, the woman was saying, a burning cigarette dancing in between her lips with every word. *Get your ass up and get movin'!*

Ellie shook her head, but a calm washed over her.

She squinted in the room on her right as she faced back down the hallway. The faint light of the moon came in through a window, barely perceptible. She turned to her left and there was nothing but darkness. She squinted further and raised the candle, walking back down the hallway a few feet.

The last room wasn't a room at all, but another short hallway. She entered in it tentatively, the darkness in the alcove swallowing up any light from the hallway. She raised her candle up and squinted. As she inched forward, the back wall of the alcove began to materialize in the darkness.

She strode forward and reached a countertop with a series of locked drawers. Abandoned and forgotten, some of the drawers were missing or wrenched out onto the dirty tile floor. She found a sink, cracked and old, and above it on the wall what appeared to be an old poster, half ripped from the wall. A patch of black mold crawled from the bottom right corner closest to the sink, the left shredded away to only reveal half the faded poster.

Beauty is Therapy, it stated, warped with the curl and yellowing of time. The words below were faded and ran into the tear, the rest of the message missing. She raised the candle further and saw a busted out cabinet hanging off the wall, holding on admirably with one last screw into the stud. The cabinet was covered in mold as well, swallowed up.

The roaring behind her increased as she backed out of the alcove, and moved on toward the darkness. Stepping over more debris, Ellie entered another hall that stretched as far as she could see in the darkness. Holding her candle up, she moved forward quickly down the hall, trying to focus only ahead, not behind her or to the side. She raced down the hallway as far as she could go. The corridor was dark, but laid out the same as the one she had just left. The hallways appeared to swing out, offset and stacked: hallway, little alcove, another wing. They fanned out away from that entrance she had identified through the window. It occurred to her now how she was getting further from this goal with each step.

She ran down another row of dark rooms, the moonlight bleeding in from the darkness through barred windows, casting haunting shadows in the rooms.

She slipped on plaster and went down, sliding on her hip like a baseball player into home plate. Her knee burned but she managed to keep the candle lit and bounce back to her feet. The noises continued to grow and she could hear hooves running toward her, the pace quickening.

As she reached out the end of the hallway, she stole a glance back. The darkness swallowed up the light past fifteen feet. The monster was not within that distance yet, but that brought little comfort - she had no confidence that it wasn't just beyond her sight.

She looked to her right and saw the stairwell door propped open. She quickly stepped through the stairwell and tripped over debris unseen. She fell forward and caught herself with her left hand and followed by her chest on the hand rail as it looped from the steps around across the landing. An audible *oomph* blasted from her lips and she realized she was holding her breath again.

She paused to orient herself, the candle miraculously still lit. A loud *click* behind her caused her to whirl around. The door back to the floor she had been on (*the second? Could she remember?*) had closed. She turned her attention to the descending stairwell and started to move down. She hit the top step when she heard a loud thud. Followed by another.

And another.

The sounds echoed in the stairwell and it took a few more to isolate that they were coming from below. A loud nasal exhale followed, floating up the stairs. Ellie was holding her breath again. She backed up the step and went back to the door. She gently leaned on the crossbar, trying to get back out to the hallway where she could put a solid structure between her and the monster.

The door did not budge. She leaned harder. Nothing.

When the door had closed behind her, it had locked.

That's when the monster appeared on the landing below. It stopped its slow, thudding pursuit and looked up at her, just standing there, its heavy breathing echoing through the landing. Ellie, frozen where she was, stared back. The monster's eyes glowed red in the dark, peering up at Ellie with malevolence. The ax hung at its side, dangling in its right hand. The monster's shape seemed to swirl in the darkness, like a silhouette that wasn't quite solid. That is, except for its head, a long snout, a row of white teeth streaked with a dark substance, slobber dripping. The red eyes, piercing through the darkness, and the horns. The horns reached upward, almost shining.

The monster twirled the ax in its hand, and then leaned forward in a ear splitting roar, its large mouth opening, spittle flying, ragged teeth flashing. It seemed to be relishing her fear, soaking it in.

Ellie didn't hide or crumble to the floor - she threw the candle as hard as she could straight at the gaping mouth and bolted up the steps to her right. She was halfway up the first set of steps when she heard the candle connect and the animal cry out. Then it roared again and its hooves beat on the steps. She grabbed the railing and twirled herself across the landing to the next set of steps, her feet not even touching the landing. She leapt up the steps two at a time and crashed through the door (*unlocked thank you, Lord*) onto the third floor. She was at the end of the building so she ran to her left. She felt her pursuer's breath on her neck, its hand reaching out, ready to grab the collar of her shirt and pull her back.

She felt crawling on her neck and upper back, like that of an outstretched hand.

Not sure if it was her hysteria or real, she pushed harder. She slipped on debris and slid on the floor, crashing into the doorway of one of the rooms. She pulled herself in, wind knocked out of her, stars floating in her head.

As she crawled, she saw she was in an open room, with another door in the back. As she crawled for that door, she heard another roar echo down the hallways. She scrambled quicker, frantic and unable to even pick herself up. Her hands cut on the plaster, brick, and debris on the floor, she crawled into the back room. It appeared to be an old community shower. There were no pipes anymore but there was a tiled off section in the back right corner. She crawled across the tile floor, over the drain in the middle, and around the opening to a small privacy room. She pulled herself all the way to the back corner, panting and curled up. Trying to control her little sobs, tears streaming down her face, she worked to regain her breath from the ragged gasps escaping her.

She waited to see if her pursuer would find her. She couldn't go any further, she had fought and done the best she could do.

She sat and composed herself, wondering if those awful red eyes and shining horns would appear around the tiled wall, determined to stand tall to the end and not cry out.

If death comes, I will stare it down until the end.

Her voice trembled even in her own head and her body shook uncontrollably, an melodic tapping as her fingernails tapped the tiled wall behind her. She tightened her hug across her chest. Even her teeth chattered in fear.

I'll fight it. I won't cower.

That sounded a lot braver than she felt.

Eleven

Ellie sat on the floor regaining her breath for what seemed like an eternity. The third time she heard a roar, it was soft and barely reached her, and she began to believe that she had escaped again - at least for the time being. She slowed her breathing and drew in until her lungs were on the verge of bursting, then let it out with a *whoosh* that echoed off the old shower walls. Once again, she surveyed her body, head to toe.

Her headache had faded but her ribs ached, each ragged breath sending shooting pain through her. Sliding into the doorway had reawakened the pain from where she had hit the desk. Her hands had minor cuts on them from crawling across the floor. Beads of blood trickled and her hands burned, but nothing looked or felt serious.

Still here in one piece.

Every time she felt herself coming back, felt an inner fire start to burn, she was shoved right back to the ground. She would conjure her strength in this awful place and as it started to build, the monster would show up or she would melt into the Other World and be told she was dead - a ghost. It made some sense that this would be a version of hell. She felt as if she was constantly being tormented, dark and demons dancing in every corner, a monster on the prowl through this old asylum (*if this Helen character is to be believed*).

This labyrinth of rooms swirling with darkness and decay, she felt like she was running in circles. Her goal had been to get to the first floor and now she was at the far end of the southern batwing on the third floor. The more she ran and the further away she seemed to end up. She needed to get off the hamster wheel, stop running in place.

How do I get out of here? Can I get out of here?

She surveyed the room. She was in a small alcove in the corner of what appeared to be a community shower room. The alcove was made of large yellow bricks and extended about halfway to the fourteen foot ceiling. There was a broken, decaying opening against each wall. The ground sloped to a drain in the middle and the floor in the entire room was a dark yellow tile with a flower pattern with pale yellow petals and a faded blue center.

Ellie stood and left the alcove and out into the main bathing area. As she crept across the threshold, she scanned left and right, trying to peer across to the exit. Shrouded in darkness, she could not see anything. Though she had heard the roars off in the distance, her mind imagined that the monster was just out of sight, lurking in the shadow. Grinning its slobbery, toothy grin, it would wait until she approached close enough to reach out and grab, dragging her off to wherever to be devoured.

The darkness swirled as she squinted into it. Then it began to lighten, as if her eyes were adjusting to the lack of light. However, she had been in the dark for the last half hour sitting, and the light kept growing until she could see all the way into the small entry room off the hallway. As the light grew, the tiles began to brighten. Large pipes grew out of the walls and capped at shower heads sprinkled around the wall. Pipes materialized and ran along the ceiling. The yellow tile became crisp and the blue shined.

Suddenly, water began to rain down from the shower heads and two women were underneath them. The women were dazed, almost looking asleep on their feet as they stood. A nurse stood at the doorway observing.

Ellie walked through the entry into the staging area for the communal shower. She saw a series of benches lining the walls for changing areas and a small cabinet area for the nurses. She passed through and out into the hallway.

This hallway was much different from the one she had been in earlier. It lacked the flowers and the piano. The art on the walls was smaller and placed up high, out of reach. She saw a few benches and chairs lining the walls. She neared the closest one and saw that it was attached to the floor and the wall.

Ellie jumped as the sounds of screaming emerged from one of the rooms down the hall. A woman came running out with nurses right on her heels. She ran into the wall and bounced off. Her hair was cut short and uneven, and she had a large scar down the side of her face. She was skin and bones, her eyes sunken and dark, her upper lip drawn back in a look of terror as her eyes flashed wildly about. Her top row of teeth were darkly discolored where there were teeth at all. She screamed again and ran down the hall.

She approached where Ellie stood and grabbed the chair next to her. The woman yanked on it, and when it didn't budge she wrapped her arms around the chair and climbed into it, sitting sideways in the chair against the wall. She began to sob, rocking back and forth. Her wails echoed down the hallway.

Ellie had instinctively been backing away without even realizing it. She stood in front of the room across the hall as the nurses came running after her. Ellie ducked into the room to avoid the three nurses rushing to the woman, though they could not see her.

They calmed when they arrived at her, as if they had seen this before and knew the manic episode had devolved into the sobbing fit. They began to coax her and talk gently, attempting to further calm her and gain control.

Ellie turned to observe the room she was in. It had a large window, like all of the rooms, and the bright light of the day caused a glow in the space. The room was barren, just a bed against the wall, and only about eight feet wide by ten feet deep. She saw movement outside the window and approached. She was indeed on the third floor. She could tell by the light and the rising mist that the new day's sun was blasting away. She was facing west with the sun bleeding into the fields off to the south but not over the top of the building yet.

Down below and off to her right, she saw a series of cottages, including a large cottage right below her. Further to the right she saw a large railway and a building with pipes and wires running into and out of it. The rail had a cart on it with what appeared to be coal and some men were unloading it. The building seemed to be some kind of power facility. She scanned back to her left and saw people out working in the fields and orchards. Nearest to her, people were walking to and from the fields. She saw all sorts of activity and people milling about. She saw pigs and chickens, apple trees and cherry trees, and vegetable fields running into the distance.

As she stood, mesmerized by the beauty of the landscape below her and the sun shining down on the work in the fields, she noticed a woman walking back toward the building. The woman raised her eyes and looked straight at Ellie. Even from three stories up Ellie recognized the wavy graying hair and tilted head. It was Helen.

Helen began waving wildly, her whole body involved. She was shaking from her feet all the way up to her hand extended out over her head. Ellie could see her lips moving but could not hear her through the window or from so far away.

She was jumping around, waving emphatically, and a man approached her. He placed his arm on her and talked to her. She nodded vigorously and calmed down. She began to walk slowly with her arms stiff at her side, looking like a child heading for the hotel pool, trying so hard not to run. Her pace picked up as she put distance between herself and the man, some kind of employee of the asylum. As he turned away, she glanced over her shoulder and began running. Ellie leaned forward against the glass as Helen disappeared out of sight in the shadow of the building.

Ellie knew she was running to see her - Helen's Ghost. She turned and headed toward the hallway, not sure if or when Helen would make it up to this wing. The commotion had been handled and the corridor was empty.

The "shimmering" happened again at that moment (that's what she thought of it as, a shimmering of reality with when the Other World seems to melt in or out), but this time instead of going back to her dark prison, the shimmering stopped with the same hallway she had been in.

The corridor was still empty and still looked the same. Wait, something *was* different. She couldn't place it. The furniture was the same, the art on the wall had not changed.

The light was different. She turned back to the room she had left and looked in. A woman, blonde and heavyset, lay on the bed with her back to Ellie. Sunlight streamed into the room. She walked to the window and looked out. There were still people out in the fields but the number had been significantly reduced. The sun was now past the apex point and coming down on the western side of the building. It must be a bit after midday.

It was as if she leapt in time. Was it still the same day? She wasn't sure, and wasn't sure how to find out. Or if she should care. Why do these visions keep occurring? She shivered again, wondering if this *was* reality and she really was a ghost, the dark world her prison as she is tormented by the monster.

She turned back into the hallway, intent on seeing more of the asylum in this Other World.

Maybe it will help me escape the Dark World.

It occurred to her that she was labeling the two worlds, and that her brain had just decided to accept this situation as normal.

As she rounded the door frame to head back toward the middle, Helen stood at the end of the hallway. Her face lit up as she saw Ellie, and she began waving all over again. Helen rushed down the hall and met Ellie before she could take more than a few steps. She looked around and then motioned for Ellie to move back into the shower area where she had started.

The women and nurses were gone and the shower was empty. The shower was cleaned and polished, the room outside perfectly spotless and tidy. There was nothing lying around, not a speck of dirt anywhere.

The cleanliness and beauty seemed to be everywhere you looked in the asylum - the previous floor with beautiful art and flowers everywhere, the fresh flowers adding color and life in Helen's room on the inner wing; the arboretum with the beautiful trees out front; the power in the structure of the building, including the majestic entryway. There was even beauty in the farm out back, the hard work yielding fresh fruit and vegetables, bringing life into the world like the cow she had overheard about earlier.

All of this confused Ellie, and made her wonder which world was real and which was a dream. Asylums were not beautiful and clean, doctors weren't kind and genuine, playing the piano. The doctors were mad scientists and mutilated patients to create the start of the zombie apocalypse. Asylums were the start of ghost stories -

She laughed out loud at her unintended pun.

Ellie remembered being scared on her first shift into the Other World through the shimmering. She remembered wishing her Dark World would come back. Now, all she wanted was to stay here in the beauty, walk among the trees, feel the sunshine on her face.

Helen brought her around the corner, back in the community shower area. They had the place just to themselves.

"Yer back! I am so happy, I missed you!"

"You can see me?" Ellie asked.

"O'course! Yer my ghost friend! I din't know if you'd wait for me when I saws you this mornin' in the wind-er," Helen said.

"I tried to come right away, but they got me. I do laundry sometimes," she explained as if to her oldest friend. "Then I hads to eat lunch. We had soup, which I like in the winter, but it was good. Still a lil cold in the mornin'."

Ellie nodded, still a bit confused. She was getting used to Helen and could not help but like her energy and zest. She had an intensity about her but also a supreme kindness.

Helen's face suddenly lit up and she stood taller, puffing her chest out and removing her slumped posture.

"Guess what? Guess what?" she exclaimed, her whole face glowing. "I helped with a baby cow."

"Yes," Ellie replied. "I remember you saying that earlier today."

"Today?" Helen said, her face crumpled in confusion. "No, this was a lot of sleeps ago. I think almost a month."

"Oh" was all Ellie could muster in response. It seemed her jaunts into Other World jumped around in Helen's time. "Well, what day is it?"

"Ne'ermind that, I hafta tell you bout the cow. I helped with the cow, pretty baby cow, it was all slimy and gross but I helped and then I fed it. It took a whittle-itty-bitty baby bottle." She changed her voice for the end and was smiling ear to almost-ear, that left side still drooping a bit.

"That's amazing," Ellie said. She couldn't help but smile as well. The smile felt foreign and strange. Her situation was chaotic, confusing, and scary. She felt like she was losing her mind, and yet the smile came across her face and she fed off of the elation that Helen was exuding.

"No, no. That's not it." Her words came out hissing, echoing in the room as if she was trying to be quiet but could not contain herself. "They named her Colantha like I asked. Traverse Colantha Walker. She gunna be a great cow!"

All of Ellie's troubles melted away at the simple joy that came from Helen. And it *was* joy, not happiness which is a fleeting moment, but down in the bones and soul joy that Helen had and was pouring out. That pouring out electrified Ellie, giving her an energy that seemed to shove away her despair - despair at the unknown, despair of the monster chasing her, despair at not fully knowing who she was or how she got here

Despair of (*maybe*) being a ghost.

It crossed her mind that if she were banished to hell to

be tormented for eternity she shouldn't feel this kind of joy. She also felt that if she could feel such warmth for Helen, she couldn't be a bad enough person to be relegated to hell, could she?

"That's amazing! I am so happy for you!" Ellie said. She genuinely meant it, and suddenly found herself wanting to hear more about it. She snapped back to focus. "Can I ask you a question, Helen?"

"O'course!"

"What day is today?"

"Well, I know it's May because we jus' did calendars."

"And it was a few weeks since you saw me and told me I was a ghost?"

"Uh yes! It was a few weeks." She frowned. "Then you just went away. I was sad and a-scared that you was mad at me, and you wun't gunna come back."

"Oh no, dear, I wasn't mad at you at all. No, I was just surprised. I can't control when I get to see you. In fact, to me that was just about an hour ago."

She reached out and rubbed Helen's arm. She was actually surprised that she could feel Helen's blouse in her fingers.

"Wow, your warm, I thought you'd be cold," Helen said. "Yer know, bein' a ghost and all."

Ellie smiled.

"My name is Ellie."

"I know *that*. You told me that after we met. I still sorry about being scared that first time, but I'm glad you came back to visit."

"We've met before? Before when you told me I was a ghost?"

"Yes, you've visited a bunch!"

"When did I first meet you?" Ellie asked.

"Well there was when I got a-*scared,* that was Christmas. I 'member 'cause the deec-o-rations were up and we hads the dance. I was so happy you visited at the dance and wasn't mad at me. An' you he'ped me there too!"

Ellie took this in. She didn't remember any of this. Was this another memory that hadn't come back yet, or was Helen confused? She obviously was in the asylum due to some inability to take care of herself. She struggled with her speech, stood slightly stooped, seemed simple minded, and had physical ailments on the left side of her body. Maybe this was all part of her ailments?

A strange thought occurred to her, the clothes, the structures, the shower heads seeming very old fashioned.

"Helen what year is it?"

"It's May." she said and shrugged.

"It's so beautiful here, it's not what I think about when I think of an asylum." Ellie said.

"Beauty is therapy, work is therapy," Helen replied, changing her voice to add a deep quality and pulling her face back. Ellie realized she was imitating someone.

"So this place is an asylum, do you know which one? Do you know where we are?"

"You askin' a lot of questions. I do know that 'un. We in Traverse City Asylum. I know all about it."

Her voice changed again and Ellie realized she was repeating verbatim what she had heard.

"This is the Traverse City asylum... " and she began to tell Ellie what she knew. "which opened in 1885."

"That's a long time ago," she whispered, breaking her character and then switching back. "Beauty is therapy, work is therapy. We are surrounded by the beauty of the world to heal us and we work the grounds because we have meaning. Time spent in nature is good for us, and nature will help us heal. We have a farm with many animals and crops, of which we earn our keep and sell to support the facility."

Her character voice was waning, excitement growing.

"I he'ped with a baby cow. Oh, darn," she said, snapping her fingers as her arm moved in an arc across her belly. "I a'ready told-ja that. Anyway, I he'ped with the cow and named 'er!"

She was grinning again, shaking her head in affirmation to push the point.

"Anyways. I get to help on the farm. I like the am-di-bles." She cautiously pronounced the word, drawing out *animals*. "Anyway, better 'an the veggies. I dun't go out every day, but the day room is fun too! I gets to meet other people."

At that she leaned in close to Ellie, put her hand by the side of her mouth and whispered fiercely, making the sound louder than when she was talking.

"You gotta be careful, though, people in here are a bit crazy. Watch out for Hans, he'll yell at your for stealin' his u-chickens, and then Willie'll strum is ole gee-tar. Most awful sound." She shook her head sadly.

"That's what we do. We be a-workin', be a-talkin' to the doctors. They's really nice. They asks us lots o' questions, and hep us appr-e-shee, shee" her face scrunched while she struggled through the word. "Appreciate." She smiled and nodded triumphantly.

"Appreciate what?" Ellie asked.

"Beauty. We gets to see the beauty in life with the am-dibles, with the veggies, gets to see hard work makes things like food. We gets to see all the pretty flowers and the sunshine. That's my fav-o-rite, the sunshine. I could jus' sit by them windows over there and close my eyes, feeling the sunshine make me feel sleepy and warm."

She smiled again.

"The doctor says the sun is important for healin'. I am gonna heal fast with all the sun I get. Even in the snow, I likes to look out at the cookie-wagon going by -"

"Cookie-wagon?" Ellie asked.

"Uh-huh. The cookie wagon brings milk around. There is a lil' boy who helps sometimes. Big barrels of milk and food. I gets to see the horses pullin' it."

Face brightening from a sudden realization.

"Nows that I am here and go outside, I bet I could say hi to that boy. I'd say 'hi boy!' and he say 'hi' back. Maybe I can even help shovel with the coal scoops. I seen them doin' that after the big snow and it looks like so much fun!"

Helen's voice trailed off and her face reverted back to a more serious demeanor. She smiled her half smile at Ellie, cocking her head to the side and looking up at her.

"We's can't be here. I get in trouble. This be the *difficult* wing," Helen said, taking her by the hand. "Peoples be comin' back up soon."

"What does that mean?" Ellie asked.

"So's, the far away rooms be fer *difficult* peoples." Helena answered, emphasizing the word difficult in the deep voice as if repeating what she had heard. "They sometimes break things, get all mad. They say as you move to the middle, you be closest to getting out."

Ellie began to understand. The patients that needed the most care or presented the most danger to themselves or others were in the outer wings of the facility.

"I start over here, but nows I am over dere" she said pointing. She smiled and puffed her chest out, a sense of pride. "That's why I gots to be at the dance, and now I gets to be outside and with the am-dibles."

"How long have you been here?" Ellie asked.

"I dunno. I know I had an acc-i-dent" she said, pointing to her scar that shined white in the late day sun. "But, I supposed to be in the Day Room now and then it's almost supper time."

"Helen! What are you doing over here? You know you aren't supposed to be here," a voice called, as if on cue. "Who are you talking to?"

A nurse was coming straight for Helen, a mild look of concern but no anger on her face.

"No one, ma'am. Jus' thinking out loud." She gave a winning smile and a quick side wink at Ellie. The nurse took her by the arm and led her away, not seeing Ellie at all.

Ellie followed her around the corner, through the alcove,

and into the next wing. The paintings returned in this wing, as did the flowers on the wall at head height. She walked to a set of flowers on the wall and breathed in. The wonderful smell filled her nostrils like an unexpected summer day's breeze that pushes the stale air of winter out. She smiled and took another deep breath. The air filled her lungs all the way down to her belly, the scent filling her with calmness. The pain in her ribs even seemed to melt away.

She reached her hand up and felt the red and white petals of the flowers. The silky material felt soft in her hands. It all felt so real.

As if triggered by the very thought filling her head, the flowers began to darken. The petal in her hand wilted and turned black. Its dry brittle texture caused it to crumble in her hand. The color of the flowers ran down the wall, mixing with the paint on the wall and ran to the floor. She turned, looking up and down the hall. It was devoid of the nurse and Helen, the walls running with colors dripping to the floor. The entire hallway appeared to be bleeding. The walls, the art, and the flowers. The furniture seemed to liquefy and melt to the floor. When there was no color left to bleed, the floors cracked and splintered, the pools of color running through the cracks like a drain.

And she was back in the Dark World.

Twelve

Her heart jumped as she spun around, looking for the creature. She was alone. Her relief led to despair as she realized she missed Helen and the Other World. The contrast of light and dark, life and death, love and emptiness seemed so stark. She was already longing for the next *shimmering* to occur.

Can I make it happen? she thought.

She closed her eyes and concentrated, squeezing her eyes. *Bring me back to the Light World,* she thought. The words echoed in her head, almost as if she was yelling.

She opened her eyes and the darkness remained.

She repeated again, shouting in her head.

Open sesame! she thought. *It always worked in the books, right?*

Again she opened her eyes to the darkness and she felt silly.

With all the shit that's happened, why should I feel silly?

Still, regardless of her self-deprecating thoughts on the matter, she pined for a return to the Light world, the land of fresh smells and bright colors. If only she could figure out how it occurred. What was it? A particular spot, a special time, or when she said a certain phrase? Or was it completely random?

Unless of course, she was already dead, or maybe she was in the hospital in a coma and this was all a dream. Some great tumor in her head, or Zach finally beat the shit out of her enough that she couldn't recover. It had almost happened before. There was the time that he pummeled her so bad she peed blood for a week.

Dead and in Hell, living through this miserable place, the shimmering just a part of the overall story of suffering that she was being forced to participate in? Would it be that this scenario put the fresh flowers under her nose just so she would know the pain of them wilting away? A metaphor of death that she must endure over and over? She could en-vision Hell being the repeated teasing of beauty to have it wrenched away, causing her to die repeatedly.

Again, she wondered in her head how long eternity was.

At this point, she told herself, it didn't even matter. She had to see if she could get out of here; she had to keep pushing forward. She gathered herself a bit and tried to force herself to think.

She had started on the third floor. She had been near the middle of the building when she had awakened. She had run from the creature the first time and found the stairwell that she had fallen down. That would have been at the end of this wing.

She was right around the corner from where she had started.

The thought depressed her. She was battered and bruised. She had run from the creature, fallen down stairs, been choked, had an ax swung at her, slid into the door frame, and cut her hands on the debris in the bathroom.

God only knows the grime and germs in those cuts.

This was in addition to the initial beating from her abduction.

Or maybe murder? She returned again to the feeling that she was already dead and serving an eternal penance.

She pushed down the feeling of defeat and took another deep, cleansing breath. Except it was really a mildew and stench breath, far from the flowers in the same spot a few moments ago.

She stepped into the nearest room to look out the window. *Maybe someone will be out there and can help. Or if this really is hell, do I even want to go out there.*

She remembered the little yellow house in the distance, her goal, her beacon, *her salvation.* She strode toward the window to look out when she realized in the middle of the room was an object. It was hard to see in the dark and gloom, but she could make out the shape of a small person, hanging down from an exposed beam in the ceiling. It was a very small person, or more accurately, a doll.

She was a porcelain doll with a white face, rosy cheeks and

golden blonde hair. She had a wry smile, a white dress with frills down the middle. The doll was old, an antique.

As she approached the doll hanging, she heard the high pitched sound of maniacal laughter floating in the door from the hallway. She turned around quickly, her heart beating fast. She was on high alert and slowly moved back toward the door.

"*ELLLLLLLIIIIIIEEEEEEEE*" drifted down the hallway like a mist. It was faint and could have been the breeze through a barred and broken window. "*ELLLLLLLLLLLLIIIIEEEEEEEEE....*"

Apprehension telling her to stop, that she didn't *want* to see what was coming. That part lost out on the part that was ready to take the challenge head on, ready to fight.

As her eyes cleared the doorframe, a massive roar thundered in her face. She jumped back out of the door, expecting the monster to be there, almost able to see the glint of light of the blade of the axe. As the roar faded it was replaced by a new laughter, deep and baritone.

Laughing at me, she thought. Her body was shaking, the roller coaster of emotion, confidence then despair and back again, causing her to shudder. A wave of sweat rolled over her, the adrenaline washing through her body.

"Screw you, you bastard," she hissed, though not even convincing herself.

She didn't creep around the doorframe but strode right across the threshold, poised to fight or run. Her eyes searched the hallway, right then left.

The hallway was empty. The laughter continued to echo down the corridor, but she was alone. She turned on her heel and reentered the room. The doll swung in the gentle breeze coming in through the window. The moon light rode the breeze into the room, illuminating the doll and causing its white cheek to glow.

Ellie shivered in the cold air and she could hear the gentle whisper of fallen leaves blowing outside the window, its susurration providing an ominous non-diegetic number as she honed in on the hanging object in front of her. Approaching the doll, her breath began to show in front of her, casting a mist around the doll in the moonlight.

The doll stared back at her, its little smile seemingly unaware that its head was bashed in above the right temple.

It took Ellie back down memory, to a little stand outside of the opening preseason Eagles game that she went to with Zach. To a little Asian lady, a doll that looked similar, and to the rage. She had wanted the doll and picked it up on the way by. Zach had been talking to a client and drinking after tailgating before the game. She had been thoroughly embarrassed as he had his hands on her, teased her, called her names, and pinched her ass in front of his friends and client that he was hosting. She had drifted to the back, looking at her feet when she passed by the makeshift booth.

The doll had called out to her. Her blouse was frilled baby blue instead of the white the current version wore, and the eyes seemed to shine. She was moved by an inanimate object and felt an infusion of joy that she hadn't had since the coffee shop. She had picked it up and turned it over in her hands. The doll seemed to have the joy that her own life lacked and she couldn't help but think that if she had the doll that some of the joy would be hers. She could take care of it, love it the way she had never been loved. A triggering of a maternal instinct, perhaps.

That had ended as quickly as it began, when it was wrenched from her hands by Zach.

"What the fuck are you doing? We're trying to get into the game" he hissed at her. He moved in close enough so he could drive his thumb into her ribs without anyone seeing. She gasped as her wind escaped her.

"Over this stupid, ugly ass thing?"

"You pay for that mister" the old Asian woman said.

"I'm not paying for this ugly piece of shit."

"You broke it, you buy it!" the lady shouted. She was a fierce little woman, with scrunched up face behind large glasses. As usual, Zach started to back down when he was stood up to. He looked at the doll, part of its blouse ripped open.

He pulled his wallet out.

"How much?"

"Twenty-five dollars"

"You have got to be shitting me? This garbage isn't worth a quarter." His face reddened and he was getting angry.

"Fine. For you, thirty dollars and get out of store," she shouted back, waving her hands at him.

Ellie felt an elation build up in her belly as Zach threw thirty dollars down and turned away with the doll. He walked away and she jogged to keep up.

"Can - can I have the doll" she asked after a few moments of walking behind him, waiting for him to hand it to her. It came out like a whisper.

He spun around with such rage in his eyes that she stopped cold. She knew what was coming and it was much more than a violent poke in the ribs that would leave a bruise that no one would see.

He held the doll up, turned and spiked it into the curb, his entire body into it. The doll shattered into a million little pieces, raining like broken dreams all over the road. When he met her eyes, she saw triumph in them. To emphasize his point, he stepped off the curb and stomped on the remains, then ground his foot into them. He never broke eye contact, the maniacal joy at her pain in his eyes.

"There," he said. "There is your fucking doll, and now I'm late to the game." He sneered and turned on his heel, walking away.

The pain she felt from the broken doll at her feet overwhelmed her. Not even the beating she received when they ended up home after the game hurt as much. At least for that he had been drunk for so long that he didn't have much left in him.

Now, in this dark room, this asylum hell, she held a very similar doll. She looked at its bashed in skull and noticed a shard wedged in the damage looked out of place. She squinted in the dim light and pulled the doll closer.

A piece of a china plate.

Her hand instinctively rose to her head where just past the hairline a thin white scar sat. Another Zach Weston courtesy. This one several years ago before the doll incident. She had spilled dinner, a plate of spaghetti and it had fallen on the floor. Of course he had been drinking, but he had grabbed the nearest plate and flung it at her like a frisbee, striking her in the head. He had called her a clutz and an idiot, a worthless piece of shit that couldn't even serve him a shitty dinner right.

The blow shattered the plate, slicing open a cut that had required stitches. It had rung her bell and she had sat down in the spaghetti mess. Blood poured down over her face while he went back and finished the game. Once it was over, he realized he would have to take her in, he had silently put her in the car, crafted a story on the way there and let her know what would happen if she deviated from it.

It had taken nine stitches to close it up.

The doll.

The plate.

She was convinced now. She was in her own personal hell.

All the mistakes I made, I am paying for it. I am in hell, reliving the pain of everything over and over while I am chased by a savage monster that keeps hurting me. I keep running but I'm going nowhere. I am running in place, stuck on a hamster wheel just waiting for the monster to find me again, hurt me some more, and have the cycle start over.

She sobbed uncontrollably, feeling despair creeping back in.

How long is eternity?

Frustration boiled over. She took one more look at the doll and yanked it off the line it was hanging from. She wound up and threw it across the room and against the far wall. It shattered, taking a chunk of the plaster wall with it. She strode through the dust cloud to the window, a steely determination coming over her.

She looked out, the clouds having cleared a bit and the

moon shining down. She could make the outline of the yellow house out in the dark.

Is it a mirage? Is it even really there?

The leaves rolling in the cold, gentle breeze seemed real enough. She found herself missing Helen again and the light, welcoming world she was in.

Is there even a way out?

There had been a way out last time. The doll had been it. She remembered now, she remembered when she had decided she had had enough. The doll in this room, perhaps meant to torment her further in despair, would have the same effect as the last one.

She would fight, and she would break free.

*   *   *

The event with the doll had been it. She wasn't sure why. It seemed so trivial, it was just a cheap porcelain doll at a stand up booth off the road outside the stadium. Somehow, it had put her over the edge. It had seemed to represent a joy that was almost in her fingertips, she could just about touch it. And then Zach had gleefully destroyed it. He had destroyed it because she wanted it.

Somehow that had seemed like a joy she was meant to have, and then it was gone.

She had been beaten on by Zach for six years. She had been pulled out of the coffee shop, forced into his apartment and then condo. She was barely allowed to leave, she cooked dinner and cleaned. She did not have any friends or outside contact. The heat had been turned up and it was boiling.

He knew how to find the right spot on the ribs or hit the kidneys. The perverse joy he received from hurting her only seemed to fuel itself. It was like a drug, and each time he required more to get the high. He came to the point where he couldn't perform in the bedroom and the only way he could get off was violence. It wasn't the plate, it wasn't when she had been late and he was worried she was pregnant so he pummeled her belly. It wasn't when he put out the cigarette on her arm like Ms. Bath from the Shyt House.

Even with all of that, it was the doll that had finally made her leave. It didn't build up, it didn't fester or get planned. She woke up the next morning after the doll incident and was leaving.

She wasn't even surprised by it. It was as if it was the most natural thought that she could have. Hindsight, after all she went through, a smashed doll seemed to pale in comparison. And yet, that morning while Zach went off to the firm, she left the condo for the last time.

She wasn't sure what possessed her to do it. It seemed natural, but also not her. It was what she imagined an out-of-body experience might feel like. She wasn't in control, but just an observer. Had she been of her mind, she would have kept doing what she always did - crumple to the floor, wait, and leave it all the same.

Or would she? She had left Shyt House. She had been the

age where she just didn't matter anymore. She was almost eighteen and would have had to leave anyway. She had been unwanted and ignored and just walked away.

Where am I going? she thought as she moved through the condo to the door. She was floating over the ground, her own thoughts bouncing in her brain, sounding muffled as if talking underwater. She felt far away from reality. Her feet across the carpet, the closing of doors, everything sounded dampened.

She moved through the living room and across to the mantle. She popped the "secret" drop shelf on the bottom of the mantle that Zach didn't know she was aware of. She pulled out a stack of cash, crisp one hundred dollar bills in large stacks. There was probably ten thousand dollars in the drop shelf along with a firearm, a safety deposit box key, and several cell phones.

She took a quarter of the stack and left the rest of the items, replacing the shelf. She strode away into the bedroom, grabbing a backpack and stuffing a few changes of clothes. She went into the bathroom and grabbed her toothbrush.

In her head she was incredulous - *steal a couple thousand dollars, leave my home, back to the streets but at least I didn't forget my toothbrush.*

She floated to the door, opened it up, and walked through. She stood in the hallway, wondering how she would get down four floors and out the door. She knew that the door-man kept an "eye on her" when Zach was out. While she was pondering the dilemma, her feet were already moving. Her subconscious seemed to be running the show, guiding her out of body experience. She decided to just let it, though she didn't seem to have a choice in the matter anyway.

Letting go and retreating back into her head, she just observed, like watching a movie. She didn't even feel any of the pain from her beating after the game the night before. Her ribs had screamed all night and she had had to breath in short, choppy breaths. Her kidneys felt like a rock in her lower back, immovable and grinding pain throughout her whole body. Her chest hurt and even her breast and nipples were on fire from being hit and twisted in the rage. Her buttocks and legs hurt from where she had curled up on the floor, throwing up on herself as the beating raged on.

All of that was suddenly gone as she moved about, completely giving up control.

Her feet carried down around the corner. The walls were a darker cream and the red carpet detailed in square patterns. She had never noticed it before, but now the red, the dreary walls, the dark light fixtures all felt like a tunnel in her personal purgatory. Her feet found each square as she moved around the corner and came by a maintenance cart. A man was on a ladder working on a light fixture. He was oblivious to her as he was focused on the fixture, squinting through thick glasses balanced on a chubby, red face. She floated by silently, grabbing the keyring on the side of the cart without breaking stride.

She moved to the end of the hallway, and to an unmarked door. As she watched herself, the first key she tried opened the door. She propped the door with her foot, and turned back to the hallway. She tossed the key ring into a potted plant in the hallway.

She moved through the door, hearing the click of the door closing echo through her head. There was a maid elevator ahead - no cameras, no doorman.

She rode the elevator down, holding her breath that it would not stop on the way down. Thankfully, when the doors opened, she was on the first floor. She strode out and saw large carts and laundry machines. The room was dark and dank, housing a small maintenance shop area on her left, shelves and cleaning supplies in front of her, and a path to a set of doors with the label *Lobby* by it.

She moved to her right and weaved her way through containers and carts. She felt a draft of air and continued forward. A slamming noise followed and she heard a grunt.

"Hurry up with that. We're already behind schedule."

She rounded a stack of palettes and saw two men unloading the back of a truck. She moved quietly to the wall and wove her way to the dock door. As the men headed into the truck she slipped down beside it and hurried away from the building. She was on the backside, away from the main street. Glancing around in the early morning cold, she headed down an alley between the buildings.

She continued to watch herself, noticing that she never even looked back. She turned right and then left or maybe right again. She crossed streets and headed down alleys, she crossed a campus and over a river. She headed through a park, crunching through fallen leaves.

She had no idea who was making these decisions for her, all she knew was that it wasn't her conscious mind. Something else was in charge, steering her across town. She had no idea where she was going but it seemed to her that she was on a course.

And then she was there. It was as if she was given back the reins, that she came back up front to be allowed to control her mind and body, dropped back in from her out of body experience. It happened with a *whoosh* as she swept back in, like zooming back in on reality.

She blinked a few times, and glanced around. The August air was already heating up with the sun shining down. Heat was rising up from the concrete; it was going to be another hot summer day, and she realized she could feel the heat and air again. As she reentered herself, the noise came back in as well. Horns blared and trucks roared as she stood on the sidewalk. She jumped as the melancholy silence was cut so abruptly. With the feeling also came the pain. She suddenly doubled over in pain. Everywhere, head to toe, screamed out at her. She could smell exhaust and the warm dampness of the wet concrete from the early morning's rain.

She stumbled forward to the curb, and fell to her knees, throwing up in the gutter. She panted as she finished, raising her eyes to figure out where she was. Everything was very familiar, as if from a long ago memory.

The rows of storefronts up and down stirred a familiarity in her brain. She turned around and looked behind her, on her side of the street. She was looking at a wooden door with a drape on the window. A large glass window was off to the right and a series of tables existed inside. The interior was about a half full of people sitting and chatting. The door swung open a familiar bell tolled, followed by a soft, stern voice that carried on the morning summer breeze.

"It's not pumpkin spice season yet" the voice said, no malice in it as it wasn't capable of it, but with a firmness that ended the conversation.

He never was one for the PSL craze.

It was Joe.

She was back in front of the coffee shop.

Thirteen

She stood and continued to look out the window, back up on the third floor in the middle of the three wings of the building. She recalled the fear when she exited that dream-like state and realized she was in front of the coffee shop. The fear was debilitating, back on her own, afraid of Zach coming after her, afraid of what would happen, afraid of having nowhere to go. The road had been tough, but it had been the best thing that ever happened to her.

Back where I started, just like the coffee shop. Right back where I started. No one to help me this time though.

The thought made her miss Helen. She also missed Nora and Anna. The whole picture was starting to come back and she now remembered a bit of who they were. The fog was almost clear and what were shapes and silhouettes in memory were coming into focus. She remembered the coffee shop, she remembered going inside, and she remembered the journey that first step had started.

No time for that right now, she thought. *It's time to take the step on this journey, out of the gates of hell.*

She realized she was one wing away from where she started. After everything she had been through tonight, she had moved a hundred yards from where she woke up. She wasn't any closer to the yellow house, she wasn't any closer to that front entrance she had eyed out the window after waking. This seemed to be a recurring theme of her life. When she did try to move, she ran and ran only to realize when she stopped to look around that she was on nothing but a hamster wheel, never really going anywhere.

It seemed that she was destined to just sit down and curl up on the floor.

No. No, I will not sit down, I will not give in or give up. I don't care if I am getting no where, I don't care if I am losing ground. I am need to keep pushing on.

She stuck her head out in the hallway and saw nothing. She strode the length of the hallway and the stairwell was there. She ran her hand along the wall and found the hole from the ax earlier. She shuddered at the sharp feeling of the edges of shattered plaster.

She moved through the darkness back to the original hallway she ran down. She recalled the doorway at the end of the hallway, her original destination. She again felt a tremor pass through her, and she could feel her pulse quicken as she recalled the creature pushing through that door in her original confrontation.

The almost out wing, she thought, recalling what Helen had told her. *Hopefully that holds true.*

She chuckled involuntarily, the sound shaky and uneven in the empty hall. It betrayed her true feelings of anxiety, lacking humor in any way.

She moved onward down the corridor. The light flickering in the room where she had originally found the skull of the steer, the pentagram, and the vile insults cast shadows into the hallway. After what she had been through, the skull made more sense. This creature chasing her seemed to be her own minotaur in her personal hell, this dark and decrepit version of the asylum her labyrinth.

She passed the door without looking, the next room the one she awoke in. Another light flickered in the next room down, one door from her starting point. She didn't recall if there was a light in that room when she was here last. She had turned this direction, made it almost to the door when it had opened and the creature had emerged.

No, she was pretty sure it was not lit up. However, in this strange world where there are creatures chasing her, where a shimmering to a different version and time occurs at random, and where she is trapped in this run down building, who knew if it was strange to have a room light up?

Her heart began pounding in her chest as she knew this was for her. There was another message, another consequence, another reminder of her mistakes and how *small* she was. She slowly approached the door frame with the flickering light, this one on her left, facing west instead of the rooms on the east side where she awoke.

She paused just before the door frame and strained her ears to listen. She heard the thudding of her heart, and nothing more. She closed her eyes and focused further, trying to hear or sense the approaching creature, another threat, or *anything* that might surprise her.

She took a deep breath after a moment of complete silence and stepped around the door frame and into the room.

As she crossed the threshold, there was a soft crunching under her foot. Looking down, she saw a pile of paper on the floor. The whole floor of the room was littered with what appeared to be newspapers, except for a series of candles in the middle of the room with a large circle of bare floor around them.

She leaned down and grabbed a handful of the papers and lifted it to her eyes. It appeared to be a series of articles from several different periodicals.

She read the headline, and immediately dropped it. Her hand went to her mouth and she gasped in horror. She crumpled to the floor after all. Lying there in a heap, the strength left her and she didn't know how to take another step. She clenched her eyes tight as every part of her body weighed too much to hold onto, her very soul suddenly attached to an anvil.

She began to sob uncontrollably.

LOCAL COFFEE SHOP OWNER FOUND MURDERED

Fourteen

Ellie stood on the sidewalk in front of the coffee shop after leaving Zach behind. Once again on her own, she moved to the door with trepidation. Her hand shook as she raised it to the door handle, pushed down and opened the door.

The familiar sounds floated out to her. The hissing of the pressure from the espresso machine, the clinking of silverware, the movement of people, and the sound of voices. Standing in the doorway, she felt unworthy to cross the threshold. The smell of pumpkin spice and coffee beans floated across to her. If there was a smell for *warmth* and *family*, this was it. Apparently, Joe had relented on the PSL.

Behind the counter stood Joe, his back to her. He suddenly tensed up, stood up straight, and began to turn around. As if he sensed her very presence, he immediately made eye contact and smiled. His soft, forgiving eyes comforted her. He swiftly moved around the counter, his large size moving with the agility of a much smaller man.

Ellie felt a wave of exhaustion overcome her. She began to cry and sink down in the doorway. Somehow Joe covered the distance, or, more accurately, seemed to materialize at the door and caught Ellie in his arms.

He held her tight for a moment, not saying a word. Then he guided her inside, behind the corner and into the employee rooms in the back.

The room was much as she remembered it, small and cluttered. Several filing cabinets stood against the left side wall and a desk took up the area on the right. A two seat couch was against the far wall, an obscene crimson with tears in it. She remembered sleeping on that a few times when she first was getting settled or after a long shift. It was much the same though faded more than she remembered.

She sank into it now, the comfort of the soft, billowing cushions wrapping her in the familiarity. The couch smelled old and somewhat musty, but it was a familiar smell of family and coffee. Her sobbing slowed as Joe showed up with a warm cup of coffee.

The smell further strengthened her memories and she felt a wave of safety that she wasn't even aware had been missing for so long. The steam rose off the cup to her nose as she wrapped her hands around the mug. Despite the summer day, she had felt cold and the coffee warmed her before she even took a sip.

"Calm down, you're safe now," Joe said in his gravelly voice. The sound was so soothing that Ellie smiled in spite of herself. "I'll be back in a few minutes and we'll figure out what's next." The word materialized beneath his mustache, his lips not even appearing to move.

She nodded and sank further into the couch, bringing her feet up next to her and leaning on the arm rest, caressing her cup of coffee. It was as if Joe already knew the story though she hadn't told it. She found that astounding yet comforting, felt both safe and ashamed. He knew the story because he expected it, dating all the way back to the night she had left those years ago.

She flew back into years past, of time in front of the fireplace sipping coffee in the morning, hot chocolate or hot cider on cold evenings with Madelyn and Joe. She could almost feel the warmth of the flames, see the orange warmth of the flickering light, and the comfort of being a part of a family. It was a short time and she didn't even realize the impact it had had on her all those years ago.

She allowed herself to breathe, waves flowing over her of both relief and exhaustion. When Joe returned, she told him everything that had happened over the last six years. For his part, Joe simply listened, stoic behind his large mustache. If you looked closely, you could see his face tightening and his forehead clenching, the vein starting to pulsate below the surface.

She recounted every single incident, verbal abuse, and physical beating. She talked into the afternoon, never stopping. As she told each story that had made her feel small, weak, and unimportant, she began to feel a strength coming over her. It was as if telling her story released its power over her. She began to feel better about herself, she began to think she wasn't *nothing,* and she began to think that there was a way out, a way to better.

That is, until the bell on the door rang violently. So violently, in fact, that it was cut off mid-ring, as it ripped from its mount and flew across the room.

Joe, whose face had remained stoic, was patting her hand on the couch. As soon as the door was flung open, his face clouded over and he was unable to keep the mask any more. He rose from the couch, turned on his heel, and headed for the door.

Almost cartoon-like, he pushed up the sleeves on his shirt.

"Stay here" he said without looking back.She rushed to the edge of the door, her heart pounding. She looked across and saw Zach standing, anger over his face, the fading afternoon sunlight creating a shadow over him that seemed to consume all light that came within range. In the shadow, she could see his face was red and contorted with rage.

"Where is she?" he yelled, spittle flying from his face.

"Get out of here" Joe replied. He didn't raise his voice but it reverberated through the shop anyway. All other sounds stopped - voices halted, drinks froze halfway to mouths, and the hiss of the espresso machine cut off.

Zach faltered for a moment at Joe's voice, but his bubbling rage took over. He stepped to the side and flipped a table. Mugs flew in the air and shattered. The table crashed to the floor and slid through the cafe.

"I want her out here now! I fucking know she is here. She doesn't walk out on me. Mess with the bull and get the horns, is that what you want piece of shit? Don't mess with me!"

He raised a hand and pointed his finger, shaking it right in Joe's face. Joe's face stayed stoic, showing no emotion.

"Get out."

"Fuck you!"

Zach poked Joe in the chest, which crossed Joe's line. Still with the same languid expression on his face, his left hand shot up and grabbed Zach's hand. The speed was surprising for Joe's size and soft demeanor. He bent the finger back violently, and audible snap echoed through the coffee shop. Before Zach could scream Joe's right hand drove forward into his stomach, just under the rib cage.

Zach crumbled to the floor, his hand still held in Joe's massive fist and his face contorted in a silent scream that his lungs had no air to make a reality.

Joe reached down, and grabbed him under his arm, crushing his hand in his fist. He took two steps forward and launched Zach out the open door to the coffee shop. Zach went spiraling across the sidewalk and into a parked car on the curb with a *THUD*.

"She's not here. I wish she was, I wish I could have stopped her from ever meeting a piece of trash like you. And it warms my heart to hear that she moved on," he said through the door. "You are not welcome here. Do not come back."

Joe calmly stepped forward and swung the door shut, then strode over to turn the table upright. He calmly began cleaning up the shards of the broken mug and spilled remnants of coffee. The large window to the left of the door showed a limping and broken figure push past, retreating wounded.

Ellie stood in the doorway from the back of the shop.

She watched over the counter as Joe calmly cleaned up. As he came back behind the counter with a rag and handsful of broken mugs, Ellie emerged from the back. Joe dumped the broken pieces in a garbage bin, and dusted his hands off. He turned to Ellie, his face still calm.

"Are you OK?" they both said to each other at the same time.

"I'm fine," Joe said with a smile.

"I'm sorry. I shouldn't have come here. I should have known he would come here first to find me."

"None of that now," Joe soothed, patting her shoulder. "You're where you should be."

"I'm sorry about the shop and that you had to deal with that."

"First of all, we have a liberal mayor and governor, so I am used to dealing with criminals. Second, don't say sorry. Sorry implies some kind of fault. You have no fault for that awful person. Don't you dare bear that burden."

She hugged him and winced when he hugged back. He pulled back and his eyes narrowed.

"He won't be touching you again," he stated.

She nodded and replied, "I don't know what to do. He'll find me, I can't hide here forever."

He looked at her, met her eyes and looked through them. She felt him looking all the way down into her soul. He nodded as if he had found what he was looking for.

"Let me make some calls. I think it's time you move on from Philly."

With that he walked away to the office in the back, closing the door.

Leave Philadelphia, Ellie wondered as she stood there. *Where would I go?*

She thought for a moment. *Why would I care? What would keep me here? Outside of this coffee shop, is there anything that has brought me any joy? And what has happened to the shop because of me, the damage –*

"Excuse me, can I get another mocha?"

The words cut through her thoughts. She turned and looked to see a young man with a ball cap and backpack standing there, his shirt proudly announcing his allegiance to Penn. She looked up and down the counter for a moment. He was tentative after witnessing the scene between Joe and Zach.

"Extra shot in that?"

The man smiled, relieved.

"You know it."

She grabbed the portafilter and tamper, getting right to work, her hands flying without thinking about it, the muscle memory guiding her as if she had never left the shop.

Like riding a bike, she thought as the familiar hiss of the milk steamer and the gurgle of the pressurized water pushed through the tightly packed beans filled her ears.

She smiled. It felt good to be back in the shop.

*   *   *

Ellie was sitting back on the couch in the backroom. A big rush had come in after dinner with the college kids just getting back to school, already in for late cappuccinos and studying. She had worked feverishly, the work cleansing her. She felt good - no, she felt great. It was incredible how her senses had honed in on the shop - every sound like a magnificent symphony in her ears, every smell magnified to the point where she even relished the smell of the oak tables, every smile radiating warmth as she handed over some form of coffee concoction.

She felt an emptying of her burdens as she poured into the work. Joe worked with her, never saying a word about her situation, acting as if she had always been there. He stayed back and let her wrap herself in the work, quietly recognizing the effect on her it was having - making her feel back to *normal.* The flow of the work, the hiss of the pressure from the espresso machine, the smell of the coffee, the sound of mugs and plates, all of it working together in a familiar symphony to Ellie. The familiarity made her feel home and gave her a rhythm to align herself with.

Now she sat, tired but happy. The ache in her ribs had even faded with the work. She sat, snuggled into the fluffy couch, with a hot chocolate between her hands, fingers clasped around the mug. Joe came in and took his seat in the old, brown desk chair. It was an antique, with tears in the leather and stuffing coming out. It leaned slightly to one side and the arms were worn flat. It groaned under his weight as he sat down and leaned back.

He regarded Ellie with a soft smile. His face showed a constrained joy, having enjoyed the evening but knowing that what was coming next would be difficult on Ellie.

They made small talk for the next hour, sipping their drinks and chatting about the coffee shop, the coming fall, the inevitable return of pumpkin spice everything. Joe made comments about foo-foo drinks and how the generation should toughen up and drink their coffee black like a man, but also acknowledging how he liked what he called the PSM - Pumpkin Spice Margins.

Ellie could see he was starting to shift uncomfortably, and she knew it was time to get to the crux of the matter - *what was next?*

"How is Madelyn doing?" she asked, attempting to segway the conversation to the matter at hand.

Joe smiled. "She's doing well. She was upset, of course, after you left. She felt very protective of you and wasn't too fond of that asshole, as you know. She ended up getting into a program to catch on at Penn and earn her degree. She met a nice guy there, and they have since graduated, got married and moved off to start a family and their careers. She moved up and is the marketing director at a mid-sized company that runs outdoor stores. Hunting, fishing, camping, that kind of thing. She settled out west, Montana somewhere."

"She calls from time to time, always asking if I have heard from you. I think once we get this settled, you should reach out. I'll help arrange it. For the time being though, I think it's best for you to move on."

He leaned forward, his face taking a solemn look.

"I saw the crazy in his eyes. He is a weak, pathetic man, but he feels he owns you. Leaving him was an affront to the manhood that he seems to think he has. I don't think he'll stop looking for you around here. Coupling that with the trauma that you went through, that you've been through all your life, I think a fresh start in a new place would be best. Of course, it's your life and your choice."

He sat back, regarding her, gauging her reaction. He folded his hands across his belly and furrowed his brow. The chair groaned as he leaned back, studying her.

"I'm sorry to put you in this position, Joe. You have always been so good to me, and I feel like it's my fault that you are dealing with this. All this trouble because of me, and you and Maddie told me not to go." Her eyes filled with tears as she tried to hold back from crying.

The corners of Joe's mouth turned up a bit as his brow furrowed and his lips pursed. He let out a deep sigh.

"Oh El, I won't hear any of that." His deep voice seemed to reverberate through the room, its deep bass carrying off the walls and back. "You can say that you went along, but you didn't do the deeds. He did. I certainly wish you didn't go through it, but you can see that it has strengthened you. You're here aren't you? You made the decision to leave, you found the strength."

"I don't know about that. I couldn't tell you why I left. I don't even think it was me, it was as if someone or something else was controlling me. I felt like I was watching a movie of my life but someone else was driving. I don't remember thinking about any of it, and then suddenly I was out front."

Joe waved his hand dismissively.

"That doesn't really matter, you're here. You aren't to blame because he broke some glasses in my shop just like you're not to blame for him abusing you. You're not to blame for your mother not taking care of you, or for what you endured at that youth home you were at."

He saw her shiver a bit at the mention of Shyt House.

"So it took some doing, but I do have some friends in this city. I had some conversations with some folks on the police force and at City Hall. They were able to dig into the goings-on at that youth home. That woman was charged and the home was fully investigated. The latest I heard, she's going to be going away for a while."

He frowned.

"I know that doesn't right what happened to you and Maddie, but take solace in knowing that others won't be going through what you went through, and because of your strength in getting away and talking about it."

Ellie forced a smile. Part of her did feel good about it, but part of her also just felt empty from the pain of the experience. She was glad others didn't have to go through it, to be beaten, humiliated, put in the room under the stairs, and emotionally battered, but she felt a sort of jealousy that she had to go through it to spare them.

She allowed a thought to creep in. If she was so used to the abuse from Shyt House, maybe that's why she allowed Zach to abuse her. As if she had some deep desire to be abused, as if she deserved it and needed it to fulfill her image of herself. What made her think this time she would break the cycle? She might have run from Zach, but what situation was waiting for her up ahead? What would she do this time -

would she end up in the same situation but different, abused and beaten because that is what she deserved? Perhaps it was a self-fulfilling prophecy and she'd never allow herself to get away from it.

And now, people that she cared about were being hurt because of her propensity to find abusive situations. Who would she hurt next? She deserved whatever came her way.

Joe, in his typical uncanny way, seemed to know just what she was thinking.

"What happened wasn't good, but we learn from the past and own our future. What matters is what happens next, what you do with it. You can do one of two things. You can let your trials define you, or you can push forward."

He shifted in his chair and leaned forward.

"There is no doubt you've had it tough. The question is, do you want to lean on it as a crutch and use it as an excuse for what happens next? Or do you own your circumstances and pursue your purpose? Certainly, it's easier to wallow in the tribulations you've had, to lean on the crutch. To blame the wounds and hold on to it. It's certainly easier to fail, to sit in self-pity, blame your circumstances and lean hard on that crutch. Quite frankly, that's what most people do." He paused briefly, his face having reddened a bit.

His face brightened a bit as a small smile crept across his lips.

"No, that's not you though. I can see it. You may have been pushed down, but underneath that, I see strength. And you'll need it. The road you are about to embark on is hard. Letting go of the crutch and venturing out into the unknown, into the wilderness, takes courage. It's scary and hard. You will have new challenges, new demons to overcome. There will be storms and high winds, but there will also be sunshine. You'll see the beauty that is out there, but you have to put down the crutch and leave the cave to do it."

Ellie had never heard him say so much in a day, let alone in a single breath. She could see the iron determination and raw passion in his face. She realized how much he loved her, and how he felt his purpose lied in helping people like her. He wouldn't allow her to wallow in self-pity, to be a victim and give in, allow it to be an excuse to be mistreated. Or to mistreat herself.

His love and grace washed over her, and as she met his gaze, she felt a conviction overwhelm her. She could not let him down. She had to fight forward, she had to persevere, whatever that meant. But with all he was doing for her, and all the love he was showering her with, she had to fight for him.

"And, forgive me, but I am going to help you leave the cave, like it or not. I am going to push you out of the entrance, throw you from the nest. I believe in you though, I believe you'll fly just fine."

His smile had grown large now, and he sat back.

She didn't know what to say. She just stood from the couch and went around the desk, giving him a hug and breaking down in tears.

"I'm scared," she whispered.

"I know. But I have people that will help you, they'll help you find your footing." he replied. "Here's what we're going to do."

*　　　　　　*　　　　　　*

Ellie stood in the room, all the newspaper clippings crunching under her feet. Tears welled up and overflowed, and she stood shuddering. She tried not to feel responsible, but somehow, she felt that by him knowing her, helping her, was the reason he was gone. As she stood in her personal Hell, this punishment was about her feeling the agony of being the reason Joe was dead.

She didn't want to but read the articles anyway; it was like a car wreck that you just couldn't look away from even though you tried to. The Philly Sentinel, Philadelphia Gazette, and the Pennsylvania Tribune all had articles strewn about the room. As she scanned them, she pieced together the various versions.

Joe had been closing up the shop by himself a bit early, letting everyone else enjoy the Halloween festivities. The fall afternoon had been bustling, everyone gearing up for a night of trick-or-treating or parties. Parents caffeinated themselves on the way out of downtown, ready to take their children out and about. College aged kids fit in their necessary mochas and the like before heading off for parties in their costumes.

Joe loved the evening, she remembered. Seeing everyone in their costumes and talking with them about what they were wearing, especially the little ones. He would always hand out candy throughout the day, throw extra espresso shots in on-the-house for parents hauling multiple little witches, skeletons, and superheroes around.

In her recollection, she realized how much joy Joe felt for helping others smile. He was always extending a hand, be it to her or Madelyn, customers coming in, or parents frazzled and worn out but doing the best they could for their kids on Halloween. He was the epitome of the jolly, helpful shopkeeper, extending joy far past the coffee he served.

The tears escaped Ellie's eyes as she remembered him. She tried to wipe them away, but many blotted the articles as they tumbled off her cheeks.

By himself, with the store closed, someone entered the store. A passerby thought it was a homeless person as they wore a big hat and a large overgrown coat. The man was filthy and worn as it was said. The passerby said Joe was mopping and the door was unlocked. He thought nothing of it and kept on his way. About fifteen minutes later as he was exiting a sandwich shop a couple blocks away, he saw the smoke and orange glow. He ran back and saw the fire, calling the police.

After putting out the flames, they found Joe's charred corpse inside. They had managed to put the flames out quickly and were able to identify a large, open slice wound in his back. He was lying on top of his mop.

Footage from a camera across the street at an ATM showed the man enter, remove something from his coat that was large, and swing it at Joe's back. Joe dropped and the man left the screen. The place was in flames a few minutes later and the attacker was not seen leaving the front entrance. The theory was that a random person, possibly homeless, went maniacal and hit Joe with an ax. The register was still closed, partially melted from the flames but full of cash.

Ellie dropped the clippings back to the floor. Joe was like the supportive but firm father she never knew, and now would never know again. She shook with anger and frustration. Her mind bounced back and forth from hardening with anger to feeling weak with sadness and despair. The room full of the clippings was another ring of her Hell. When would it end? And what lay ahead?

She looked around the room again, the draft blowing through a broken window causing the clippings to swirl about her legs.

"I will not break!" she yelled. "You cannot break me."

She actually began to laugh, albeit while crying at the same time.

"Bring it on," she hissed through gritted teeth, and strode to the door. She stepped into the hallway, her heart hammering and feeling the heat of adrenaline. She had her hands raised, ready to fight, expecting the monster to be right there.

I can't take this much more, let's get it over with, she thought.

The hallway was empty.

"It's allll yourrrr faulllllltttt...."

The sound floated to her, quiet like a whisper riding the wind. The sound was so low, she thought at first she was imagining it.

The voice increased, it was feminine and childlike, and taunting her.

"Why Ellie? Why did you kill him?"

The sound increased to a shriek as the high pitched

laughter blasted through the hall, making her jump. She spun around looking up and down the hallway. Blackness enveloped the edges of her sight lines. She squinted, straining for every detail to come into hyper-focus.

"Why does everyone who knows you dieeeeee..."

The voice transitioned from the feminine to a distorted, low sound, dragging it out. The air filled with the sounds of pained screams and shrieks. The sounds of suffering were accompanied by the crackling sounds of flames. The laughter overlaid onto the sounds, the volume so high Ellie had to close her eyes and clamp her hands over her ears.

She spun in circles, the whole hallway spinning around her, the doors gaping and black, pulsating to the sounds.

Where is the creature? her mind screamed at her.

She backed down the hallway, still spinning and searching.

The stairwell was just a few feet away, the same door that opened and released the creature after she woke up. She stared at the handle as she closed in on it, willing it to stay still so she could escape the screams, flames, and laughter.

She reached for the handle as she passed the last room, removing it from her ears. Out of the darkness, a black gloved hand shot out, its fingers splayed as she walked right into it. The animal smell followed as she felt her shirt twisted tight by the hand and she was spun. Her eyes found the darkness of the room and the red eyes that glowed. She heard a snarl as she was wrenched off her feet, and pulled into the gaping darkness.

Fifteen

Ellie looked out the window of the bus, watching the cornfields pass by as she left Iowa. The land seemed impossibly flat, as if she could see for miles. She was on her third different bus after two days of travel from the Joe, the coffee shop, and everything she had known in the greater Philadelphia area for the past fifteen years.

With two more days of buses ahead of her, she had already been through three of the books she had bought at stops along the way. She had rediscovered her love for reading, falling back to the days when she would camp out in the library as a deposed youth to have shelter from the day. She would envelope herself in the book, forgetting the rest of the world's troubles.

The trip from Philadelphia to St. Louis had been filled with that, along with the four hour stop in Indianapolis.

She had bought a ticket under another name in St. Louis and headed up to Des Moines. She had rushed quickly to the bus to Minneapolis and then she was to go on to her destination.

At least she was feminine again. That first trip she had tucked her hair up in a large hat, dressed masculine to get through as Billy McIntyre. Joe had had a friend buy the ticket and given her directions.

It turned out that Joe, through his contacts around the city, had found that the firm Zach worked at had significant influence with the police. Zach had already leveraged that to keep an eye out for Ellie. He wasn't backing off. To throw him off the scent, Joe had devised a series of routes and made her memorize them.

He had also discussed with her avoiding cameras and staying near walls, blending in with the crowd and keeping her face hidden. She had followed his instructions to a tee until Des Moines, but she couldn't take much more and had removed her hat and overcoat for this portion of the trip.

She felt dirty, sweaty, and unkempt. She had worn several layers, losing a layer at each bus station to ensure she looked different.

"It's unlikely that they will track you past the bus station, but if they do, this way they won't track you to the next. By the time you get off the last bus in Grand Rapids, having used four different names, outfits, and hiding your face, you should be impossible to track."

He had told her what to do when she arrived, which she went back over in her head for the millionth time.

She sighed deeply, looking out the window as the sun

illuminated the corn. At least it was light out, though she was hungry. She was going to wait to eat until Minneapolis. She would arrive at dinner time after a series of stops. She would eat then as it would have to last her a while. The bus would leave at 8:30p and continue through the night on to Chicago. Then it was the bus to Detroit, but she would get off in Kalamazoo MI, head up to Grand Rapids before switching again and on to her final destination.

Joe had again made her memorize the next steps, specific paths after she departed the bus, specific phrases that had to be said. She felt it was all very cloak-and-dagger, but he said he did not want any trail following her so phone calls, emails, and other forms of communication were out of the question.

"Perhaps it's overkill, but I would rather be far too cautious than the other option."

So she had memorized it all, and repeated it back to him over coffee, hot chocolate, lunch, dinner, and the final hug goodbye.

There would be a brief stop in Ames in just a few minutes. Perhaps she should grab a snack and another book. The bus continued to barrel up I-35 as she watched the unchanging landscape of corn. It was tall and almost ready for harvest.

She thought of Joe again. He had always treated her well, loved her when she needed it, but led with a quiet discipline when she needed that. She wished for the hundredth time that she had listened to him with Zach years ago.

"Thank you," she had said that last time, sipping hot chocolate before heading to the bus station. "You've loved me like the dad I never had."

"Girls need fathers. To love them, show them what it

means for a man to treat them right. To show them how a real man protects and provides. To be their first love. I am sorry you never got that. I am honored that you feel I had a small part in that." he had said.

He had leaned forward and met her eyes. The intensity shone in his eyes like she had never seen.

"I think you give me more credit than I deserve," he said, his bushy white mustache dancing with each word. "The road ahead is going to be tough. But you are tough, and you learned that on your own. No matter where you are on that road, remember that you are loved, you are tough, and you can make it through. You matter and make sure not only that other people treat you that way, but you treat yourself that way. Don't for a second think you aren't worth it. In the grand scheme of things, you have a part to play and your story matters. I, for one, believe you are destined for great things. I can see it in the way you carry yourself, and I can see it in your eyes. When, that is, you let them shine."

She had promised him she would, gave him an extended hug, feeling the safety and warmth of the big man one last time, and left. She longed for that warm presence now as she felt lonely on this long journey.

She exited the bus at Ames, looking for a snack to tide her over. The early August heat was oppressive. The bus station announced that the departure would be in about thirty minutes, so she left the station and turned onto the road. She could see an advertisement for Iowa State students, lofts, and shops all around her. She turned on the next road and traveled down a block. There was a Kum & Go on her right, and a Jimmy John's on her left. Having never had much money of her own, she wanted to make what she had last. She had no idea what was ahead of her. She ducked into the gas station.

All around her were college students milling about. It reminded her of the coffee shop and the swaths of students from Penn that would come in and out. They were so full of hope, believing that better things were ahead. She wondered what that was like.

She was unsure if better things were in her future. They couldn't really be any worse than what she had been through, but it always felt like they ended up the same. She left home young, ended up in the Shyt House. She left Shyt House, ended up abused by Zach. She left Zach and - what? Why would it be any different?

Maybe it was her. Maybe she invited it, or brought it on.

You can knock that right off, she heard Joe's voice in her head. *You don't have time to be a victim.*

She replayed their conversation from a couple days ago. It made sense then, and she was invigorated, but at that time she had a cup of warm coffee, the comfort of a fluffy couch, and friendly, familiar surroundings. Now she was a random gas station in the middle of nowhere with the future ahead seemingly held by the murky darkness of the unknown.

She sighed, wondering what lay ahead, hoping that this time, *this time,* it would be different. She finished making a slurpee and grabbed a tin of assorted nuts and a bag of Chex Mix. She longed for a cup of coffee from the shop, an Americano perhaps.

Well, at least I have a hearty, health dinner, she thought to herself, failing to stifle a laugh. She scurried out of the store amid a few sideways glances.

Jammed in between all these stories of her life was the coffee shop. That was her beacon of happiness between the storms. She wished she could just be back there, instead of wherever she was headed.

She watched a few of the students laughing together as they strolled down the sidewalk, not a care in the world.

I just want to find that. Some laughter, and no worries. Just for a bit.

She headed back to the bus stop to head onward in her journey.

Alone.

*　　　　*　　　　*

Her back hurt, her head hurt, her legs ached. She stretched into her seat, shifting around for the millionth time, trying to find comfort. She had already worn every part of her body out, ran out of books, and couldn't look out the window anymore. Her trip from Minneapolis to Chicago found her next to a rather large, hairy, and sweaty man with more hair shooting out the back of his t-shirt than on his head. It had been a long ride, especially after he had "accidentally" had his hand roam out of place a third of the way through.

She had surprised herself, saying "Touch me again and you'll be pick your teeth out of your seat." His eyes had gone wide. He saw something in her face that struck fear in him. He turned away from her and kept his eyes down for the rest of the trip.

He was obviously a bully and a predator, taking her downcast eyes and closed off demeanor on the bus and at the stops as an opportunity to take advantage of her. She would have agreed, and shocked herself with her fiery response. She felt that bubble in her starting to grow and rise, and it wasn't from two days of gas station food culminating in the largest burrito she had ever seen before leaving Minneapolis (*not my best decision in life,* she laughed), it was her inner strength and confidence.

Maybe I'll be OK after all.

Now all she could think about was a shower and a mattress. There wasn't a lot of time between buses in Chicago or Kalamazoo, though she had had three hours in Grand Rapids. She had spent her time piling on with a fantastic burger and a beer at Founders around the corner from the bus depot. She was back on the road, the final leg of her journey, shortly thereafter and now she had finally left the last stop in the small-nothing-town of Kingsley. Her next stop would be her last, the three and a half day journey full of misdirection, wardrobe changes, and bland names would be over.

The bus braked and pulled in, the hydraulics hissing. It came to stop and the sound of the doors opening filled her with anticipation.

"Thirty-five minutes and the bus departs for St. Ignace" came over the speaker.

Not me, she thought to herself and smiled.

She bounded off the bus, energy renewed, muscles screaming from the new exertion. She headed out to the road, looking left and right. The sky still glowed orange from the sun, even though it was after seven in the evening. As she came out on Hall St. she was drawn by the smell of the bay. Turning to her left, she headed down and looked out over the sparkling water in the setting sun. Boats were scattered across the bay with large floating platforms attached, kids jumping off the bows, and jet skis buzzing around them. The sound of laughter filled the air.

She crossed 31 and walked into the park. Off to her left she saw groups of people playing beach volleyball. The sounds of summer, of community, and *family* filled the air. She smiled to herself, feeling both alone and filled with hope at the promise ahead.

She stood, stretching and gazing out over the bay for quite some time. She snapped out of her trance by the realization of setting sun. She headed back the way she had come, away from the bay and down toward Front St. She saw a series of shops, restaurants, and dessert places.

Traverse City Pie Company, she read as her stomach growled again. Burger or not, there was always room for pie. She tucked it in the back of her mind and continued on. She turned left and found herself in a neighborhood. The houses filled the blocks with porches and windows lit, families enjoying each other. As she wandered on with a few more rights and lefts, zigzagging her way southwest of the bay, she stepped out onto a sidewalk running along a busy road.

Almost there, she thought. The sun was almost gone now and the evening had a soft glow from the dying light.

She saw the road sign: eleventh and division. She carefully crossed and headed down eleventh. Her destination was up ahead on the right. She was to ask for Nadine, and tell her the network had sent her. Joe had explained that it was a nation-wide network helping women in need.

She came upon Elmwood, and could see a large building ahead of her with towers reaching for the sky through the trees. She glanced around before crossing and heading right on Elmwood. The Women's Resource Center was on her left. It was a strange looking building with a steep roof that came low over brick walls. It almost appeared as two buildings connected by another low, flat roofed lobby connecting them. A large brick section stuck up in the middle of the flat roof with a bench and a flagpole out front. The building was dark, somewhat hidden by bushes, and as sad as the despair carried to its doorstep.

She regarded the building for a moment. After such a long journey, she struggled to take the next step to its finality. She loved and trusted Joe, but she didn't know these people. What if they took one look at her and sent her away? She shook her head to clear it. She didn't think like that anymore. She willed herself to take the next step.

Based on the white sign out front, the building housed a childcare center and a church. She walked to the door and peered in. There was a light in the main area, but the rest of the building was dark. She pressed her face against the glass. She scanned inside, looked for movement, light from under any of the doors, any sign of life.

Nothing.

She walked around the building looking in all the windows, knocking on them.

There was no one there. She was too late. Her dawdling at the bay had seen everyone leave for the night.

What's one more night? she thought. It was a warm summer evening in the middle of August and she had slept outside in much worse conditions.

She decided she would walk around for a while, noting the beautiful trees off to her right, approaching the building with the towers that she had noticed earlier. She headed that direction.

She found a nice tree with soft grass and figured she could sleep there when she was ready. Having been cooped up in the bus, sleeping off and on, for the last several days, she wasn't ready to retire for the night.

She glanced up at the building and shuddered. It looked like a once beautiful and now decrepit structure. It had an odd, flat and low front and then quickly rose into four stories of ornate design. It fanned out in a batwing shape with an exorbitant amount of windows. Windows were broken, the building dark and peeling. It seemed to pull any remaining light in and exist in a shadow.

Ellie shuddered again and headed back the other direction. *There will be somewhere else to sleep.*

As she walked, she saw a yellow house with some lights

on. It was just across Eleventh from the Women's Resource Center. It had a series of rectangular windows on both floors and cement walk up to its steps. The left side of the house curved out and was further covered with windows. A post out front read *"May Peace Prosper on Earth"*.

She felt drawn to it and could see a light on in the main front window. She peeked in and saw a plump woman with gray hair sitting at a desk. She felt compelled to knock on the door, unsure of what was driving her.

She found herself standing at the door with her hand raised. She paused, not even sure what she would say if someone came to the door. Then she knocked, timidly at first and then increasing in intensity.

"Coming," sang a cheerful voice from inside.

The door swung open and the woman she saw through the window stood with her arms spread wide, one on the door and the other on the door frame. She had a large smile.

"How can I help you?" she said.

Ellie stood motionless, unable to speak. Her brain spun, trying to find words but she could come up with nothing. She turned and looked back at the brick building across the street behind her, and then back at the woman.

Her shoulders slumped.

"I'm sorry to have bothered you - " she began.

"Nonsense," the woman interrupted. She reached her hand out and grasped Ellie's shoulder. Her stubby, plump fingers were gentle but firm. She pulled Ellie forward and across the threshold.

"It's OK, I know," she continued. "You're welcome here,

and safe." She led her straight back past the desk and the bookcases, and through an archway to the back of the house. It led to a kitchen. A sink was over a back wall and dining room through another large archway off to her left. A small two seat table was at the near wall opposite the sink. The woman pulled out one of the chairs.

"Sit, dear," she said. "You're in luck, we just got some cider. It's a bit early in the season but I can't wait. It's store bought, we'll have the good stuff in another three weeks."

She smiled her radiant smile as she poured apple cider into a small pot on the gas range. She sprinkled some nutmeg in and tossed a couple cinnamon sticks in, stirring gently.

"It's a great time of year. I love the summer and the beach, but there is nothing like when it starts to cool a bit, the leaves fall, and there are colors all around. Yellow, and orange, and blazing red, leaves, and cornstalks, and pumpkins. Oh my, I can't wait!"

She turned, her eyes absolutely shining, and leaned forward toward Ellie.

"And, as you can see," she said pointing at her rotund belly, "plenty of pumpkin doughnuts!"

She laughed at her joke, her whole body shaking with a melodic laugh. Ellie was smiling and laughing too, before she even realized it. This woman was an angel - Ellie went from despair to overcome with joy in the few minutes in her presence.

"My name is Virginia Gray, you can call me Ginny, everyone else does." Her eyes sparkled. "Welcome to *Stronger*

Together women's support. We've been helping women for going on eight years now. We know why you're here."

"You do?" Ellie responded.

"Of course."

"Did Joe call?"

"Joe? No, I don't know Joe. We know why everyone knocks on our door," Ginny said, waving her hand and curling her lips. "Oh, the circumstances are different, and always important. But the *reason* you're here is the same. You need a family, you need support, and you need to heal. We'll help with all of that."

She smiled again.

"You're safe here."

"I was under the impression that Joe knew this place, that he was sending me somewhere he knew someone. I was supposed to go to the Women's Center across the street, ask for Nadine?"

She waved her hand. "We work with the Women's Resource Center, but Nadine has moved on, a few years ago actually. We are different from them, providing more hands on and targeted support. We don't just help you, we give you a family. This Joe, he may know someone here, or our founder and president, Carey Hughes. But it may just be that he knows The Network."

"The Network?"

"Carey can tell you about it tomorrow when you meet her. The cider gets you settled in, like liquid warmth and love, but now that we are past that, why don't I fix you something to eat?"

"That would be wonderful. I didn't think I was hungry until I saw that pie company on the way over here."

Ginny laughed, a jolly, melodic sound. She headed over to the refrigerator again, and pulled out a large container. Tossing a pot on the stove, she poured a large helping out of the container to begin warming.

"You can really tell I am ready for the fall, I already have soup ready to go." She laughed to herself. "There is nothing better when coming in from the cold than warm apple cider, but a steaming bowl of soup might be a close second. Even though it's still August, you're coming in from the cold. You might not even know how cold, but I can promise you, here at *Stronger Together*, you'll feel warmth like you deserve."

Her hands whirred through the air as she grabbed various spices out of the cupboard and blended them in while stirring, and singing to more than speaking to Ellie. Ellie could not stop smiling in the woman's presence, and she giggled as Ginny danced from the stove to the table to deliver the soup. She spun to the cupboard and returned with a baguette.

"There is nothing better than a nice piece of french bread to soak up that broth."

The soup was delicious, full of chicken, rice, and vegetables. The celery had just the right crunch and the heat of the spices and broth warmed her from the inside out. She remembered the shiver when looking at the abandoned building, and realized that it never left until this delicious elixir warmed her soul. She felt welcome for the first time since leaving the coffee shop.

As she scraped the bottom of the bowl, leaving it almost

as clean as when it left the cupboard, she stood and threw her arms around Ginny. She felt as if she had known Ginny as a favorite aunt rather than having met her an hour ago. She was a female version of Joe.

"Oh! Well that was unexpected." Ginny said, embracing her back. "The power of soup! Vindication for me."

They laughed together and she patted Ellie on the shoulder.

"Now, how about we get you a place to freshen up, maybe a nice bath, and I can show you where you'll sleep tonight. Tomorrow, you'll meet Carey. It's not all cider and soup, but if you think it's a good fit for you, and I think you will, we'll get you right to it."

Sixteen

Ellie opened her eyes, looking around the room at the Stronger Together house. The mattress was firm, the blankets billowy and warm. She smiled and stretched, not wanting to move. The sun streamed in through the windows, and the room was covered in bright colors. A chair sat in the corner with a large stuffed bear on it, the curtains were light pink, and a large bureau with a mirror on top made the room seem even larger.

She threw back the blankets and let her feet hit the hardwood floor. The nightgown she wore was a bit big, but the slippers fit like a charm. She could still smell the rose body wash and shampoo from her shower last night. She felt revived, renewed, and ready. Energized even. She slipped out the door and headed down the stairs, sliding her hand gently down the curved banister.

She heard sizzling as she reached the bottom of the stairs and the sweet smell of maple syrup and bacon filled her nose. Her mouth watered involuntarily. She may have traveled a dozen states, but she had been eating better than she had in a while.

She entered the kitchen to find Ginny right back at it. She looked the same, with her hair done up and a large white blouse over a pair of jeans. Bacon sizzled and a bowl of oatmeal with bananas and strawberries on top sat steaming on the little table.

"Good morning," Ginny sang. "Have a seat and eat up. Carey will be here in just a few minutes to meet with you."

Ellie sat down and started in on the oatmeal. It was so sweet, tastes of maple syrup, brown sugar, and a touch of vanilla filled her senses. The fresh fruit burst in her mouth with a cool sweetness. It was creamy and warm, filling her belly and warming her entire body.

All this over oatmeal? she thought. *I am going crazy.*

Except she realized it wasn't oatmeal, it wasn't craziness, it was joy. She felt *good.* She hadn't felt good... ever? She may have touched it at the coffee shop, but she was so guarded back then she didn't believe it. This lack of belief is probably why she put herself back in the situation she did - it was easier to be miserable than to believe in happiness that wasn't real.

But now, she was stronger. She had escaped, she had picked herself up and left. She had ridden buses across a dozen states, and made it here. She had carried herself away from the abuse, decided that she had had enough. She was strong enough to do all that. And she was strong enough to feel happy. She couldn't help but think that Ginny's infectious demeanor contributed as well.

"So, Carey will be here in just a few minutes," Ginny said, sitting down across from Ellie with two cups of coffee. "I know I come across very bubbly. I can't help it, I have always been the kind of person that finds the good in things. I believe we are doing God's work here, and my little contribution to the lives of those around me brings me such joy and fulfillment."

"Now, I have the blessing of being this way because of Carey. She has been doing this for a while now and she has seen the good, the bad, and the ugly. I am telling you this because I am all smiles and giggles, but she is a little bit..." She trailed off, as if looking for the word.

"Harder," she finished.

Ellie furrowed her brow. "Harder?"

"It will be okay, but just know that she will come across more sternly. Just be honest and be prepared to be put to work."

"I'm not afraid of work."

Ginny smiled and patted her arm. "You'll be just fine."

Ellie stood and took her dishes to the sink and began to wash them, as if demonstrating her work ethic. As she finished and placed the dish and mug in the drying rack, the door rattled open behind her. Carey Hughes strode into the kitchen.

Ellie was immediately struck by her presence. It was

strength personified. She carried a confident aire about her. She stood tall with short auburn hair flecked with gray, looking to be in her early to mid-fifties. She had the beginnings of crow's feet around her eyes, which were sharp and piercing. Her jaw was set tightly and she entered the kitchen in a dark pantsuit over a cream blouse. She had a double golden necklace on and bracelet to match. She was taller than Ellie by several inches but seemed to tower above everything. All the light in the kitchen seemed to dim a bit, as if she was in a spotlight.

"Ellie?" she asked, extending her hand.

"Yes," Ellie replied, shaking her hand. Carey's handshake was firm and her grip strong, not in a dominating or intimidating way, but exuding strength and confidence. Ellie wasn't sure how to match it and felt overwhelmed.

"Please come with me. I'd like to discuss your situation and *Stronger Together's* role in helping our community and those in need."

With that she turned on her heel and headed out of the kitchen, long strides echoing on the floor. Ellie glanced at Ginny, unsettled and unsure. Ginny smiled, and nodded slowly, patting her on the shoulder.

"You'll be fine," she whispered, ushering her after Carey.

Ellie left the kitchen area, following through the dining room and into the office space she originally saw through the window the night before. Carey closed a sliding door behind her. Ellie saw bookcases on the wall, a set of double doors that led to the foyer that were closed, and the large desk against the back wall. Carey settled into the large desk chair and motioned for Ellie to sit in one of the chairs across the desk.

She slid slowly into the chair, again feeling intimidated. Her strength she felt earlier seemed to have evaporated at the glowing figure in front of her. Ellie raised her eyes to meet Carey's and felt them piercing into her. She resisted the urge to look away, the gray-blue seemingly reaching down into her soul, sizing her up.

Carey's face was hard. She radiated a powerful beauty, elegant and in control. Her face said that she could not only handle anything that came her way, but dominate it, beat it into submission. There wasn't anger or contempt, but a fierceness that told the story of a woman who would not be denied and missed nothing.

After an excruciating minute, Carey leaned back in her chair.

"What do you want from us?" she asked.

"I - I don't know." she stammered. "A friend of mine helped me get here, I don't know what to do."

Carey nodded slowly. She held her hand out, indicating for her to go on.

Ellie stared at her, not sure of how to proceed. After a moment of staring at her, she opened her mouth and just let the words fall out.

"I have been in bad situations my whole life. I always kept my head down, tried to stay out of the way, make myself small in the hopes that I would just be looked over. The one time I finally had the opportunity to be loved, I was too young and stubborn, or too weak and ended up back in another bad situation. I don't think I trusted that it could be real and so it was easier to head into what I knew - the abuse that was overt rather than think I had something and have it disappear, to have been a mirage. I finally got up the courage to leave. Well, that's probably a lie - I don't even know what came over me, I just found myself gone. The next thing I knew, a friend of mine helped me get out of town. In all it took to get here, I realized that I am stronger and I won't live in fear anymore."

"What do I want from you? Nothing, specifically. I am after a new start, my feet are down and I am going to find my path. I am going to be strong enough to do… something. I'm scare, because I don't know what it is yet, or where I'll end up, but in the short time that I have been in this place, and with Ginny, I realized that it's okay to have happiness. I am not sure what that is yet, other than apple cider and oatmeal, but I think there is more of it and I am ready to go take it."

She finished, shocking herself. She took a deep breath in, and then shook her head, laughing to herself.

"What's so funny?" Carey asked.

"Well, I had no idea I thought any of that until I started talking."

Carey's face softened just a bit and the hint of a smile touched the corners of her mouth.

"Okay then, why don't you go ahead and tell me your story."

Ellie felt as if she had passed the initial test. A sense of relief washed over her. She talked for the next thirty minutes, telling her story up to landing on the doorstep last night. Carey never once interrupted, sitting stoic in her chair, leaned back with the one hand on her chin and elbow on the arm of the chair. Ellie wasn't sure she ever even blinked. Her posture was open and receptive, soaking in the story in a non threatening and non judgemental manner, but her eyes blazed with passion.

Ellie knew as she started that she would have no issues due to that fire burning in Carey's eyes. She could already tell that Ellie was one of *her girls* and the pain Ellie endured was pain to Carey.

When she ended her story, Carey sat back up, taking over the focus of the conversation.

"Well you've certainly endured a lot. All the women we help have. And I believe we can help each other here. However, you must understand that we have a way of doing things. If this way is not followed, we will ask you to move on. Our goal is for you to move on eventually, when you are ready. That is to say, we always want to maintain a relationship with you, but, as you said earlier, our goal is to help you find your feet on your path to self-sufficiency."

"You will be committed to our program. You will participate in sessions with other women in our care, you will not judge or condemn, but lift up. You will practice faith. You may or may not be a Christian, but you will be while you are here. The Lord has blessed us with this ability to help and a big part of that is spreading His hope. You will not contact anyone from your old life while you are here. This is for two reasons. One, it can cause you to fall back into bad habits, and two, it can put you and the women around you in this program, in danger. You will be put to work through one of our programs. Work is therapy, it will help you feel your impact, it will strengthen you, and it will help support our community and cause. We will have several options and will help you find the right fit. You have some say, but ultimately, I will place you. Finally, there is no substance abuse. No alcohol, drugs, and no sex or men. We are not man-haters, a healthy relationship with a man is likely important to fulfilling the role God has for you. There is no better calling than coming together in marriage and having a family. Lord knows I have been blessed to be with my husband for thirty years with two wonderful children. But, right now, the goal is to help you on a path, and there are to be no distractions until after you are on your own."

"If you break any of these rules, you will unceremoniously be shown the door. This is not baseball, you don't get three strikes. We will love you, but we will focus our resources on those who want to be helped."

She paused, folded her hands in her lap. Her face was tight and serious, gauging Ellie's reaction to her stern monologue.

"Any questions?"

"When do we get started?" Ellie replied.

Ellie jumped when Carey suddenly clapped her hands loudly, smiled, and stood.

"Right now."

*   *   *

It amazed Ellie that all this flooded back in her memory as she flew into the darkness. It was a happy moment in her life, the new start she had been looking for. And now, in the terror she found herself, it was a solace.

The room was pitch black, except the red glow of eyes in front of her face. The rank breath of the creature as it breathed on her in the blackness caused her stomach to turn. She was dragged across the room. It roared in her face, deafening her and causing her to clutch her eyes shut.

She tried to reach out to fight back and found herself flying through the air. Hurled across the room, she raised her hands in front of her just before she hit the wall headlong. She crumpled to the ground, her head spinning and the explosion of stars lingering in her vision. She felt the crunch of old plaster as she crawled along the wall, pieces raining down on her. She was wrenched from her hands and knees and thrown again, spiraling across the room. Sliding across the floor, she gasped for breath. She was moving before she even skidded to a stop, crawling and trying to create space. She looked back over her shoulder, searching for the monster in the dark.

Fuck, she thought. *I'm going the wrong way.*

She saw the gaping door to the hallway behind her. All the spinning around and the bouncing off of the wall had her disoriented. Her chest exploded into new pain as she felt the boot of the creature crash into her ribs, lifting her off the ground. She rolled, gasping and trying to scream, but no sound would come out. She tumbled into the wall and planted her foot, pushing off as hard as she could, tucking her shoulder in a roll like she learned in class, right as she heard the creature smash the wall where she was.

She stumbled to her feet, teetering and unstable. The room was black but the entry way danced in her eyes, seeming to swirl around among the stars dancing in her vision. She tried to shake her head to clear it enough to get her bearings. It was impossible to escape through a target jumping every which way.

It began to stabilize in front of her and she realized she was directly across from it, all the way on the other side of the room. And then it disappeared completely, a lit rectangular beacon one second, and gone to darkness the next.

As she felt a hand close around her throat, she realized the darkness was the creature standing between her and the door.

The hand squeezed her throat and she felt the cold of steel on her neck. The blade of the ax gently slid across the side of her neck under her ear while the creature growled. The blade was gentle enough not to cut, but the pressure increased and she felt the wetness of blood begin to trickle.

She brought her right arm in a swift arc, smashing a large piece of plaster wall she had grabbed off the floor upon standing into the side of the creature's head. It grunted and she hit it in the chest with her two hands, grabbing its collar as it fell backwards a few inches. She yanked the creature back towards her, dropping down and to her right.

She surprised the creature with her violence of action, which countered its superior strength. It smashed into the window behind her, shattering the old glass. The shards rained down behind her as she darted toward the door. The creature turned and slipped on the glass, falling to one knee. It roared after her, but she was already out the door.

Running again. Through doors, down stairs, into hallways, she wasn't thinking about where she was going, only about putting distance between her and the creature. She could feel blood running down her shoulder and back from the cut as she ran swiftly. She passed landings, and barreled through alcoves. She was running on pure adrenaline, everything a blur.

Finally, she pulled over into a room, trying to be quiet and listen, calming her heart and her breathing. Her ribs screamed, her lungs burned, and now that she had stopped, piercing pain was coming from her neck where the ax had sliced.

She listened intently and heard nothing. After ten minutes, she began to look around to figure out where she was. She was in another room, looking much like the last. This one was facing the front of the building which allowed the light of the moon to come in through the window. The room was cold, the glass broken out of the window. A grate was covering the window, its bars separating the light from the moon into stripes across the floor. The room looked like many of the rest, but she could see the grass out the window. She quickly checked back into the hallway, glancing up and down in the darkness.

The creature was nowhere to be found and the hallway was silent. She saw the end of the wing and realized she was on the first floor in the outermost wing of the facility. She returned to the window and looked out, longing to be out there, out of *here.*

She looked out the window, the grass frosted a bit. She shivered as the sweat from her encounter with the beast dried and the adrenaline wore off. She wiped the blood off her neck, gently probing the cut. It was a good inch long, but not deep. It was clotting up and the blood was just a trickle. It stung, bringing tears to her eyes. The sweat dripping in it didn't help.

The window sill had a bit of old glass still in it, but she felt she could climb out and drop to the grass below. The first floor was not precisely at ground level as the sub level had windows that rose a few feet up, leaving the drop about seven or eight feet from the window sill. Still, the grass was below and she could tuck and roll.

She looked over the grate standing between her and freedom. The window frame was old and crumbling, the grate sagging already in the lower left corner. She shook it gently. It moved. Dust and debris fell down and showered her. She coughed but smiled.

She was almost out of here. She began to pull harder, more debris and the grate dropped an inch. It was heavy and she didn't want it to fall on her so she had to be careful about how she pulled -

The grate melted away. The dark, molded plaster wall melted away. The cold melted away. The glass grew back into the window and the dark colors were replaced with white walls of undamaged plaster. The floor cleared of debris and dust.

No, no, no! she thought. Except she didn't think it, she was screaming it in frustration. *I am so close.*

She was back in the light world. Her exit was gone, the window closed off with glass, a gentle snow falling outside of it and the ground covered.

And there was Helen, sitting on the bed, staring at her terrified as Ellie yelled in anger.

Seventeen

Helen was screaming and waving her arms, her face terrified. Ellie paused mid-yell, cocked her head, and realized what she had done. Her shoulders slumped, and she felt awash of guilt at scaring her friend.

"Oh, Helen, I'm sorry," she soothed.

She reached out to put her arm around Helen to comfort her. As she reached for her, Helen shrieked louder and shrunk away.

"I didn't mean to yell, I was just frustrated. Helen, please calm down."

"No, dun touch me, help! Help! No!"

She continued to yell, and wave her arms, flopping on the bed violently. She fell to the floor, writhing.

"Please, Helen. You're going to hurt yourself. Please calm down," Ellie pleaded. The more Ellie tried to help, the more hysterical Helen became.

The door burst open and three nurses rushed in.

"Hep muh!" Helen cried through gritted teeth, her eyes wide. "Dum let 'er get me!"

The nurses rushed in, one rushing straight through Ellie. It was a strange sensation to see a person materialize out of her, like a light washing over her. She felt nothing physically, but was startled by it.

The nurses grabbed Helen by the arms and legs, and lifted her onto the bed, trying to soothe her and calm her down.

"Helen, it's okay, you know me, I'm not going to hurt you," Ellie said.

"Dun touch me," she screamed, writhing on the bed as the nurses attempted to hold her down. "Ya come fer me? Please dun't take me. Please!"

Her eyes broke from Ellie and she began to sob. The nurses administered something to calm her down, the view blocked from Ellie as she backed away with her hand over her mouth.

Helen's breathing slowed and she sobbed, the nurses backing off just a bit with the pressure but still holding her on the bed. A few minutes past and the sobbing moved to a whimper, and then to slow shallow breathing as she succumbed to the medicine and stress, moving into a sleeping state.

"She's out," one of the nurses said.

"What was that about? She has been doing better, hasn't had any fits in months. That was rough," another said.

"She was yelling about something in the room. Hallucinating? These new calming drugs do that sometimes I've heard, people start seeing things."

They all turned and looked right at Ellie. Well, not at her, through her.

"I don't know," the first nurse replied. "She hasn't had any of those."

She shrugged.

The group regarded Helen one more time on the bed and then moved to leave the room.

"I'll stay in this hall and keep an eye on her," one of them that Ellie hadn't heard from yet offered.

The other nurses nodded assent and they left.

Ellie stood there, the shock of Helen's behavior still creating a state of paralysis. She had been at this asylum all night

(how long had it been? Was it still just the same night?)

and she had not felt so alone as she did right then.

She stood at the foot of the bed and watched the gentle rise and fall of Helen's chest. The scene was serene compared to the chaos from moments ago. Ellie's heart was still pounding as she tried to regain control. In just a moment, she had moved from escape within her grasp to being completely alone, her only friend in this nightmare terrified of her.

She stepped out of the room and saw the nurse standing as a sentry a few feet away, reading a book. She leaned down in front of the nurse and saw her immersed in the story, a novel named *Michael O'Halloran* by Gene Stratton-Porter. She shook her head - she had never heard of it. Somehow though, she thought she might tuck that nugget away in her brain for when (*if*) she made it out of here. Or maybe it wasn't even real.

She continued down the hall and around the corner. The other two nurses were in the nurses station, washing their hands and preparing for their rounds.

"Of course she offered to watch, gets 'er out of 'er rounds and she can sneak more of her book," one nurse said, laughing. She was young and short, with short hair and the permanent markings of a smile written into her cheeks and eyes. Her english accent only made her seem even more jolly. "Anything to get out of a bit of work."

The other nurse, an older woman with tight lips and stretched back forehead that made her eyebrows look perpetually surprised, simply clucked and shook her head.

"Well, we have work to do, more now with Helen's fit."

"Oh bah, it'll be fine. 'elen'll be fine too. She's a good soul. I 'ate to see 'er like that. I wonder what got into 'er? It was like she saw a ghost."

"Don't you start that now! You'll be riling everyone up," Crotchety Nurse warned. "We don't need that kind of trouble, the patients in this wing are a handful enough as it is."

"Oh bugger, you worry too much. It'll be fine. You 'ave a nice Thanksgiving?" Jolly Nurse asked, trying to connect with the cranky woman.

"Aye, just another day. Edward and I just had a nice quiet dinner."

"No family? No roast turkey or cranberry sauce?"

"Bah!" Nurse Crotchety said, waving her hand.

Nurse Jolly furrowed her brow, suddenly looking concerned. Her voice was lowered.

"Do we 'ave to report 'elen's outburst?"

"You know we do."

"You don't think 'ey'll keep 'er from the Christmas ball, do you?"

Nurse Crotchety dropped her hands and turned to Nurse Jolly with her lips pursed, a borderline look of contempt on her face. Even she softened when she saw the deep concern and sadness on Nurse Jolly's face.

She sighed.

"I don't know."

"Can't we do something, she's been looking forward to it so much? There has to be something we can do?" Jolly pleaded.

Another deep sigh.

"I'll talk with them and see."

Ellie saw the nurse she thought of as Jolly perk up a bit, and then the nurses left the station and began their rounds, checking on patients. She followed Nurse Jolly down the hall until she broke off into a patient's room.

In the middle of the three wings, the halls were lined with holly and ivy, tinsel and ornaments, wreaths and garland. The smell of the garland filled Ellie's nose as she wandered the beautifully decorated corridor. She trailed her hand on the garland, smiling and feeling the warmth of Christmas. She looked outside and saw red and white candy cane stripes on the trees, more colorful holly wrapped around the outside of the windows. The ornate and towering entryway looked much the same. A sleigh was being pulled by as she watched.

"Ahh the cookie wagon is here," she heard from behind her.

"What's that?" another voice asked.

"It's what brings the drums of milk around."

"Those boys'll be mighty hungry after clearing that snow with the coal scoops. Looks so pretty out there for the Christmas season."

Ellie recalled Helen telling her about the coal scoops and cookie wagon. She wondered if the boy was with it that Helen spoke so fondly of. *'Hi, boy!' and he would say 'hi!'*

"Bah! How long until Spring? Tis just cold out there," came the response.

A laugh came back.

"It's just December yesterday, you have a bit to wait. It'll get worse before it gets better."

She pulled her face from the window and continued down the hall. She was just wandering, following the festive decorations and feeling the warmth of the holiday season. She had left the hall and entered a large common room. Sitting in a large chair was a man in a dark suit with a large bushy mustache and a top hat. His legs crossed, he was reading a newspaper and was chatting with another gentleman sipping from a cup and gazing out the window.

"John, have you tried this Goebel's beer? The newspaper has all kinds of advertisements on it."

"No, but I believe Dr. Gordon has. You should ask him," John said. He clucked and shook his head. "Can you believe this snow? It was warm on Thanksgiving and then here comes the snow. It is pretty for Christmas though, but I don't care for the cold."

"Yes, I preferred the warmer weather as well. How about this train to California?" the other man said, lifting and shaking the paper. "Leaving from Chicago it has *'Itineraries of some of the forty ways and more California Expositions'.* It's warmer out in California, isn't it?"

"I am sure that is a bit expensive, James."

"Needn't worry, the advertisement is old. The last train left last week on the 27th," James replied. "Oh, and Miss Dunkelow is selling a wing piano. That would be nice for this room."

Ellie listened with mild interest, still engrossed in the Christmas decorations.

Goebel's beer? she thought. *Never heard of that.*

It was Christmas season and she had heard multiple comments about Thanksgiving last week. The last time she had visited Helen it was spring. People were working in the fields, the weather was warm, and Helen had said it was May. It was after Thanksgiving, that would be late November or early December.

Maybe Helen just didn't remember her? Maybe she had forgotten about her encounter from the previous spring?

Ellie moved in and peered at the front of the paper while it was open.

Leelenan Enterprise, W.C. Nelson Pub. Leland, Leelanau Co. Michigan Thursday December 2, 1915.

December 2nd, 1915.

She was in the old state asylum, her personal hell or her

light world of hope in 1915. She sighed deeply. It was overwhelming.

Why am I here? How do I keep getting here? What purpose does this have? If I am in Hell, why do I keep getting to this place? She shook her head, again trying to make sense of it all.

She could feel the warmth and beauty in the place. She could smell the evergreen and fir, she could hear the hooves of the horse pulling the Cookie Wagon.

Why would all this *good* be shown to her while tormenting her in the decrepit Hell of the other side? Is it just to give a taste of hope, and then crush it? Is that why she came here when she was about to escape? There was no escape, and if she was almost there, the world would flip.

James pulled at his bushy mustache and laughed as he set the paper down. His laugh echoed and then changed, as if through a damaged tape, drawn out and deeper. It was as if it was skipping and grinding. It melted along with the man, running to the floor, striking Ellie as macabre. The furniture and Christmas decorations followed.

She was heading back to the Dark World.

The melting pooled and drained away leaving the Dark World all around her.

And the creature stood right before her, less than three feet away.

Eighteen

The world melted away and the Dark World returned. The room was the same shape and size, but instead of the bright, warm atmosphere of 1915 Christmas season, the walls were broken and dark. Mold crept out of the corners, spidering its tendrils as if reaching up and wrapping its fingers around the walls, consuming them. Broken plaster lined the base of the walls and shards of glass lie underneath broken, grated windows. Cold air blew in from the darkness of the night. She was back in her hell.

And the creature was right there.

It's hideous face, long snout and red eyes. It's darkness, head to toe in black. The ax wasn't in its hands, as it stood facing her.

It jumped as she appeared, shrieked in surprise as Ellie

stood there. She didn't wait. Her instincts took over and she didn't cower but instead struck forward.

She stepped her left foot forward as she bent into a fighting stance. Her left forearm rose to protect her face and she drove her right hand forward, exploding her hips and driving the heel of her hand at the creature.

The creature, shrieking in surprise, pulled away, diminishing the blow but wasn't quick enough to avoid it entirely. Her hand struck the creature in its throat and she followed through, using her momentum to turn on her heel and run.

She heard the grunt at the strike, and the creature fell backwards, hitting the ground. The sound of glass and plaster crunching echoed around her, but she was already out through the entryway, and turning down a hall. Choking and gasping sounds followed her as she pushed through a door and into a stairwell, heading up and away from the creature.

She ran, but this time with a purpose. She knew the lay of the land now, and felt comfortable in the asylum. She wasn't scared and running blindly, but knew where she wanted to go, feeling almost at home from her time wandering the asylum. She could almost *see* the halls from 1915, as she ran.

Then she realized she *could see* the halls from 1915. They were pulsating in and out, the hallway a collage of each world in little patches, growing and then receding as she ran. Light and darkness, beauty and ruin, in and out.

She darted down the hall and took another stairwell, putting space between her and the creature. She had made a lot of noise on her way, and now she slowed and crept through the door. She gently closed it, depressing the bar to mute the click of the closing.

She quietly took the stairs, marveling at the light this time through as it was plastered with Light World. She exited on the third floor, and headed further down the hallway, pausing to listen.

She listened intently, her eyes searching the corridor. She wasn't afraid. Her eyes were zeroed in, ready. A small table materialized next to her with a beautiful vase filled with flowers, and then it wiped away as if by windshield wipers on a car. When it wiped back, there was a poinsettia and a wreath.

The entire hallway was flashing before her eyes, in and out of Light World and Dark World. As Light World came back, it differed each time. Sometimes spring flowers and a wave of warm air, then a blast of summer heat, next the hall filled with Christmas wreaths and garland, then cornstalks and fall decorations.

It was as if multiple channels were bleeding through on the TV, overlapping each other and blending. Ellie watched the scene in wonder, listening for the creature. She was not afraid, almost enjoying the display before her.

The scene began to calm down as her heart slowed from the escape. She could not hear the creature and felt confident that she was not being pursued, or at least if she was, she had thrown him off her scent.

She took a few deep breaths, the adrenaline wearing off. She felt strong, having stood up to the creature. She had not cowered or dropped to the floor, but her instinct had been to fight back.

She thought a bit more about the encounter. The creature had shrieked in surprise. It hadn't known she was there. That meant that when she was in the Light World, she wasn't in the Dark World. Part of her had wondered if she was hallucinating, having some kind of breakdown, perhaps as a coping mechanism that put her in a trance state. However, she was not in the Dark World when she was in the Light World or the creature would have seen her as if she were "sleep-walking."

Furthermore, the creature wasn't in control of every-thing. It didn't know where she was when she was in the Light World. If the Light World was a torture mechanism for her Hell, the creature didn't know it or control it. It was genuinely surprised by her appearance. She thought of it jumping back, caught unprepared. Furthermore, it meant that the creature wasn't *in the Light World.* She was safe in that world, in 1915. The creature couldn't get to her there, it couldn't enter that world.

She thought more about the Light World. She wondered what caused her to go there, and she wondered again if she could control it. While she was running and her adrenaline flowing, the world had been going in and out. Did she do that? Was her emotional response somehow related to the world flipping? It had never gone in and out like that before. She thought of Helen and laughed. What would she have seen? If she had been there for all those different times, would Ellie have just flashed in and out briefly over all those times.

She couldn't be controlling the shimmering though. The last time she flipped she was almost out of the window. She could have escaped, and yet the world flipped from an open window to when the window was impenetrable for her. If she was controlling it, she wouldn't have prevented her own escape.

She paused again, deep in thought. She felt a wave of pride come over her. She was strong, she had stood up to the creature. She had surprised it, fought and won. She remembered the last time she felt that strong. It had been at *Stronger Together*, with her friends. With Anna, who taught her to be strong, and taught her to fight. It had been Nora, who wouldn't put up with anything less.

Nineteen

She stood in the doorway, leaving her room. Unpacking had taken about thirty seconds as she had no possessions. She had moved into her room at the *Stronger Together* home. It was a few blocks away from the yellow house and the office space, having a series of rooms for the women in the organization's care. They had two rooms open, and she had taken one. She was all checked in her room and waiting for a person named Anna to give her a tour of the building.

She stood in the entry to her room, facing the hallway upstairs. Rooms lined the hallway of the big house over off Sixth St. The upper floor housed the women, several of the big rooms having been converted into multiple rooms to house women in need. Her room consisted of a bureau and a bed. The bathroom was shared down the hall at the end and a large wooden stairwell sat off to her left. The hard wood floors ran all through the upstairs.

The stairs creaked and a hand appeared up the railing along with the head of Anna. She reached the top and smiled at Ellie.

"Whatchu doin' just standing there?" she said. "We got shit ta do. C'mon now."

Anna was short and slight, but every bit of it lean muscle. Tattoos covered her caramel forearms and she had jet black hair. She wore a sleeveless shirt and bluejeans, and she carried an air of get-it-done. She moved briskly and with confidence, her face serious and her mouth like a sailor.

Though intense, she was friendly and caring beneath the hardened exterior. She grabbed Ellie by the arm and pulled her like a sister.

"Upstairs? Just a bunch of rooms like yours. Who cares? The most important thing is the kitchen downstairs. You have to know how to get chow."

She half dragged Ellie down the stairs, chattering her ear off. Ellie tried to keep up, as much to keep herself from tumbling down as to trying to match Anna's energy.

"So Carey told me to get you settled and break you in today and tomorrow, because Monday we're putting you to work. So we'll get you the lay of the land here and out on the town. Tomorrow we'll head to church and get this place in order for the week, more on that in a bit, and then Monday we'll meet down here in the living room to talk about your work assignment."

"OK. What will I be doing?" Ellie asked.

"You know, I took one look at you and knew I'd like you, so I pulled some strings. You'll be heading with me over to the Bay View, helping out with the ole' folks. It can be some dirty work, but it is a lot better seeing a difference in these people's eyes."

She paused and smiled.

"And it beats the hell out of setting beds and washing sheets at the Sugar Beach or Continental. Don't get me wrong, I love Sugar Beach, but laundry and sheets get old fast."

"OK" she said. She had no idea what Anna was talking about. She talked so fast, never stopped moving, Ellie was on sensory overload. Everything was coming so rapidly, she was having a hard enough time tracking Anna's hands moving with her energetic speech, she almost missed the last step and fell off the stairs.

The stairs dropped right at the front door. There was an open area with a couple chairs and a table, fresh flowers adding color over top of a dark area rug. Past the chairs was an archway that led to a larger room that was mostly open.

"That is where we'll have group sessions. You'll be expected to be there and participate. We meet three times a week, Tuesday and Thursday evenings for group sessions, and Sunday evenings for a bible study. You'll be expected to be in church on Sunday mornings and will likely be assigned some kind of job. We help with all the events - fundraisers, bake sales, community outreach, Christmas programs, decorating the church for various functions and seasons. The church will be like your second home."

She led her off to the right down a hallway that entered

into the kitchen. The kitchen was large, with an island. Off to the right was a hallway that led to a bathroom on the left and ended in a large room lined with books and a large desk. To the left was a large dining room with a long, wooden table. A light hung down in the middle and the walls were a dull red.

"There are seven of us here right now. Down the hall is Carey's office, she doesn't lock the door but no one is allowed in there unless you talk with her first."

"Does Ginny stay here?"

"No, she has her own place, but you'll find she is around a lot. We are like one big family, and she is the loving, cheerful aunt of the place."

"Pretty simple rules, don't make a mess. Keep your room clean, do your own laundry, and clean any dishes you use. We do a big dinner together every Sunday before the Bible study. You'll be asked to help with that, and once you're comfortable, have a hand in planning it. Saturdays we all clean the house together, top to bottom, dusting, sweeping, cleaning the bathrooms, kitchens, sinks. The whole nine. This includes the outside, pulling weeds, mowing the lawn, planting flowers," Anna continued as she pulled items out of the fridge.

Ellie stopped a moment while Anna cracked eggs on the side of the pan. Saturday? She had no idea what day it even was.

The football game had been on Sunday, she had left Monday morning. She was at the coffee shop overnight and left Tuesday evening, arriving on Friday evening. She had met Ginny, stayed over at the yellow house, and had come over here this afternoon after meeting with Carey.

As if reading her mind, Anna said "Yeah, great timin'. You just missed all the cleaning fun."

She poured milk in the bowl with the eggs and began to dunk the bread. She continued to talk, telling her about the people at the home with them.

"There are a bunch of rules but you get used to them. We have Charlotte, Cynthia, Tamara, Angela, and Kayleigh. All are pretty nice, but all of us carry around our own baggage." Her faced darkened a bit. "Except for Cynthia, watch out for her. Something ain't clicking with that one."

Her hands flew as she perfected her dish. She turned and handed a plate full of french toast to Ellie, the crisp edges softening under the deluge of maple syrup and the light dusting of powdered sugar like the first flurries of winter trying to hold onto the grass.

Ellie smiled and headed to the table with Anna having her own plate in tow. The crisp crunch and soft interior of the bread with the woodsy sweetness of maple syrup erupted in her mouth, her senses overwhelmed with bliss. She grinned at Anna, syrup dripping off her chin. Anna had powdered sugar on the tip of her nose.

Ellie snorted, and they both burst out laughing.

*   *   *

Ellie averted her eyes from the glare from across the circle.

It was her first session on Sunday evening and everyone was in a set of chairs in a circle in the main room. Ginny had brought donuts and apple cider, warmed on the stove. The smell of cinnamon filled the room and it felt like fall, despite the mid-70's temperature outside.

The evening was warm and a gentle warm breeze flowed through the door from open windows in the kitchen. The ones in the room were closed so the discussion wouldn't carry, but the breeze made the room pleasant and carried the smells from the kitchen into the room.

Despite the warmth from the cider and the late summer air, Ellie had felt a chill. She had listened intently to everyone's stories, trials, and challenges, and then had been invited to speak about herself. She had heard how Charlotte had felt down about herself because someone at Tom's Food Market had called her a derogatory name when she wasn't checking out fast enough, and she had heard about how Kayleigh was feeling about staying sober. She had taken a deep breath and told some of her story when asked, urged on by Anna. She wasn't ready to meet anyone's eyes, so she had found a small spot on the rug to focus on, about five feet in front of her across the circle.

When she had finished, she was given some kind words by Carey, Anna, and even Ginny, who was milling about with more snacks. Ellie had smiled weakly, and felt a small welling of confidence in her. That is, until she felt the chill. She raised her eyes up and saw Cynthia, directly across from her, glaring at her with intense, hate-filled eyes. The eyes were so fiery that Ellie involuntarily drew a sharp breath and pulled back. She quickly lowered her eyes back to the floor.

The rest of the session droned on, but Ellie barely heard a word. Cynthia never spoke, declining with a shake of her head when asked. Ellie would occasionally glance up at her, eyes still dripping with hatred. No one else seemed to notice.

Ellie sat there, not knowing the source of the animosity, but feeling the old feelings coming back. Shyt House and the bullies. She tried to sink into her chair further.

As the session ended, she rose and said some pleasantries and slipped out into the main foyer. She took a deep breath and shook off the old feelings.

I escaped, I traveled hundreds of miles, I am on the path to a new life. I am a new person.

On that thought, she felt a hand on her shoulder. It spun her around, and two hands shoved her up against the wall. A forearm pushed across her clavicle and pinned her. As Ellie looked down upon her attacker, Cynthia's raging eyes shone back.

"You think you're something special, don't you bitch," she hissed through gritted teeth. "You march right in here with your sob story, boo-fucking-hoo."

Ellie pulled back further, the stench of her breath bringing tears to her eyes. Cynthia's hair was half-purple, half green. She had studs in her nose and eyebrows flashed in the dying evening light. Up close, Ellie noticed that her face was mottled with marks and acne, covered by heavy make-up. Her black eye-shadow made her raging eyes look like fireballs in the middle of a blackhole.

"You ain't shit. I don't want to hear you talkin' any more here."

She took her arm off of Ellie, and gave her a push in the chest.

"Pay the toll, bitch," she said as she began to grab at Ellie's pockets, trying to see if anything was in them. Ellie folded her arms across her chest to protect herself with her hands up by her throat and forearms out. Spittle flew from Cynthia's mouth through gaps of missing teeth, the rest black and gray.

Cynthia was suddenly wrenched backward and away from Ellie. She fell backwards, skidding across the hardwood floor of the foyer. Anna stood over her, hands on her hips and leaning forward.

"You got a problem? You keep your hands off her, you goddamn tweaker."

Anna's face was tight with anger as she towered over Cynthia on the floor. Neither woman was tall, both shorter than Ellie, but Anna had seemed to grow ten feet tall. Her muscular arms were taut and she looked poised to strike. Cynthia stayed down, glaring up at her at first, then averting her eyes. She scooted back away from her and then crawled before running out through the foyer to the back of the house. A moment later, the backdoor opened and the storm door slammed shut.

Anna turned back to Ellie who was still standing with her back against the wall, arms across her chest. Her eyes softened and her posture came out of the fighting stance.

"Are you ok?" she asked.

Ellie nodded.

Anna came and put her arm around her shoulders, pulling her off the wall.

"You got to stand up for yourself. It's a big, mean world

out there. You gotta know how to get mean and fight back or the world will run you over."

She smiled at her.

"Don't worry about it, I'll help you out. We'll get you as bad of an attitude as I have. I go to a place, not only do I learn how to defend myself, but it helps get that aggression and frustration out."

Ellie looked at her with confusion as Anna grinned.

"C'mon, don't worry about it. Or Cynthia, she won't mess with you, she has a comfortable amount of fear of me. She is a bit of a crazy bitch. As you probably gathered from her teeth, she is a recovering tweaker. Or at least she better be, Carey won't put up with that shit in here. She is really on her thin ice anyway, I expect that bitch to be kicked out of here in short order."

"C'mon, we have stuff to do. I am showing you a fun night before the work starts tomorrow. Grab your stuff, we're outta here."

Ellie shook herself, and headed up stairs. She splashed water on her face, grabbed her purse and headed back down. Anna was waiting back in the foyer for her, a completely different person. She was dressed for the town in a pair of jeans and a sleeveless white shirt, showing off her tattooed arms and taut muscles.

"Here we go," she said and turned on her heel.

They strode out through the front door and headed east.

"Where are we going?" Ellie asked.

"I figured we'd grab some dinner, then gorge on dessert. Head down to the bay. It's not going to be this nice much longer."

"Oh?"

"Yeah, it gets as cold as a witches tit here pretty soon."

Ellie giggled.

"The beaches are great if you can get over some of the woke, bullshit culture here. Food is good, the bay is amazing. But come winter, hunker down or you'll freeze that little ass of yours right off."

They turned north, heading toward the bay.

Not skilled at making conversation, Ellie struggled to find things to talk about. Then she thought of something.

"What's the deal with that creepy building over by the yellow house?"

"The asylum?"

"Yeah, that."

"Well, it was a major employer here for a long time. It shut down in 1989, just shut the doors. Over time it was deemed it became 'less relevant' to other methods," Anna replied, her fingers making air quotes. "They just cut a lot of patients loose when they closed. For a time patients would return and bang on the doors to try to get let back in, but they were closed up and no one was home. Pretty sad shit."

"It was a big deal around here for a long time. Something about Perry Hannah, and jobs, and the farm. I guess local people fell out of love with it after a while, farmers were up-set at the free labor that allowed the asylum to sell stuff from their farm cheaper than farmers could. It was slowly disman-tled for many years until it finally closed," Anna continued. "The big claim to fame is a giant cow, Traverse Colantha Walker. She won a bunch of awards and they got an asinine amount of milk from her, some kind of record. Her grave is still on the grounds somewhere and you can go see it."

"A cow is the big accomplishment?" Ellie laughed.

"Yeah well, I guess she was a helluva heifer." Anna said with a grin.

They came out on Front street and headed east again.

"Of course, there is the Hippie Tree over behind the asylum, so maybe there's more to it," Anna teased.

"Hippie Tree?"

"Yeah, it's this creepy, old willow tree that runs along the ground with a big old trunk and branches. They are all painted. It is said to be a gate to Hell." Anna was animated with wild eyes and waving her arms. "According to legend, if you walk around the tree in a specific way, a portal to hell will open up beneath its roots."

Anna shrugged. "We'll wait for it to get dark and then I'll take you over there."

"No!" Ellie cried out, pulling back.

Anna laughed again. "I'm just messing with you. I'm in the mood for wings and beer. Here we are, just ahead."

They came up to the brewery and pushed through the glass door. As they entered, they took a quick left up a small set of stairs. The brewery and restaurant was dark and stretched out before Ellie. Tables were all around with a big bar in the middle. More tables stretched toward the back away from the bar.

"This building was originally a candy factory back in the day. The brewery took over a while back. Traverse is known for its cherries and their cherry barbeque wings are fantastic," Anna explained.

After a beer, the wings arrived and were as promised.

While Ellie sipped her beer and cringed with the hoppy flavor of the IPA, Anna drained hers swiftly. After finishing her second, amid a pile of wing bones, Anna regarded Ellie seriously.

"Before I get too far off into the fun, I want to talk to you about what happened earlier. No more letting anyone beat up on you. You're going to stand up for yourself. Wednesday night, I am going to take you out with me to the dojo. SMA Academy. It's a martial arts place that I go to. I get to train, it's a great workout. They offer several different arts, and I have taken a variety. Right now I am doing Brazilian Jiu Jitsu and it's a hell of a workout. I am going to have you talk to Sensei Sparks but I think getting you into Krav will be the quickest way to get some skills and confidence in you. He is a great guy, really cares about his students and has an energy that just makes you feel good. You down with that?"

Ellie met her gaze, paused a moment, and then nodded. She realized she was thankful for her friend taking the reins and forcing her to do this. She wouldn't do it on her own. Her life had changed so drastically in the last four days, but she still wasn't ready to fully take the reins.

"Good, because I can't stay serious like this with that barbecue sauce goatee you have going on there."

Twenty

Ellie recalled all this and felt sure that she didn't swear like a sailor until she met Anna. The memory of the hoppy bitterness from the beer and the sweet taste of the barbeque wings came flooding back as she stood in the hallway. Her stomach rumbled at the memory and she realized she was hungry. When was the last time she ate? Is that why all her happy memories seem to revolve around food? French toast, oatmeal, apple cider, barbeque wings.

Maybe I can get into the Light World at dinner time next, she thought. *Did they have BBQ wings in 1915?*

She laughed to herself, shaking her head at the thought, and more so at the realization that the crazy thought seemed not crazy.

No, she needed to get back to that window down on the first floor.

She moved to the door to the stairwell, opening it gently and listening. She slipped inside and gently closed the door behind her.

She stopped inside and listened again, straining to hear. The thundering silence echoed back to her until she could hear nothing but a rhythmic thumping, increasing in cadence. She realized it was her own heart beating in her chest and tried to take a deep breath while remaining silent. The stairwells were dangerous - dark, enclosed, and nowhere to run.

She strained in the darkness as she slowly headed down. Her calves strained as she tried to walk on the balls of her feet, minimizing any sound. She realized that her head was pounding, her ribs ached, her hands stung, her shoulder throbbed.

She felt a wave of exhaustion come over her and fought the urge to just sit down in the darkness and rest. She knew if she stopped, she might not get started again. Besides, who knew how those red eyes could see in the dark. What was darkness to her might be clear as day to it.

She shuddered at those big horns glinting in the moonlight.

I hurt it once. Remember what Anna said, stand up for yourself. Remember Nora, fight, always fight.

The thoughts calmed her a bit as she headed down the steps, straining in the dark to hear anything and poised to bolt back up the steps.

Fight.

She remembered Anna again, and that first night when she started to learn to fight. She wished she had had more time, two and half months wasn't enough to learn to fight this battle she was in now.

She longed for that breeze off the beach, belly full. She longed for the dojo, where she had just begun to learn.

She pushed on, though her mind began to wander back to that first week of her new life.

*   *   *

Ellie's education occurred on two fronts - physical and mental. The first, she received from the Krav Maga classes with Anna, the second from her faith and from Nora at Bay View Independent Living Center. Ellie remembered the rest of the night, a night where she felt safe and realized that she was never alone.

Pie followed the brewery, where Anna insisted on treating her after she insisted on getting dinner with some of Zach's money. After, an evening walk down to the beach on the bay along with a beautiful sunset, warm sand on her feet, and a gentle breeze off the water. The night seemed to both fly by and stand still, the sounds of the surf and their laughter drowning out everything else.

The sun sunk out of sight and the mosquitos began to buzz as the night began to wind down.

Ellie laid back on the sand, looking out at the bay. The

water lapped gently on the shore and the surf was like a dark sheet spread out toward the night's horizon.

The calmness enveloped her and she felt a deep sense of serenity. It was an odd feeling, one she was unaccustomed to. Most of her life had been about survival, existing in between dangerous encounters. Tranquility had never been in the picture, and when the opportunity may have presented itself, say in her time in the coffee shop, she had just been waiting for the shoe to drop. In fact, you might argue, when it didn't she had found it herself. She had a sense that instead of waiting in anticipation, at least by initiating it with Zach she wouldn't be surprised.

Somehow that one morning, that one doll, had shocked her system and forced her to finally take action. It was an action that she was ill prepared for, but she found support in friends that she didn't even know she had.

Joe. Ginny. Carey. Now Anna.

She closed her eyes and let the sound of the waves on the shore drown everything else out. She smiled and breathed in the bay air all the way to the bottom of her lungs. She felt content, calm, and in control. *Happy.* Something she wasn't sure she had ever truly felt.

She was free from it.

"You still there?"

Anna's voice shook her from her meditation.

"Huh?"

"I was just chatting away, but you were somewhere else," Anna said.

Ellie looked at her and smiled.

"Sorry, I was just enjoying this. I'm not sure I've ever felt so relaxed, so in the right place," she replied. "I'm sure that sounds strange."

"Not at all. You've been through some serious shit. We all have, that's why we're here. But God brought you where you belong and He never said it would be easy."

Ellie hesitated.

"I'm not sure if it's okay to ask" she trailed off.

Anna just nodded knowingly.

"What shit have I been through?"

Ellie nodded, looking away.

"It's okay, it's not like you're asking a woman her age or weight. I don't mind telling my story," she replied. "Thirty-two and one thirty by the way."

"My story is pretty simple, and not nearly as rough as yours from what I have gathered so far. Mine was all self-inflicted, you seem to have been dealt a continuously shitty hand. Mom and Dad never married, mom pregnant too young. She worked hard and did the best she could, but the current state of families in this country is a huge cause of our problems. If good Christian families stuck together, a great percentage of our country's ills would be rectified. Anyway, I fell in with a bad crowd, got into drugs. I was always too strong a personality to be abused by a man, but I did fall in with a few bad apples."

"After several years of self-destruction, I had two events happen simultaneously. I OD'd on some shit and a good samaritan got me to the hospital. He saved my life, but I cost another. They were able to save me there, but I found out I had been pregnant, not very far along, but I lost it. Amazingly, realizing that I cost a life, my selfishness took a poor child's chance at a life, rattled me out of it. Not my own life that I almost lost, that didn't seem like much, but knowing that I caused that, it was the worst feeling in the world. The same good samaritan helped me get into rehab. He was associated with the nationwide network that your friend is. Joe I think it was? Anyway, they helped cover the bills at the hospital, get me detoxed, and relocate here to *Stronger Together.*"

She paused, the emotions flowing over her. Ellie tried to keep an even face, but it took all her effort to keep from crying.

"I've been here for almost eighteen months. It has changed my life, that's for sure. I'll carry what I did and who I hurt for a long time, but God's forgiven me and He has my back."

"How can you believe in God with all that's happened? You buy into all that, or just because you have to here?" Ellie asked. "I find it hard to believe that He's there with all this going on."

"Believe it? It's a lot more than belief. It's truth. God is all around us, and putting my faith in Him is what changed my life. When I lost the baby, realizing what I had done, I had some dark moments. I am not proud to say, I was within moments of taking matters into my own hands. I didn't feel like I even deserved to live. I was raised to believe in God, but it wasn't a very active part of our life, and I fell away when I got into my teens. Things may have been different if I hadn't, but God brought me here, where I help others now. He sent an angel in my life, a tough nut at the hospital. The nurse was very firm but adamant that God will forgive me if I give it to him."

"That feeling you get in your chest? That moment when you feel so confident in what you are doing? That deep tranquility? Those moments of pure peace and joy? Or that moment when you are doing something good for others or yourself, and you aren't even sure why or how you are doing it? That's God working in you. That's the Holy Spirit in you. Always with you."

Ellie contemplated this and thought back to her escape from the condo, how she felt like she wasn't driving. She wondered if God had been steering, and laughed a short chortle.

Anna looked over at her.

"I wonder if God was fed up with me not listening and took over when I left. I still don't even know how I got back to Joe to get help," Ellie said.

Anna nodded knowingly, having heard of her out-of-body experience in the group session.

"It seems hard though, to believe in something you can't see or touch. It almost feels irresponsible, as if shifting your responsibilities to something else," Ellie said.

"Who says you can't see or touch it? God is all around us. How would we be here if not for God? Something had to start the universe, something outside of it to cause it. Speaking of science, science says that things don't change unless something changes it. Who changed the nothing into something to start this?" Anna replied. "Besides, the Big Bang sounds an awful lot like *Let there be light!* from Genesis, doesn't it?"

"Furthermore, look at all the beauty around you. How could that just happen? Do you ever see something spontaneously appear out of nothing? I can see beauty and design all around us. If you walked down the beach here and found a watch, would you just think it happened by chance, or would you see design in the watch face, the gears, the hands? You would believe that someone designed it. Well, our world was designed too, and by God."

Ellie contemplated all of this, and felt something. It was almost like something falling into place, and she could hear an audible click in her head.

And she smiled.

She didn't feel alone anymore.

*   *   *

Ellie froze on the stairwell.

Her smile faded as the sounds of snorting came from below her, drifting up the stairwell and echoing off the walls. She was halfway between the third and second floors. She strained to see in the dark as she crept backwards to the wall. It was too dark to see very far, however, and the more she strained, it seems the more the shadows began dancing and playing tricks on her.

The snorting stopped. It was replaced by laughter, a deep

throated sound reverberating off the walls as it increased in intensity.

She stood, trying to break free from the fear freezing her in place, and debating if she should try to quietly head down the flight in front of her to the second floor or head back up to the third. The second was closer to her goal, but also closer to the creature.

She leaned forward, trying to hear footsteps (*hoof steps?*) on the stairs to aid in her decision.

The laughing ceased.

In a loud but hissed whisper, she heard *"I seeeeeee yoooouu-uuu"* echo up the stairwell.

She was moving before she even processed the sound, heading back up the stairwell, not caring about the sound she was making. She threw open the door and stepped into the hallway.

She felt hands and was wrenched off her feet, thrown across the hallway. The whole room spun in front of her, the candles swirling orbs and she careened across and crashed into the plaster wall. The wall crumbled and showers of plaster rained down on her. She was yanked off her knees and thrown again.

She heard snarling as the room spun again. She tried to stand up and fell back down, dizzy and disoriented. She was struck hard in the stomach and doubled over. She looked up to see those red eyes. The snout snarled at her again as it backhanded her across the face, sending her sliding down the hallway.

She rolled and came to her knees, gasping for breath. Blood

trickled down her face and her right eye burned, welling with tears. She leaned forward, vomiting between her hands.

She struggled to see, and tried to compose herself.

Move now! thundered in her head and she rolled away just as a violent kick flew towards her. The kick would have ended it, but her roll caused it to glance painfully off her ribs.

She reacted, swirling on her hand and kicking out. She caught the inside of the creature's knee, and it buckled, sending him down to one knee and roaring. Seizing the opening, she climbed to her feet and staggered away. She had to move, her body couldn't take much more abuse.

The end of the hallway was her goal, bouncing in front of her as she tried to run.

Almost there, almost there, please God, please God, she screamed in her head.

She pushed on.

Thirty feet.

She couldn't see or hear anything else, she had no idea if she hurt the creature or if it was pursuing her.

Twenty feet.

Dammit stay still, she thought as the end of the hallway jumped around from her disorientation and lack of depth perception, her head still spinning and ringing in her ears deafening.

Ten feet.

Five.

Fingers grasped her hair and yanked her backwards. Her feet kept going forward and she slammed down on her back, all the air going out of her. She felt like she was drowning, willing her lungs to pull air, but nothing came except wheezing. Her head screamed from the hair being ripped out.

The creature stood over her as it came to halt, a fistful of her hair glinting in the fading candle light. The other hand had the ax and it began to laugh as it raised it over its head.

It's laugh was short lived, however, as Ellie reacted with as violent of a palm strike as she could muster. Grunting and screaming the little air she managed to draw, she turned her whole body in it, driving straight up between the legs straddling her and into the creature's crotch.

As she connected, she continued to roll and drove her shoulder into its knee, getting a foot up on the ground driving upward, throwing the creature as it doubled-over in pain back over her shoulder, using its own momentum to topple it. The ax rattled to the floor.

She turned, ready to grab the ax and end this, but the creature's paw grabbed it, as it lay on the floor moaning. It brought its knees up to its chest and screamed at her, trying to get its feet underneath it for another attack.

She ran again.

The creature rose and shuffled after her. Both moved down the hall, looking like drunks kicked out after last call, shuffling, staggering, moving side to side as much as forward. The slow motion pursuit rounded the corner into a rotting nurses station.

Ellie fell on the pieces of plaster. She hit the ground and all her energy was gone. She had nothing left to give, she couldn't find the energy to run any more.

She pushed herself back to the wall, sobbing.

"No!" she yelled at herself. "Get. Moving. Keep. Fighting." The words came one at a time, riding her gasps.

She moaned as the creature staggered around the corner. It roared. And then it began laughing.

Laughing. She was on the ground, beaten. On the ground, being laughed at.

No, I left that shit behind!

She reached up the wall, grasping at any purchase to raise herself up.

I will not go out lying down.

She felt a depression in the wall, and wrapped her fingers around it. She pulled herself up. As she pulled, she felt another piece of the wall give way. It slapped back against her fingers.

What the hell?

She pushed again as she slowly rose, the creature laughing and advancing on her slowly, savoring the moment and her struggle against inevitability.

She pushed the portion of the wall and it swung away. She felt inside. The hole had a bottom. She didn't dare look as the creature advanced, fifteen feet away now, shuffling in obvious pain. It favored its knee and leaned forward slightly.

She stood violently and threw herself into the small hole. The creature charged, raising the ax at her. It was slowed by the damage she had inflicted and the wall panel slid back down as she jammed herself in, sending her to blackness and blocking the creature's advancement. She had just enough time to envision the ax piercing the panel, driving into her face as she was wrapped into a tiny ball to fit the tiny space, tucked in a seated fetal position. No way to defend herself, no way to fight back, no way to escape. An ax hacking her over and over again. The vision was vivid, but it didn't last, as her weight started the ancient dumbwaiter down.

She slid down as the roar and a crash from the ax hitting the wall echoed behind her. She fell fast, much faster than she expected. Her stomach dropped as if on a roller coaster cresting a hill. She screamed as she fell. She didn't have enough room to even brace herself.

She heard a loud grinding sound and the dumb waiter slowed and then halted. She reached out to push the panel out of the way to get out, relieved to have not been crushed at the bottom, resigned to dying broken in this tiny box shaped coffin.

Except, the panel didn't move. She pushed harder.

No, it wasn't that the panel didn't move, there was *no panel.* There was just the wall of the shaft.

Her heart began beating faster, then racing. In the darkness she could see the walls closing in, getting smaller and smaller. She couldn't move, she couldn't breathe. Everything hurt and now she would die here. Her face stung and was wet with blood, her head hurt, her cut neck from the ax earlier had reopened and was bleeding. She wondered if she would go crazy, starve, drown in her own blood, or suffocate.

She began pounding on the walls, maybe she could break through. The box made splintering sounds, but nothing budged.

She stopped, beginning to sob and moan. There was nothing left to do. She didn't have enough room to shift her weight and try to force it down further, to try to get to the next floor.

Then a sound. A scraping sound.

Is it sliding down more? she hoped.

It began to move. Her heart beat faster, she felt lifted with hope. She was moving. She reached out to the wall, trying to feel for the panel as she moved.

The dumbwaiter was moving slowly, in jerking motions.

Wait, why is the wall sliding down?

The dumbwaiter wasn't going down, it was going *up.* The creature was using the pulley to try to lift her back up to him. She could hear grunts coming down the shaft. It must have heard her sobbing and realized she was stuck.

Her heart raced, she moved painfully to try to shift her body. She had to be fast, when the panel appeared she had to launch out. She would either be on a floor without the creature or she had to attack. Would the creature's ax have broken the panel? If there was a panel did that mean she was on a different floor? She didn't know, but her life depended on preparing to fight and flee.

Another foot. Another scrape. Another grunt.

Another.

Another.

And then at the top of the opening, a panel. She didn't lift it, afraid the creature would be there. As it got to the halfway point, she threw it up and began wriggle out as violently as possible. She got stuck halfway, but one more pull up and she tumbled out onto the floor.

The room was empty.

The dumbwaiter scooted away in a hurry without her weight holding it down. The creature would realize this and understand that she had gotten away. She stood, trying to orient herself to her surroundings. She wasn't in a nurses station this time. She moved out of the alcove and saw the windows were much smaller than previous areas, and they were in the top third of the wall.

The top third was the ground. She was in some kind of basement.

Twenty-One

Ellie looked around at the basement. She had fallen all the way to the bottom, grinding just before hitting the bottom of the shaft but past the last panel. As she scanned the area, the dumbwaiter crashed back down again. The creature had let go and realized she had gotten away.

Being partially subterranean, the walls were a yellow brick, not the plaster of the higher floors. A draft came in from a broken window, glass pooled beneath the bars. Her body ached and the breeze reminded her of how cold she was. She could see her breath in front of her as she shivered. She wanted to get moving, and away from where she had emerged from the dumbwaiter. She didn't want to be here if the creature rushed down after her.

Ellie moved through the basement, hearing dripping

water and smelling the dank, moist aroma of a basement. The chipped faded yellow brick stretched out ahead of her with rooms on the left and right staggered. Doors hung on some, many were open. She peeked inside, squinting in the dark. She didn't see much. The rooms appeared to be empty, perhaps used for storage in some previous time.

Blood trickled down her face from being struck, dribbling her nose and mouth, and her ribs ached with each step. It ran down her shirt from her neck, making her feel wet and cold down her chest and arm. Her head was pounding in time with her heartbeat as she rubbed the spot where her hair was ripped out.

Damn girl, you a fucking mess! she heard in her head in Anna's voice. *Yep, yep I am.*

She moved away from the middle of the building, hoping that she would find a stairwell ahead, a path to get back to the first floor and the open window. The hallway narrowed on the left side cutting into the hallway that had a door, this one solid and not hanging. The remaining portion of the hallway continued another fifteen feet before it ended in some kind of boarded up entryway.

As Ellie approached, she realized that there was an opening on her left. The hallway turned ninety degrees, and then ran for fifteen feet before another ninety degree turn back to the right. She looked at the strange door jutting out and decided to follow the corridor around.

Seems to be the right way. At some point I should find one of the stairwells. The further to the end I get, the closer I am to my exit.

She peaked around, peering into the darkness that took

over after about fifteen feet, took a deep breath and stepped into it. The windows in this section were barred, but after the first two, were also boarded up, cutting ambient light to almost nothing. She stepped forward again, ten feet to the darkness. Five feet.

God don't let that thing be waiting in here.

She didn't have to wait long for an answer. She heard a grunting echo from behind her. It sounded far away, but getting closer. She ran back through the bend and peered back to where she started. The sounds echoed down.

Down the hallway beyond the dumbwaiter she had crawled out of, she saw an open staircase. This one wasn't enclosed in a doored stairwell, and she felt sure that this is where the sounds were drifting down from, floating warnings telling her to get a move on.

It won't find me. Please go the other way.

She watched, holding her breath. Trying to decide whether to run into the darkness.

I heard the sounds on the stairs, ran up and the creature was right there. Is there more than one?

This struck her and she went cold all over.

There is more than one, she thought. *They tricked me, one herding me into the other. What if the other one is in that dark hallway? This one is pushing me toward it.*

She couldn't move.

Then she noticed speckles out in the hallway on the floor. Right down the middle, away from the dust, broken chunks of brick, and shards of glass, a trail of dark speckles led straight toward her as if ratting her out - *she went this way!*

She reached up and touched her face, and pulled her hand away. It was wet with blood. She had dropped a trail of blood right to where she was standing.

The sounds were getting closer. The creature was looking for her, being slow, meaning it didn't *know* where she was.

Think dammit!

She wiped her face again, getting as much blood as she could on her hand. She walked back toward the dark hallway, shaking her hand to extend the trail of blood, making it more reconizable. She took a breath, and moved toward the dark. Just before the light cut out, she put her wet hand on the wall, leaving a smeared handprint of blood. She wiped again, and walked into the darkness, swinging her hand to the ground to push the trail into the darkness.

She hoped the creature didn't work on smell, or couldn't see in the dark where the trail abruptly stopped, ruining the ruse.

She ran as quietly as she could back, up on the balls of her feet, trying to move as little of her upper body as possible to not create a new blood trail to where she was going. She glanced around the corner. She could see a shadow from the little light that was left at the landing of the stairwell, coming down. Scurrying across the open space, she approached the strange door she had seen earlier.

Please don't creak, please don't creak.

She pulled it open soundlessly.

Finally, something going my way.

Glancing at the door, she noticed the old hinges looked wet. Puzzled, she paused but was hurried when the sounds increased behind her. She slipped in, gently closing the door behind her.

She looked in the door, stunned for a moment. On the left was a narrow stone staircase that went *down* into darkness. On the right was a smooth ramp that fed down next to the stairs. The staircase was only about two feet wide.

If I am in the basement, where the fuck do these go? she thought. The steps were uneven and looked old. They were chipped and broken, made of old stone an descended into darkness.

Ellie shivered as the last of the light was choked off and the door clicked shut,

Whatever, doesn't matter, out of options, out of time, she thought as she entered.

She heard the creature come off the stairs. She gently cracked the door, watching through a slit with one eye as it moved about, searching. It walked over to the alcove with the dumbwaiter and went inside, its ax swinging at its side with each step like a pendulum of death counting the strokes until it got to strike.

The creature didn't stay long. It came out at a quicker pace; it had found the blood. She imagined that the dumb-waiter and the floor around it were covered. It walked swiftly down the hall, looking at the ground.

She held her breath.

The creature moved past her at the door, almost at a trot, and onward to the next hallway.

She closed the door, unable and unwilling to head back out, not wanting to expose herself in the open hallway.

She turned in the dark and headed down the staircase. She was still holding her arm and head up to keep from bleeding, but as she checked, the bleeding was slowing. She moved down the narrow staircase and further underground. She stepped off and moved forward in the darkness. As she stepped off the last step, the ground was curved and uneven. She knelt down and felt bricks, sloping to the middle and back up the other side.

She was in some kind of tunnel. She moved further into the darkness.

What the hell am I doing?

She kept moving forward slowly, the smell of moisture and earth becoming stronger.

She peered into the darkness, wondering if the tunnel would take her out of here.

Is that a light ahead?

Then it was gone, her eyes playing tricks in the darkness. She kept shuffling along the tunnel. Suddenly behind her, the door was flung open. Light poured into the tunnel, not reaching where she was. She could see the tunnel now, and it was indeed a round tunnel made of brick, about eight feet high. There were electrical conduits running across the ceiling and she could see lights. She retreated into the darkness as the footsteps reached the bottom of the stairs.

Oh my God it knows I'm down here.

She felt along the wall until there was a recess. She climbed up a couple feet into the recess and felt a small metal door or panel. It had a small tab, not a handle. She tried to pull it, but it didn't budge.

Must be some maintenance panel, no hiding there.

Suddenly, there was a click, and the whole hallway lit up. She held her breath. Her hiding spot was still dark as the light right outside was burned out or broken.

Finally some luck? she hoped. If the creature was looking for her, it would surely find her here. She had nowhere else to go, no energy to run.

The creature entered the tunnel. She heard the ax dragged momentarily against the brick and heard it shuffling down the tunnel, still favoring its injury from their encounter earlier.

Good you miserable fuck, I hope it hurts, she thought, trying to make herself feel braver than she really was. She held her breath as it came within fifteen feet.

Ten feet.

Five.

And it was right there, so close she could have jumped out onto its back. She clamped her eyes shut and willed her body to be completely still. She swore for a moment that even her heart stopped beating as it passed.

The creature strolled right past her, never even looking her way.

She resisted the urge to let her breath out in relief. The creature continued down the tunnel another forty feet until it turned off to the left in a tributary, moving out of sight.

Only then did she let herself breathe again.

Where is the other one? There must be two of them, the one at the bottom of the stairs laughing and taunting me, and the other one at the top of the stairs that assaulted me.

She strained to hear and leaned out of the darkness to look

up and down the tunnel. Other than shadows from the lights dancing down the brick, there was nothing. Then the lights went back out.

She sat in the dark, trying to collect herself.

There must be two. Even if I concede that monsters exist and this is seemingly supernatural, it couldn't be at the bottom and then the top. If it could do that, it wouldn't have needed to chase me.

She couldn't reconcile it any other way. She tentatively moved out of her alcove, and moved back into the tunnel. Part of her told her to follow the beast, see where it's going and try to understand all that's happening to her, but the other part, the part that said *get the hell outta here*, won out and she moved back through the darkness to the door she originally came through.

She moved slowly, the darkness enveloping and consuming her. After stumbling and falling on the smooth ramp, sliding painfully down on her knee, she felt along the bottom lip for the first step. Bracing herself against the wall, Ellie started up the narrow, uneven staircase.

She eased the door open and peaked out to see an empty hallway. Ellie moved forward, not wanting to be back in the darkness of the other hallway, heading instead for the open stairwell the creature initially came down.

Reaching the landing of the first flight of the open stairwell the creature had come down minutes before presented another door.

That'll work.

The door was boarded up with plywood, the smells of fresh air and dried out leaves tantalizing as it drifted through.

Running her fingers along the board and finding it solid, she hooked the tips of her fingers and pulled.

It didn't budge.

Yanking again, the wood panel remained steadfast. It was as if the only thing not rotting in the cursed place were the exits.

So close, please just open.

The wood refused to yield, and the noise was already making her nervous. Putting her finger in her mouth with its nail broken off from pulling, the copper taste of blood and shot of pain brought her back to face her plight.

A realization washed over her as she spun on her heel and headed up the rest of the stairs to the main floor.

She wasn't afraid anymore. The old version of Ellie would sink to the floor and wait for it to pass. She might sob or cry out, feel sorry for herself. She would definitely be over-whelmed. She remembered doing just that a few hours ago, earlier in the night.

As she regained her memory from that early fog, she found her strength. The defeat feeling was gone, the resignation to victimhood cast aside, the cowering was over.

In fact, as she reached the top of the stairs and opened up on the first floor, she recognized something else - anger. It had begun a few hours ago, in her encounter with the creature. An instinct or a reaction. She didn't just run but *struck back.* That reaction had loosened something inside of her, awoke a small beast that was buried deep down, a small flicker of a match or a lonely ember under all the ashes of her life.

But it was there, and that had blown away some of the debris covering it. And now uncovered, it had begun to burn a bit more. Her mind started churning, taking all she had learned from Nora, from Anna, from her brief month in Krav Maga, and from her own survival over the years.

Exiting the stairwell on the first floor, there was a short hallway off to her right followed by an open area. She took a deep breath, choking on the mildew odor that permeated the lower level, but feeling her heart slow slightly. Being out of the darkness of the tunnels eased her mind and helped her re-focus. The immediate goal was to put some distance between her and the creature, while also being mindful that there was likely more than one. In doing so, she needed to work her way back to the open window on the first floor that was her escape.

Striding across the checkered floor, a renewed energy enveloped her, pushing her forward with a purpose.

Escape. Freedom. Almost there. I am going to make it through this.

Still unsure as to whether there *was* an escape, thoughts of being in Hell were pushed down, a singular focus on reaching that window entered her mind and took over. Keep it simple, to the point, and relentlessly pursue it. That was an Ann-ism which she had tried to instill in Ellie. It certainly fit Anna, Ellie found it could work for her too.

She felt a surge of adrenaline and a laser focus take over. Her heart felt light and she realized she was smiling. A bounce formed in her step and she moved away from the stairwell.

Escape wasn't enough. Simple survival wasn't enough. She

wanted to fight, to inflict damage, to show the creature what she was capable of. The creature had a fight coming; she was going to hit back.

A smile broadened on her face as her mind plotted. She would head to the first floor, come up with a plan and if she encountered the beast, she would fight.

I am a warrior, and I am bringing a storm.

Ellie followed Anna through the door of the Bay View Independent Living Center. She was dressed in a cheap, white pantsuit that felt sterile and cold. Company issued en masse, it crinkled while she walked and made her feel like she was covered in paper. Her hair was pulled back tight, pulling her forehead and eyebrows. Anna waved her away when Ellie said she felt like she looked perpetually surprised, eyebrows chasing her hairline.

The front doors slid open and a half circle reception desk. The carpet was a light beige and soft lights hung from a high ceiling. The atmosphere felt like forced welcoming, a façade in front of a cold, sterile interior.

Bay View Independent Living Center started as a small twenty-five bed hospital back in the 1930's known as Board-man Hospital. It was expanded and repurposed in the late

1950's, renamed to Boardman Valley Medical and focused on the needs of the elderly. In 1998, the building was revamped and renamed yet again as Bay View Independent Living Center.

Bay View focused on their residents needs and encouraged independence as much as possible. The reality was that this would be the last stop for most of the guests, but the organization was rooted in the community and driven by its core values of compassion, integrity, and stewardship. This led to the partnership with Stronger Together. The organizational leadership, led by the Director Jennifer Hall, partnered with Carey Hughes to create a collaboration that allowed for the women of Stronger Together to serve, gain confidence, and help those in need. Both sides benefited, but the driving force was the two women's desire to positively affect those they served and the community as a whole.

Ellie fell behind Anna, almost hiding as she approached reception.

"Hey Bets, this is Ellie, she's starting up today."

The girl behind reception smiled warmly, her plump round face pressing her large glasses up and causing her eyes to squint. Her dusty brown hair hung around her head like a bowl with the first streaks of gray catching the soft light hanging above her head. She had to brace herself to get her obese body up out of the chair. She shuffled around the desk.

The receptionist startled Ellie with a high pitched voice.

"Ooooh welcome honey!" she squeaked, drawing out the words. There was a hint of a southern drawl in there. "You come on now, let's get-choo settled in then." She waved her arms in a circular gesture, around the reception desk as she stooped forward.

She shuffled forward, having to bring herself forward and then pull her leg along. She leaned forward a bit and seemed to favor her left side.

"Oh dear now, I don't move like I used to with this hip," she lifted her head to smile again, her face turning red from the exertion. "C'mon now, let's get-choo all good."

"I'm Betsy, unless your Annabelle there, then I'm jus' Bets." The woman wheezed a bit, as she shuffled back with a stack of paperwork. "Anything you need, you just let me know. I am like the mama of Bay View here. I don't do none of that medicine stuff, but I know how to keep this machine a-runnin', be it where the lady products are when ya need 'em, to what nurse is crabbiest in the morning to who's dealin' with family problems or who's kid has a big ball game comin' up. You need to know what's-what, and I can help you out."

The red-faced smile beamed out at Ellie again, her eyes looking up past the top of her glasses as she stooped forward. You couldn't help but smile back at this woman's energy and enthusiasm.

"Here you go, you fill this out quick as best-cha can. Then we'll make the rounds so everyone'll know ya." She turned and shuffled back toward her seat, looking back over her shoulder.

"Then we'll put-cha to work!" she called, a shrill cackle escaping her, causing Ellie to jump.

After being led to a small room, Ellie sat and worked through her paperwork. A wave of loneliness came over her and a small tear to her eye. The last time she had to figure out some of this was when Joe had helped her get into the coffee shop. It was so long ago, but the fact that he still cared enough about her to help her find her way out of Philly warmed her heart.

Twenty minutes later and after both Anna and Bets stopped in to see if she needed any help, the forms were complete. She was led back out to the reception area and to a hallway on the far side. The building was laid out with a large reception area in the middle and a hallway on each side weaving to the north and south in an arc. Each of these intersected with another hall that ran away from it, lined with rooms.

The lighting was soft and the carpets gentle and light brown. The hallways were lined with plants and basic art, attempting to push away from the clinical feel of a nursing home. Ellie felt the shift from the reception area, along with her attitude, and began to see warmth in the set up. As Ellie was led down the hall, utility closets pointed out periodically, she attempted to stow away "clean sheets are there" and "cleaning supplies are there."

Toward the back center wing of the property was a kitchen, cafeteria, and a parlor for the guests ("do not use the word patient") where those able could meet and dine. The cafeteria was another gentle room, though with tile floors and round tables periodically set. The hallways were wide to accommodate wheelchairs and the like.

"This room is also where we hold larger activities. The parlor is used for gathering and small games such as cards or shows. We try hard to make the guests feel active and involved in their life. Some are not able to and we try to bring it to them," nurse Dalton told her.

She led her into the laundry room, past the kitchen to the south hall in the back wing of the building. The entire atmosphere changed. Hard tile floor ran the length of the room and harsh fluorescent lines lined the ceilings. In the middle was a large set of tables and rolling laundry bins of varying sizes were everywhere. Large washers and dryers lined the outside of the room on three sides.

"You'll spend a lot of time here. Make sure you are wearing appropriate gloves and sterilizing. Some of what you'll be washing will be, uhh, unpleasantly dirty." She forced a wry smile and shrugged. "Comes with the territory, just remember that these guests deserve your respect and their dignity."

Nurse Dalton was just a bit older than Ellie, in her late twenties, with a big smile, freckles spattered on her face and bright red hair trying to be pulled back in a pony tail but revolting against her. She was slim and medium height, about the same as Ellie, but she walked with an exuberance and energy.

She stopped in the hallway and turned to Ellie.

"Get all that?" she said.

"Yes, ma'am," Ellie replied.

"Call me Emily. We'll be seeing a lot of each other I'm sure."

"Yes, Emily. I think so." Truth be told, she was completely overwhelmed. She wished she could be behind the counter at Joe's hearing the familiar hiss of the espresso machine instead, but she kept her mouth shut.

"Listen, it's okay if you don't. All you have to do is work hard, stay in your lane, by which I mean don't try to be a nurse, and ask if you have questions. Most of the people here are here for the same reason, to help."

Emily had graduated with her B.S.N. and ended up in the Emergency Room for a few years down in Ann Arbor. The blur of faces and emergencies had deadened her connection with people.

"Everything had become a clinical problem, no people were involved. When losing a patient had stopped hurting, I had realized that I wasn't fulfilling my mission when I set out to become a nurse. So, I left. I can say that I definitely found it again working with elderly patients here."

Emily's eyes flashed up as an older woman walked by on the other side of the reception area when they entered.

"Most people are here to help, anyway," she muttered, not so much to Ellie but to herself.

Ellie looked at her and then to the stout woman at the end of her gaze. The woman was short and round, with a head of mangled gray hair. She seemed to almost scoot across the room rather than walk. She carried an aura about her, one that seemed to suck in the light and consume it. She was surrounded by a colorless gray and people seemed to unconsciously move away from her as she approached.

"I'm not going to lie to you, though, people will be a bit leery of you until you prove yourself. The girls from *Stronger Together* have been really hit and miss. Anna is amazing, as hard a worker as they come, and she has helped overcome the stigma, but we've had a few that don't show up, show up drunk or high, or are just plain lazy. That girl Cynthia was awful and we had to send her packing after a week." her eyes sparkled. "I feel like I can tell just by looking at you it won't be a problem, but you'll have to earn it from some others. Plus, Anna speaks quite highly of you and she's a tough nut."

Ellie simply nodded.

Emily wasn't deterred and continued.

"Last warning, sometimes things happen here. This is the last stretch for our guests. We make them comfortable, give them as much meaning as we can, and then oftentimes they pass on. It can be hard if you haven't dealt with it, and even harder if you develop a relationship with the guests. Be prepared, and if you need help dealing with it, let us know."

Ellie looked again at the woman across the room.

"Who is that?" she asked.

"Nurse Harmony. Ironic name, you'll want to avoid her. She's Medusa, don't look directly at her."

Too late, Harmony Winstadt had noticed Ellie looking at her and was heading her way. In her early sixties, she had a permanently turned down mouth, her jowls hanging around her frown. Her neck fat jiggled as she walked, creating the illusion that her face melded straight into her clavicle. She moved slow as her movements moved as much side to side as forward, walking on stiff knees.

"Oh boy, here we go," Emily said as she rolled her eyes.

"Nurse Dalton!" she yelled, even though she was only five feet away. "What is this scavenger standing around for?"

She waddled the rest of the way up, squinting her eyes at Ellie, sizing her up.

"Scavenger?" Ellie replied, taken aback.

Nurse Harmony sneered at Ellie. "Get to work."

The words were out of her mouth before she knew she was talking, surprising herself.

"Excuse me, but I don't appreciate you talking to me like that."

Nurse Harmony stepped closer trying to intimidate her.

"Oh you don't street trash? I don't give a damn what you like. Feel free to march your little ass right back out that door and go back to the gutter you crawled out of."

"That's enough you two," Emily started.

"Get rid of this trash, get her out of my ward."

"That's enough!" cut across the room. Everyone turned to see a tall woman with short hair in a pantsuit standing by the door to the hallway that led to the offices. Her lips were pursed and her face tight with anger.

"Nurse Dalton, please help Miss Ellie get started, Nurse Winstadt come with me now." Director Hall turned on her heel and went back through the door.

Then a devious smile spread across her lips, at least Ellie thought it was her version of a smile. It looked more like a rabid dog bearing its teeth, but the corners of her mouth did curl out of the perpetual frown. Ellie shuddered.

"Clean and bathe room 314." She cackled briefly as she turned on her heel, and followed the director.

"Goddam scavengers, come in off the street, useless," she muttered as she waddled away. "I don't know why we tolerate this trash."

Ellie turned back to Emily.

"I'm sorry, I don't know what came over me," she said, her eyes cast down.

"That's all right, Lord knows that woman deserves it and

a lot more. She has always been a nasty, bitter old woman, but she was worse after the pandemic. That vile Governor woman who pushed all the patients in the nursing homes, we lost a lot of people, including a few that she was close to from her growing up. That really pushed her over the edge."

"Besides, she's going to hear from Mrs. Hall." Emily grinned. "She is proud of the program we have to help *Stronger Together*. She and Mrs. Hughes have been friends for a long time. Unfortunately, she has a soft spot for Nurse Harmony after what she has been through. She'll reprimand her, but I doubt much will change. It's the small things though, right?"

As they entered the hall together, Ellie couldn't help feeling pity for Nurse Harmony. It would be sad to live in such a dark existence, filled with hate and anger. Ellie certainly had flaws, and with Anna's help felt like she was working on them, but to choose to exist in a cloud of darkness would be a hell like no other.

"Where are we going?"

"Room 314," Emily replied, trailing off.

"Why does that sound ominous?"

"Well, room 314 is a bit special. She and Nurse Harmony have some pretty epic battles. She tends to make things... difficult. She's really not that bad, but she has spirit and isn't afraid of anyone. That tends to bother Nurse Harmony. As you can see, she is used to bullying people."

They arrived at the closed door of 314.

"What's her name?"

"Nora. Oh, you'll find out about Nora. This is one of those

situations where Anna would say, and pardon my language, shit rolls down hill."

Emily's eyebrows raised up, she sighed deeply, and pushed open the door to 314 and Nora.

Twenty-Three

"**Y**ou put your hands on me again and I'll bite your damn fingers off!"

Ellie's first introduction to Nora was a threat of violence. As she entered, she saw a wheelchair and a head of wavy gray hair in a silhouette facing the window.

"Go easy Nora, it's me Nurse Emily. I have a new team member for you to meet today. We are going to get you all freshened up."

"Fine, you just keep that wretched witch away from me." A crooked, scraggly finger waved in the air. The dark silhouette gave an eerie appearance, like an apparition. Ellie entered the room behind Emily, a bit tentative. She had no idea what she was doing here. Slinging espresso shots and bringing a pumpkin to life in latte art she could do, tend to a crotchety old woman in a nursing home? Her confidence was low, and her first experience was going to be with a woman already threatening to dismember her at the first mistake. Where was a nice, old grandma? Couldn't she start there?

She crossed the threshold and scanned the room. The room was quaint and small. Nora covered most of the window, facing it and looking outside on the landscape illuminated by late summer sun. The window was lined with white curtains and had a flower box underneath, housing some kind of fern. The rest of the room was a blend of cream and crimson. The bed had crimson sheets and a nightstand with a lamp coming out of the corner on her right running along the wall toward the window. A bureau sat off to her left and an armchair sat next to the window. A bathroom sat on the wall to the left and a set of drawers with a television on top lined the wall between the bureau and the bathroom.

The room was jam packed and looked much like the other rooms Ellie had peaked into during the tour. A picture of a small girl with a middle aged couple and an older woman sat on the drawers under the TV in black and white. A cross with Jesus was hung on the wall above the bed and a well worn bible rested on the nightstand, tabs sticking out of the top and sides marking pages. There were no other personal effects in the room. The room's attempt to be cozy came off as cold, or perhaps it was just that Nora ensured it as such.

The woman sat in the wheelchair, hunched forward with her back slightly curved, her body appearing slight and frail. Her silver hair in tousled waves around the sides of her face and extending down to her shoulders, she appeared harmless. Until, that is, you saw her eyes. While her body appeared worn and near decrepit, her bright green eyes appeared sharp and piercing. Those eyes caught Ellie's attention in a squint as she and Emily came around the front of the wheelchair.

Nora scanned Ellie up and down, appearing to size her up. Her lined and weathered face tightened and her lips pursed. Her steely eyes met Ellie's and seemed to bore into her. Ellie was mesmerized by the green orbs piercing her. Unable to break the gaze, the two stared at each other for an eternity until Emily broke in.

"Okay, let's get you started here Nora. No scratching this time."

"Hmpf!" Nora replied, turning away from Ellie and back to the window. "Don't be rough and I won't bite back."

Emily talked through everything with Ellie, who was there just to help in the non-medical sense - get another towel, take care of this, or run and get that. It was obvious that Emily was a pro - she was methodical and smooth despite the sporadic obscenity or lashing from Nora. Small in stature, but solid as an oak, Emily managed Nora who, for her part, offered little resistance other than the sharp tongue.

Ellie cleaned the room and changed the sheets on the bed with barely a word. She was unnerved every time she saw Nora looking - no, *glaring* - at her.

Emily finished her duties with Nora and moved to the door.

"Please clean the bathroom with the supplies there. Then please grab that tray and run it down to be cleaned." She pointed to the lunch tray on a small table by the window. "Then come find me and we'll run down a couple more rooms before the end of the day."

She glanced at the watch on her wrist. "I have another guest to get some meds to." With that, she disappeared out the door and could be heard scurrying down the hall, echoes fading into the distance.

"Don't you talk?" Nora asked, startling Ellie.

She met Nora's gaze. Her green eyes seemed to be on fire, drilling into her.

"I talk when I have something to say."

"Seems wise enough. You don't have anything to say to an old hag like me?"

"Seems to me your sharp tongue has been doing enough talking for the both of us," Ellie shot back, shocking herself. She almost looked around to see if Anna was there before she realized the words came out of her mouth.

Nora snorted. "Touché."

Raising an eyebrow, Nora continued. "So, you're not a nurse, you must be one of those troubled girls that come and go."

"I'm here because I'm *not* in trouble anymore."

"I see. They don't usually send the troubled ones my way unless they really don't like them. I ran the last one off in under a week."

Ellie gave her a full face grin. "Challenge accepted."

Nora's eyes narrowed for a moment, before she pushed her head back and let a throaty laugh.

"We'll see dear. We'll see."

She regarded Ellie with a side-eyed look, a smirk on her face as her sagging lips, curled up. Ellie finished up the list Emily had given her, and moved to leave. She glanced back at Nora, who sat smirking in her wheelchair, regarding Ellie with a raised eyebrow.

Nora's sharp and demanding demeanor didn't scare Ellie, and *that* made her nervous. She somehow felt immediately comfortable with Nora despite her abrasiveness.

Sitting in her chair, feeble and hunched over, Nora should seem frail. Yet, Ellie could sense a power emanating from her. Her skin hung off of bones, most of her muscle deteriorated in her age and condition. The pallor skin, a dull gray that seemed cold, made it easy to just pass right over her at first glance. Until the green eyes shone, made ever brighter by the surrounding ashen appearance.

They stood eight feet apart watching each other for an eternity, each digging into the other and trying to figure her out.

Finally, Nora broke the silence.

"Check the hall, let me know if that Nurse Witch is coming."

Ellie stuck her head out and found the hall empty, turning back to see Nora rooting around in her wheelchair. Her fist came out clutching a small white package as she pushed herself close to the window.

"Crack this thing open for me, would ya?"

Striding across the room, the mid-afternoon streaming through the window, she rotated the crank to open the window.

Nora pushed a lighter into her hand and slid a cigarette in her mouth. She waved her hand impatiently at Ellie.

"C'mon dear, we don't have all day."

"Won't I get in trouble?" Ellie asked.

"Dear, you need to stop worrying about everyone else so much. You sit and worry about everyone else and you'll get nowhere. Now quit yer blabbering, and light me up. It hurts my damn fingers to do it myself."

Ellie raised the lighter and looked at the shiny silver casing. The outside had been engraved with the words *Nora & Roger Sept. 15 1956.* Above the words and date was a cross with intertwined circles and a shining star in the middle.

She was struck for a moment, as if a revelation that this hardened old woman was still a person. She flicked open the lid and struck the flint wheel, a flame immediately jumping to the wick. The orange glow danced in front of her face as she lowered it to Nora's cigarette. The tip glowed orange and Nora took a deep drag.

She leaned forward in her chair and blew the smoke out the open window.

"Not sure that'll take care of it. They'll still smell it," Ellie murmured.

"They can piss off!" she hollered, waving her hand in the air and sending ash fluttering away like snow flakes. "They don't own me. These cancer sticks are a bit of pleasure in my otherwise boring existence." She tapped her cancer stick on the edge of the bowl sitting on the lunch tray. It might have been soup in at a previous time, but now it just looked like congealed slop.

"I'm a bitter old woman, sitting here just waiting to die at this point. I'm going to enjoy the things I can enjoy. The sun-setting, the birds outside the window, the burn of a nice hit of whiskey, and these," she announced, holding the cigarette up in front of her face. The smoke lifted off and reached for the ceiling.

Ellie waved it away from her face, trying to usher it out the window.

"So, that's you then. Worrying about what everyone else will think of you?" She shifted in her chair, trying to raise her stooped head a bit to look in Ellie's eyes.

A choice to make, engage this woman or simply leave. A part just wanted to run away, get away from the smoke, from getting in trouble and getting yelled at, get away from the woman's piercing eyes, get away from her questioning stare and bitter demeanor.

Another part, a new part it seemed, wanted to stand fast. In her head she was leaving, like she always did, be small and out of the way, fade away or run away, so she was surprised to find herself in a chair she dragged over. Lowering herself so Nora didn't have to strain, she met her gaze.

"What is it then? You want to know your worth from how someone else thinks of you?"

Nora narrowed her eyes, as if concentrating the force of her stare to increase the depth it would drill into Ellie's soul. Ellie let her eyes drift away toward the window sill, following some of the smoke drifting out.

"No, that's not it. You aren't shallow like that. Something else then. Maybe a simple lack of confidence, not belief in your own worth at all." She paused. "Or perhaps you are just a kicked dog, beaten so much that all you want is to stay out of the way of anyone's wrath."

Ellie's eyes inadvertently shot back to Nora, ever so briefly but she didn't miss it.

"Ahhh, I see. Struck a nerve there, did I?" Another deep drag created a pause to let the tension hover in the air between them. She exhaled a deep cloud with an audible *whoosh* and chuckled a bit.

"Well, then, let me tell you. Life is not easy, was never meant to be. God didn't promise us an easy go of it. Turns out nothing worth having is easy. You need to face and fight battles to find out who you really are, to mold your character. Anyone can have character in easy times, it's the times of suffering and trials that develop you. Your character is forged in the fire of adversity."

"There isn't a person on this earth who hasn't had to fight. It's what separates the strong from the weak, not winning the fight but persevering to fight again. Getting back up when life knocks you down."

She paused for another drag.

"I've certainly led a successful life, but not without its challenges. But I have always pushed harder, and it's because I know my life has purpose and meaning, God brought me into this world with a purpose. Jesus suffered more than I, and He did it for me. I can take a little suffering in this world knowing He is with me."

"Basically, I am telling you two things. First, no whining allowed. We all struggle and if you sit and wallow in self-pity, you are wasting the gifts God gave you. Whatever those are, follow Him and find your purpose, and do His work to the fullest. Second, fight for it. If you project weakness, you will be a target for others. People are not inherently good, they are inherently selfish. If they can dominate you, they will. You need to stand up, forge forward, and, if necessary, fight."

She cackled again. Then leaning forward all the way in her chair and pointing her fingers right in Ellie's face with her eyes blazing like green fires, she hissed:

"And if you're gonna fight, you fight like you're the third monkey on the ramp to Noah's ark, and baby, it just started to rain."

Twenty-Four

"**F**ight like you're the third monkey on the ramp to Noah's ark, and it just started to rain."

Ellie repeated it again, out loud. The sound echoed softly through the empty room of the rundown asylum. She had a loose plan forming in her mind to fight back if necessary. She had to find the right spot, something to weaponize, and enough time to set up. She moved through the corridor on the first floor and found a door off to her right.

Upon entering, she found a large room. It was dark and cavernous, Ellie had to squint to make out the far side in the gloom. She stood on the subfloor, whatever original flooring had been there was long gone. Wooden flooring was rotting and warped, flowing almost up and down across the open expanse. The ceiling was high and every step seemed to echo from all around her. She stepped cautiously to the middle of the room. Scanning around the space, first looking for danger, second for a possible way out, and third for useful items to fight back with.

There was a door at the back of the room, but it was thin and jammed shut. It did not appear to be an external door. She pulled on it, yanking with her weight. The door groaned in the frame and snapped open, sending her tumbling backwards. The sound seemed thunderous in the open space, causing Ellie to hold her breath to listen for oncoming danger in response. After a few moments of nothing but her beating heart she stepped through the door.

The internal room was even darker as she peered in. The room was rectangular and ran about two thirds the width of the larger room. It was only about ten feet across and appeared to be for storage. It was empty, other than dust and mold. The room smelled dank, offering no prospects to Ellie. There was no way out, nothing to use as a weapon.

Except that small wooden crate. And that larger open crate against the far wall.

Blinking, Ellie squinted. She heard voices behind her. She spun around, her heart jumping in her chest. The room wasn't dark anymore, it was well lit with flickering light. And it was milling with people.

She looked back and the storage room was lined with boxes, many empty, some with Christmas decorations, tablecloths, and other assorted items.

She stepped back into the hall and there was a rumble of voices and the gentle playing of piano music. Ellie stood back and saw men on her left, women on the right. All standing and milling about, looking anxious.

The flooring was back and the light posts were lit up. Christmas garland and wreaths ran around the walls and fixtures, a table sat on the back wall to her immediate right with red flowers and poinsettias. The warm glow of light reflected off the decorations and the festive mood of the room warmed Ellie. The room itself was cozy, and Ellie rubbed her cold arms. She strode through the door and into the party. Her eyes scanned the space, an orderly brushed past her, not even seeing her.

That was okay, she was feeling warm for a few minutes at least; she was back in the Light World, 1915. It was still Christmas, judging by the decorations. All the men on her left were dressed in suit jackets, slacks, and ties. The women wore a mix of dresses, some red, some white, some with flowers on them, others still with patterns or plain. Some wore hats or bonnets, some had their hair done.

One had a nice big hat with a large red flower on it and wrapped with a red ribbon. The woman wore a white dress with a large flower up the right side. The woman was smiling a radiant smile, though one side didn't quite reach as high as the other. Her eyes were locked right on Ellie.

Helen waved at Ellie from across the room.

Two doctors stepped forward between the two groups. Ellie recognized Dr. Sutherland from earlier. He raised his hand to the men's side, and in a gentle sweeping motion, gestured to them to begin. The men moved slowly across to the women, and politely began to ask the women to dance. The piano began to play louder and the men and women danced.

The patients danced while Ellie watched, song after song. The smiles were radiant, and the awkward, stiff movement loosened after a few minutes. Each time, the men politely asked for dance, the women curtseyed, and the dance began. The joy was palpable, the mood so light Ellie forgot about her plight, forgot about being chased or in an asylum, forgot about the pain in her whole body.

She found herself infected with the atmosphere. Men and women dancing to Christmas music, laughing, and singing to the piano music. Even Dr. Sutherland and his cohort, while trying to keep an eye on everyone along with a group of orderlies and nurses, were getting wrapped up in the festive spirit. Dr. Sutherland sang under his breath with a smile on his face.

Ellie drifted through the crowd, listening to the laughter and joy. She ended up on the far wall on the right side of the room, and leaned back, taking in the warmth and atmosphere.

Suddenly, she felt she wasn't alone. She turned and Helen was standing next to her smiling.

"Hullo again."

"Hello Helen."

"I been watchin' you. I dun't think I need to be a-scared a-you."

Ellie smiled, remembering how scared she was last time.

"You don't have to be afraid of me. We're friends."

"Oh-kay" Helen said drawing the words out. "The nice doctors kind-a threw out my fit when I seen you last. I still got outta the bad wing. That was nice of 'em, huh?"

Ellie looked at her, puzzled.

"The bad wing dudn't get to do the Christmas dance. I's so

glad to move! I love the dance!" She clapped her hands and bounced on the balls of her feet.

Helen wore such a smile on her face it warmed Ellie's heart. She tried to think back. She could hear Dr. Sutherland asking the nurse about the voices, the young lady and the monster back when she first met Helen.

And Helen knew who she was. She had talked to her like she already knew her. It was spring and she was out on the farm, plus she remembered the nurse saying she hadn't heard anything in a while, and that Helen had been doing well in the middle wing.

December 1915, Helen was scared of her.

Spring on the farm, Helen knew who she was.

The meetings were backwards for me, Ellie realized. Her first meeting through this strange time rift was not Helen's first meeting. The spring must have been after the first meeting, after now.

Ellie shook her head, trying to reconcile all of it.

No wonder Helen freaked out, she thought. *I appeared out of nowhere and talked to her, knew her name. That's why she called me a ghost the next time. To her I am just an apparition that keeps appearing. In my timeline, I saw her in the spring but that was the third time she had seen me.*

"They say the dance lets us be like reguluh people. It's good for us. Such fun! I love wearin' this dress. Do you like my dress? Am I pretty?" Helen asked, her eyes dancing in the gentle light.

"You look beautiful Helen. Simply beautiful." Ellie replied, and she meant it.

She had been in the darkness all night long, the joy in the room lifted her spirits and made her feel alive. Ellie didn't realize how down she had felt, meandering through the dark halls of Hell and wrestling with her internal hell as she struggled to remember. The dance and Helen's happiness lifted her up.

She soaked up the room, seeing all the smiling faces, the old fashioned light fixtures with their ornate curves and brass color. She could smell the sweet smell of the wreaths, even through the suffocating smell of overdone perfume on Helen.

"Do you like me perfume? Nurse Nicole and I be good friends and she let me have some. She said it's white something. White flower…" Helen's face contorted as she struggled to remember.

"It's very nice," Ellie replied. She found herself basking in the atmosphere, the first time all night that she wasn't stressed out and overcome with anxiety, fearing for her life, or her soul if she was already dead.

"Rose! White rose!" Helen cried suddenly. "By Ba-carn. Bacarn. It's sophis-uh-cated." She shook her head to emphasize the word.

They laughed together, Ellie resting her hand on Helen's arm.

"Who are you talking to Helen?" a voice said, startling them both.

Ellie turned, still laughing with Helen and saw an orderly in a white uniform, head to toe standing before her. The man was young, maybe late twenties, with brown thinning hair combed over. He had large wire glasses with circular lenses covering the top third of his face. He had a smile on his face.

As Ellie looked him over, it was more of a smirk, the corners turned up in a devious manner. Ellie immediately felt on guard, something off about the man.

Helen's hand pulled away from Ellie's arms violently. Ellie turned, her smile fading from her face, and looked at Helen. A wave of anxiety flowed over Ellie. Helen's eyes showed fear, and her lips were pulled back, exposing her teeth. Her shoulders hunched, and she leaned backwards away from the orderly.

"Are you seeing someone again Helen?" the orderly said. "I'll get you back to my wing, now Helen." He laughed.

"No..." Helen whined. Tears appeared in her eyes. "No. No hurt."

Helen started blubbering, saliva dripping out of her mouth. "No, no, no..."

"Yes, Helen, you'll be right back in your room, and I'll come check on you."

His hand shot out and grabbed her arm violently. Helen yelped in pain.

"I'll be right there to check in on you." he sneered. He twisted her arm, and Ellie saw the skin fold like an old Indian rope burn she used to get from the bullies at the Shyt House.

Ellie had flashbacks to Cheryl, sneering and laughing at her. Twisting the skin on her arm. She thought of Zach, pinching and twisting her breasts, punching her kidneys, or simply throwing her down. She had flashbacks to lying on the floor of the condo, lying in the yard or on the concrete, flashbacks to the room under the stairs, sitting in the dark.

She thought of Cynthia, the bullying she received after

getting to the *Stronger Together* house. She thought of the first time, when Anna stood up for her. Anna, who stood up for who was weaker and couldn't stand up for herself.

Anna who took on the bullies.

Ellie's arm shot out and grabbed the orderly by the arm.

No one could see Ellie except Helen in the 1915 world, so she didn't even know what to expect. She imagined her hand passing right through the orderly as she stood in front of him, like a ghost in a movie or cartoon.

Her hand struck his arm. She felt it solid, and wrapped her fingers around it. Pure rage flowed through her for the bully, hurting her friend Helen.

The orderly cried out in surprise. His face was overcome first with shock, then swept with absolute horror. His whole face contorted in terror, and he suddenly became white as a sheet. His eyes opened wide as he stared into the face of a young woman, who appeared out of nowhere right in front of him. Her face held a fire of rage and her eyes were slits of anger.

"Whuu-uhh-t? Who are you? Where did you come from?"

He began shrieking and trying to pull away.

"Let go, let go of me. Stop!"

Ellie twisted his arm into wrist lock, spinning him around, driving him forward into the wall. She pinned him up. He was surprisingly light, shaking with fear.

"You don't like it when it happens to you, do you?" she screamed in his ear.

"No, no, no."

"Answer me!" she bellowed, twisting his wrist further.

"No, I don't!"

"What did you do to her?" she yelled.

"I.. I.. I hurt her?" he stammered.

"Hurt who?" Her voice kept rising.

"Helen! I hurt Helen! I would go into her room, I would twist her arm! I would pinch her! I put a cigarette out on her, where no one would see it! Please let go of me!"

"Why, you sick fuck, why would you do that to such a sweet woman?" He writhed as she twisted further, the wrist straining, close to snapping.

His face glistened in the gentle light, his face ghastly pale. He was close to passing out from pain and fear.

"Because I liked it! I like the power over her! God, please stop!" the orderly cried, tears streaming down his face.

Ellie pulled him back and then slammed him forward into the wall, his face smashing into the plaster. He cried out a grunt and slid down the wall as she let go of his wrist. She turned around, shaking with anger, and saw Dr. Sutherland and another doctor standing a few feet away, watching the whole thing. She turned back to the orderly.

"Don't you touch her again."

He didn't answer as he got up. He brushed off his pants with his good hand, and then held his bad wrist with his good across his body. His eyes darted left and right, searching.

He mumbled and looked around. He turned and glared at Helen.

"Hey! I said don't touch her again."

He didn't respond.

He can't see me again, she thought. *As soon as I let go, he can't see me anymore.*

His death stare at Helen told Ellie she might still be in danger. She stepped forward toward him. This time she grabbed him by the throat and shoved him backwards.

His eyes told Ellie he saw her. His whole body went rigid.

She screamed straight into his face.

"IF YOU TOUCH HER AGAIN I WILL COME FOR YOU!"

She struck him again, straight in his sternum. He bent forward and she grabbed his chin. Lifting his pained face to meet her raging eyes, his body shook with fear.

"Every moment, I will be watching you. When you least expect it, I'll come back. I will destroy you and haunt you forever if you even think of touching Helen or any of these patients ever again!" she shouted.

With that, she bounced him off the wall again and let go.

Krav Maga class, target the soft areas.

She didn't want to gouge an eye out, so she instead drove her knee directly into his crotch on the rebound of the wall, driving with all of her weight.

He crumpled to the ground, shaking and coughing, holding his crotch.

The doctors came over.

"Glen, are you ok?"

He didn't respond, his eyes were empty and far off. He kept blubbering to himself, unintelligible musings in between tears and painful coughs. His body shook uncontrollably and his face was deathly pale. Spittle dripped off his chin.

"He crazy" someone said behind, drawing on the word crazy so it sounded like *crayyyyyy-zeeee*.

"All right everyone, it's going to be all right. We are going to get back to our rooms for the evening. Thank you everyone. I hope you had a wonderful, festive evening." Dr. Sutherland said. To another orderly, "The dance is over, let's get everyone back to their rooms, and lock down for the night. We need to rid Mr. Oesterle there of his keys and hold him for observation."

The orderly did as he was asked, crouching down to Glenn, and seeking the keyring to the facility off his belt. Ellie realized that Glen was the only person who could see her. She couldn't imagine how everything had looked to Dr. Sutherland.

The orderly tried to help Glen Oesterle to his feet, but the man began shrieking and pulled away. His ramblings were incoherent as his eyes darted around the room, unfocused. It took several orderlies to get him to his feet. He turned and jerked, off balance and lurching around the room as if trying to escape but being lost. After several minutes, two orderlies held him down while another administered a sedative.

The shrieking finally stopped.

Dr. Sutherland, a worn look on his face, scratched his head and breathed a deep, troubled sigh.

He turned to Helen.

"Helen, are you all right?"

"Yessur Dr. Suth-er-lin."

"All those things he said, are those true?"

"Yessur Dr. Suth-er-lin. He hurt me lots" she whispered, and tears rolled down her face.

"Not anymore Helen, not anymore," he replied, a concerned look on his face. He turned back to Glen Oesterle with a sharp look. "He won't be hurting anyone anymore."

Ellie, still standing as an observer no one could see, looked into the doctor's eyes. She saw a deeply determined rage and she felt confident that Mr. Oesterle would be dealt with.

Helen turned and looked at Ellie, smiling at her, eyes radiating an appreciation to her hero.

"Nope, I guess he won't."

With that, 1915 melted away, the mold crawled back up the walls, and Ellie felt herself drop a couple inches to the subfloor. She was back in her Dark World. The floating image of Helen stayed imprinted in her eyes for a few moments as the darkness enveloped the room.

She felt good, she stood up to a bully and helped Helen. What a feeling to see the look on Helen's face!

She remembered how Anna had helped her. More importantly, she remembered how Nora had helped her help herself.

Twenty-Five

"**C**an I ask you a question?"

"Would it stop you if I said no?" Nora responded, not looking up from her book. Her gnarled hands clutched the binder awkwardly, but when Ellie had tried to help, she shooed her away.

Ellie stopped and thought for a moment.

"Probably a couple weeks ago, but now that I've endured you this long, nope." Ellie had lasted more than a week, she was on week three at Bay View. She worked in many rooms, but made sure to stop by to see Nora every day. Their friendship was unusual, the timid girl trying to gain confidence, and the raspy, matter-of-fact take-no-shit old woman, but despite it's atypical nature, they got along. Yin and yang, Ellie thought.

As she brought in towels for the bathroom and restocked the bathing supplies, she continued.

"You sure talk about God a lot for someone so surly."

Nora closed her book in her lap and looked up, her lips pursed and an eyebrow raised.

"I still didn't hear a question."

"Well, shouldn't you be happier for someone who believes in God?"

Nora reached out and set the book on the table, shifted to face Ellie better in her wheelchair and folded her hands in her lap.

"What does God have to do with happy?"

Ellie shrugged.

"Besides, I am happy. What you call surly is just that I used all my patience up with people and outlived it. Is that really the question you want to ask?

Closing the small closet in the bathroom, Ellie returned to the main room.

"What do you mean?"

"Something tells me that's not the real question, that's a scratching at the surface type question. Be out with it, girl, tell me what's on your mind, don't make me guess."

Ellie once again thought about it.

"I've never been to church, but now at the house, we do bible studies and go to church on Sunday. I don't really know what to believe. Don't get me wrong, I *want* to believe it. The idea that someone, something out there is watching over me, loves me and all that. Just seems like it might be a coping mechanism for the harsh reality."

Nora nodded, a solemn look on her face.

"Well, having heard what I've heard of your story, I can understand your skepticism. But God only put you through it to strengthen you. He never says it will be easy, He never says there won't be suffering. But He's there, I don't just believe it, I know it."

"How can you believe it with all the bad stuff in the world? How can you believe it with people like the Shyt House, people like Cheryl, or like Z-" Ellie couldn't finish.

Nora didn't make her.

"Well now missy, you knock off the water works. We don't have time for that. Life is hard, no one ever said it wouldn't be, or if they did, they were a knucklehead. Anything worth it is going to be hard. Life is worth it. You had a worse hand than many, but not everyone. You were blessed with a good head on your shoulders and God has certainly dropped angels in your path. Was it just a coincidence that you ran into that Madelyn girl that day? What about your friend Joe? Maybe you turned your back on your angels to go with that monster. But God brought you out of the desert. You said yourself, you had no idea how you left the condo that day."

Nora signed.

"God is there, don't you waste a moment of your precious life thinking he isn't. Now, I have a different perspective. My Roger was an engineer, a very analytical mind. Made a nice living for himself up at Worley's there, designing widgets and what-nots. Now, we were both Christians but he came to his faith a bit different than I. He was too logical and too analytical to just feel the Holy Spirit in himself."

"He used to talk about philosophical arguments like the Uncaused Cause, the idea that something had to start this. He would talk about physics such as the argument for design and fine tuning, talking about inertia, and the first law of thermodynamics saying that energy isn't created or destroyed and only transferred. If the universe had a cause, it had to have a first cause, and if anything not in motion can't become in motion unless acted on by an outside force, and if energy can only be transferred, well then what got it moving? God must be behind it."

"If that didn't get you, he'd talk about the second law of thermodynamics and how finely tuned the strong nuclear force was, or the weak nuclear force, and how if the slightest differences had occurred, we'd only have hydrogen or something. If that didn't convince you, well, he would just keep going on."

Ellie was perplexed and having a hard time following along.

"But in the end, I think the most convincing questions to prove it to me are *how did it all start if not for God* and *why are there moral values at all without God?* Think about it - why would something come from nothing without intervention of a perfect being like God? Things don't spontaneously appear now, so why would they back at the dawn of time? And why do people have moral values? Why isn't it just survival of the fittest? Why do we have a conscience? There is no benefit. Yes, people argue community benefits, but really that's a stretch. I'd benefit from taking by force as the strongest at my leisure. Without God, there is no right and wrong. We know better, so God must be there."

Nora paused, her voice even more raspy than usual. She sipped some water.

Ellie sat back, taking it all in. Nora met her gaze, waiting patiently for her to reconcile all her words.

Then Ellie smiled. "Well, you make a pretty convincing argument."

"God's there for you, but you have to put in the work. Pursue Him, and He'll provide for you."

"Sometimes it feels hard to believe that part."

"Well, the best way to find it is to look for it. The best way to look for it is through gratitude. Whatever you are doing, do it the best you can and pour yourself into it. Like right there, you're doing a shitty job setting the bed." She pointed at Ellie. "How you do anything, is how you do everything."

"Tuck the sheet under the corner, fold that into a triangle, there you go. Tuck it in there. Okay, now fold that sheet back. Smooth it out."

Nora kept on until the bed was tucked tight, so tight you could bounce a quarter off it. The bed was smooth.

"See, do it right. Feel good about what you do, do it right and have a good impact. That's how you serve God, use the skills he gave you to do the best job you can at something worthwhile. That's why man can create beautiful things like works of art or architecture. Pursue God's perfection and land in beauty. And express gratitude in all things. It's just a matter of perspective. Look for the good in something, and you'll find it. Look for the bad in something, and you'll find that instead."

Then she smiled. Maybe it was more like a sneer.

"And you'll just be a whiny bitch."

Nora shrugged.

"I used to tell my Roger, people can bitch and complain once, then do something about it."

Ellie laughed.

"Who knew behind that rough exterior, you were a philosopher."

"Have a purpose in serving God, show gratitude, fight like hell, and put up with no shit. Pretty basic, but effective rules for life." Her finger stabbed the air as she talked.

"Now, you tired me out with all this and there's a horse in my throat" Nora croaked. "Don't tell my secret."

She dug into her wheelchair and pulled out a flask from under the cushion. She screwed off the silver cap and raised it to her lips. She took a deep pull and grimaced, feeling the welcome burn warming her scratchy throat and warming her chest and belly.

She offered the flask to Ellie. Tentative, she took it and had a sip. The sharp flavor was burned like fire in her mouth. She coughed violently, aspirating the bourbon, setting her entire chest aflame. She doubled over in a coughing fit, tears running down her face as she tried to catch her breath.

Nora was trying to catch her breath too, but due to being doubled over in her wheelchair laughing hysterically.

"Easy there Doc Holiday," she cried, taking the flask back and tucking it under her cushion, just as Nurse Emily came in.

"Everything okay?" she asked.

"Everything's fine," Ellie stammered in between coughs. "Just had a drink go down the wrong way."

Nurse Emily stood back a second, looking between Nora and Ellie.

"Uh huh," she said, and gave a knowing glance at Nora, mocking disapproval.

Nora raised her hands in a "who, me?" gesture before she and Ellie burst out laughing again.

Emily shook her head, and left the room.

*   *   *

Smiling in the dark as she stepped back out of the hall, she found herself both lonely and comforted. She missed Nora, that woman sure knew how to put things in perspective and there were no wasted words. She didn't give a damn what you thought of her, but you were getting what *she* thought.

On the other hand, her faith in God had strengthened Ellie, teaching her to have faith as well. This made her feel less alone as she tried to strong while she was hunted in the dark. Remembering all this lit a fire in her. With her faith, there was no way she was in Hell, right? So there must be an escape.

The inner strength she felt that overcame despair at her situation was the knowledge that she wasn't alone, that she had a purpose. Maybe all her life had been building to this moment, iron sharpening iron to strengthen her will and her soul to battle this monster.

The window. Right now, her main purpose was to get to the window. The bars had been pried away, she was right there, when she flipped back to 1915. She needed to get back there while she was in the Dark World.

So close.

She turned back down the hall and headed back on the first floor toward her goal, the sweet taste of freedom and the autumn smell in the fresh air.

No more of this dank, moldy smell of death all around me.

Moving to her right and down a short hallway, Ellie noticed the hallway ended and opened up into a small open area. Past the open area was another hallway in the far corner, just past a set of doors. As she began to walk through her world flickered again, in and out, dark and light, present and 1915, hell and paradise, good and evil. A large kitchen materialized in the light through the doors. Christmas decorations adorned the entry and each side of the door was framed with poinsettias.

She followed the light and into the kitchen. Off to her right were a set of long tables running in parallel, one along the wall with a gap enough for preparers to work, and then another. A group of women were working to wipe down and clean up the stations from the Christmas celebration dinner that Helen had mentioned previously. They wiped and carried off utensils and containers. The women all wore white long white aprons, stretching all the way to their ankles, over top of light blue or gray blouses and full length skirts. Each had a white hat pulling their hair back away from their faces. Most worked silently, a few solemnly, but a couple were humming or singing Christmas tunes under their breath.

The room was warm, hot even. It smelled of food, but underneath was the aroma of hard work. The women's hands flew as they completed their tasks. Ellie had the feeling that Christmas was almost upon them and this may be the culmination of the season before they went to their own families and homes.

She turned from the focused women and followed the black and white checkered floor further into the kitchen. A small group of men stood around preparing tables in front of a large oven and hood. Groups of cubbies with metal bins stood on one wall, the large ovens on the other. The small silver handles glinted in the light and the men glistened with sweat. They all were adorned head to toe in a white shirt and pants, and covered with the white apron. Two of the men had large dark mustaches and serious expressions, while the third was tending to a series of pitchers on the table.

The whole room hummed with work, the operation that kept the patients in the asylum fed. Large pots sat on the counters and the whole room smelled of baked chicken and warm soup. The atmosphere made Ellie feel hungry but warm.

The scene was hurried but organized as everyone in the room seemed to be in sync as if in a well practiced and choreographed dance. They seemed oblivious to each other and yet moved together. If anything, this trip had made an impression on the function of the facility, and the impact on its patients.

Beauty is therapy. Work is therapy,

Beautiful nature, large windows, a farm to work, crops to tend to, cows to take care of.

Everyone seemed to have a purpose at the asylum, they seemed to know their work had an impact, and possessed a healthy respect for the impact.

I wonder what my purpose is? Ellie thought. She thought of Carey and her purpose, Joe and his purpose. She made a promise to herself to figure it out if she got out of here. As Nora had told her, she had a purpose bestowed on her, she just had to seek it. That was what life was all about, serving through the gifts she had to fulfill her purpose.

When, not if, she corrected.

The warmth went first, as it faded the intoxicating aromas of food dissipated as well, and finally the people, color, and furnishings. The room was dark, black, and molded. The floor was torn up, covered in debris, and curled in the corners.

Dark, cold, and mildew.

She turned back and stepped back out of the kitchen, scanning the environment, looking for signs of the beasts. She leaned into the open area, straining to hear for the sounds of shuffling feet, heavy breath, or the demonic laughing that had followed her off and on throughout the night.

Nothing but thundering silence.

An encounter was inevitable, it had been a while since she had run into the creature. She realized at this point that it was playing with her. It would appear, torment her, and she would get away. It always seemed to know about where she was, appearing just when she was getting comfortable to punish her and start the pain and fear all over again. The clock in her head was ticking louder, as if her body had figured out the cadence of the attacks.

Squinting through the darkness and around the corner, Ellie could feel her senses sharpen, her hair rise on her neck, and a tingle in her fingers and feet. Her body was ready, though she couldn't ascertain if a subconscious trigger was trying to warn her, or if it was simply the increasing ticking of the clock in her head.

Her mind was sharpened to her surroundings, a situational awareness that prepared her for battle. She noticed more, the dripping of water somewhere in the distance, a breeze that flowed through the dilapidated asylum, and the smell of mildew.

This heightened sense of awareness was new to Ellie - instead of crumpling to the ground or lowering her head and hoping it passed, she felt ready to battle.

If you're going to fight, fight like you're the third monkey on the ramp to Noah's ark. And, baby, it's starting to rain.

Twenty-Six

Ellie recounted the events to Nora over a cup of coffee after her shift. Mid-way through her third week taking care of Nora and others, it had become a common occurrence that she would stay after her shift to visit with Nora.

A codependency had formed in their friendship, the color returning to Nora's face, her hunch less pronounced, and her speech less raspy - not to mention less sharp. Ellie had gained confidence and had a parental figure that she had lacked most of her life. She confided in Nora and in return, Nora advised her, strengthened her through the cultivation of her moral character, her finding of her faith, and the ownership of her circumstances and results. There was no complaining, no self-pity, and no victimhood with Nora - if you had an issue, you solved it. It didn't matter what the fight was, you took it head on.

On this day, Ellie was struggling. She had poured herself into her work and the exploration of her faith. She had tried to "turn the other cheek" and reason with Cynthia, but it only made the situation worse.

Ellie had left Nora the day before and walked back to the home. The air was starting to crisp in the early fall and the sun was lowering behind the horizon earlier each evening. The wind had a slight fall bite to it and the leaves were bright and colorful. As she strolled along, she was taken by the blazing colors around her and lost in her daydreams.

Her apartment.

She was close, it was almost time to leave *Stronger Together* and have her own place. She had never had her *own place* before, she had been on the streets, in an apartment with Madelyn, in the condo for those years. Nothing had been *hers.* She never intruded on Madelyn's property and she lived in constant fear of doing the wrong thing in the condo, not that it even took a *wrong thing* for her to have to pay.

She dreamt of her own bed and small kitchen table, art on the walls, and the smell of a scented candle. She envisioned herself in the kitchen making dinner, a glass of wine on a small island. She imagined herself gazing at the setting sun next to a window with a good book - they already knew her name at the library and she had a stack of them in her room at the house. She felt the warmth of home, her home. She had begun to dream of being like Anna, returning to help at the house even though she didn't reside there anymore.

She smiled as she lurched forward, her dream shattered by violence on her arm. As the real world filled back in her consciousness and the confusion abated, she saw a small framed person yanking on the purse around her arm. The person had on ripped black jeans, tight to thin legs, and an oversized, dirty hoodie.

The pulling yanked Ellie forward. Sticking her foot out in front of her, she braced against the pull, and rotated her body. Three weeks at the dojo, she felt more comfortable in her body, having begun to learn to use it as a tool to protect herself. Driving her hips away from the attacker, she stood her ground and pulled the assailant back toward her.

Driving off her back foot she rotated her hip low and into the attacker as he or she stumbled back toward her. Her assailant spun down to the concrete sidewalk and rolled away, letting go of the purse. Ellie was ready to flee when she noticed the hood had been pushed away in the fall, exposing her attacker's face.

Cynthia.

"Cynthia? What are you doing?" she said.

Ellie was paralyzed by the violence for a moment, and just stared at her attacker, shocked it was someone from the house. No stranger to violence, of course, she was just beginning to trust again - trust her friends, trust her environment. Cynthia's eyes bore through her, seething with hate, as she cowered on the ground in front of her.

Overcome with pity, Ellie reached to her.

"C'mon, let's get you back to the house. We'll work this out." She had enough confidence not to cower anymore. She felt strong and sure of herself. She could handle this, they could work it out. Maybe Cynthia just needed help, maybe this was how she manifested her pain -

"Say what?" Nora interrupted. "It just sounds like she needs an ass-kicking!"

Ellie shook her head and continued

Cynthia had just continued to stare at her with hateful eyes.

The moments passed in slow motion until Cynthia crawled forward and ducked her head. A moment of confusion passed over Ellie until she felt hands on her back and she was flying through the air, overtop of Cynthia on the ground. She hit the sidewalk, fire burning through her hands and knees. She kept her head from hitting the cement, and rolled onto her side.

Cynthia and another hooded girl, this one a much heavier and stout, quickly descended upon. Ellie tried to roll, but too slowly as the girls attacked. She covered her face as Cynthia kicked her in the ribs and the heavy set girl stomped on her stomach.

Her breath left in a violent *whoosh* as she rolled and tried to protect herself. As quickly as it started, it was over and she could hear footfalls on the cement away from her.

She lay there, rolling and crying, trying to catch her breath. She felt as if she were drowning, and her stomach was tightened into a little ball that wouldn't release from the stomp. After a few moments of gasping short, choppy breaths, the air began to come easier. She filled her lungs and sat up. Her hands were bleeding, scraped to cherry red. She felt the same burn on knees through her jeans.

Her purse was gone.

She sat a moment by herself, no one else on the stretch of sidewalk between Bay View and Division. She didn't know what to do - this was supposed to be her safe space, she had won the fight and made it here. She was starting over, how could this happen?

"Honey, the fight never stops," Nora interrupted again. "And if you ask me, or even if you don't, that girl needs herself an ass-beating. You can't fix assholes, you need to face your problem head on."

Nora shifted in her chair and pointed a finger at Ellie, a long piece of ash on the end of her cigarette shaking and threatening to let go.

"Don't go thinking just 'cause you won a fight that it's over. The war of life is made of many ongoing battles. Battles with yourself, be it confidence, addiction, or whatnot. Battles with others who want to take advantage of you or hurt you, or just don't care if you are in their way. Battles *for* others who can't fight for themselves. There is always a battle to be fought. Until you are called home, you are in a constant battle for your soul."

"What about turning the other cheek? Isn't that what we are supposed to do?"

Nora snorted.

"Hardly. You don't need to seek trouble out, but evil exists in this world, and if you don't do something about it, will someone else? Don't be afraid to fight back, use your gifts to help others fight back, just know your limits. Don't fight unnecessarily, but, as Edmund Burke said, 'All it takes for evil to triumph is for good men to do nothing'."

She waved her hand in the air as she sat back.

"Or something like that. Even C.S. Lewis states that tackling evil requires a fight. Besides, God meets you, you have to meet him too. Just remember not to fight out of envy, pride, or vengeance. But protecting and standing up for yourself, bah, get after it. Like my Pa used to tell me, don't ever start a fight, but damn well finish one. If you're going to fight, fight like you're the third monkey on the ramp to Noah's ark. And, baby, it's starting to rain."

She laughed.

"Think of it this way if it helps you. God blessed you by creating you in His image, you have an obligation to protect the temple that is your body created as such, to ensure that you can live in the purpose He designed you for."

She smirked at Ellie and held up her hands.

"There. How's that? Personally, I like the ark metaphor better."

Ellie slinked across the room and sat on the bed, putting her head in her hands, heaving a big sigh. It was so confusing, so much to think about. Letting it fester in her head, it made sense. Her expectation from going through the tunnel of darkness and coming out the other side into the land of milk and honey had been shattered. The fight was still on, she could either be a part of it or let it overtake her yet again. How long would it take her to wake up this time?

No, she wouldn't be a victim anymore.

She lifted her head and made eye contact with Nora, who wore a look of concern.

"Do you need anything? Do you need money if they took it?" Nora leaned forward. "Believe me, I have plenty that I don't need."

Eyebrows raised, Ellie said, "No, I am okay. I only carry enough for what I need for the day, and a bit more just in case."

"What's with this all-this-money business?" Ellie inquired.

"Bah, I have plenty. I told you I have been blessed. My Roger was an engineer and did pretty well, but I inherited my parents business and ran it. Turns out my attitude translates quite well to the business world, I am loaded as you might call it."

"Why are you here then?"

"Why not? I have to be somewhere?"

Ellie gave her an impatient look. "You know what I mean, why not at a place having someone take care of you? Why not with family?"

Nora shrugged.

"I don't have any family left. My Roger passed away some twenty years ago, and my son, William, God rest his soul, in a car accident not too long after. This is just the way life is sometimes, but God led me here for a reason."

She thought for a moment, and smiled. "Maybe to find you. I've grown quite fond of you, so maybe you're my family now."

Ellie beamed.

"I've never really had a family. I like the sound of that."

"Me too."

Overcome with too much emotion to sit still, Ellie rose

and went to Nora, hugging her in the chair, trying to not squeeze the old woman too hard.

She needn't have worried, Nora may have looked frail, but she had an iron grip, and she held Ellie back just as fiercely.

Ellie's healing felt complete.

Twenty-Seven

Fight she would. Moving in the halls of the old asylum, Ellie felt complete again, her old self felt fully back. Whatever had been in that rag to knock her out had caused her some momentary amnesia, but remembering the hug from Nora had closed the gap in her memory, and she felt herself again.

Assuming, that is, that she isn't dead and in Hell. She felt reasonably confident that that wasn't the case.

But how to explain the monsters then?

She struggled with that as she slowly and cautiously moved through the asylum. It was a pertinent issue, however, if she wanted to achieve her goals.

First fight, then escape.

She was ready to fight and had a loose plan. She would set a trap and lead the monster into it. An outline, a sketch as it were, existed in her mind but the lines were faint in pencil. They would have to be redrawn and erased based on what she could find along the way. And she had to plan for two creatures. She didn't think there were more; it seemed that she would have more encounters if there were. There had to be at least two though, as she had run from the one she heard at the bottom of the stairwell and opened the door at the top to another.

What did she know about the monsters?

They had red glowing eyes and a large snout. They stood tall, towering over her. They grunted and made animal noises. Rabid animal noises, not that she knew what that meant but it seemed to fit in her head. These were demons, horns rising high off their heads.

They blended into the darkness, head to toe in black except for the glow of those demonic red eyes and the glint of the steel of the ax head.

Don't forget the ax. She shuddered. Of all the ways to go out, chopped up by an ax was not really high on her list.

She had hurt one of them, hitting it, pushing it into the window, and kicking it in the crotch.

Well, I guess that's universal.

This was important because it could be hurt.

It. Singular.

She paused a moment, letting that ruminate. But there were two? Or were there?

Thinking that over, she realized she had never seen them together, just heard one and ran into the other. What if the other one wasn't the same? Had she encountered both of them at different times? Or had she just encountered the same one every time? What if the other one was completely different?

She shook her head. *Sometimes you have to make the best decision with the information you have at the time.*

Head toward the exit, plan your trap along the way, and get out if you can. Fight if it - or they - are in your way.

Now that she felt back to herself, her whole self, she thought about what she knew. This was the asylum, or some version of it at least *(present? past? future? something else?).*

What did she know about the asylum? She thought back to what Helen had told her, and what she had witnessed through the 1915 / 1916 world she had been in. And of course the conversations with Nora, the asylum out her window, through the trees, and across the grassy landscape. As the leaves fell, the asylum became more prominent out her window, and Nora would gaze out at it.

Nora loved the trees and the landscape, pointing out trees that were brought back by Dr. Munson to the grounds due his belief in *beauty is therapy.* How many times had she heard that tonight? On the walls, from Helen, from the doctors when the shimmering took her back to 1915 / 1916, and now the recollection from Nora.

Perry Hannah, the father of Traverse City, was a Scotsman born in Erie Pennsylvania. After moving to Port Huron Michigan with his father, he ended up working for a lumber baron, and moved to Chicago. He met his future business partners here and ended up founding Hannah, Lay and Company, a lumber firm with property at the head of the Grand

Traverse Bay and along the Boardman River. They eventually bought the Boardman sawmill, investing in and growing it. This growth fueled the area and in 1853, a post office was christened in the new "Traverse City." It wasn't until 1881 that Traverse City became a village.

As Traverse City grew, Hannah, Lay & Co. offered more jobs, such as general mercantile and banking. By 1856, the company was the largest employer in the area, making Traverse City a company town. If someone wanted a job with Hannah, Lay & Co., he or she would receive one in Traverse City. The company invested in the area, building the infrastructure along present day Front Street and the Boardman River.

Perry Hannah wasn't done, however, as he entered the political arena in 1857 and became the village president in 1881 followed by the first mayor upon city designation in 1895.

Hannah was busy in 1881, as he also used his significant political influence to bring the Traverse City Asylum to Traverse City. He saw the writing on the wall as the logging industry in the area began to die, with the harvesting of logs getting further and further from Traverse City.

The state determined that an additional asylum was needed to support the Kalamazoo State Hospital (at that time known as the *Michigan Asylum for the Insane*) opened in 1859 and the Pontiac State Hospital (*Eastern Michigan Asylum for the Insane*) that opened in 1878.

To ensure that the people of Traverse City would have a means to support the community and themselves, Hannah made certain he was on the selection committee and used that influence to secure the facility for the people of Traverse City. Awarded in 1881, the hospital opened in 1885.

It was the first of the hospitals that utilized the Kirkbride Model and was planned by the famous architect Gordon W. Lloyd. The first building, known as Building 50, was constructed in Victorian-Italianate style according to the Kirkbride Plan. This is where Ellie had been spending her time this evening, in both the dilapidated, moldy version of the present after its closing in 1989, and the thriving version in 1915 and 1916 with Helen.

The batwing architecture came from the Kirkbride plan. In the focus of beauty on therapy, light was an essential element. The plan utilized a bat wing structure to maximize the number of windows that could let natural light in. The design, advocated by American psychiatrist Thomas Story Kirkbride, were contingent on his theories regarding the healing of the mentally ill, in which environment and exposure to natural light and air circulation were crucial. The typical floor plan had long wings arranged staggered, so each connected wing received sunlight and fresh air. This was meant to promote privacy and comfort for patients. The building form itself was meant to have a curative effect, with the grounds having tasteful ornamentation.

Ellie recalled Helen's talk earlier in the evening about the sunlight in the windows and how it was healing. It made her feel safe and warm, she had said. As she moved slowly about the dark halls, there was nothing safe and warm right now, that was for sure. She found herself missing all the flowers and vegetation that adorned the halls in the 1916 world.

The asylum was built with local bricks from Markham

Bricks. Between 1874 and 1907, James Markham produced the bricks at a company along the shores of nearby Cedar Lake. For a time, it was the largest brick factory in northern Michigan. More than eight million bricks were used to build the hospital.

Dr. James Munson, the first superintendent of the asylum, believed in beauty as therapy and filled the grounds with exotic trees and plants from their own greenhouses. Ellie recalled the first conversation about Helen's favorite trees in the arboretum.

Munson expanded the facility and the patients were treated with kindness and comfort. He expanded the farm with animals, plants, crops, a canning facility, and furniture construction. Restraints were forbidden.

As the years went by, the farm and other services came under attack as it was viewed as "free labor" and undercut the local farmers who could not compete with the pricing. The farm was shut down in the 1950's, and the hospital closed in 1989. Patients were turned out on the streets, which contributed to a homeless population. As Anna had told her, many patients returned to the hospital after closing, banging on its doors, trying to get back in.

Now, Ellie was trying to get out.

The many windows were all sealed up to keep kids and homeless out. The police had responded to many calls of people, mostly teenagers, horsing around in the building, daring to stay over the night in a *Haunted Hill* type, or getting lost in the tunnels.

The tunnels! It made sense now that she had it all back.

She was down in the tunnels earlier, she had hidden in the little alcove in the wall that led to some kind of maintenance hatch. The tunnels were run under the grounds and used to house all the steam pipes to bring heat, water, and air circulation to the buildings.

Those tunnels, she heard, were a bit of a maze. The creatures were lurking down there as well. The one had walked past on his way somewhere - it did not appear to be searching for her, but on a mission, heading to a specific place. The other times she had run into it, it had known where she was, or so it had seemed.

She did not want to get lost in those tunnels, there were almost two miles of tunnels beneath the campus. She needed to cautiously move through the asylum to the first floor window and slide out. If she was in the real world, she would be free. If not, well who knew what would happen.

Nora loved gazing at the grounds. Ellie loved Nora, and thought of her again. She had helped her learn to fight. Sure, she had learned *how* to fight at the SMA Academy, but she learned *to* fight from Nora - to fight for herself.

She remembered that lesson, and how even then it took more help.

*   *   *

"Hi-*yah!*"

Her fist pounded the pad, and she drew back again.

The SMA Academy was run by Sensei Sparks, a short but high energy man full of positivity. His bubbly personality energized you, and Ellie was eager to hit the mat from the moment she met him. His infectious smile lit of a thin face under close cropped hair flecked with more silver than black. Three weeks into her training, she had jumped into the lessons. It wasn't the violence as much as it was the movement, the sweat, the racing heart. She loved being with other people and learning, all while leaving the mat both exhausted and exhilarated.

Of course, feeling the confidence of being able to take care of herself, to defend herself, certainly was an added bonus. While a lifetime of cowering couldn't be erased in a few weeks, her new found love of controlling and using her body to her advantage coupled with the incredible community had her visiting as frequently as she could. This was her third day in a row at a class as she had attended her first Brazilian Jiu Jitsu class the evening before. That was an incredible experience, so much tact and patience as you could not just brute force it by trying to overpower your opponent. While Krav seems more immediately practical, she felt a connection with the little bit of grappling she had done even more than the striking of Krav Maga. Perhaps because she was on the floor, something she knew quite well, but this time she was using her familiar environment to fight back. Or perhaps because it was an art that evened the playing field with those who were stronger.

The atmosphere at the dojo was incredibly welcoming. Martial artists that were far up the ranks treated the new people with such care, genuinely interested in their learning. Egos did not exist and everyone mattered. It was another community for Ellie to be a part of, and she relished it.

This community was her favorite part of the experience. While she worked with three different black belts, people of such experience and discipline, they were the most patient and down to earth people she had met. They were gentle in their instruction and understanding as she worked through the form, all the while they were people that could snap her like a twig if they so desired.

Sweat dripped off her nose as class was called. She lined up, paid respect to her teacher and to her classmates, and was dismissed from the mat. She packed her bag and stayed a bit late to help clean the mats. By the time she left, she had to throw a jacket over her sweat soaked clothes and the sun was set. She moved down the road toward the house, a fifteen minute walk.

The fifteen minute walk would be less in a couple days. She was officially moving out of the house and into her own apartment. She was earning a decent wage at Bay View and she was about to pick up a second job working part time at the local coffee shop. She knew her way around an espresso machine quite well and the owner had been very impressed with talking to her. She had just stopped in for a warm cup on the cool fall evening over the weekend and had ended up in an informal interview.

She missed the environment of the coffee shop and had an instant longing to be back among the wonderful smell of brews, hiss of the espresso machine, and friendly community atmosphere of the shop.

The whole world was different in just eight weeks. Starting with a single step outside the door, on a journey that was so long and yet not much time had passed. In that time, she had gained her freedom, met new friends, established a support structure, found a motherly figure in Nora, gained new skills in a new job, and gained confidence in herself. Now she was about to be back in a coffee shop and have her very own place.

The wind picked up and a chill ran down her back. It took a moment, but Ellie realized the chill was not from the wind. The hair on the back of her neck stood. Self defense was about being aware of your surroundings, tuned in to changes or deviations from your normal, an identification of a potential threat looming.

Pay attention to your subconscious, it often notices things amiss while the front of your mind focuses on something else. If it sent up a flare, you had better be ready to react to it.

She spun, sensing movement behind her, the feeling of tension and the rush of air, a vacuum whooshing behind it. Out of the shadows was a dark blur, masked by the dark and heavy cloud cover.

Ellie bent her knees and brought her arms up as a shining pair of white hands emerged from the dark, reaching for her. Pivoting to her left, the momentum carried her assailant toward her. She grabbed the outstretched hand by the wrist and spun further, throwing her hips and causing the attacker to fly past her, skidding down on the cement.

An animal screech erupted from the attacker that Ellie recognized. It was another show down with Cynthia.

Strike first, use violence of action to end this quickly.

Ellie drove forward as Cynthia stood up, striking forward with a palm strike to her face. A sickening crunch was audible as her nose exploded in blood and her head snapped back. Whirling on her heel, Ellie struck out with her right foot, learning from last time and covering behind her. Sure enough, another hooded attacker was charging, this one only slightly larger than Cynthia.

Elliie connected full force on the side of her knee, and she crumbled to the pavement. Backing away to ensure both women were in front of her, Ellie scanned the situation. She was almost to the house, perhaps a half block around the next corner. She could run, especially in the moonless night. The house felt like safety, a sanctuary from the violence.

Should she attack again? Put an end to this once and for all. Both women were staggering to their feet. The new one's face was all mottled with acne, her sneer showing no teeth. Blood was pouring from Cynthia's nose, which was off to one side. Her eyes were tearing up, but the red rims around them were not from the fight.

These girls were both strung out, or coming down from a binge. They were not going to stop unless she put them down for good, which was not something Ellie wanted, nor did she think she was capable of doing it. It was time to go. She began to move toward the corner to get to the house when another shadow appeared out of the dark gloom. It was the larger black girl with the short buzzed hair that had surprised her from behind in the previous encounter.

Then another shadow, smaller. Then a third, this one visibly shaking, an anxious and strung out laugh chittering from her.

"You goin' no where, bitch," the large woman stated. An audible click echoed through the evening stillness. The glint of steel caught Ellie's eye. "You goin' bleed this time."

The woman sneered, and began advancing slowly.

"Cut 'er up," Cynthia called, blood spraying with each word. "Look what she did to my face. Cut dat bitch up!"

"Shut up. Yo face looks like shit run over anyway, she done did you a favor," the woman laughed.

"C'mon cut her up, then let's get some. I need a hit, c'mon get her done," Cynthia mewled.

"I said shut the fuck up," the large woman bellowed, causing Cynthia to shrink back as if struck.

Ellie stood her ground and got in a fighting stance. She was surrounded, there was nowhere to run. She would have to fight against a bigger, stronger opponent who was armed with a blade.

In her books, this is where the hero would show up just in time, riding in on a white horse with sword in hand. The fire breathing dragon, the evil sorceress, or the man in the black hat would never stand a chance, she would be saved, good would triumph over evil.

But this was the real world and Ellie knew better than most, no one was coming to save her. The difference now was that instead of curling up and taking the punishment and hoping to survive another day, she had to fight for herself.

Her target picked, she darted over her right shoulder, driving low on the small fidgety girl that stood there, mewling to herself and shaking. This was the weakest link and also the furthest from the knife in the large woman's right hand.

She hit the timid little thing with her shoulder right below her belly button, as if she was bringing down a rumbling running back coming through the line. The girl was so light that Ellie stumbled off balance. They both tumbled to the ground with a thud on the grass, barely clearing the sidewalk. The girl's head hit the ground on the way down and she immediately went limp. Ellie rolled over the top of her and tried to regain her footing.

She slipped on the grass, and fell to one knee. Rising back up, one of the other girls jumped on her back, wrapping arms around her throat and legs around her waist. Ellie's subconscious took over, her hand shooting up to the one clutching her clavicle. She wrapped her fingers around the outside of the thumb and rotated it outwards as violently as she could. At the same time, she threw her upper body forward in a bow while throwing her outside hip up and back.

The girl was propelled over her shoulder and landed on the sidewalk with an audible *thud.*

There was no time to admire her work. Before she could finish her first stride, her legs were wrapped up from behind and another girl jumped on her back. She went down to the grass. She flailed, throwing elbows and fists, driving her knees. She connected on several, and the grip began to lessen. One girl fell off at a knee followed by a kick that connected with soft tissue. She scratched the face of the other assailant, raking down the side and feeling skin give way.

The attacker howled in pain and released her. She was almost free.

Her stomach exploded in pain as she was about to scramble to run. The large woman had stomped on her again. And again. Then a kick to the small of her back, the toe of her boots driving into her kidney.

Everything in her turned to jelly. She couldn't move, couldn't breathe. She still had the will, but nothing in her body was responding to her demands.

"Get that bitch up. I gonna carve my name into that pretty face."

She was lifted to her feet. Her eyes cleared from the fog of pain. She saw a battered group in front of her. The small girl was still lying in the grass, Cynthia was doubled over in pain from the knees and kicks. The other girl was just now pulling herself off the sidewalk and holding her wrist against her body.

The fourth was holding her right arm, fingernail marks down the side of her face, leaking blood. Her eyes were already swelling shut and turning a pretty shade of purple.

In front of her was the large woman, her face twisted in perverse delight as she twisted the knife to and fro in front of Ellie's face.

Well, five on one, at least I did some damage. This is going to be bad, but I went down fighting.

She tried to struggle but the kick to her kidney was still reverberating through her body. She felt like a big plate of jello out of the mold, jiggling back and forth. Her whole body was made of gelatin and her muscles refused to respond.

Nora would be proud, I fought all right. Fought like the third monkey. Unfortunately, this storm is just too big.

She felt sadness overcome her, and found herself thinking that her only hope was that Nora would understand and know that she fought hard.

The big woman advanced now, the sadistic sneer contorting her face into a pure ugliness. Her face was deformed into a dark smoke, with no definition, just swirling evil.

The scene was broken by a racking sound from behind the group.

The big girl froze, her face recognizing the sound. Her body tensed up, and she slowly turned toward the noise.

"I suggest you put her down before I put you down."

There was no steed or Excalibur, no white hat donning cowboy ready to stand for morality and goodness. But there was the modern equivalent - the racking sound of the action being pulled to load a shell in the Remington Wingmaster, the stock braced against the shoulder of Carey Hughes.

Ellie was always struck by her strength of presence, and this time was no different. There was no fear in her eyes as she gazed down the sights of the shotgun.

"Bitch, you best put that down befo' you get hurt."

Carey took a stride closer, the large woman recoiling. Trying to regain her composer, the ringleader of this sad, strung out group whined "you can't get us all."

"Just you. Drop that blade or I'll put a hole straight through you. The rest of these meth heads might get me in a rush, but

I highly doubt that anyway. Looks like they all already had their ass kicked tonight. Any way you look at it, you won't be around to see."

The knife clattered to the ground and Ellie's arms were free. She crumpled a bit before steadying herself, and moving around to the side of Carey. The other girls fled back in all directions, limping away.

"Ut-uh. Not you. Get on the ground before I turn your knee into oatmeal and you say goodbye to walking another step."

The big girl lowered herself to the ground, arms extended. Moments later, the first police car arrived and Carey lowered the shotgun.

The woman, Nikole Bass, had a rap sheet as long as Ellie's arm. Battery, assault, possession, possession with intent to distribute, the list went on. As it turned out, she had another warrant out for attacking an elderly man on the street un-provoked.

Ellie gave her statements to the police, as did Carey, at the police station. After a few hours of getting everything answered and documented, she sat with a cup of hot apple cider with Anna, waiting for Carey to emerge.

Anna was concerned, of course, but Ellie assured her she was fine. Surprisingly, she was. In fact, she was better than fine. She didn't want to say that and she couldn't quite put words to it. She certainly wished she had just made it to the house, taken a shower, and gone to bed dreaming of her apartment. On the other hand, she had faced down evil and emerged victorious. She had fought for herself, and won. For the first time, she had not crumpled or curled up in a ball, but had fought back and *won*. Well, she had help, sure, but that just spoke even deeper into the connections she had made.

This was evil's last gasp effort to pull her back, but she had not succumbed to its grasp. She had stood for herself and put it behind her. She didn't want to feel *good* about what had happened, but there was a feeling of strength and triumph.

This was the corner, and she had turned it. Her life was good and if evil reared its ugly head, she knew she could fight it.

Twenty-Eight

Ellie snorted in the darkness at that thought. *Evil is behind me.*

Right behind maybe, breathing on my neck and ready to take my head off.

She still had a fight ahead of her.

That had been a turning point, however. She had learned to fight from Nora, learned how to fight at the dojo, but all that had been *theoretical*. That night had changed her, putting all of that into practice and defending herself. You could talk all about standing up for yourself but when the rubber meets the road, how do you know how you'll react until you do? That evening had given her a new set of confidence in the harshness of reality.

It had also made her really understand the depths of love. Carey had been there for her, stood up for her, putting her life on the line as she stood behind that shotgun. That woman was fearless.

As Ellie crunched over some fallen plaster in the hallway on the first floor of the asylum, she recalled Carey after the event. She had taken Ellie in and made sure she was all right. They stayed up far into the night and the dark hours of the morning, sipping on apple cider and talking about - well, everything.

Carey had carefully led the conversation, making sure that Ellie was all right. She pried out the feelings of triumph that Ellie had, and had approved of them.

"There is nothing wrong with feeling that way. You stood up to a monster, and you took care of yourself. As long as you have the discipline to understand that fighting is a last resort. Some people get the taste of blood if you will, and can't tell the difference after. It changes them. Don't let that be you, and you'll be fine."

"To be honest, I am proud of you. The big challenge for you when you arrived was confidence and self-respect. You aren't a timid mouse, you are a roaring lion. I have no doubt you are ready to be out on your own," Carey finished.

Ellie had felt better about her own feelings, having them validated by someone she held in such high esteem.

And of course Nora had cheered her on the next day.

"Great! I heard that you really kicked their ass! I am proud of you, standing up for yourself," she had said. When Ellie expressed a bit of uncertainty, Nora continued. "Think of it like this. What if their next target was someone who wouldn't or couldn't fight back? Who was the next elderly man on the street that was going to get hurt by these idiots? You not only stood up for yourself, but you stood up for them. You stopped that future pain on people who can't stand up for themselves."

Everything wasn't sunshine and roses after, however. A few days after that night, she was moving to her new apartment. She had made a few trips over and was back to double-check that she had everything out of her room at the house. Her room empty, she dropped down to Carey's office to leave her key on the desk.

The door had been closed, which was odd. Upon turning the knob and opening the door slightly, she had heard a soft, muffled sob from inside. She had tried to stop, pull it back like it never happened, but her momentum brought the door open enough to make eye contact with Carey.

"You might as well come in," came a slurred voice.

Ellie had pushed open the door, and saw a different version of Carey than she ever had. It hurt her to see the red rimmed eyes, the disheveled blouse and messed hair. Her nose was running and her lips wet. She blinked slowly as her hand rested on the neck of a bottle of Wild Turkey.

"At least shut the door so no one else sees me like this."

Ellie had done as she was told. Carey didn't even wait for her to sit.

"I try to save everyone. I try to save them all. You can't save them all. You can't, no matter how hard you try. You can't save all of them." Her voice had wavered and slurred, her eyes far away as she stared into the amber liquid in the bottle.

She had raised the bottle to her lips and took a pull, wincing as the burning liquid punished her throat for her failures.

"They have to want to save themselves. You can only help

that along, give them support, tools, love. But in the end, you can't do it for them."

"Is this about Cynthia? It's okay, I forgive her. We can still help her," Ellie had pleaded. She hated to see Carey, someone she thought of as her hero, in this state.

"No, no we can't, not anymore," Carey trailed off, her eyes distant.

"We can't give up on her. I can help," Ellie pleaded. "We can get her some help, detox her. That other woman is going to jail, maybe getting away from that crowd will do it."

Carey had met her eyes, the dreamy look sharpening. She suddenly, like the flick of a switch, had become stone sober.

She shook her head slowly, her eyes never leaving Ellie's.

"Cynthia's gone, Ellie. Dead. We did all we could, but people have to want to be saved, you just can't do it for them." She had shifted in her seat and sighed, a deep sound of melancholy that had yanked right at Ellie's soul. "The police went to find her, and find her they did. OD'd, rubber tube around her arm, needle on the floor. They figure she had done heroin and either overdosed on it, or the heroin was laced with fentanyl. It's an epidemic in this country, coming across due to the open borders and lack of leadership in Washington." She had waved her hand in the air. "One of many problems with the lack of leadership I guess. The toxicology will come back later, I guess but it is irrelevant. Anyway, Cynthia had meth issues, we were trying to help her but she relapsed a few months ago. It was bad. Trying as we did, she hasn't been quite the same since. It took a bad turn last week and I told her she needed to be clean or not to come back. I hadn't seen her since until tonight. I guess after she ran off, she found what she was looking for."

Ellie had visions of her own mother, dying the same way so many years ago.

"Anyway, she is gone, beyond saving. She didn't want to be saved. I know that, and I know that there was nothing I could do. It still hurts. It's amazing how much it still hurts." Her voice had begun slurring again. "I think it hurts because it's hard to understand. Someone that doesn't want to be saved is a hard case - extrinsically you can't force them to want it. It has to be intrinsic, and all you can do is help stoke the embers to hopefully build a burning fire inside them that consumes whatever their darkness is - addiction, lack of confidence, whatever. But when there is not even a single glowing ember and there is nothing to fuel, it doesn't matter how much you try to blow on the flames, the fire won't start."

"You, you want to save yourself, that's evident," she continued, her eyes once again meeting Ellie's. "That's why you are finding such success. I have heard all about you and Nora at Bay View, about the job you are doing, about your training at SMA. I had the coffee shop owner call me and rave all about you, wanting to make sure the vibe she was getting wasn't wrong. I applaud you for what you have done for yourself, and I am honored to have been able to be a small part of it, the catalyst for your success, if you will. The force to get you over the inertia of inaction."

She had laughed at that.

"That's why she hated you, you know? Because you were everything she wasn't. Like so many self-described victims today, she didn't want what you had, she just didn't want *you* to have it, and she wanted to blame you for her lot in life. She didn't want to change, just wanted to blame someone else for it. So prevalent in our narcissistic and hedonistic society today unfortunately. Most people don't want it to be better because then there would be nobody to blame. They might have to take responsibility, be accountable for their choices, and have to *work.* No, it's much easier to just sit, point the finger and say 'there, it's that person, group, insert whatever here's fault that my life is shit.'"

Carey had reached for the bottle again.

"Anyway, I am going to have a drink. I know how it is, but it still hurts every time. We help them all. We lose a few like Cynthia, and some truly thrive, like you. Most just get a little better. It still hurts to fail."

Ellie had sat with Carey, eventually removing the bottle, and helping her to bed in her old room. She had slept on the couch that night, checking in on Carey several times. When she awoke the next morning, Carey was already up and her normal self, no worse for wear. They did not speak about the previous evening, and Ellie had made breakfast, cleaned up, and headed off for work.

Even the strong had their moments of vulnerability. Life wasn't all success but you fought for every inch and kept pulling yourself along.

The same message rang true now; she had setbacks through the night, but she was close, so close, to escape. She couldn't wait to get out, go find Carey, Nora, and Anna.

A sound in the darkness derailed her train of thought. She

froze in her tracks. She was at the end of the first batwing fan out on the first floor, ready to swing into the next wing. The sound was from ahead, but it was strangely familiar. It echoed through the hall, a scratching sound of metal.

She flashed back to the night of the attack, the racking of the Remington Wingmaster action, loading a shell into the chamber.

Carey! She was here to help again, she had found Ellie.

She started to run toward the sound when a new sound erupted. The Wingmaster fired, the thunder of the shotgun discharging deafening in the silent building. Ellie came around the corner and peered down the hall. She could just smell the sulfuric scent of the fired shell. The reverberating sound of the fired weapon faded, replaced by slow footfalls on the floor. About half way down the hall, black boots emerged from one of the doorways.

Ellie's breath caught in her throat, a soft whimper escaping her lips. It wasn't Carey. The dark boots were followed by dark pants. Then the torso, head, and horns materialized through the threshold of the room. The head turned toward Ellie, red eyes glowing, and the ax settled on its shoulder.

The creature threw its head back, and began to laugh. The laugh traveled down the hall to her, increasing in intensity until it was all around her, pounding in her ears. She was completely enveloped in the laughter, as if it was coming from all around her and not just from down the hall. She clapped her hands over her ears, wincing. The creature turned on its heel and walked away from her, turning to head into the final wing and out of sight, laughing the entire way.

Ellie stood frozen for a moment. The laughter began to fade until the hallway was quiet.

A deep breath, a step forward, a sense of foreboding. The creature was playing with her, it seemed. Something was waiting in the room, waiting for her. Another step, the sound of crunching plaster echoing off the walls.

Another step.

She had a sense that she was on stage, being watched by many observers, the spotlight shining right on her. The audience knew what was coming but she did not. They sat on the edge of their seat, waiting for the big reveal. Based on the night, she was in a horror movie. That didn't bode well for the "big reveal."

She approached the doorway the creature left. The smell of the shotgun was strong, it had been fired right here. Taking a deep breath, she cautiously moved forward toward the threshold. The room slowly came into view, foot-by-foot.

The far corner emerged, the Remington resting in the nook, a thin wisp of smoke leaving the barrel and drifting toward the ceiling. Another deep breath, another foot came into view. This foot contained a giant hole in the wall, also smoking. The round fired from the shotgun made short work of the old plaster, exposing the decimated brick between the room and the outside world.

She felt a sense of relief at the hole - the shotgun had hit nothing but the wall. She stepped the rest of the way into the room.

Her eyes found a shape on the far wall, just to the left of the window. She couldn't even scream.

A dark shape was splayed out against the wall, held up

by arms that were driven into the wall. It was a person. The head hung forward, preventing Ellie from seeing the face. The crown of the head showed short auburn hair flecked with gray.

Oh no.

Ellie rushed across the room, reached under the chin and lifted the face.

Skin with gray pallor looked back at her with milky, unseeing eyes staring far beyond her. Blood was on her chin, having poured from her mouth, but it was long dried. Ellie's eyes teared up and she began to sob, stepping back.

A large dark spot of dried blood sat right at Carey Hughe's belly button, her stomach torn open from a shotgun blast at close range. Her arms had stakes driven through to hold her on the wall, but very little blood.

Ellie at least had solace in knowing that the wall crucifixion came after she had been killed, apparently by a shotgun blast to her abdomen.

Because of me.

She was here because of Ellie. Joe and now Carey. It seemed her Hell was systematically eliminating everyone she cared about, leaving the remnants to torture her with - all because of her.

The whispering voice came back, echoing through the halls, raspy and barely audible.

"It's all your fault. I will torment you, and take everything you love, and when you have gone crazy from the pain of knowing it's all your fault, you will beg me to end it. AND. I. WILL."

She sank to her knees and sobbed, crying for Joe, crying for Carey.

Twenty-Nine

Moments, minutes, or hours could have passed while Ellie kneeled by Carey. She stopped sobbing after a few minutes, just mourning on her knees in front of her. The laughing had carried on for a few minutes, but she had blocked it out, retreating inside her head as she used to as a child during beatings at Shyt house. Running through the memories of her mentor and friend, she paid a silent tribute.

Then she arose, took a deep breath and moved her eyes to the shotgun. It was a message, as the shell fired had been a call to bring her to this spot. It didn't hurt to check. The old Wingmaster felt heavy in her hands, and foreign, like it didn't belong there. She had never fired a gun of any kind, but she would be fine with pointing this at the creature for her shotgun-christening.

She managed to check the chamber and saw it empty. She racked the action, checked the chamber again and it remained empty. Unwilling to put it down, she carried it out the door, glancing back at Carey one last time.

I'm sorry. I'm sorry this happened to you, I'm sorry that the world doesn't get more of you. I am sorry for all the girls that you would have helped, I am sorry for them. I am sorry for your family.

She took a deep breath and let it out. Hearing Joe's voice echo through her head, it's message was clear: *this is not your fault. You are not responsible for the evil happening to others around you.*

How can you say that, she thought. *You're gone and now Carey, and its because of whatever is happening to me, because you knew me and helped me. I am the common denominator here!*

Joe's face flashed in her mind, his bushy mustache perched on a frown and his head shaking.

No, whoever or whatever did this is responsible, not you.

She nodded to no one in particular, steadying herself.

Turning to Carey's corpse, she tipped her head one more time and walked out the door, still cradling the shotgun in her arms. She looked to her left as she exited the room, now Carey's tomb, attempting to discern if the creature was there, hiding or waiting for her. The hall appeared empty.

Should she go the other way, take a circuitous route back to the open window to avoid the creature? Would the creature expect that? Would it be safer for her to go directly at the last point she saw it, outwitting it?

Did it matter? If there were two, one could simply be

ahead of her while the other flanked her, waiting where she had been.

She wasn't sure how much time had passed, but the shotgun barrel was still quite warm, indicating it hadn't been too long since it was fired.

In paralysis of indecision, her feet were rooted in the threshold of the door. The shortest path is a straight line, and the creature would expect her to go away from where he was last seen, so direct to the escape path she would go.

Her first step brought upon another shimmering.

The walls melted away and color returned. She was no longer frightened by the effect. Instead, she felt frustration boil, once again so close!

Maybe I can go to that room and wait to flip back, then I'll be away from the beasts and ready to escape as soon as it happens again.

This made sense. In fact, it was a great plan. She smiled to herself. She seemed to be able to move freely in this time and eventually she always returned to the Dark World. All she had to do was wait it out - go to where the window was, and just wait. When the shimmering brought her back, as it inevitably would, she would be able to vault to her escape.

The feeling of hope faded as quickly as it came as she surveyed her surroundings. The hospital did not look the same as it did before. Hallways had beds in them, many occupied by sweating, sickly individuals. The air was hot and sticky, the sun poured in from the windows. Nurses milled about briskly, looking tired and worn out under masks covering their mouth and nose.

The bed in front of Ellie by the window had the shape of a person, but the sheet was pulled up over the face. A nurse slowly walked by, appearing tired and worn out.

"Help needed in the day room!" came a yell, causing the nurse to break into a trot.

Ellie followed, not comprehending what was going on and why everything was so different from her last trip. She moved quickly through the hallway, back toward the middle of the building.

The nurse pushed into a door on the left and into a large room. The day room was long and rectangular lined with windows on the west wall, catching the late afternoon sun and refracting it to look like gentle white lasers into the room. Chairs and tables were pushed to the far walls and stacked haphazardly. It appeared that these were moved in a rush and replaced by what were now a series of beds, most filled with a sickly patient.

A wet cough echoed throughout and the stink of sickness hung like a wet blanket over the entire room. The nurse rushed to the side of a bed housing a small, stout man. He was mostly bald, with longer hair sticking out the sides of his head, pasted across his cheeks and forehead by sticky sweat. He began to cough violently, his chest rattling. The cough sounded as if his very lungs were ready to explode and release the tidal wave that knocked within. His whole body violently shuddered and his gray, pallid skin seemed to become almost translucent. The nurses were trying to tend to him, but his body shuddered a final time and became still.

The two women attending to him had their shoulders drop in unison, visibly fatigued. The smaller woman pulled a white sheet up over his face. They turned and a profound sadness startled and frightened Ellie.

What was going on?

She came closer, hearing the nurse.

"Another one. Bloody flu. This is worse than the springtime. We are fighting a losing battle." A slight Irish accent, normally sounding like a gentle song to Ellie, instead delivered an overwhelming sense of melancholy.

"Well, we can only do what we can. You know Dr. Munson lost his only son to the flu earlier this year. He was a captain in the Army and caught the flu over in New York. Poor soul, losing his first wife all those years ago, and now his only son. You know he is going to keep us helping as many of these poor people as we can."

"Aye, and on top of that awful war. The War to End all Wars, let's pray it's over soon. It's been, what a year of that? When did it start?"

"Last year, last summer."

"Aye, seems like just a constant news of death and dying. Let's pray that the good Lord takes care of us all, 'specially with the fall and winter cold coming soon."

The air in the room was heavy, the mood somber, and the stench of death suffocating.

Ellie thought for a moment. She read a lot of books, she remembered the war to end all wars, World War I. Not that they would call it one yet if it only started last year. She had stepped forward again. She had met Helen in spring 1916, visited her at Christmas time 1915, and now here she was in 1918.

Helen.

Ellie was suddenly filled with panic. Where would she be? She had to check in on her.

Please don't let her be sick.

She moved throughout the room, checking all the patients. Helen wasn't here. She left the room in a sprint. If this was the flu ward, she wouldn't be here as a regular patient.

Moving to the middle of the building, she took the grand stairwell up to the second floor. She was blindly running from room to room, searching for Helen. The stench of death was dampened, but still hovered in the air, making the environment feel heavy. Ellie felt as if she was moving in slow motion, trying to run under water.

Everywhere she turned, nurses with grim looks on their faces and sullen eyes moved about. There was no light in their auras, no jump in their step. They moved as if tired and bearing the burden of the world on their back, slumped shoulders and feet dragging along the floor.

She felt like she was in a horror movie with slow and sloth-like zombies ambling about. It struck her that she *was* in a horror movie in the Dark World, and this was supposed to be her respite from it, but now her Light World too was subject to chaos, darkness, and death.

She moved down the hall of the second floor pushing her way through. She reached the middle wing, noticing that the abundance of plants that adorned the hallways were missing, the few that were there showed signs of wilting and abandonment.

Slowing to a walk, she began to cry without even realizing

it. The asylum had been a beautiful place to her, a refuge from the darkness and creatures of the Dark World. It hurt her to see it this way, under siege from the flu pandemic.

This was her room, I'm sure of it.

She stood in the doorway, peering in. The room was empty. It might not be her room anymore, even if Ellie remembered specifically which room she had been in among the many. Helen had moved before, from the outer wing to the middle wing. Who was to say that this was her room anymore? Maybe she wasn't even at the asylum anymore.

"How's Helen doing?" a hushed voice floated down the hall behind her.

Ellie spun, her hair flying across her face. She strode toward the sound in time to see two nurses walking side-by-side, the one on her right shaking her head.

"Oh dear. I miss seeing her up here," the other said.

"Aye, she was a bright one. I heard she is still downstairs in the sick wing, but it doesn't look like she'll make it through this," the other replied. Her voice trailed off as she finished her sentence, her words hushed but heavy.

Ellie recognized the voice. It was Nurse Crotchety from earlier. Even she carried a new shroud of darkness across her shoulders. She seemed somehow smaller to Ellie.

"Such a sad thing, how did she get downstairs?"

"I dunno. She said she was looking for her ghost friend, she thought she might find her down there."

The nurse again shook her head. "I just can't believe she was in that room, all the sick patients. If she just hadn't gone down there -" her voice trailed off as she slammed a fist into her palm. The nurse's shoulders dropped and she sighed. So much loss to see, she seemed to shrink further before Ellie's eyes.

First floor.

Ellie moved back to the stairwell and down. She passed the sick-bay day room and began moving through the wings, searching for Helen. She scanned rooms as well as the beds in the hall - nothing.

Two nurses moved away from a bed near a window as she entered the middle wing on the first floor. The light shined on the bed through the window, and the sheet running its length outlined the silhouette of a person. The hall had a lack of color except for the illuminated bed before her. The sharpness of the white sheet called to her and she could see the curve of the person beneath the sheet. It was the same bed she had seen earlier, right after the shimmering that brought her to this wretched time.

Creeping forward, the silhouette grew bigger and sharper as the background faded further away. Part of her didn't want to know, trying to will her feet to stop. She had already lost so many people she cared about. Turn around, walk away, ignorance is better than knowing she had lost another.

Her feet didn't seem to listen or care, as they kept stepping in front of each other toward the bed. Besides, she already knew.

She could feel her toes dragging slightly on the ground and hear heart thundering in her ears. She stood beside the bed and could feel the warmth of the sun streaming in from the window. She saw her left hand extend forward, her fingers wrap around the end of the sheet, and her arm drag it back. None of this felt like her doing, it was as if she was in a first person movie, unable to affect the outcome.

Helen's pallid and expressionless face stared back at her. Empty eyes stared past Ellie and toward an unseen horizon, the light and love extinguished. Her face was pale to the point of translucence, a sheen of sweat glistening in the sun. Her lips were colorless, her hair wispy and dry despite the sweat, like straw after a rain.

Tears were running down Ellie's cheeks, dripping off her chin and onto the sunken skin across Helen's clavicle. Gently, Ellie replaced the sheet over Helen's face, and then sunk to the ground.

She sat and pulled her knees up to her chest. Face buried into her legs, she wept.

*   *   *

She raised her head at a loud clanging sound echoed from a distance away, as if something metal was dropped. The hallway was dark again, she was back in the Dark World. Everything had transitioned while she had wept dry tears. She had nothing left after losing Carey to cry for Helen. She pulled herself up and tried to gain her bearings. The shimmering did a number on her sense of direction and location.

She laughed. It came out strange, dry and raspy, almost

sounding more like she was choking than laughing. The sound made her wonder how much she had left in the tank. She was on the precipice of a giant chasm, hanging on by a thread to her sanity. The darkness of the abyss seemed almost welcoming at this point - chased by creatures, flipping worlds, reliving her abuse and escape cycles, and watching everyone she cared about being destroyed and dying.

The laugh felt more like a slide, a bit closer to falling into the darkness of insanity. She wondered how much more until she just let go.

Well, at least I am in the right place!

She laughed again, the sound edging on maniacal.

Her initial laugh had been at the realization that after all the running in the Light World, she had ended up beside Helen's deathbed exactly one window away from the room she had found Carey's body in. It seemed to sum up all her efforts so far - run and end up back in the same place, on this sadistic hamster wheel.

It seemed this place was eating away at her sanity, driving her into the abyss of chaos. It was as if the goal was to first destroy her spirit, crush her very soul, before the final end. She felt her grip starting to slip with each loss, with each realization that for all her effort she went nowhere, with each let down.

Shaking her head, she admonished herself.

None of that. I won't give in, I won't give up. No matter what, I will scratch and claw. This place may swallow me, but it will be the most painful and bitter thing it's ever had. Win or lose this shitty game, I will make sure whatever is doing this me wished it never messed with me.

She tried to remember what she was even doing when the sound of the shotgun had interrupted her. She searched her scrambled brain, but it didn't seem to want to put a coherent thought together anymore. It was as if Helen's death had finally turned her brain to mush.

A wind blew in through the broken glass of the window, chilling her. She rubbed her arms as she shivered, dried blood from the cut on her shoulder flaking off. From the warm sun to an icy late autumn breeze through the same window, moments apart in Ellie's world.

The window.

She was heading for the window, the exit and her salvation. Looking down the hall, she had one more wing to get through. The metal sound echoed around her, the sound floating from somewhere. Was it one of the creatures? Regardless, it sounded far away. She needed to get moving, but she hesitated still. She had to go the same way the creature had gone after leading her to find Carey. She remembered its laughter - the bastard was tearing her apart.

Ellie balled her fists and gritted her teeth, then she hurried down the hallway. She tried to stay up on the balls of her feet to reduce the noise of her footfalls and crunch of the debris underneath, but also to be poised to move if another threat appeared.

Approaching the transition between the middle and the outer batwing, she pressed herself against the wall. Listening, all she could hear was her own heartbeat. She lowered herself to the floor and pressed her ear to the ground, trying to listen for vibrations of footsteps (*hoof-steps?*) on the floor. She had a brief flashback to a movie theater and some action flick with Anna, causing her to smile. There was none of that *rom-com* crap with Anna, it was a Krav session or some rolling on the mat followed up with some kind of action film, culminating in barbeque wings and beer.

She heard nothing, felt no vibrations, and she didn't feel a presence. Sticking her head into the enclave between wings quickly and pulling it back, she saw nothing but darkness. She felt warmed by her memories of Anna and almost swore she could smell the buttery goodness of a giant, overpriced popcorn bucket.

Moving into the wing, she could see a splattering of light as rays from the moon shone through the windows. The checkerboard path of light and dark looked like a road leading her toward freedom. She felt herself grinning, maniacally, a giddiness almost overtaking her.

Freedom.

She came to the room and slid inside, not even thinking to check for vibrations or any of that other spy movie stuff - she just barreled right in and headed to the window. The grate was hanging where she left it. She reached up and pulled. Plaster pieces rained down and the grate slid several inches. She pulled harder and two of the corners gave way. It swung on the upper right corner for a moment before giving way. She grasped the bars and attempted to guide it down, but it was too heavy and crashed harder than she would have liked. She jumped back to get her feet out of the way. The grate sat leaning up against the wall to the right of the window, pressing into the corner of the room.

The window was open.

It gaped in front of her, leaves blowing gently across the grass. She looked up, the moon shining from the other side of the building and down onto the grass a hundred feet from where she stood. The darkness of the building shade seemed to swallow up the distance.

Climb through the window, sprint across the darkness, and enter the light. It will all be okay if she can just get to the light.

She put her hands on the window sill, and took a deep breath. She ducked her legs down, ready to vault it, and roll after the eight foot drop.

And stopped.

She stood back up, her brain nagging her.

Poor Helen.

She shook herself and poised to try again. The fresh air was a delicious elixir, filling her throat with the taste of salvation, expanding her lungs and cleansing them. It was right there.

But she couldn't bring herself to do it.

She stood at the gaping window, thinking about Joe, Carey, Helen.

Helen.

She had been timid, a whipping boy. Madelyn had given her a chance, and Joe had helped her find her own strength to take care of herself. Anna had helped her protect herself and taught her to fight. Nora had shown her that she had *worth,* that she should fight for herself and that she had value in the eyes of God. Carey had stood up for her, and shown her that someone else cared enough to fight for her.

All of this she had learned, been taught by people around her. She had fought for herself, and tonight, in this hell, she had used this to keep herself going, moving forward. Without those lessons, she would have been swallowed up shortly after waking.

But that wasn't enough. It wasn't enough to fight for *herself*. The skills you learned weren't about serving yourself. It was about serving a greater purpose, it was about serving God, and to do that, she had to be in service of others. She had to help others, like others had helped her. That was the purpose, the impact, that was *why*. None of the sacrifices of Joe, Nora, Carey, and Helen mattered if she didn't use them to serve. She couldn't keep them for herself.

Why was this stopping her now? Why couldn't she just jump through this window and run to the light, then help others out *there*?

Helen.

She had to help Helen. She couldn't leave her friend like that. How many times had she flipped to the Light World? Every time she had been in a different time, and not in a chronological order. The first time she had met Helen hadn't been the first time Helen had met *her*.

If she left through this window, she wouldn't be able to help Helen. Something about this place, maybe this night, or the full moon, whatever it was had this strange connection in a rift through time (or some other Sci-fi channel craziness) that was allowing her to move back and forth between the worlds. She needed to do it again, this time to a spot before the flu pandemic and somehow let Helen know not to go into that day room, to not get around those sick people.

She stared out the window again. The line where the darkness ended and the light of the moon began ran jaggedly across the lawn in the shape of the top of the asylum. It beckoned her.

You'll have to wait, she thought. *I have more to do here.*

She turned from the window and walked back across the room to the hallway. It wasn't time to go just yet.

Thirty

Anna jumped ahead a step, energized by the action of the movie they had left. The two of them had taken the day to go shopping, have lunch and catch an early matinee. A typical action movie, zombies had run amok, and the hero who just wanted to be left alone reluctantly learned about himself, showed up just in time, and saved the day. Crisis averted, the gates of Hell closed once again.

Ellie had not really been that interested, but Anna was a fighter and a girl of action, so, though the day was about her taking care of Ellie after the ordeal with Cynthia and Carey, she just couldn't help herself when selecting the movie. Ellie had feigned interest and excitement, and, despite herself and her attempt to mainly focus on the head sized bucket of popcorn, had actually enjoyed the mindless action as a way to distract her from all the thoughts swirling in her head.

A late fall day, the sun was shining and the last gasp effort of summer to warm had turned the afternoon unseasonably warm. The smell of fall was heavy in the air and when the breeze blew, it had the sharpness of Old Man Winter's breath. They strode down the strip, feeling the crisp air swirl in off the bay. A glance between the buildings and across Boardman river showed the dark water of the bay, a violence settling just underneath the waves, waiting to be unleashed by winter.

"It's still early, I'm not ready to call it yet. The clocks change this weekend, and I doubt it will be this nice out again until after Easter," Anna said, a bounce in her step.

Ellie nodded in agreement. "I'd like to drop this off to Nora. I don't think I can wait until Monday to give it to her."

Both being frugal, "shopping" had been browsing, trying items on, laughing, and then putting them back before moving on. Ellie did, however, come across a picture frame with an engraving of a heart and two birds across the thick wood base of the frame, with the inscription "Friends Forever" on it and purchased it for Nora.

"Don't you think you should actually put a picture in it first?"

"Yep, but since I can't wait that long, let's drop it off and take the picture while we're there."

The two women skipped along the sidewalk, turning away from the bay and riding the wind down toward Bay View. They chatted throughout the twenty minute walk, talking about the latest Krav class and Ellie's new affinity for grappling, about the tragic story of Cynthia, about the good the *Stronger Together* did for them and others. Of course, Anna wanted to include discussion on a variety of movies. Though different in the aggression in which they approached the world, the two girls had become inseparable.

After chit-chatting about this and that, Anna stopped talking abruptly.

"Ellie, I care a lot about you. Carey asked me to show you the ropes when you arrived, but I feel like there was a connection right away. Now, don't get me wrong, I don't do all that mushy shit, but I really feel like we're sisters," Anna said, smiling. "Well, maybe sista's instead of sisters."

She turned and looked Ellie right in the eye.

"I guess what I'm throwing down, what I want you to know, is that I've been clean for pushing up toward two years, as you know, but meeting you is one of the best parts of it. I was supposed to help you, but you helped me."

Ellie looked at her, a bit shocked by the emotion Anna was displaying. Usually it was only toughness on display.

"I love you too," Ellie replied, wrapping her arms around her in a hug. "Sista'."

"All right, no more of that mushy shit now," Anna said, pushing her away.

They walked through the doors to Bay View Independent Living Center to see Betsy manning the counter.

"Hey ladies!" she cried, pushing her glasses up on her nose. "What're y'all doin' here? Isn't it your day off?"

"We wanted to stop in and see Nora. We have something for her," Ellie replied. "Can we go see her?"

Betsy frowned and lowered her eyes, her chin jiggling.

"Well, I heard she had a rough night so I'm not sure she's in a state to see you. Go ahead and head down that way, but don't go in until a nurse meets you there to make sure it's okay."

"Rough night?" Ellie asked.

Betsy softened her expression into sadness seeing the concern on Ellie's face.

"She does well most of the time, but she's had a tough go and has episodes every once in a while. You'll have to talk to the nurse. Sorry, dear."

Ellie half ran toward Nora's room, Anna on her heels trying to slow her down.

"Slow down, El, it'll be okay."

Her friend's reassurances didn't have much impact and she arrived at the door to Nora's room almost out of breath. The door was closed and all was quiet. She reached for the handle, but Anna grabbed her arm.

"Bets said to wait for the Nurse, we need to respect that. They know what's best for Nora. We don't want to make it worse or startle her."

They stood outside the door in the hallway for five minutes with Ellie chewing her lower lip and pacing. Nurse Dalton appeared around the corner.

"Thank God it wasn't Nurse Bitchy," Anna muttered.

Nurse Emily Dalton approached and held her finger to her lips.

"Try to keep quiet. Nora had quite the night. I think she is sleeping right now, we had to give her a little something to calm her down last night and again this morning."

Emily cracked the door gently and all three women peered

in. Nora was sound asleep in her bed, her face pale and stricken.

Shaking her head, Emily gently closed the door. Her face looked tired and her shoulders were slumped.

"I'm sorry, but you can't disturb her. You can leave your gift with Betsy or come back tomorrow. Hopefully, she'll be back to herself again." Emily put her arm around Ellie and began to steer her back toward the reception area.

"Can you tell me what happened? Is she going to be alright?"

"I think so. When she came to us a few years ago, she would have spells where she wasn't completely lucid. They were few and far between, they didn't last long, and she came out of them well. She was just in a sort of la-la land."

"Then recently, back in late August, the episodes increased in frequency and instead of being out of it, she began to be afraid. She can't remember anything when she comes out of it, but she is afraid of something. The fear slowly got worse, and then last night was by far the worst I have seen. She kept screaming about horns, and burning eyes. She was incoherent, talking about a tree. She threw herself around and we were worried about her hurting herself. We gave her some medicine to calm her down and she went to sleep. Even sleeping, she kept murmuring about horns."

"When the medication wore off, it started all over again, and we had to give her more. She seems to have calmed down and is just sleeping, the medicine should have worn off."

Ellie's lip trembled.

"Please, I won't make a sound, can I just see her for a moment?"

Emily stopped, looked at her with hard eyes. Then they softened.

"Fine. Do not wake her. This is against my better judgment and if Nurse Harmony finds out, there will be hell to pay so, *do not wake her.*"

Ellie gently passed through the door and set the picture frame on the nightstand without a sound. She stood over Nora, and said a prayer for her safety and a return to the lucid world. Nora looked peaceful, lying on her side facing Ellie at the side of the bed. Her knees were drawn up slightly and she lay under a blanket. Her eyebrows were moving and Ellie could see her eyelids twitch.

She began to turn to leave when she heard a gentle sound. It was so low she couldn't make out what it was. It took a moment to realize it was coming from Nora, her lips moving slightly. The sound was barely audible.

She leaned down close, her ears almost touching Nora's lips, and heard her murmuring quietly.

"You mess with the bull and you get the horns."

*   *   *

Anna and Ellie left Bay View in a somber mood. Ellie didn't repeat what she heard and drew within herself. She was walking without even paying attention, and before she knew it Anna asked.

"So, where are we going?"

Ellie looked up, startled a bit, realizing that they were on the asylum grounds. The building loomed above them.

"I, I don't know," she stammered.

"Well, it's still light out. I want to show you something, follow me," Anna replied. With that, she jogged ahead, past the asylum, past the remaining cottages on the campus, and toward the trees behind it all. Anna linked her arm through Ellie's and they walked together, arm in arm.

Ellie's mouth watered as the smell of a nearby bakery floated by, and then they were off the road and onto a small trail. Leaves crunched under their feet as they walked, a gentle breeze blowing them like tumbleweeds tickling their ankles.

They headed through an archway created by wood branches and into the woods. Trees were suddenly surrounding them, choking the early evening light and leaving a gray gloom hanging around them. The woods were eerily quiet, as if they had entered a different world. The sounds of the far away traffic was shut out as if a switch was flipped, and the rustling sound of leaves disappeared. No birds sang or squirrels scurried about. It was as if time had ceased moving and everything was still.

The trail led back through the trees, winding deeper into the woods. The trail split and Anna moved to the left, dragging Ellie with her. The trees broke into a small clearing. No wind blew, and not a blade of grass moved or swayed. The autumn sun the women had basked in on the way to see Nora didn't seem to penetrate into the clearing and a shimmering gray hung heavily over the area. It reminded Ellie of seeing a mirage shimmering off in the distance on a hot day, except it hung everywhere. She shook her head and squinted but the lack of color and *vagueness* of existence remained like a fog hovering over the ground.

Anna seemed unfazed and led Ellie back into the trees on the trail past the clearing. As they entered the trees, a trunk on the right had colorful graffiti on it, stating *HIPPIE* in blue with a red background on one side of the dual trunk, and *TREE* running vertically next to it. Ellie shivered as they walked past.

Then they were there. It wasn't far from the stagnant clearing, but the air seemed even denser. "Welcome to the Hippie Tree," Anna whispered. "Told you I'd bring you."

The tree stood before Ellie. Or rather, it lied, wound, and arched before her. The Hippie Tree was an assortment of branches and trunks, climbing up from the ground, and a large downed trunk. The assortment had a variety of colors that appeared to be spray painted on them in psychedelic color schemes. The pinks, greens, red, and blues made the array in front of her appear more like something out of a Dr. Seuss book than in a small woods in Traverse City.

The giant trunks and branches rose and curled up, reaching up off the ground extending taller than Ellie could reach. The branches curved and widened, creating a few platform areas that could be stood or sat on.

The Hippie Tree is an old willow and legend has it that the big tree has spiritual capabilities. The tree received its nickname due to local legend that conjurers and spiritual visitors, called "hippies" by the locals, gathered around the base of the tree. The experiences inspired the conjurers to paint the trees in the array of colors Ellie was seeing before her.

The colors stood out to Ellie while everything else held the same, shimmering faded gray. Ellie blinked, but the colors only seemed to brighten. There was a colored halo around the drawings as if Ellie had jumped out of a chlorinated pool and looked at lights in the dark.

The legend held that the tree held the restless spirits of people who resided at the asylum. The colors pulsating in the gray made it seem to Ellie that the spirits were trying to escape the trunk, break free and into the world around her. Her anxiety continued to grow, and she began to shiver. Her skin crawled. She began scratching her arm nervously.

The air still hung still around them, no sounds drifting amongst the trees. Even their own footfalls seemed to be completely swallowed up. Ellie heard, or more accurately *felt*, a deep bass thrumming all around her. Anna seemed to be ignorant of all that Ellie was feeling, unaware of the presence lurking around the tree.

"They say if you walk around it a certain way, the gates to Hell will open," Anna said. "Something like, this!"

She walked around the big, sprawling tree with her arms in the air. Ellie felt her heart race and held her breath. After a minute, Anna circled back to where she started, and she stomped her foot down at the initial point.

"Open sesame!" she hollered, laughing.

As her foot hit the ground, a large wind blew through the

woods, rocking the trees and rustling the leaves. Ellie felt her hair billow in the breeze, and a shudder rode down her spine. Though the leaves rustled and the trees moved, they did not make a sound.

Anna's eyes went wide.

"Ok, sorry, that's not funny. Let's get going," Anna stammered. "It's getting late anyway, I definitely don't want to be here when it gets dark."

Her brow furrowed and her face contorted in confusion. She was looking at her watch.

"Damn thing. It stopped working."

They both looked at the Hippie Tree again, its colors seeming to dance and swirl on the trunk and branches.

"Let's get the fuck outta here."

Ellie didn't argue.

Thirty-One

Inside the dark asylum, Ellie was contemplating how she could help Helen. She needed to cause the shimmering again, and somehow control the time she went to. It had to be close enough to the pandemic to affect Helen's choice to look for her. If it was *years* before, she wasn't sure that Helen would remember.

What happened each time she flipped? Was it in a certain place in the building? She was in a variety of old patient rooms, was it the presence of Helen in a room? A place she had been? Perhaps she should return to a spot that the shimmering had occurred before. She headed down the hall of the first floor outer wing, trying to sense if the creatures were around.

The closest spot the shimmering had occurred was for

the Christmas ball. She just had to get back through a couple wings and down the main stairwell.

As she walked through the hall, she remembered the way the sunlight streamed in the windows and the plants added color and life to the building. She could almost see it. And then she could see it, just for a moment. The colors swept from the ceiling down to the floor, like a starburst. Anything within the starburst and tail appeared in the Light World as it swept down. Colors on the wall, sunlight through the window, a table with a fern on it underneath.

As the tail swept by, it left the Dark World back in its place.

Woa.

Then she remembered the kaleidoscope of worlds flashing when she was sprinting away from the creature. That definitely didn't have to do with a place. Was it some outside force that decided when it would occur?

The open window was right there and then the shimmering and boom! - she couldn't leave. Was it that something didn't want her to leave?

Was it the same something tormenting her with the creatures?

She went back to already being dead and in hell, but that just didn't jive with the joy she felt with Helen and the Light World.

Unless losing Helen was part of the pain, give me the joy to just take it away.

She felt too confident that she could fix this, she wasn't in despair or hopeless. She could feel the determination running through her, hands tingling, laser focused.

Determined.

The starburst of the Light World.

She stopped walking again and thought through it.

Overwhelming fear when she was running, elation when she was about to go through the window, anxiety in the ballroom. The shimmering seemed to happen when Ellie was in some kind of emotional state. It seemed to have to be almost suffocating her. The feeling of fear that was so strong that she couldn't feel anything else. The feeling of despair and hopelessness, the feeling of loneliness.

Ellie's eyes narrowed in determination. Now, she would try love.

"I want to go to the summer of 1918 to save Helen," she shouted. She closed her eyes and repeated it again.

When she opened them, she saw - mold, mildew, and crumbled plaster.

Frowning, she sighed deeply.

Concentrate.

She closed her eyes. Picturing Helen's face when she came in from working with the animals. The cow she was so proud of naming. The joy on her face as her eyes tilted up toward Ellie and her slightly crooked smile filled her face. She imagined smelling the flowers and feeling the warmth of the sun. She felt that rising love in her chest when Helen would tell her something with such exuberance.

Ellie felt herself smile, unintentionally. The thoughts filled her with the joy that she felt when she was right there. She could here Helen saying,

"Hi-ya!"

Ellie opened her eyes, seeing Helen standing right before her. She looked surprised to see her, but her smile was large.

"It's been long time, I missed you," Helen exclaimed.

Ellie grabbed her, tears streaming down her face, and embraced her in a big hug.

"Hi to you to Helen, I am so happy to see you."

"Did you get away yet? Away from the monster?"

Ellie shook her head.

"Almost, there is just something I need to do first, and that's talk to you. Do you know what year it is?"

Helen shook her head. She did look a bit different from earlier, the lines on her face a bit more pronounced, the silver hair a shade grayer. Ellie looked out the window, which was propped open and warm air streamed in.

"Helen, is it summer time?"

"Yee-ep. It's so warm and nice with flowers and birds. I jus' love it right now!" She clapped her hands with excitement.

"Helen, this is really important. Has anyone been sick lately? A bunch of people feeling yucky?"

Her face darkened at the question, her lips tightening.

"Yeah, a bit ago in spring, a lot of people got sick. It was baaaad," she leaned in and hissed, "some people died."

She shook her head sadly.

Ellie sighed with relief. It seemed she was between the spring and late summer outbreak. Helen was fine and had not yet been exposed.

She patted Helen's back, placed a finger on her chin and

lifted it to look right into her eyes. Their faces were only a few inches apart.

"Helen, this is really important. I need you to listen really carefully, and please make sure you don't forget it."

Helen nodded, her eyes widening.

"I am not a ghost, I am a person, from a long time from now. So I know what's going to happen. More people are going to get sick. A lot more people. Many of them will come here to be taken care of. Do you understand that?"

Helen nodded again.

"Okay, this is the important part. I will not be back during that time. If you think you see me, you didn't. Do not go to where the sick people are. Stay away from the sick people, no matter what. Do you understand that?"

Helen smiled, nodded her head vigorously.

"I can do that."

"I know you can. It'll happen soon, probably in another month or so, toward the end of the summer. Stay away, please Helen, please stay away."

Ellie had her repeat it all back.

"Oh-kay, you get away from that monster then." she told Ellie, stabbing her finger in the air as she spoke.

"I'll try. I have to go now, I think I can get out of this place now." Ellie smiled, hugging her again. She had her repeat everything one more time.

"If I don't see you again, Helen, please know that I love you. You are amazing, and a great friend. I will always re-member you."

Helen smiled brightly at that, beaming pride and love.

"I love you - "

She didn't finish her sentence as the shimmering happened again, and Ellie was back on the first floor, forty yards from the room with the open window and her escape.

As the Dark World materialized in front of her, the creature stood between her and her escape.

Thirty-Two

"**W**hat the fuck? Where do you keep coming from?" a voice growled with rage. The creature jumped backwards, dropping the ax. It roared at her and lunged. Instinctively she lashed out, striking it as its hands wrapped around her shirt. She felt herself thrown up against the wall.

Stars exploded in her head as hands tried to wrap around her neck. Lacing her fingers together, she brought her fists up between hard, striking the creature under the chin, and then driving her elbows down into the crook of the creature's arms.

The hands released as the arms folded and she swung her elbow back across her body. The creature tried to roll away and her strike glanced off its shoulder.

She didn't wait. She was sprinting down the hall, vaguely aware that she was running *away* from her escape window.

Again.

She came to the alcove between the wings, and turned. Her foot hit a piece of loose plywood, the entire sheet moving from her force. Ellie crashed to the floor. The plywood had slid a foot away, exposing a hole in the floor that ran from the base of the wall. She hadn't noticed it or hit it right on the way through the first few times, but her momentum and the crash carried her straight down.

The wood tilted toward the ceiling and she slid further into the darkness on the floor. Her legs dangled out of sight as she grasped for purchase on the rotting floor. The dust, grime, and chunks of plaster simply slid into the hole with her as she continued to grasp at the floor. Her hands were sweaty from exertion and she felt herself slipping further.

Over her own screams she heard footsteps coming toward her. In her head, she saw the creature standing over her, raising the large ax over its head, and raining it down on her skull while she struggled above the hole.

So she simply let go.

And she was swallowed up by the darkness.

*   *   *

Ellie didn't fall far until she landed hard and was jerked away from the hole above. It knocked the wind out of her and she slid down a slope. She slid fast from all the dust over the years that had accumulated on the shaft and exited the chute through an opening feet first. She hit a hard concrete ground on her ribs, sending a fire up into her brain that made her think of fireworks.

It took several minutes for the pain to subside and her vision to clear. She lay on the ground panting in a heap. When her head finally cleared, her heart slowed down, and she could breath normally, Ellie sat up.

Pitch black surrounded her. She felt along the floor and felt loose chunks of stone or brick. She reached up behind her and found a brick wall leading up to the hole she came through. The hole felt rectangular but was crumbling out of shape. It seemed she had landed and then ridden some chute, perhaps for garbage or laundry in some other time, and landed in this dark room. Tracing the wall to a corner, she followed it slowly around to another, tripping over chunks of brick and debris. The wall was only about six feet, maybe eight at the most. She continued to trace around the brick room and came to a cold, flat service.

A door.

She traced around the metal surface, feeling seams. She searched for a handle, but the door was completely flat.

She tried to calm herself. The darkness all around her felt like it was closing in, the room getting smaller. She felt around the door again. There was nothing to grab, no way to pull. She dug her fingers into the seams but there was no give, no purchase. The door was solid and was not moving. She threw her shoulder into it, gently at first, but more violently when it didn't move.

Panic began to set in. She could herself whimper as she threw herself against the door. The whimpering turned into crying, the crying into screaming. She crumpled to the ground, barely aware that her shoulder wound from the ax earlier in the evening had reopened and blood was running slowly down her arm and chest.

She sat on the floor and wept. Suddenly aware of the cold in the dark room, she rubbed her arms with her hands, and her teeth began to chatter. She pleaded with herself to calm down but the panic overwhelmed her. She tried to concentrate on causing the shimmering, at least maybe there would be some light.

Nothing happened.

She sat in the dark, feeling it surrounding her like a snake, tightening around her until she couldn't breathe. All she had fought for, so close to escaping, and being done in by a laundry or garbage chute.

A soft voice, muffled, floated her way from off to her left. *"Ellliieeeeee..."*

She turned her head. That was the wall she hadn't checked yet. She traced the wall away from the door in that direction, finding the corner and tracking along the wall.

"Ellliieeeeee..."

The voice was soft, not like the taunting voices she had heard before in the halls of the asylum. Attempting to follow it, her fingers found a hole in the brick, open air beyond it.

Trailing her hand around the opening, she found it was only about three by three. She would have to crawl on her hands and knees, a thought that caused her heart rate to climb again.

The air smelled faintly of wet dirt. It was stale and hung in the small tunnel, as if it hadn't moved in ages. Drawing a breath of the musty air, she crawled forward. The debris cut into her knees as she moved slowly into the tunnel. She could feel the walls of the tunnel surrounding her as she entered, the feeling of suffocation enveloping her. She couldn't see in the darkness and was crawling blind, moving slowly forward and probing with her hands as she went.

Ellie imagined the walls closing in around her, choking her off and pinning her before crushing her into oblivion. Her hands shot out to the side walls every few feet to make sure they were still there.

Then she saw herself falling forward as the tunnel disappeared or dropped off into a bottomless pit. She imagined falling down, landing at the bottom to slowly lie there, broken and waiting for death in the dark.

She pawed at the ground in front of her before moving forward. Her breaths were short and ragged, her heart pounding in her chest. The darkness seemed to swirl around her, disorienting her. She stumbled to the side, her shoulder hitting the wall.

It's getting smaller, I know it.

She had only covered about ten feet and had to stop, clenching her eyes closed and willing herself to calm down. After a moment, she pushed on.

Nowhere to go but forward.

Her hand struck dirt and debris. Chunks of brick and stone piled in front of her. She trailed the wall of the tunnel around in the dark, panic setting in that she would have to crawl backwards to where she started. The tunnel wall turned jagged about halfway up. She ran her fingers along the ceiling, finding where a small cave-in had occurred. Reaching out, she found space above the debris pile and below the jagged loose rock and dirt. Following the space, she thought there was just enough room for her to get through.

But what was on the other side? What if she became stuck? Could she crawl back out? She didn't know where else to go but the thought of getting stuck in the debris in a subterranean coffin under the asylum terrified her.

I need to go back, find a different way. Maybe I can crawl back up the chute.

"*Ellliieeeeee...*" floated through the small opening.

It was friendly, and now Ellie was sure that she recognized the voice as Helen's.

"*Ellliieeeeee... You can do it.*"

"I can't, I can't do it. I'm scared, I don't want to die down here," she sobbed.

All she could think of was getting stuck. How much should she trust Helen? She was in an asylum, for God's sake! Besides, how could she even be real? Maybe this is the culmination of her condition, in her coma and this buried-alive scenario is her end. Really, she was in a hospital bed, beaten to a pulp and this hallucination or nightmare or whatever was the culmination of the doctors pulling the plug on her...

She shook her head violently in the darkness.

"Get a fucking hold of yourself," she said aloud, and then listened to it echo in the tunnel. She pictured Anna, her muscled and tattooed arms grabbing and shaking her. "Knock this shit off, get yo' ass moving!" Saying it out loud, she even heard Anna's voice instead of her own.

Drawing a deep breath in, she reached through the hole, pressing her ribs into the debris as far as she could. Pawing in the darkness, she could feel the cave-in all around. She didn't think the hole narrowed, but she also could not feel it open up on the other side.

She pulled herself up on the debris pile and wedged herself into the small opening. The dirt and rubble pressed in around her as she pulled with her arms and wormed her way into the small opening. Scooting along, her arms were above her head, grabbing for purchase and pulling, while she bent her knees and dug in her toes to propel her forward.

Six inches at a time, she pushed through. Once her whole body was in, she felt the opening narrow. Suddenly, she couldn't bring her arms back toward her sides. The passageway pressed into her ribs.

Mistake, mistake, go back, her mind screamed.

Except she couldn't, there wasn't enough purchase from her hands to provide a push strong enough to go back. She tried again, but went nowhere. She drew a breath in, and pulled forward. Scooting another six inches, her hands reached around and felt the tunnel opening up. She pulled herself forward and moved her arm around. The tunnel definitely opened up. She couldn't scoot backwards, forward was the only option. She pulled again, feeling the tunnel dig into her ribs. Digging her fingers in, she tugged her body, but didn't move.

A small cry escaped her. She was stuck. She panted short, ragged breaths. Panic set in, the walls were pressed all around her, digging into her ribs and shoulders. She kicked with her legs. She tried to back up, but was wedged too tight. This was her final coffin, there was nowhere left to go.

Calm down and think.

Sitting in the pitch black, she blocked out the swirling purple darkness and thought back to her walk with Anna on that beautiful fall day. It was clear in her mind as she realized that was just a week ago. The leaves blowing on the ground, the warm sun, the love of her friend.

Her breath calmed a bit and her heart slowed. She dug her fingers in, and pulled. She scooted forward, but barely any. Her ribs were stuck on the debris walls of the passage.

Already breathing short breaths due to the pressure on her ribs, she dug her hands in and exhaled as far as she could, timing her pull with the bottom of her exhalation. Making herself as small as possible, she would either get through, or be unable to draw another breath and suffocate.

She strained, pulling with everything she had. Stars exploded in her head in the dark, and she dug in her toes, pushing, reaching…

And then she slid forward. The pressure on her ribs eased and her hands dangled over the edge of the widening section in the darkness. She gasped a breath in, feeling the sweet feeling of her lungs expanding. She took a moment to catch her breath and then bent her elbows to gain more leverage to pull.

Sliding forward, she pulled her upper body to the edge of the narrow passageway. Her hips were caught where her ribs had been, but she wriggled back and forth until they squeezed through. She stumbled in the darkness and fell forward, sliding down the debris as if she was rolling down a hill.

Chunks of brick and rock tumbled with her and she came to rest after a few feet. She lay still, panting and collecting herself. She tried not to panic, it was still dark and she had no idea what lay ahead. She certainly could not go back.

Calmed slightly, she began to explore this new area. Running her hands along the bricks away from the debris pile, one side was solid brick. The other side she felt the archway of another tunnel, but her heart sank when she found another cave in, this one packed tightly floor to ceiling in the small tributary tunnel.

The wall across from where she had squeezed through also had dirt and debris piled up on it. She could feel it in the dark.

She had traded one tomb for another.

The room she was in wasn't quite tall enough for her to stand, but she could stoop or squat. She felt the ceiling and it was solid brick. The whole room seemed to be sealed off. She sat down in defeat, suddenly exhausted. There was nothing left to do and she was too tired to think or fight. She crossed her legs, shivering in the cold and rubbed her scraped arms and legs.

"Ellliieeeeee..."

It was definitely Helen's voice.

"Why did you do this to me? Why did you bring me here to die?" she cried out.

"Dun't give up! Yer almost here!"

Ellie turned to the sound. It was louder than before, floating through the dirt pile on the opposite wall from where she had crawled through.

"There is nowhere to go," she cried. "The only connecting tunnel is completely caved in."

She rose to a crouch and duck-walked to the wall, grimacing as sharp pains shot through from all the small cuts and scratches on her knees and legs. Now that the adrenaline had worn off, the pain and fatigue wasn't masked anymore.

She felt along the debris pile as it led up to a brick wall.

What the hell? There is nothing here.

"C'mon, Ellie" came Helen's cry, more in a hushed whisper now. *"They's gonna find me and make me go back. You gotta hurry."*

Helen was definitely on the other side of the wall.

"Helen, I don't know what to do, the wall is solid, there is no way through." Ellie was getting frustrated.

No response.

"Helen?" she called. "Are you still there?"

There was no response in the dark, and Ellie felt alone.

"Please Helen," she pleaded. "Please don't leave me here. You brought me here, please don't leave me now in this tomb." Tears welled up in her eyes as she sat in the dark.

"Please Helen, I don't want to die down here," Ellie murmured.

Ellie sat there in the dark, feeling around the wall again and finding nothing. She closed her eyes, trying to feel the shimmering to see if the Light World would present her an option.

Nothing happened. She remained in the dark.

Frustrated, she screamed in the dark, grabbing a brick from the debris pile and threw it across the small room. Then another, and another. She grabbed handfuls of dirt and threw them in every direction while she yelled.

Finished with her tantrum, she sat there panting again in the dark, dust floating around her and sending her into a coughing fit.

Except it wasn't dark. Well, not *totally* dark. There was the faintest of lights leaking into the small room. It wasn't enough to see, but enough to make the black and purple dark a lighter shade of gray. The faint glow was coming from the debris pile, up against the brick wall. She had cleared some of the debris out in her rage.

She began to dig. Throwing dirt behind her, chunks of rock, pieces of brick. Fueled by her panic, she began to clear large pieces of the pile, exposing the brick wall behind it. Her nail snapped off and she felt her finger wet with blood, but she didn't stop.

As she dug, the light increased. At first it was bleeding through the cracks in the brick, and then space between the bricks, and eventually, through an area devoid of bricks at all.

She continued to dig. She stopped to rest a few times as her muscles burned, but the thought of escaping this tomb energized her to keep going.

After twenty minutes, she had cleared to see a sizable hole in the brick. The bricks at the top of the hole rattled as she pulled them, a few falling out to widen the opening. She lay on her back and kicked with both feet. The bricks gave way, shooting into the tunnel beyond.

She crawled through the opening, her aching ribs scraping on the bricks. She tumbled out and down the arched wall of the tunnel beyond. She stood feeling around in the dim light. She was in one of the main tunnels, it was large and curved, similar to the one she had explored before when she had hid from the creature. Down the tunnel she could see it connect with another larger tunnel, which was where the light was coming from.

Overcome with fatigue, she sat down on the tunnel floor, leaning back against the curved wall. She took a deep breath and a moment to rest before she figured out what was next.

Thirty-Three

Ellie zoned out for a while, resting in the dimly lit tunnel. Her back was pressed against the cold brick and the air was dank in the tunnel. She gazed across at the hole in the brick she had crawled through, but wasn't really seeing it. Her mind was wandering through time, thinking of Anna and Nora, wondering if she helped Helen escape the death clutches of the flu. She hoped so - it had cost her her freedom.

After some time had passed, she became aware of a stinging creeping in through the fog of consciousness. It grew and cut through her thoughts until it returned her to the present. She drew a sharp breath, the outlines of the bricks in the wall coming back into focus, and looked down at her hand. Her nail had torn off digging through the rubble, now raw and bleeding. She shook it to stop the stinging and wiped it on her shirt. She wrapped her shirt around it and squeezed, hissing at the sharp pain.

Her body screamed as she tried to stand. Unclear on how long she had been sitting in the tunnel, it was apparent that it had been long enough for every muscle, tendon, and joint to stiffen up from the evening of abuse her body had undergone.

"Evening?" she snorted. "Is it evening still?"

She had no idea and being down in the tunnels, there was no way to check.

"The longest night of my life," she muttered. "What I wouldn't give to see the sun."

She sighed, brushed herself off and scanned the tunnel. The shaft ran off into darkness on one side, and ran into a T-connection with another tunnel on the other. The light was leaking from that tunnel.

Go toward the light? Or will that be where the creatures are?

She recalled earlier how the tunnel had been lit and the creature had turned the lights on and back off.

Strange. It always seems to know where I am in the dark asylum, but it used lights down here? Is this just some monster that lives below the asylum?

She felt like one of those awful monster movies on SyFy with some government-experiment gone-wrong that was lurking in an abandoned place and seemed evil but really just wanted to be left alone to live a normal life.

Ellie chuckled, the sound echoing throughout the tunnel.

That's not how reality works.

This made her laugh again, who was she to talk about reality with the night she'd had?

"This way…" Helen hissed.

Jumping, Ellie looked around. She was still in the Dark World, or so she thought. She couldn't see Helen.

"Helen?" she called, squinting into the darkness. She saw nothing in the swirling purple and black.

"This way, c'mon," Helen's voice came again. "I dun't have much time."

The voice was coming from ahead of her, toward the tunnel's T-junction. She followed.

"Helen, I can't see you," she said.

Then a wave swept from the ceiling to the floor, like the starburst and tail from earlier. For just a moment, the brick wasn't crumbled and dirty, but clean and solid. Pipes materialized along the ceiling and Ellie could feel the heat coming off them.

And there was Helen ahead of her, beckoning for her to follow.

Then it was gone, everything back to dark, dirty, and crumbling.

Ellie moved quickly down the tunnel to the junction. Peering around the corner, she saw lights strung off the ceiling in both directions. They were dim bulbs, fifteen feet apart haphazardly hanging from any purchase that could be found in the ceiling.

Stepping out into the lit tunnel but staying close to the wall, she waited to hear Helen again. She was poised to jump back into the dark tunnel at any sign of the creatures.

"C'mon El, this way."

"Helen, is that you? What are you doing down here? *How* did you get down here? You can't be here!"

The wave swept again. There was Helen before her, smiling her crooked smile, a woman in uniform coming down the tunnel after her. Helen looked younger than a few minutes ago when she had warned her of the flu pandemic.

"It's a good thing I was coming for the wash and found you. You could get hurt, and in a *lot* of trouble down here!" the woman called.

"Hurry, El. Go down here and turn at the next tunnel. Go up. You need to know!" Helen exclaimed, pointing down the tunnel. "Hurry, I can't help you down here anymore!"

"Helen, who are you talking to? Oh no, are you talking to your ghost again," the woman bemoaned.

"No nurse, just wanted to help and got a little lost. I's sorry," Helen replied. She turned and winked, and the wave passed by, leaving Ellie in the dim tunnel alone.

A memory from earlier struck her as she stood there.

I gots in a lotta trouble for being in that tunnel, Helen had said. Ellie had been confused at the time as it was the first time in her chronology that she had met Helen, but based on conversations with Helen, it had been the *fourth* time. First was when she had scared Helen, then the Christmas ball, followed by this, and then Ellie's first time meeting Helen.

It made her head spin.

She looked down the way Helen had pointed. She shrugged to herself, Helen had saved her countless times already that evening.

Everything about tonight has been bat-shit crazy so why not?

She snorted laughter again as the thought in her head had been in Anna's voice.

She moved down the tunnel, listening for the creatures. It was silent except for her own soft footsteps. One of the bulbs had fallen and swung against the wall on the cords connecting the string, busting out. It was dark between them except for the shimmering of broken glass on the floor.

She moved through the darkness and saw that the tunnel curved off to the left ahead. She couldn't see around the small curved junction so she moved forward slowly. Peering around the forty-five degree gentle curve, the lights and the tunnel ran off in the distance. She squinted in the dim light. It looked familiar.

She noticed a stairwell and steep ramp at the end in the gloom. She was pretty certain that this was the tunnel she had hid in earlier. It was easy to get disoriented in the tunnels, her mind was probably just playing tricks on her.

Looking to her right at the curve, she noticed there were a few stairs, and another door.

She recalled how she hid in recess in the tunnel wall and the creature had walked through, turning at the junction. This was where it had gone.

This was where Helen was leading her.

Ellie shuddered, a chill rolling down her spine.

She wondered if she was being led into the belly of the beast. Her strong feelings toward Helen made her doubt this, but what if Helen was just a pawn in this awful game?

To hell with it, she thought. *At least we'll take it head on.*

She walked into the little enclave and climbed the steps.

The door opened quietly, surprising her. She looked it over and noticed that the hinges appeared wet. She touched them, pulling her fingers back and felt the slick texture of oil.

The monsters know how to use WD-40 I guess.

It occurred to her that if she kept laughing at her own jokes in her head, she may belong in the asylum anyway.

Another short set of stairs rose up and turned on a landing. She slowly climbed them, peering around the corner for any sense of movement or threat. More stairs led to another door, this one oiled as well.

She emerged in a basement. The construction was the same yellow brick and long hallway laid out in front of her with rooms on either side. The rooms had brick walls, but most were open, with half walls she could see over, or an opening that spanned half the room. She walked forward slowly, the big heavy wooden beams looming over her head.

Spray paint graffiti littered the walls, the rooms looked large and dark. Continuing forward, she worked her way slowly down the hall, glancing into rooms on her left and right. A large room came into view on her left. Inside, there was a half wall separating a section. Squinting in the low light, it appeared to be a community shower. She pushed on and the room on her right had a cave in. Debris and broken floorboards littered the floor and stretched down from a hole in the ceiling. Ellie dodged a pipe that was hanging low, broken off and jutting out from the wall.

A smiley face was painted on the wall past the room, but it looked angry and possessed, not inviting. Her trepidation increased as she pushed through, the demonic smiley face seeming like a bad omen warning her against continuing. Past the smiley face was a small cubby, filled with dust, broken wood, and debris.

She was about halfway down the hallway when she noticed through the gloom that there was a stairwell at the end going up. She walked toward it, eager to leave the basement, see where she was and hopefully find a way out.

Something caught her eye as she passed a large room. She spun toward it, her heart stopping. A single white chair sat in the room. She swore it was rocking by itself, an unseen visitor resting in it. She shook her head, her fear getting the best of her.

Of course, who was she to say there weren't ghosts here? She was one, right?

She entered the stairwell, following it up slowly and checking around the landings for any surprises. Reaching a landing, she saw the stairs continued up to floors above. Seeking a way out, she stepped out onto the first floor.

She followed a short hallway away from the stairs and stepped into a long corridor, splitting the building. It extended the whole length of the building, back over the area she had covered in the basement. Doors lined the hallway, and there was a large open area in the middle that she couldn't quite see into from where she stood.

Glancing in the first door, she realized she was in a room. Striding to the window, she found it barred and impassable. Looking out, she could see the moon lowering and the first dull purple of morning overtaking the black of night.

Almost through the night, she thought to herself.

She could see the asylum across the grass and road before her. She realized - the tunnel had taken her to one of the cottages behind the asylum. Those were added onto after the initial build of the asylum and housed more patients.

I made it out! she thought.

She felt exhilarated and almost giddy. She was out of the asylum, she had done it. Helen had led her out. She just had to find a door or window she could get out of the cottage.

She strode out of the room and down the hall. The main room would have a front door, she could get through it and be out in the fresh air of freedom. She passed a bathroom and shower, and more rooms. Glancing in each one, the bars covered the windows.

I can check to see if any of these are loose like the other room and pull them off, she said to herself. *Let's check the front door first.*

She covered the rest of the hallway and the main room loomed ahead of her. Emotions overrunning her logical thinking, she didn't slow down to check the room before bursting into it.

She crossed the threshold and stopped cold. Her hand shot to her mouth, the joy melted from her. It took a moment to comprehend what she was seeing.

When it happened, it explained everything.

Thirty-Four

Munching on a cinnamon roll from the bakery, Anna and Ellie had already put the events at the Hippie Tree behind them. It was just a strange coincidence that the wind blew, and the murky feeling was chalked up to the build up in their heads about the supernatural powers of the tree. None of it was real, the cinnamon roll, *now that was real.* And it was fantastic. They cast aside the strange occurrence, and barely even talked about how Anna's watch had stopped frozen, and they certainly refused to acknowledge that the time was the same time the wind blew.

As big as Ellie's two fists together, the cinnamon delight was warm and soft in the center and crispy on the outside. The cinnamon smell itself was intoxicating and the gooey frosting along with bits of apple crumble on top was heaven.

The Cinnaholic Bakery knew how it was done. Anna had

marshmallows stuck to her nose as she tried to bite on her giant s'more cinnamon roll. Bits of graham cracker rained down to the sidewalk as they walked.

They were chatting and laughing again, not a care in the world. The discussion moved back to grappling in BJJ, and then to missing kayaking on the bay with the winter coming.

"You gotta see Christmas out at the resort though, they do that shit right. Lights everywhere, enough to power a small country. Holy shit, I bet you can see it from space. Oh, and we'll go out to Gallagher's and cut down our own Christmas tree this year. You ever do that?," Anna was like a kid in a candy store, rambling on to Ellie.

Ellie shook her head. She certainly hadn't grown up with Christmas and they didn't do anything when she was with Zach. She smiled at the thought of it, Anna's energy infectious. It seemed surreal how much her life had changed in just a couple months, all because of the first step out of the condo she took.

"Just wait until you see the church, all done up for Christmas. It's beautiful," Anna was saying, the sun dropping down and dusk settling in. They walked by Bay View, noticing Nurse Emily walking out the front door.

"There she is," Ellie exclaimed. They had been heading to see Nurse Emily with a cinnamon roll for her. Ellie and Anna had both acknowledged that Nurse Emily was a good friend and had helped them at the nursing home. She was always in their corner, and helped them fit in.

She was a good soul, truly cared about the residents of Bay View, and had to battle with attitudes like Nurse Harmony. Nurse Bitchy, as Anna called her, making constant comments and judgements could surely eat away at the joy of doing... well anything. Anna and Ellie had only minor run-ins with Nurse Harmony but poor Nurse Emily had to interact with her on a near constant basis.

Ellie had come up with the idea in line at Cinnaholic, and Anna had emphatically agreed. They had debated only briefly before agreeing that Emily had definitely earned the Cookie Monster - frosting, cookie dough, chocolate chips, and chocolate sauce.

The bag felt like it was carrying a small anvil. She chuckled at the thought of Emily trying to finish it in her small frame.

Ellie stopped in her tracks when they approached Emily. Anna, still chattering away, ran right into her. Emily's face was drawn and gray, bags were under her eyes, and her normally sunny demeanor was clouded. She wore a deep set frown and was basically dragging her feet through the parking lot.

"Holy shit, she looks like a zombie," muttered Anna.

"Hey Nurse Emily," Ellie called, ignoring Anna. "Wait up."

Emily jumped at her voice. Her eyes were glazed over, and it took a moment for her to focus.

"Are you okay?" asked Ellie.

"You look like shit, Nurse. Long day?" Anna asked.

Emily gave Anna a smirk and sighed.

"It was exhausting. Nurse Lucy called in and with Nora having an episode - or rather episode after episode, I have been here a lot longer than I supposed to be."

"Well, you looked rough when we were here earlier, but you look like something the cat dragged in. It's only been, what? An hour?" Anna asked.

Emily sighed deeply, her shoulders slumping and a look of defeat coming over her.

"It was a rough hour."

Ellie held out the bag.

"Well, we brought you something to cheer you up, and to thank you for everything you do for us. And for the residents."

Emily took the bag, opened it up and peered inside. When she raised her face, there were tears in her eyes.

"Thank you. You don't know how much this means to me. It's been a tough day. This makes it a lot better."

Ellie beamed a smile at her.

"Truly an angel at a dark hour," Emily said, giving Ellie and then Anna a hug. "Now, forgive me, but I am going to head home, take a bath, get in comfy pajamas, eat my gigantic cinnamon roll until I'm sick, and then chase it with wine and a bad movie until I fall asleep on the couch. My kind of Friday night after a rough day."

They all laughed together.

Ellie thought for a moment, her smile fading.

"Wait, what do you mean it was a rough hour? Is Nora okay?"

"She seems to be now, but after you left, she had another episode. It was awful, she was throwing herself around, completely out of control. She was somewhere else, almost like she was having a nightmare. Throwing herself around, she bruised her arm pretty bad. For being so frail looking, that woman is strong. She ranted about a bull, red eyes. She talked about a giant ax and being chased through a maze. She couldn't find her way out. We tried to calm her down but nothing seemed to help. This went on for twenty minutes or so, and then suddenly, she stopped. Her eyes stared forward and she said something about the bull and getting the horns. Then she said *it has begun* and passed out. It was creepy as hell, I felt like I was in Poltergeist or something. I was exhausted and had to get bandaged up, the woman's nails left some nasty scratches on my arms. I am just glad she didn't get my face."

Emily sighed again, the story exhausting her all over again as if she were going through it again.

"It's getting more and more, worse and worse. If this keeps going like this, I'm not sure it's safe for her or us to stay here."

Ellie looked at her with a shocked expression.

"Oh no, you can't send her out!" she exclaimed.

Emily held her hands up. "I'm just saying, it's not in my control. I don't want it either. But it was pretty bad today. I know how much she means to you. You two definitely have a special relationship."

Ellie's lip quivered, Emily noticed it and sighed.

"Listen, I am tired and beat up. Don't read anything into it right now. I am going to recover. I'll be back on Monday and things will look better."

Emily turned to go.

"Thanks for the cinnamon roll. It'll help my recovery."

Anna suddenly looked up, her brow furrowed.

"What time did all this happen?" she asked.

"Well, the fit started a few minutes after you two left. It stopped at quarter after six," Emily answered.

"Exactly 6:15?" Anna asked.

Emily sent her an exasperated look. She was getting weary with the conversation.

"I know, I'm sorry. I was just wondering," Anna replied.

Shaking her head, Emily said, "Okay fine. I remember when she stopped, her bedside clock showed 6:14, okay? Close enough to quarter after. Now, ladies, I'm sorry I don't mean to be short or rude, but I am done and out of here."

She turned and strode away, rushing to gain some distance so they wouldn't ask any more questions.

Anna turned to Ellie, eyes wide. She held up her wrist, showing the watch to Ellie.

Frozen at 6:14p.

Ellie shuddered for a moment, then said, "I don't want to talk about it."

*   *   *

She remembered Nora's fit. Ellie had checked in on Nora the next day and she was resting, then again on Sunday and she looked like she was back to normal. She had left her alone but had the courage to go see her when she was back to work on Monday, and carefully prodded her about the events. She remembered none of it, even asked Ellie how she had bruised her arm.

Ellie had steered a regular conversation toward the events

to no avail, even becoming bold enough to drop in some of the words she had said, hoping to trigger some kind of memory while not triggering another episode.

Neither happened.

It seemed Nora had no idea what had happened the previous Friday. Ellie couldn't shake the bad feeling that it was her fault. That was ridiculous, the Hippie Tree was just a local legend and Ellie's imagination blew it out of proportion.

Ellie tried to let it go, and by Tuesday, it had drifted away and the first light snow had fallen, the last gasp of summer long gone. By Thursday, she had let it go completely and had a great class at grappling at the dojo. Friday was a fulfilling day at work followed by a warm fire in pajamas and a bottle of red wine while Thanksgiving was being planned. A big family Thanksgiving dinner with the girls of *Stronger Together* sounded amazing and Ellie was already dreaming of succulent turkey, warm stuffing, and mashed potatoes.

Then Saturday had come and she was hanging in the yellow house. She and Ginny had been chatting. She had risen early, gone for a cool, windy walk down by the bay in the morning sun. The light snow was long gone, but it would be back as a stiff wind came in off the bay. She had swung by the library and checked out a few new books before seeing how she could help at the house.

The morning had been serene, comfortable and warm with friendship. A perfect fall morning in her new life.

That's when the door had burst open...

Thirty-Five

Standing in the central room of the cottage, it explained everything.

Well, not everything, but a lot.

She was a few feet into the large room, looking at a setup of gear on a series of tables. The blinking lights flickered in the dim glow of the screens, cables ran along the floor and the tables. She felt frozen to the ground, not sure how to proceed.

Three foldable tables sat in a U-shape. On each lay a series of equipment. Several screens were glowing along with a few laptops. Cables ran to and fro, interconnecting the gear. A microphone sat next to one screen and power cables ran off to the wall, and down through the floor. The third table had papers covering it. Approaching, she saw it was full of print-outs, blueprints, pictures, and newspapers.

She walked over to look at the various papers when the largest of monitors caught her eye. It was hooked to one of the two laptops. On it she saw the screen was broken up into a series of boxes, as was the laptop screen. Each showed the inside of the asylum.

Tapping the keyboard, she was able to cycle through a series of images. She saw the room she woke up in, with all the vile words on the wall and the skull inside the pentagram. She saw the hallways she had been in, and the stairwells. She saw Carey's body, she saw the first floor, and she saw the ballroom.

Something flickered on one of the images. She zeroed in on the panel, clicking it took up the whole screen. It was a live feed of the first floor, and she saw the creature in it, striding through the hallway. She followed it to the next camera.

She saw that with movement, each camera would light up and she could move through it to follow the live feed. The ax dragged along side the creature as it was glancing into rooms.

The creature was looking for her.

What the hell was this place? She moved over to the other laptop and scanned the screen. There were a series of files, an equalizer, and a list of what appear to be locations.

> *North Stairwell*
>
> *Third-Floor 1st Wing*
>
> *Ellie's Room*
>
> *Meddling Bitches Tomb*

Looking at the files, she began to understand. The list of

files were something listed as *WAV* files. They had names
like:

Roar-1.wav

Growl.wav

Snarl.wav

Laughter-low.wav

Laughter-high.wav

She saw in the target list, a location called *Control Center*.
Taking a breath, she selected *Laughter-high* and the target as
Control Center. The speaker that sat on the table began to emit
a high pitched, demonic-like laughter.

She shuddered at the sound.

Clicking on the equalizer, she played with the settings,
increasing and decreasing. She was able to replicate the
laughter she had heard in the hallways earlier.

She shut it off. She felt like a great epiphany was about to
occur, but was just out of her reach. She checked the cameras
again, the creature was still on the first floor. She had some
time. She moved to the table with all the documents.

The first set she picked up were stacks of pictures. She
gasped as she saw herself in them. Her at Bay View Independent Living Center, through Nora's window, at the *Stronger
Together* home, at the yellow house. She saw her and Carey
talking in the yard, her and Anna at the bay and at dinner
together. She saw her at the front desk with Besty and going
into SMA for one of her classes.

She saw herself in her apartment as well. Standing over the stove, she could see she was singing as she mixed up her stir fry. She cringed a bit at the look on her own face, eyes scrunched and mouth open wide.

Rocking out, she thought.

There were many more. She felt violated, her whole life being cataloged in the stacks pictures. Walking into Oleson's - she remembered that one. She headed in there so she could make her new favorite fall meal, bison chili. Ginny had given her the recipe and it was amazing.

Her morning walk on the bay, a cup of coffee and a book last Sunday morning, and her and Anna scarfing giant cinnamon rolls on a walk.

She dropped the pictures back to the table. All of the pictures had been taken within the last two weeks. Angered, a sound she had never heard erupted from her and she swept all the pictures off the table. They flew around the room, floating to all corners.

She turned back to the table.

Stacks of documents and newspapers were piled up on the right side of the table. She began to scan them. Several of the pages were of companies, organizations, and nonprofits. In the margins were notes, tracking and connecting the various organizations.

One margin had musings like *Follow the money, everyone has bills to pay.* Another sheet had *Joe?* written in red and circled. Below it became a rant of obscenities that devolved into maniacal scribbles.

The notes kept talking about the *Wunder.* One showed

Wunder = Women's Underground and Ellie began to understand that this was the national organization that facilitated her relocation. Rifling through the papers, she found a series of bus schedules to various spots around the country for the day she left and up to a week after. The papers had various bus routes circled in different colors until she found her own route with stars next to it. The next sheet had her route mapped and a final flow chart that showed *Joe* with arrows to the various bus routes up to Traverse City, and finally, *Stronger Together* circled, and with a series of forceful, violent *X's* carve through it, ripping the paper.

A final memory began to scratch in her head. She saw Ginny at the yellow house before the door had burst open. Ellie had been standing at the bookcase, and Ginny was behind the desk, reading her an email. What was it? The memory stayed just out of reach. It felt so important, she strained to remember. It just wouldn't come to her.

She shook her head and moved to the stack of newspapers.

The first set was similar to the one she found in the room of the asylum. The one that talked about Joe and his murder.

The next were a series of cut out articles featuring *Stronger Together*. Several talked about the good the organization did, one was a complaint about the organization bringing in problems to the city, and several featured Carey prominently at various events - community work, fundraisers, and company organizations that supported the cause.

The article with a quarter page picture of Carey in front of a podium at a large corporate event to raise money and awareness had the word *BITCH!* scrawled across it in violent red letters.

Rifling through the newspaper clippings, she came across an article folded in the paper. It was from Philadelphia. It read:

Police Seek Financial Analyst in Connection with Bauschor & Allen Murders

Philadelphia police are seeking Zach Weston for questioning in relation to last week's murders at Bauschor and Allen, a large financial firm that manages hedge funds in downtown Philadelphia. James L. Stocking, a partner at the firm, and Philip Resling, an associate, were found murdered in Stocking's office. Resling was found on the floor after brunt force trauma to his head while Stocking was found in his chair, cut with a letter opener from his desk.

The two men were found by Mr. Stocking's administrative assistant upon her return from lunch. Mr. Weston was seen hurriedly leaving the building on security cameras within the hour in question.

Through the police investigation, it appears that Mr. Weston's involvement in some questionable business practices had led to disciplinary discussion, an internal investigation, and likely criminal charges. It is suspected that this may have led to an adverse reaction by Mr. Weston, and that he may now be on the run.

Do not approach Mr. Weston and consider him dangerous. If you have any information about his whereabouts, please contact the Philadelphia Homicide Taskforce immediately...

Ellie's hand went to her mouth in horror. Zach certainly had a temper, and she had feared for her own life plenty of times. Could he really be capable of that?

The next clipping held another story. It didn't mention anything about Zach, instead it discussed a police officer who was murdered in his own home. The officer was on suspension from the force for improper usage of resources and excessive force. He had been on a narcotics task force. Found stabbed in his home, the officer's blood alcohol had measured 0.21 and a mostly empty bottle of bourbon had been found on its side on the floor. The theory was that it was a robbery gone wrong as the office he was found in was trashed, and the idea was that the disgraced officer had been too drunk to defend himself, and just drunk enough to think he could.

She finished going through the clippings, another talking about the murders Zach was sought for and a picture of him from before, smiling around the partners of the firm. All the clippings from Philadelphia were from just over two weeks ago, a few days before she recognized the pictures of her.

The research into her whereabouts, the finding of *Wunder* and *Stronger Together*, the article about Joe, the clippings of Carey, the pictures of her being stalked, and the articles about the firm and murders. The fog lifted, she remembered the rest.

*   *   *

"Ellie, you need to hear this. I got an email from Carey last night, I didn't see it until a few minutes ago. I tried to call her but she didn't answer. I haven't been able to get a hold of her at all. I am a little worried. But I need to share this with you," Ginny said.

Ellie turned with a smile on her face, standing by the bookshelf with a stack of novels in her arms. Her smile faded to concern when she saw Ginny's normal joyous face showing deep lines of concern.

"What's going on?" she asked.

"Carey said she received an email from Joe, your Joe from the coffee shop."

"Huh? I thought no one knew each other, so you guys couldn't even communicate?" she asked.

"Well, yes. That's why we are just getting it now. The whole of *Wunder* is the decentralization to protect the women we help and relocate. We are just a participant as is Joe. It took over two weeks to get through all the layers to get to us. Plus, it's highly irregular, so it took a while, but it's something you need to hear," Ginny said.

Ginny began reading, but Ellie didn't hear it in her voice, she heard the deep bass of Joe's soft voice float across the room toward her. And she began to tremble with terror.

"Ellie, I am sorry to have to reach out to you like this, I pray this message makes it to you. Hopefully, I am being overly cautious, but I have a bad feeling. What am I about to tell you shows an unstable man, capable of great violence and he is looking for YOU."

"As you know, I make the coffee shop about community, and participate in Wunder, Women's Underground. This is a nation-wide decentralized network that allows for assistance in the relocation of people who need help, usually battered and abused women."

"With this, I have developed many friends and contacts around Philadelphia, Pennsylvania as a whole, and even across the country. Zach has visited the shop several times since you've been gone, seemingly more unstable at each visit. He is looking for you. He started with small inquiries, began to ask about various organizations that had ties to Wunder, getting closer each time. He asked about buses. I think he is getting close. He isn't doing this because he wants you, I get the feeling he wants to *hurt* you because you beat him. He is angry that you got away, that you showed him up, that he is too weak."

"Due to these concerns, I have talked with many of my contacts, several of which are in law enforcement. It turns out he has a contact there as well, a man named Miles Lynch.

He is some kind of narcotics officer. He is just Zach's type as I hear he is about to be investigated for use of excessive force. Either way, Lynch has been using his police resources to inquire about Wunder and you. I fear that the two of them are getting close."

"With all this, I began to feel like I needed to find a way to contact you and let you know. But then, the other shoe dropped. Zach went off the deep end. What I am hearing is that he was in some really shady dealings at the firm he worked at. The whole company is under investigation as he launched a crypto element at the firm and promised big returns. He pushed for funding a new company that had its own crypto currency. He funneled funds from the hedge fund to invest in the company to fluff it up, which in turn increased the hedge fund. Basically, he funded the company, bought into the company, and then sold stakes in the company fluffed up by his own actions. It was a house of cards, as people bought in at the inflated value, he took lavish vacations and bought cars, funneling the rest of money invested back into the crypto to falsely inflate its value. As happens with these pyramid schemes, they eventually fall apart. Rumbling got out, rumors started floating, and there was a run to cash out before it fell apart. The organization didn't have enough to cover the cash in, and the values plummeted."

"The partners at the firm were furious. Zach had charmed his way through and they didn't care as long as they were making money, but suddenly, they were out over a hundred million dollars, clients were pulling everything from the firm, and people were angry. Not to mention the SEC was breathing down their necks and asking lots of questions. They fired

Zach, and told him they were turning him over for charges. They cut him loose and let him take the fall, not that he didn't deserve it."

"My sources feel confident that he lost it when they told him that. They apparently didn't understand his violent tendencies that you and I know all too well. He apparently cold-cocked the lower level associate in the room when he smirked at him, then grabbed a letter opener off one of the partner's desks, stabbing him in the throat repeatedly. He then circled back and bashed in the head of the associate with a paper weight. The administrative assistant to the partner came back early from lunch and saw the whole thing through her boss's door. She was so terrified she hid in a supply closet until he was gone and then called the police."

"My feeling is that he has lost it, completely lost control. The police cannot find him and he is on the run. I am worried that all of this will turn toward his obsession with finding you, punishing you for having the audacity to leave, to stand up to his abuse and take away his power over you."

"Please, be careful. I am always thinking of you, I pray that you are safe, well, and happy, and that at some point, our paths will cross again. Love, Joe."

Ginny finished reading and looked up, a concerned look on her face. Ellie stood frozen by the bookcase. Zach had killed two people. He had been looking for her. He was filled with rage and hate and evil, seeking to make her pay for his pain and shortcomings. He was wanted for murder and fraud.

They'll find him and put him in jail, she didn't have anything to worry about. That's what they do, they'll find him.

Zach also had nothing to lose. He would —

The thought didn't get the chance to finish in her head as it was interrupted by the door bursting open.

It had begun.

Ellie stood in front of the monitors, dropping the last of the newspaper clippings down. This was the control center, this is where it all started from. The cameras throughout the asylum showed how the creature knew where she was, the sound system played the roaring and snarling, the laughter and other sounds.

She scanned all the cameras again, looking for movement. The first time through she had only seen the one creature and now she was all but certain there was only the one. She was also certain *who* that was.

Something supernatural was afoot, the evidence being the shimmering between the two times. She wasn't sure if the creature was something that was a part of that, if a deal with the Devil was made, or some other explanation. Noting the speaker labels, she had noticed the one for the base of the stairwell. Playing that sound had driven her up the stairs and into the arms of the creature.

If the goal was torture and pain, it made sense why the creature had been toying with her all night long, herding her into the various parts of the asylum to find the clippings about Joe's murder, the broken doll, and Carey's body.

The creature, however, didn't seem to count on her disappearing and reappearing from her trips to the early twentieth century. This was unexpected and frustrating — it had screamed at her the last time. She wondered if she could use that to her advantage.

Ellie needed a plan. Now that she had a clear picture of everything going on, she needed to formulate what to do next. She could get out of here and go to the police, let them take it from there. They were already looking for Zach, she could point them here and let them find out what was going on.

Where was the creature? She scrolled through the camera feeds, not seeing the creature on the first floor hallway, nor in the stairwell or the various rooms. She came to a feed focused on an enclosed room with large windows, a sort of enclosed balcony with windows on three sides. The feed was from the back corner nearest the entry to the hallway. The room was empty except for a slumped shape near the center window.

As she peered at the feed, the slumped shape shifted. Squinting, Ellie made out what looked to be a person in a bulky chair.

"Oh no," she moaned.

It looked like a wheelchair.

Laughter came from behind her. She spun around to see the creature standing behind her. It laughed at her again, then lunged forward swinging the ax. Ellie dove out of the way, to her left, vaulting over the table and taking the laptop, sound system, and microphone with her. She landed on the electronics, hearing them crunch beneath her.

Rolling to her left, the ax crashed through the remains of the laptop where she had just been. There was no more toying with her, this was the end game. The last piece of torment was on that laptop screen and she had found the lair - the creature wanted to end it.

She rose to a squat and scanned the room. The creature was still in the U-shaped tables, but the ax had split the table and laptop in two that held the cameras when she dove out of the way. The creature moved to step over it. As he did, Ellie grabbed a fistful of the cords on the floor and yanked them from her where she crouched.

The debris moved forward as the creature stepped over it, catching his feet and he went down on top of the busted contents and table. Ellie was already running.

The creature jumped between her and the front door. She darted back toward the hallway she had entered. As she crossed the threshold, she felt a *whoosh* of air and the ax slammed into the door frame. She stumbled and fell, skidding across the floor. The creature filled the door and stood over her, eight feet away. She was on her backside, feet in front of her and hands behind her, in a crab walk posture. She was frozen, with the creature looming over her, sucking up the light and looking like a large black shadow with red floating eyes.

She darted to the wall, surprising the creature and dove

into the rotting cubby. She crashed in, the dumb waiter sliding down fast. The cubby crashed into the debris on the bottom, shards of wood, clumps of dirt, and bits of stone flying in every direction. Ellie tumbled straight out and rolled down the debris to the floor.

Dumb waiter two, fucking monster zero, she thought.

She was on her feet before she knew she hit the ground, running back toward the door she had come through originally. She hit the door and looked back, seeing the creature emerge from the stairwell at the far end of the cottage. Flinging open the door, she headed back for the tunnels.

Adrenaline taking over, Ellie was running blind. She sprinted down the tunnel under the bulbs. She had to get back to the asylum, she had to help Nora. She came to a branch in the tunnel. The lights burned out ahead and the tunnel became dark. To her right, was a tunnel that intersected at a T.

Where the hell is the door?

She heard the creature coming open the door and ducked into the dark connecting tunnel. She peered around the corner.

Shit! I went the wrong way.

In her haste, she had turned the wrong way at the tunnel, away from the door to the asylum that she knew about.

Fuck fuck fuck, she thought, the words echoing in her head in Anna's voice. *At least the creature will think I went the other way.*

She peaked around the corner. The creature looked both ways at the door. She pulled back, but it was too late. The creature laughed as it jumped down to pursue her. The sound of the ax dragging on the bricks bounced off the tunnel walls. She turned into the dark tunnel and ran. She passed the hole in the wall where she had emerged earlier, and kept pushing into the darkness.

The darkness swirled purple around her, the tendrils of shadow encircling her. She slowed but kept moving. She turned, looking behind her to see the creature's silhouette appear in the junction, the ax by its side. It followed.

She moved to the wall, her hands trailing along it as she moved. Her foot struck an old pipe, the clattering sound echoing through the hall.

"I seeeee youuuu," floated down the hall.

Then she heard an audible *click!* and turned to see a beam of light stretching down the hall.

That damn thing has a flashlight.

She moved a little more rapidly down the tunnel, her sense of urgency increased. The bricks were chipped and broken down, the tunnel narrowing. Old pipes lined the walls and ran along the ceiling and she had to turn sideways to get through them. The creature continued pursuit.

Her hand struck something solid. She flattened her palms against it and pushed. It was packed with dirt and brick. The tunnel had caved in. She felt along the wall, looking for an opening. Her hand struck a broken pipe, and she pulled back, shaking her hand.

Well, add tetanus to the list of I ever get out of here, she thought.

She dropped to her hands and knees, trying to find any

kind of opening. She stood again, frantically trying to find somewhere to go.

The blockage lit up. There was nowhere to go, the ceiling caved in and bricks laye littered about, dirt filling in through the hole in the brick. The light splashed along the whole cave-in and a voice followed the beam.

"Dead end, emphasis on *dead* you dumb bitch," growled the creature.

Ellie stood there with her back against the blockage in the narrow tunnel. The creature sauntered forward. Reaching up, it wedged the flashlight on top of a dial on the set of pipes, pointing the beam at Ellie.

The creature then lifted the ax, shifting it in its hands, tossing it right to left between its hands.

"Time to go to hell, I am going to enjoy this. I am going to split you in two," the creature snarled, and wound the ax up behind its head.

Ellie watched the blade glint in the light as it traveled in an arc toward her. She thought of Helen and the Light World, her final thought as the ax screamed toward her face was wondering if she had made a difference to Helen. Had she managed to save her from the flu? She hoped so, at least that would give her some meaning, something positive out of the night.

"You never should have–"

The blade finished its arc and slammed into the empty dirt and brick, wedging the blade into the debris. The creature screamed in rage.

Ellie was gone.

*   *   *

Ellie stumbled backwards and fell, landing hard on her backside. The tunnel was lit and the debris was gone, as was the creature. It took her a moment to realize she was alive and another to understand what had happened.

She had caused the shimmering and was back in some version of the early 1900's. The tunnel was open in both directions, but packed tighter with conduits and pipes than in the Dark World. A series of pipes ran alongside the wall with a large steam pipe running opposite, separated by a series of metal supports running from floor to ceiling. Sets of conduit ran along the curve in the upper third of the chamber, making for a packed tunnel and another sense of claustrophobia waving over Ellie.

If I can make it crawling through the collapsed tunnel earlier, this is nothing.

She walked down the tunnel. If she flipped back now, the debris would be between her and the creature. Of course, who was to say that the cave-in didn't run the length of the tunnel, and if the shimmering occurred, she wouldn't be buried in a twenty feet of rubble?

The thought made her shudder and suddenly, her feet

were in a half-run. She pushed down the shaft, seeing another intersection of tunnels ahead.

I could be lost down here for days, she thought.

She stopped. Something caught her eye on the left. She turned and noticed the shape of a door. Moving toward it, she heard activity behind the frame. The sounds of machines running, belts whipping, and the whine of voices. The faint smell of sawdust filled her nose as she ascended the stairs. Pushing open the door at the top, the dry smell became stronger.

She entered a room filled with various tables, lengths of wood, and men in dark shirts and overalls. Half a dozen milled about, working on various tasks at the tables or carrying lengths of wood. No one looked at her or acknowledged her as she wove her way between saw-horses and ducked under a two-by-four that swung through as one of the men turned.

Looking to her left, there was an arch that opened to another room with lengths of pipe and a some kind of metal working or blacksmith shop. On the right stood large paneled windows. The sun was shining outside and the ground appeared wet. Small pockets of snow sat in shaded areas. The trees were budding, but were still mostly bare, allowing Ellie to see the asylum across a narrow road.

Stepping into the hallway between the carpentry room and the smith shop, loud noises filled her ears and drowned out the wood-working noises. She followed the deep rumbling and into some kind of engine room. On her left, she could see into the boiler room and a large coal shed at the back.

A door sat off to her right. Covering her ears, she rushed through it and out into fresh air.

She was free, finally. She pulled in fresh air to her lungs, savoring the taste of spring. She smiled uncontrollably. She felt like she was in a movie as she strode away from the building, her arms out wide and spinning around. She gazed up to the blue sky and enjoyed the cool spring breeze washing over her. Covered in dirt, grime, and blood, the air was refreshing and cleansing.

Turning around, she saw a large smokestack reaching for the clouds. Off to her left, there was a well standing between the cottages and the power building, and a series of train tracks ran near the power building to deliver the coal to provide energy to the campus. She recalled the coal being shoveled off the train car earlier in the evening from a window of the asylum. She had come up from the tunnels into the power building.

She laughed with joy until her chest ached, which wasn't too long due to all the damage to her ribs. People milled about as she stepped out into the sun, which was on a down-ward arc of late afternoon. Patients returning from the farm brushed past her, completely unaware of her presence. She moved off the road as the cookie-wagon came rumbling by, the little boy abreast the driver and smiling in the spring sun.

Hiya boy!

The world was the antithesis of the chaos of her own Dark World, and brought a sense of peace and calm. Once the cookie-wagon passed, she crossed the road and onto the grassy area leading up to the asylum. She sat down in the grass, crossed her legs and closed her eyes for a moment in the sun.

After a few moments, she felt calm and in control. It was time to think of what was next. She was outside and free from the asylum, but she wasn't in her world, she was in the Light World of the early 1900's. At this point, she thought she would be content just staying here, though she did not think she actually *could* since no one saw her except Helen and she could not cause the shimmering when she was away from the asylum. The phenomenon seemed to be connected to the asylum.

Could she get close to the asylum and cause the shimmering, being outside? Could she do that and be free in her own world?

That only solved one of her problems, however. As she couldn't leave without trying to rescue Helen from the flu, she couldn't leave without rescuing the person in the wheelchair. She knew who it was, another scene set up to hurt her. She knew it was the escalation of what she loved and her new life over the past few months.

Nora.

Rising and dusting herself off, she knew she had to get back into the asylum, find Nora, and somehow get her out of there.

Then she could determine what to do next. She couldn't discount that the creature was some strange supernatural conjuring related to the same phenomenon that brought her to this time. However, with the camera, speakers, and set up, it seemed less likely. Plus, the voice yelling at her from the creature sounded very familiar. Was the creature some abomination from a deal Zach made with the Devil? Did the supernatural phenomenon come from her and Anna's actions at the Hippie Tree? Did that same force morph Zach's inner evil into a physical manifestation?

These strange thoughts swirled in her head as she walked across the grass, joining the rank file of patients, caretakers, and orderlies returning from the farms, fields, and greenhouse. Glancing up, she scanned the outside of the building, trying to determine where Nora was. Squinting, looking for a detail that would jump out and signify this as the location from the video. She wanted to get as close to the location as she could before trying to flip back, lowering her exposure to the creature.

Unfortunately, nothing jumped out.

Climbing the stairs, she was both determined and felt a longing to stay outside in the air and sun. Streaming into the rear entrance with the returning groups, she paused looking around. Everything had occurred in the southern wing, the women's side. Nora would be there. The few sunroom style rooms jutting out of the rear of the building were up on the second floor. She moved to the large stairwell to begin her search.

Hang on Nora, I'm coming, she thought and stepped up on the first step.

Thirty-Seven

Ellie strode through the halls to the first room.
Her plan was simple: head to the first room, shimmer back to her world and see if Nora was there. If she wasn't, flip back and head to the second room. Repeat.

Once she found Nora, she would tend to her to make sure she was all right. If she shimmered back to Light World, could she take Nora with her? She wasn't sure, but maybe if she was holding onto her, she could. Would the wheel chair come too? All of this was strange, she wasn't sure she could discount either thought. Ellie was hopeful though, as that would give them a veil of protection from the creature.

Either way, she would begin moving Nora to the first floor window to get out. Once she was safe, she could contact the police. Would they find a creature in the building, or would they simply decide she needed to be checked into the asylum?

It didn't really matter. What mattered was getting Nora to safety. She had to be careful, however, as it was obvious that Nora was some form of sick torture or bait to draw her in. She felt like she had a leg up on the creature though as it was down in the tunnels and would have some ground to cover, despite her wasting a few minutes in the fresh air and sunshine. Furthermore, she had no idea how much time passed when she shimmered between the two worlds. Perhaps it was one-to-one, or perhaps the time was skewed in some way. She couldn't take anything for granted.

Ellie was confident that the creature was confused by her disappearance in the dark tunnels. Perhaps it was searching for her down there and that would give her time for her escape. She wondered for a moment what it would take to cause a cave-in to trap the bastard down there for good. She let that thought fester, hoping it would grow in the back of her mind into a plan if she needed it while she focused on Nora.

Her first target was just ahead, causing a jump in her step.

Ellie felt that the end game was near. The creature's rage in the cottage and subsequent attack in the tunnels felt like the toying was over. No longer was it about causing mental anguish and psychological torture, no longer was it about inflicting painful but non-life threatening physical damage, no longer was it about herding her through the sick story laid out through the asylum.

The journey through her personal hell had reached its

climactic point; she had reached the center of the labyrinth and the final confrontation was at hand.

The creature wanted to end it with the ax, her death the final punctuation of the demented narrative.

Ellie gritted her teeth at the thought. The creature wanted to end this as a tragedy, but she had something up her sleeve that it didn't know about. In ten weeks since she had left that condo, she had changed.

She wasn't a victim; she was a fighter. She had a very different end in mind.

*   *   *

She flew into the room at a sprint, hitting the brakes and sliding on the rug that adorned the floor. The room was about the size of three of the patient rooms and had a series of chairs in the corners and around small coffee tables. A couch lay on her right and the windows had light curtains pulled open to let in the afternoon light. The room was brightly lit from the windows on all three sides, sunbeams streaming in and warming the atmosphere. It was serene and welcoming.

The room was empty at the moment, but all the tranquility would disappear in a moment. Ellie closed her eyes and focused on the dark, moldy asylum and Nora in her chair. She pictured her as she had seen in the camera feed.

She felt a rush of air as if filling an empty space, and

the scent went from dry and floral to wet and mildewy. She opened her eyes to see the dark room before her. It was amazing how different the room was. Holes covered the walls, there were no furnishings and the flooring was missing in areas, including right under her toes. She teetered over the edge, waving her arms. She backed up to keep from falling in, seeing a drop the first floor below through the hole. The windows were barred and grimy, glass broken between the bars. Graffiti covered the walls and empty beer cans fluttered in the cold breeze. Forgotten fast food bags and cups were covered in dust in the corner while black mold scaled the corner behind them.

The serenity was long gone as the stench of decay and death filled the room instead.

And the room was empty.

There was no sign of Nora and Ellie realized quickly that she did not have the right room. She sighed, disappointed. Nothing about tonight was easy.

She headed over to the south windows and peered through a large hole in the glass. She had to stoop a bit, but it allowed her to see out much better than through the grime of the intact parts of the window.

Moving her face in close she looked out to see the other room that would be her next stop. The sky was continuing to lighten, now a light violet. The gloom allowed her to see across and through the windows of the other room. She should be able to see if the shape of Nora was in there...

She pulled back and cried out. The whole window was busted out on the north side of that room and she could see clearly into it. The room was lit. In the light, she saw a silhouette standing at the window. It was shaped like a man, a dark shape climbing up through the three quarter window of the sunroom. The silhouette ran up over the shoulders of the shape, up to the head, and culminated in a set of horns. Between and just below the horns, were the glowing red eyes.

The sound of laughter floated across the space, on the next wing. It seemed so clear even with the distance. She recognized the devilish laugh, but it wasn't the same as she heard through the speakers earlier.

She watched, frozen, as the silhouette turned and behind him was the wheelchair with the woman sitting in it. The creature wheeled it to the window so that Ellie could see. She watched in horror as the ax came into view. The creature tilted the stooped woman's head back. With a one-handed short swing, it buried the ax in the stomach of the woman.

Nora lurched and cried out in pain. The creature looked up and made eye contact with Ellie. Though its face didn't change, she swore it was grinning as it ran the ax across her belly, slicing it open.

It laughed again as Nora's face was pained, her cry floating across the expanse to Ellie. He let her head go, and she slumped forward.

The creature pointed the ax through the window at Ellie. Then it laughed again, turned and strode away, the sound floating across to her and seeming to echo off every corner of the room. It enveloped her, smothering her will and causing her knees to weaken.

She heard sobbing escaping her lips and felt her cheeks get wet, but everything had gone numb. She heard nothing other than the echoing sound of laughter, wrapping around her like a wet blanket pulling her under the surface. It felt like she was drowning; she couldn't breath, could not feel anything.

Suddenly, reality rushed back in, the echoing laughter ceased, and air filled her lungs with an audible gasp. Before she realized it, she was on her feet running. Out the door, down the hall, through the alcove between wings. It occurred to her in some far off corner of her mind that the creature could easily finish her off with her hasty pursuit. It even flashed that this may have been its plan all along. That part of her brain wasn't in control however, and she flew with reckless abandon to Nora.

She came around the corner at full speed, sliding across the hall on the debris and dirt before straightening out.

At the other end of the hallway stood the creature. It was still as a statue, just watching. It didn't move or make a sound as she covered the distance to the room Nora was in.

It wanted her to go in, it wanted her to see, and it wanted her to feel.

Ellie acquiesced, flying into the room and finding Nora near the window. She slid down on her knees as she approached from the side, assessing her friend. Maybe it wouldn't be as bad as she feared. She held out hope, pushing the image of Carey crucified to the wall out of her head.

It was as bad as she feared.

Nora was slumped over, her lap filled with blood from the wound in her stomach. She lifted her head, her eyes out of focus and looked at Ellie. Amazingly, she smiled.

"Hey girly, whatcha doing here?" she croaked. Blood trickled down her lips. "Watch out, some asshole is going around with an ax." She smiled at Ellie.

"Oh Nora, I am so sorry, this is my fault. What has he done to you?" Ellie cried.

With a sudden strength and clarity, Nora raised her hand and patted Ellie's arm. A tattoo of blood from her fingers marked her forearm.

"It's okay dear, this was always how it would go."

"You're here because you know me. He is trying to hurt me. I wish I had never met you, then you wouldn't be here," Ellie sobbed.

"Don't you dare be like that. Knowing you has been one of the honors of my life. I love you and will so into the next life. You were an angel that gave me joy in the last few months. My life is at its end anyway. Don't you dare bear the burden of that monster." She coughed out the last few words, the blood leaking from her lips increasing.

Her breath became labored.

"Now, what have I told you?"

Ellie looked at her, confused.

"Fight, always be a fighter. Win or lose, you go down swinging. Don't you fold or be a victim."

Ellie nodded.

Nora continued, "Baby, fight, fight, always fight. Scratch and claw but you never back down."

She coughed and Ellie picked up where she left off, "fight like you're the third monkey on the ramp to Noah's ark, and.."

Nora joined in, and then finished it together "Baby, it's starting to rain"

Nora laughed and Ellie forced a pained smile. The laugh turned into a coughing fit.

"That's right, fight. Be smart about it, dear. Don't lose control on account of me. You need to outsmart him."

She sputtered a cough.

"Dig into my chair here, dear. Let me have one last sip 'n smoke."

Ellie reached into her hiding spot in the chair, obviously not something the creature or abductor bothered to check, and pulled out Nora's stash: the flask, the lighter, and her pack of cigarettes.

Nora's blood soaked fingers wrapped around the flask first. Ellie unscrewed the top. She smelled the strong smell of whiskey; the flask was filled to the brim.

Nora raised the flask in a toast to Ellie, "To you taking that bastard down. Put him down and put an end to this." She took a large gulp, grimacing as it burned down into her lacerated stomach.

Ellie put a cigarette in her mouth, and cupped the lighter as she struck it. The flame danced in the room, and the cigarette end glowed red. Nora took a drag, smiling slightly. Her eyes began to fade and gloss over. Ellie knew she was slipping away.

She coughed again. Ellie raised the flask back up to her lips, but she pulled away.

"No, you're gonna need that," she stated.

Her head lolled, and the cigarette slipped from her fingers. Blood dripped off her chin. Her other hand fell from holding her belly. Ellie saw purple entrails slipping out from the wound as the puddle of blood surrounding the chair widened.

"Roger..." she muttered, her eyes looking off somewhere that Ellie couldn't see, a slight smile on her face.

"Oh Nora, I'm sorry. I love you," she said.

""I love you too dear. I was always waiting for you. Don't worry, you'll make it. She told me. She told me a long time ago. Roger's come to get me now. I'll see you, but not any time soon."

She closed her eyes. Her body went limp and her head dropped.

Ellie lowered her head and cried.

Her friend was gone.

Thirty-Eight

G rief turned to white hot anger. Ellie rose up from her knees, seething with rage. She walked briskly out into the hallway, leaving her friend's body behind. She exited the room and turned to face the creature.

It still stood where she had seen it last, standing down at the end of the hallway.

She sized up the creature, looking at it differently than she had all night long. She no longer feared it. It was an adversary, and now, the subject of the rage coursing through her veins. Her eyes were laser focused, and her sense seemed heightened by the anger.

The creature didn't seem as tall as she had perceived. It was about the height of a tall man, just over six feet, pushing six and a half with the horns. The snout and red eyes lurked but no longer looked dangerous, it looked like a target. The ax sat at his side, the head resting on the ground and the handle running up to his right hand.

She just had to avoid that right hand. She had plenty of experience avoiding or softening a blow from a right handed strike from her years with Zach.

"I ripped her guts out because of —"

The creature didn't finish as Ellie screamed with rage and charged. The creature jumped at her angry cry, flinching slightly. It recovered quickly, raised the ax and made its own rush toward Ellie.

Overlapping screams filled the hallway from the two adversaries as they stormed toward each other. The thirty foot gap closed quickly. The creature running with the ax over its shoulder, Ellie's arms pumping at her side and her shoulders dropped like a linebacker.

The distance closed and the creature swung the giant clever. The steel ax head glinted in the light as it made its arc toward Ellie. She darted to her left and slid, as if doing a pop-up slide in baseball. She slid past the creature and under the arc. The ax slammed into the ground as she popped up behind the creature.

It turned quickly, its reflexes sharp, swinging the ax laterally across the hallway. Targeting Ellie's midsection with everything it had. The blade strike would cut her straight in half —

But she was already gone. As soon as she popped up, she flipped. The hallway was lit and nurses milled about. She strode forward five quick strides, spun around and flipped back. The ax made contact with the wall past where she had just been. She wasted no time, kicking up between the creatures legs from behind.

The creature let go of the ax, doubled over. She struck the back of it's knee and it dropped. She flipped, strode forward and flipped back. She was in front of the creature, who pulled back in surprise at her sudden appearance. She struck out, hitting it in the throat. A strangled cry erupted as it fell backwards. She kicked again, and again. She made solid contact, her rage fueling her forward.

Another kick and her leg stuck. The creature grabbed her foot and ankle. He roared as he violently twisted it, trying to wrench her foot from her ankle. She flipped again before the torque did damage, stepped back, and returned to the Dark World. She lifted her left and stomped on the side of the creature's face. Its head bounced off the ground and she stomped again.

The creature bellowed in pain. Then Ellie was lifted off the ground as the creature kicked her in the stomach. She landed back on her rear end with an *oomph!* The creature rose up, wounded and crouched. It charged at her. She flipped, slid to the side, and flipped back sweeping her leg out. She caught the creature stumbling forward and taking out its legs. Its face bounced off the floor.

She flipped, ran to where the ax was buried in the wall, and flipped back. She wrenched it free and strode quickly to where the creature was. She swung with all her might.

The creature felt it coming, and pushed into a roll to get away. The ax didn't connect with its midsection where she was targeting, but the black gloved hand it used to push away was just leaving the floor when the ax sliced through it, burying the blade into the exposed subfloor.

Ellie blinked at the four gloved fingers laying separated from the hand as the creature screamed. It turned, holding its hand spurting blood to its chest, and kicked out. The kick struck Ellie hard in the ribs, causing her whole world to explode. She felt an audible crunch inside her body and the air left her. She was thrown in the air with the next strike, falling backwards, her head striking the floor. Another kick struck her thigh and the lower half of her body went numb.

She couldn't breathe, she couldn't move, and she saw stars everywhere. She tried to crawl away and was wrenched from the ground. Slammed against the wall, she heard shrill screaming like nothing she had ever heard. It cut through the fog in her head. The creature had its good hand around her throat, pinning her to the wall.

Darkness began to creep in from the corners of her eyes. She couldn't concentrate enough to cause the shimmering, or to get free. Her fingers clawed at the hand around her throat. It was too tight, she couldn't get her fingers under the glove fingers. They dug in more, her windpipe cut off and being crushed. She was beginning to lose consciousness, and if that happened –

Reaching with her right hand, she found the wounded, fingerless hand of the creature. She grabbed it and squeezed with all her might, using the tips of her fingernails to dig into the stubs of the missing fingers.

An unholy roar filled her ears, but the grip on her throat loosened. She gasped a short breath to stave off the darkness, and concentrated on flipping.

She sank to the floor gasping in the well lit hallway, nurses moving this way and that. The floral smell of a vase of lilies next to her head filled her nose.

She sat gasping some time in the early 1900's, trying to recover, out of reach of the creature for the moment.

*   *   *

"Halloween's coming, you ladies planning on getting into any trouble?" Nora asked.

Ellie was setting the bed, fluffing the pillows, and generally tidying up. She had a routine on Tuesdays, and this one was no exception. She showed up and while many others worked up their pace like a heavy train slowly increasing speeds on the tracks, she was like a drag racer slamming the gas from the word go. She hustled through all her tasks, getting them done in the early afternoon so she could save Nora for last and take her sweet time finishing out the day in her company.

She found ways to linger with Nora, spending more time with her as she found ways to be efficient and productive in her other duties. This Tuesday, right before Halloween, she had come out of the gates smiling and rolling, putting her tasks behind her, working through lunch, and being done by early afternoon.

At this moment, though, she wasn't paying attention to Nora at all. Her mind was troubled, and her focus elsewhere.

"Dear, where are you at? You with me or off in la-la land?" Nora asked.

Ellie shook her head to bring herself back to the room and away from wondering about her confrontation earlier. She turned her face to Nora, blinking.

She sighed. "I'm here. Just thinking, struggling through something from earlier today."

"As long as you ain't whining, you can tell me about it," Nora replied, and followed with a little cackle. "Tell me if I need to dig out my bourbon first to get through it, though."

Ellie gave a wry smile.

"Well, I don't need to burden you with it," she replied, going back to setting the bed. Nora simply crossed her hands in her lap and waited.

"You know, that Nurse Harmony is so awful. She is just a nasty old bag, so full of herself and mean to everyone. It's as if she just lurks about, like a snake coiled in the grass, looking for any kind of slip up to strike."

Nora simply nodded along, waiting for the shoe to drop.

"Why are people like that? How can she exist in such misery, and try to spread that misery to anyone that comes in contact with her? She acts as if she needs to push someone else down to feel good. She wants to be tall but not by stretching herself, but by knocking other people down."

She began to get animated and frustrated, slamming the pillows. Her voice began to raise.

"I love being here, until I run into that witch, and she sucks the life right out of me. I look forward to the joy of being here, and it's like a nectar that she has to swoop in and take away. Arr! I despise that woman!"

"I think the pillow is fluffed sufficiently. Fluffed, beaten into submission, and perhaps completely annihilated," Nora observed. "I take it that something happened today?"

Ellie paused, her shoulders dropping.

"Well, I'm worried that I messed up and they might not let me be here any more because of her."

"Oh dear, I'm sure it's not that bad."

"Well, I was hurrying through my tasks, like I do. I work hard, take my job seriously, but I was rushing and I messed up. I made a huge mess, spilled a whole bottle of laundry detergent all over the floor. Nurse Harmony, that judgmental bitch, jumped out and was on me. She was yelling and berating me, poking me to try to get a rise out of me. She told me I was inept and useless, a homeless runt, a street rat, and a scavenger."

"Well," Ellie continued. "She got to me. Her poking got a reaction out of me and I yelled at her to leave me alone. I told her she was a miserable, insufferable bitch and that all she did was spread misery. I told her to take a long walk off a short pier and threw the half empty bottle of detergent at her. I stormed off while she told me she'd have me out of here. I went and got a mop, came back and cleaned up the mess. She was gone when I got back, and I am just waiting for her to come back to have me fired."

Her eyes teared up at the thought of losing her job here.

"Things have been going so well for me, and one mistake, letting that evil witch get to me, and it's all going to go away."

"Calm down, Ellie. Let's not get all slobbery and hysterical.

You have to be a bit more strategic. Anger is the enemy. Take a breath, figure out a strategy to attack, and then strike. Remove emotion, strike hard and with precision. Strategize and plan it out. Most importantly, *anger is the enemy.* It breeds carelessness, which leads to mistakes."

Nora regarded her while Ellie hung on to her every word.

"You will meet adversaries in your life. God never said it would be easy, but each battle will strengthen you for the next, prepare you for what lies ahead. The world is a continuous battle for your soul, and the reward at the end is eternal life in heaven. It's worth it. Now come over here and give me a hug."

They embraced and Ellie felt better. She smiled as she left.

Once she was gone, Nora picked up the phone and dialed the director. The director took her call, as she always did. Big time donors tended to move to the front of the line.

Nora explained the situation, and her request that Nurse Harmony leave Ellie alone. She had a big role to play, and she was as good as family to Nora.

Nora thanked the director after some quick small talk. And yes, she would be funding the portico project in the spring. Then she ended the call by reiterating that Ellie was her family, and she would do anything to protect her.

*   *   *

Ellie rose in the hallway of the asylum, remembering that conversation with Nora from several weeks ago, before her episodes.

Anger is the enemy.

She had some serious damage, but her anger and emotion had been out of control, and she had paid for it. Her ribs screamed and her lung felt like it couldn't draw a breath in. She had definitely paid for her haste – almost with her life.

Be strategic, strike first, and strike hard and fast, with precision.

Her eyes clouded with tears, knowing that she wouldn't get to have another conversation with Nora, who had helped her grow into the confident, self-reliant, and tough version that was willing to fight a monster in the hallway of a haunted asylum.

She walked into the community bathroom down the hall. She turned the faucet on and cold water flowed. She splashed her face and felt the relief of the cool, cleansing flow. She drank from it, her damaged throat welcoming the soothing chill of the crisp water. It occurred to her that the water she was drinking was somewhere around a hundred years old, or at least would be when she flipped back. She had felt the warmth and wind, smelled the flowers, so it stood to reason that she could feel and taste the cold water.

She wondered if she could take anything else back, like a weapon. Where would she get a weapon anyway? She needed a weapon, a plan, or both.

She wished Nora was here, she would tell her straight in no uncertain terms, how she should go about it. Or at least, what her mindset needed to be as she came up with a plan. She was resourceful as hell too, so she could have helped her fashion a weapon. She was a veritable MacGyver and would have made a bomb out of a shoelace, a piece of chewed bubble gum, and a can of soda.

Ellie laughed to herself.

"God, I miss you already Nora. Thank you for everything."

She stared at herself in the mirror, seeing a beaten and bruised body. Her face was covered in grime and small cuts along with bruises and swelling, her hair matted against her head. The cut on her shoulder once again oozed blood. She lifted her shirt to look at her ribs, revealing swollen purple skin. Sharp pain went through her as she lifted her arm, once again taking her breath away. She struggled to regain her breath. She was sure her ribs were broken, perhaps a shard pushing into her lung.

Her hands and knees were sliced in so many places. Swollen and red, they looked like large berries about to burst. Blood oozed from so many different wounds trying to stay clotted, she couldn't tell the difference from it or her sweat.

Though her body was battered and she barely recognized the woman looking back, there was one part that remained unharmed. Somehow, through all this, it looked stronger: the look in her eyes.

Determination, strength, focus, and fearlessness emanated from the orbs in their sockets. The eyes were calm and emotionless, singularly focused on one goal. That goal wasn't to escape anymore. She didn't even care if she made it out. The eyes told the story of an ice cold and relentless individual, hell bent on destruction.

She had taken its fingers, now she would take everything else. Nothing less than annihilation of the creature would suffice. As she thought of Nora and what she would do, a small smile spread across her lips.

The smile widened, as a plan formulated, and the pieces fell into place. This wasn't revenge, it was a reckoning.

Thirty-Nine

Ellie flipped back in the bathroom without breaking her eye contact with the mirror version of herself. Her smile didn't falter as the world changed all around her, though it became distorted by the cracked mirror and its filth. Once the shimmering finished, she turned and walked out of the decrepit room.

Slowly, she stuck her head out of the doorway to find an empty hall. The gloved fingers remained on the floor and she half expected them to start moving around. Stranger things had surely happened tonight.

She moved quickly and silently across the hall and down to Nora's final resting place. She entered to find the room as she left it, Nora slumped in her chair over by the window. She moved over, staying low in case the creature was peering through the window, trying to find her. She imagined it was somewhere licking its wounds, trying to recover enough to mount a counter-attack against her. She did not, however, want to take anything for granted. Carelessness had already almost cost her; she wouldn't make that mistake again.

She shuffled around the front of Nora, her body becoming stiff in her contorted posture. She lifted the flask from her lap and picked the lighter up from where it had fallen to the floor earlier after she lit her final cigarette.

She put them both in her pocket and rose to leave the room. Something else caught her eye — a silver cylinder mounted on the back of her wheelchair.

Interesting, she thought. She gathered everything she needed, then stopped and stood over Nora. She bowed her head and folded her hands, saying a prayer on behalf of her friends, asking God to welcome her into his kingdom and to watch over her. She finished by telling God that she hoped what she was about to do wasn't a sin, and that she didn't think so as she was using her given abilities to stand up for herself and her friend, but confided that her heart may be dark. She asked Him to help her, and forgive her.

She felt an overwhelming sense of calm, leaned down and kissed her friend's head one more time, before turning to the door.

Singular focus, massive action, and emotionless.

It was time to put her plan in motion.

Forty

S he was set. It was time.
A reckoning.

Moving carefully about the asylum, ensuring she didn't run into the creature before she was ready, Ellie had put her plan in motion.

The eyes that the creature had had with all the cameras were dark after the skirmish in the control room of the cottage, leaving him blind. That meant a wounded, angry creature was roaming the asylum looking for her. She had taken his off-hand out of the equation, but based on the hallway outside of Nora's room, he had retrieved the ax to use with his good hand.

It had taken the better part of an hour to set up, and the

creature could be anywhere by now. She knew she had done serious damage outside of his severed fingers, and Ellie felt confident that he was in pain. This would contribute to his rage and anger, causing him to be careless.

Anger is the enemy.

She moved through the asylum carefully now, seeking the creature. She was the bait, and needed to get his attention but stay out of his grasp. It was her turn to herd *him* where she wanted him.

It occurred to her how the tables had turned; she was in control, she had the power over him, and she was the one who had the upper hand. Her ability to jump in and out of the Light and Dark Worlds gave her the ability to stay out of his grasp, and she was pretty certain that she was in better physical shape than he, despite the fire burning on her left side. Destroying his own control center was ironic as it took away his main advantage now.

Anger is the enemy.

That is, other than fear which she had already dealt with herself, but he didn't know that.

Not finding the creature on each floor, she ended up down near the entrance to the tunnels again. A small amount of doubt crept in. She did *not* want to go down into the tunnels again. It seemed her ability to shimmer was hit and miss in the subterranean maze, and that would be a key part of being able to stay close enough to keep him angry but out of his reach for damage.

It's time to end this, she thought, taking a deep breath in.

She pulled open the door to the tunnels that she took early

that night (*how long ago was that? Could it really be just tonight?*) and descended the narrow stone staircase.

A sound echoed below her, and she jumped, flipping into Light World. She felt a searing pain on her side, the large steam pipes running up the slant that ran next to the stone stairs. There was no wall or door at the top as the steam pipes ran into the bottom of the asylum.

As quickly as she had shimmered, she jumped back. Panting in the dark, she rubbed the slightly seared skin on her right forearm that had been closest to the pipes. She needed to calm down.

She reached the bottom of the stairs and moved into the tunnel. The lights were on, but she didn't see the creature.

Creeping along, she moved down the tunnel. She was exposed and afraid here. She wasn't sure if she could shimmer, and with the big, hot steam pipes she wasn't sure she liked the potential consequences of flipping.

The fear led to other emotions and Ellie had to shove down the emotion of losing her friend. She moved back cautiously, listening for the creature. The dampness of the tunnel felt like a wet blanket around her as she crept along. Her feet shuffled along the curved floor of the tunnel, her left hand trailing on the wall and her right poised to protect herself if he jumped out. She reached the forty-five degree curve and took the stairs back to the cottage.

She stepped into the dark, dank basement. The smell of mildew persisted and she strained with her eyes and ears for any sign of the creature. She squinted in the darkness, straining to make out the walls. She didn't dare use the lighter; she didn't want to give away her position and she didn't want to run out of fluid.

Moving through the basement, she remembered how she had lost the ability to shimmer here. She had to be extremely careful. She crept along, again swearing that damn chair was *moving*, and jumped when she heard another crash and footfalls above her head.

"Ellie!" a voice yelled. It was enraged, but muffled. "I will find you, and I will gut you. No more games. You messed with the bull, you're gonna get the fucking horns! You took my hand I am gonna rip out your beating fucking heart and eat it in front of before you go to hell."

Psycho, she thought.

Except, the voice stopped and she realized she had said it out loud.

Oh well, she thought. *I guess it had to start somehow.*

"Fuck you, you sick piece of shit. I am getting out of here!" she yelled back.

She ran back toward the door to the tunnels as the footfalls sped up. She turned back to see the creature drop through a hole in the floor and roll on the concrete, the ax clanking as it bounced away.

Shit, so much for my head start, she thought and ran.

She heard the dragging of the ax being picked up, and the sound of pursuit.

Ellie made it to the west end of building fifty, found the area that led back to the tunnel. She headed down the steps and through the doorway back into the tunnel.

She heard a crash behind her and a grunt. The creature was catching up on her.

Time to go, she thought. She ran ahead in the tunnel, trying to get back to the door. She stumbled on the uneven bricks. The creature was right behind her and gaining. She reached the steps and pushed up the narrow stones.

She felt the air pass behind her and heard the ax strike the stones, showering the dim stairwell with sparks.

She burst into the ground floor of the asylum and fell forward, sliding to a stop on the far wall as the creature emerged. Panting, she flipped. She clenched her eyes and envisioned the *Light World*, Helen's world, Traverse City State Hospital circa 1916. She could smell the flowers, she could see the light, taste the clean air, and hear the voices of the staff. As she involved all her senses, the *Dark World* melted away. She heard the creature heading toward her, the footfalls echoing in the hallway, but they faded quickly.

She could make out the silhouette in the darkness as the color of the *Light World* crept in from the sides of her vision. The circular hole of the dark world got smaller and smaller as the creature approached, and then, the circle tightened to the size of a pinhead, and blinked out of sight.

She panted, back in the Light World. She wanted to catch her breath and slow her heart, but she didn't have that time without losing the creature. She moved down the hallway and ducked into the alcove. She flipped back.

Taking a breath, she peaked around the corner. The creature stood where she had been lying on the ground looking around. She chuckled a bit to herself, regaining some of her swagger.

She strode out of the alcove, in plain sight of the creature and to the main staircase steps leading up the middle of the building on the first floor, her middle finger in the air over her shoulder. The creature screamed in rage. She turned and feigned fear, picking up the pace. She heard him pursue as she slipped back out of sight up the stairwell. She hit the landing, repeating the flipping sequence. The shimmering brought her back to Light World, creature-less.

She moved up the staircase toward the first floor. She saw a pair of nurses headed down her way, but of course, they paid no heed to her approach. She kept moving and came to the main level.

She knew she didn't have much time. She had to keep the creature engaged and enraged, but flipping back and forth was dangerous if he realized what she was doing. He may be ahead of where she expected him to be and she may be in striking range.

She was indecisive at the top of the stairs. Was he following? Or did he run all the way up. She flipped back.

He was right there, less than a foot away, but his back was turned. He was ahead of her. He felt something and began to turn...

She planted two hands on his upper back and shoved, then flipped back right away. She didn't want him going the wrong way and she didn't want to be in his reach. She headed past the little hallway to the ballroom and into the open area by the entrance to the kitchen.

Flipping back, she stood twenty feet from the creature.

They stared at each other for a moment. He was being more cautious now, moving slowly, trying to figure it out.

Not good, I need him enraged and careless, she thought.

"Hey ya big pussy, can't keep up? Or are you busy looking for your fingers? Oh, here's one!" she yelled, lifting up her middle finger.

The rage came back immediately, and he bellowed as he ran to her. She turned and ran down the hallway, counting ten paces and then flipping back to the Light World.

She moved down to the end of the first wing, flipping back. He was half way down the hall.

She laughed loudly, and shook her head.

"Too slow!"

She moved into the dark alcove and flipped again.

She repeated the process in the middle wing, the creature beginning to lose control with anger.

Anger is the enemy.

She was in the final wing when she got careless. Her own ego from taunting the beast got in the way, and when she flipped back, he was ready. Guessing correctly, she flipped back *right into his arms.*

He clubbed her with his stubbed hand upside the head. She saw stars burst and the world spun, disorienting her. She was clubbed in the gut with the top of the ax, knocking the wind out of her. She dropped to the floor, the creature standing over her. Using his one good hand, he raised the ax over his head and placed a boot on her back, trying to push her down.

Ellie drove her thumb into the back of the raised knee,

knocking him off balance as he tried to swing. She drove up inside the arc of the swing, the crown of her head made a crunching contact with his chin, a strange combination of crunch and squeak, The snout of the bull bent awkwardly and the ax went harmlessly into the wall.

The creature fell backwards and she scrambled away, running the length of the outer batwing. As she was twenty feet from the end of the hall, she slowed, glancing back. The creature was picking himself up and beginning a pained pursuit.

"You fucking bitch, I am going to gut you like I did your sad, helpless fucking friend!"

She glanced out the window of the room she was directly across from. The first light of dawn was creeping across the horizon and enough light floated through the darkness where she could see the yellow house.

I'm coming, she thought and even nodded to the house, as if a long lost companion that she was reassuring she would see again soon.

"Time for you to go back to Hell where you belong," she said, partially under her breath. The creature looked at her, as if unsure if he had heard her correctly.

A pile of rotting wood stood in the hall. It was piled knee high and she had to carefully step over it and onto a smaller pile. She then stepped over another stack and back into the hallway. The sharp smell from the wood was overwhelming. The creature pursued, and realizing that the corridor ended up ahead, slowed its progress.

"Nowhere to go now," it yelled and laughed at its hideous chortle.

Ellie gasped.

The creature laughed again at her fear, its ax swinging at its side.

"You picked a fight you can't win, you dumb cunt. Now you can die slowly, painfully, watching each body part I chop roll down the hall."

She reached down and grabbed a large, heavy shard of glass that she had left, pulled out of a pile under a broken, barred window. She felt it cut into her hands but held it up in front of her.

"Stay back!"

The creature laughed again.

"Oh Ellie, you should know better than that." He came closer.

"You should never have left. You should have known your place. But I'll show you now. Oh how I have enjoyed torturing you all night long, watching you run, so scared you pissed yourself. You are nothing and never have been."

The creature continued his monologue as he stepped closer.

"It took me some time to find you, watch you, and take you. But after you stole from me, after you weren't there when I lost everything, I wanted you to suffer like no one ever has. I am going to enjoy cutting you limb from limb while you beg to die."

He twirled the ax in his hand to exemplify the point. Then he held it up.

"Your friend Joe, he died with this ax too. He thought he was so tough. He wasn't tough when I slammed the axe through him, and then burned his fucking coffee shop to the ground while he bled out."

He laughed again, stepping over the first pile of wood. Now the other stack was all that was between her and him.

"Stay back, please," she cried, her shoulder shuddering.

"Your friend Nora, well it sure doesn't pay to be your friend. Those women in the house. I thought blowing that stupid bitch with her own shotgun and pinning her to the wall was a nice touch, how about you?"

Laughter again, a few steps closer.

"At least appreciate my fucking master piece. I set all this up just to make you suffer. I fucking hate you so much that I did all this for you. Now that I have taken everything you care about, it's your turn to die."

Ellie's shoulders sagged as he laughed, looking defeated. He lapped up her hopelessness, sucking it in like the demon he was.

Then he stopped and cocked his head to one side, the snout of the bull mask smashed to the side from her strikes, it looked comical.

Ellie raised her chin and smiled at him. She reached up with her glass shard and cut through the rope she had pulled out of the dumbwaiter earlier, hiding in the darkness and tied off to the light fixture.

The creature looked up as the wrought iron set of bars from the window fell from the ceiling where it had been suspended by the rope over a beam, hoisted up a half hour before. The gate smashed him right in the face and sent him down in a heap.

Ellie flicked the lighter and tossed it on the wood. The

whiskey she had poured all over the wood lit immediately, all the wood going up in flames in a *whoosh!* as the flames sucked the surrounding air. Already old and ready to burn, the whiskey accelerated the flames.

"I'm not afraid of you," she yelled as she threw the now empty flask at the flames. She heard it clatter on the iron window bars as the creature began to scream in the flames. "Burn in hell, you monster!"

She reached through the door, into the room and pulled out the cylinder from the back of Nora's wheelchair. She opened the valve a small amount, and the hiss of oxygen added to the sound of the flames.

Ducking into the room, she swung it outside the door, tossing it toward the flames.

"Gift from Nora, you miserable fuck!" she yelled as she let go.

She turned away as she heard the oxygen tank hit and roll toward the flames. She hurried to the window. With the bars gone, she didn't break stride, vaulting through, and falling eight feet down to the grass. She rolled quickly, with just enough time to enjoy the crisp cold air, how fantastic it tasted. It tasted like freedom, salvation. The window was the gateway from Hell and she was back in the world. She kept rolling as the oxygen tank exploded, ripping outward and she felt a swell against the bricks and saw flames shoot out of windows on the first and second floor.

For Nora, she thought. She jumped up on the grass and began to run across the field to the yellow house, leaving the underworld, her personal hell, her labyrinth behind. Leaving the minotaur that had haunted her in the growing flames.

She headed to her beacon of salvation since the night started. The yellow house.

There must be a phone.

Her beacon of freedom, her beacon of escape, her beacon of *survival.*

Forty-One

She pushed through the door of the yellow house, a feeling of triumph coming over her. But instead of salvation, she walked into a nightmare.

The entire area was in disarray. She entered and saw books were all over the floor. The desk was in disarray, and there was blood sprayed on the walls. She remembered her abduction from here and saw her two friends, Ginny and Kayleigh, had been left here.

Ginny's head of gray hair was unrecognizable as a hatchet had parted her head right down the middle. Her entire face was covered in blood. She sat in the desk chair, her legs splayed and her head split open. Blood drenched the wall behind her and Ellie turned to throw up as she could see brain matter through the split.

As she wretched, she saw Kayleigh on the floor in a heap just a few feet away. Her eyes were open and empty, bruises in the shape of fingers around her neck. Ellie was frozen, horrified.

I have taken everything you care about.

Joe, Nora, Ginny, Carey, Kayleigh. All dead because they knew her.

No! Nora would never allow that. It isn't my fault, it's HIS fault. He's the one. And I defeated him.

She looked over them, frozen. Minutes passed until she shook herself free, and looked for a phone. There was one on the floor by the desk. She rushed over, picking it up. Pulling the handset, she put it to her ear.

Nothing. The line wasn't working or had been cut.

As if on cue, the door crashed open behind her. The creature entered, looking even more hideous. He was smoking from the flames and his minotaur mask had melted, partially to his face, partially away and revealing it. His face was burned and one eye had burst, leaking out onto his cheek, His other eye was maniacal, and filled red with blood. He screamed with rage as his burned skin hung from his jaw in chunks. The stump of his hand was burned beyond recognition and his side had been blown open from the oxygen tank explosion, exposing white ribs.

He rushed her and grabbed her around the throat with his good hand, still with his black glove on. He slammed her against the wall. He pulled his leaking and butchered face close to hers.

Zach screamed at her again, right in her face, spittle and

blood showering her. The heat from the glove burned the skin of her neck. He slammed her against the wall repeatedly, until he was satisfied she was dazed enough to finish her off. Stars were forming at the edge of her sight and she struggled to breath. She started to weakend and darkness moved in toward the center of her sight from the edges. She didn't have much time before she passed out, and then it would all be over.

Shimmering was no longer an option. She couldn't fathom how Zach was even still alive. He truly was a monster, a deal with the devil the only thing that could explain him remaining standing with all the damage done.

Then, satisfied that she was weakened enough, he let go and grabbed his ax off the table. He raised it over his head, ready to finish her off. Smoke drifted off his arm as he held it above his head and the stench of burned skin was strong in her nose.

But Ellie wasn't timid, she wasn't scared, she didn't wait for bad things to go away, and she didn't crumple to the floor. She was strong and would not go down without a fight.

She screamed back at him with the last of her breath, raking her nails across his damaged face. He screamed in new pain and faltered back a half step, the ax drifting down to his shoulder. It was a minor salvation, but she seized the opportunity. She reached out and grabbed the hatchet, yanking it from Ginny's destroyed skull. Swinging it in a short arch as Zach tried again to wind up his ax, she felt contact. The blade ripped through the side of his jaw, shredding his skin and bringing teeth right out of his mouth. It butchered his face further, widening his mouth several inches and exposing bone. His jaw dislodged on one side and hung at an unnatural angle

He screamed again, a strange throaty sound from his ruined face. The ax dropped. It clattered off the table and fell to the other side on the floor. She kicked as hard as she could in his stomach and he was thrown back against the desk.

She sprinted for the door, slipping and falling on the blood. She didn't look back as she burst from the building and began to sprint along the road.

She was gasping for breath and unsteady on her feet. She stumbled into the grass, falling and springing back up. She ran blindly on, all the abuse she had been through slowing her progress. She lurched more than ran.

She was passing the state hospital on her right, hoping to get behind the building to escape Zach. She stole a glance back and saw him emerging from the house and pursuing her. He was limping badly and holding his face. His whole body was torn apart, burned, and destroyed.

Just die you miserable fuck! she thought.

She pushed harder, passing building fifty on her right and heading back toward the end of the buildings. Suddenly, she felt like she was not in control again, like she was being guided.

She heard a whisper in her ear.

"Keep goin', the trail up ahead." She was sure it was Helen's voice, but no one was near her. She headed through an archway created by wood branches and onto the trail, the trees suddenly surrounding her.

She realized where she was going, and she pushed on.

The forest was gloomy but lightening. Daylight was pushing its way in, and gave the forest a gray overcast feel. There was no sound except her own footfalls on the path and her panting breath. She burst into the clearing with the dull, timeless haze. Limping down the path, she turned into the bit of woods on the far side of the clearing.

And then she was there.

The Hippie Tree stood before her with all its colors on the trunks. Its gnarled branches and trunks reached this way and that, running along the forest floor and arching up toward the sky.

Ellie caught her breath and looked around, trying to figure out what to do next.

Then she heard him. Zach burst through the trees and was right behind her. He had his ax poised and ready, his face a mangled, bleeding mess. He had a pained smile, broadened by the slice of the hatchet, skin swinging below his jaw line with bone and teeth exposed. His jawbone shined in the light as it swung crazily, and the blood poured down the side of his neck and body.

His one good eye was filled with hatred and death. It was red with blood filling it from the trauma. He dragged his left leg, as if it was a simple prosthetic.

"I will fucking kill you." he tried to say, though it came out garbled. Blood poured out of his mouth while he tried to speak and she could hear him choking on it.

He came. She climbed.

She sprung up the trunk of the hippie tree, climbing to get out of reach. She ran along the upward trunk, climbing to a natural platform by the curved trunk.

He came after her, awkwardly pursuing, lurching like the undead from one of Anna's movies.

She was about fifteen feet off the ground and looking for somewhere else to go. She began to panic, out of options, until she felt a soothing pat on the shoulder.

She turned and Helen was right there, smiling.

Zach climbed.

He rose so that his waist was at the platform level.

One more stride up and he would be there with her. Ellie held her breath. She looked around again for somewhere else to go. The trunk curved off to her right, Zach was at her left. She didn't think she could climb the smooth trunk higher. Her only option was to jump, but fifteen feet with a series of interwinding trunks and branches below would likely break a leg. Could she move faster on a broken leg than he could in his state?

Zach sneered at her, or maybe that was just the way his ruined face was now. He extended his arm, outstretched fingers reaching for her as she tried to make herself smaller.

As his fingers closed in on her, he started to take the last step up to the platform. He seemed to even smile, though that only made his face look more grotesque. Just before he could grab her, a branch seemed caught on his ankle. It almost seemed like it reached for him, but it must have been Ellie's eyes playing tricks. He grunted in surprise and tried to shake loose. He couldn't move. The tree didn't move and yet it seemed to pull him backwards. Zach was caught, careening to and fro. His arms waved wildly in the air and the ax fell to the ground. One side of the double headed ax embedded itself in an outstretched trunk lying on the ground, the opposite blade facing up.

Zach swung wildly, off balance. Then a look of confusion overcame his ruined face as he saw Helen.

"What the fuck?" he started to say, but Helen leaned over and smiled. Ellie and Helena reached out at the same time and gave him a gentle push on each shoulder.

He came loose from the branch on his ankle (or it opened up) at the same time. He careened over the edge. His good eye opened wide and locked with Ellie's. He tipped backwards and began to fall. Ellie watched the fear in him, the loss of control, and the realization of what was to come. In that brief moment, Ellie felt sorry for him, and for his damned soul.

Then he fell, twisting and extending his arms out in front, as if this would break his fall. His screams followed him down, then abruptly ended, capped by a violent grunt. Zach landed on the upturned blade of the ax, his full weight driving it into his chest.

Ellie heard a wet gurgling sound from Zach as he struggled to breath. He gasped, his body twitching over the ax. Then he went silent and still, along with the rest of the forest.

Ellie turned to Helen, who smiled at her.

"I gots you," she said.

Ellie smiled back, looked back to Zach, who was still unmoving below.

"Thank you - " she began, but Helen was gone.

Forty-Two

Ellie stumbled out of the woods and back through the archway, the sun beginning to rise but not quite breaking the horizon. The morning gray was beginning to brighten and life was beginning to move. She had no idea the time and her breath still frosted the way in front of her. She felt the morning cold, the beginnings of winter coming in but being held off just a bit by the fall sun rising.

She felt cold, but also warm. She felt conflicted, the death of Zach felt like a relief, and in her eyes, she should not feel that way. She should feel grief, or sorrow, but the sorrow she felt was that she *lacked* that feeling. She felt free, released.

She also felt guilt. How many had died protecting her, or for being her friend? She knew that it was not her fault, but the feeling in her stomach told her that others were lost because of her.

She passed building fifty and looked up at the towering asylum in front of her. It had been twelve hours of her life, perhaps a bit more, and yet it felt like the building was a focal point for her, like her life had been building to this apex and the Traverse City Asylum was the center of it. It was as if it had been a beacon she had been moving towards since she left the condo, since she left Shyt House, since she had left her mother behind all those years ago.

Twelve hours and yet it seemed like a home, a part of her. She came around the side of the building and could see the low standing front entrance. Oh how she missed the beauty of the towering front entrance from the Light World! Would she ever go to that place again? Was any of it real?

Maybe these thoughts caused what came next or maybe it was the proper conclusion to the entire experience. The world shifted one more time, the shimmering triggered. The tower came back into view, and the grounds shifted back to a previous era. The beauty returned to the building and life was buzzing about. Birds chirped and trees came into blossom. Ellie saw patients heading out to the farm to work.

In front of her was a beautiful car, black and sleek, parked in front of the entrance. A woman stood by the passenger side, young and dressed in a stylish blouse and large hat with a flower on it. Next to her was an older gentleman in a suit and hat, with a large brown mustache sitting under a set of wire rim glasses.

At the base of the steps, an older woman moved toward the young woman and the man with a nurse at her side. As she approached, the man opened the rear door for her. Ellie realized that he was some kind of chauffeur.

As she watched, the older woman turned to Ellie and made eye contact. A broad smile sprang from her face and she waved. The woman and the man turned, puzzled. Then the old woman started toward Ellie.

Ellie helped close the distance while the woman and the man stayed by the car.

"Who is that, Aunt Helen?" the woman called.

"An old friend," Helen called back. "Please give me jus' a minute."

"Certainly"

Helen's smile covered her whole face, which Ellie realized looked much older. Her skin was pallid and deep wrinkles lined her cheeks and eyes. Her hair had turned a deep gray, losing the shine of silver that sprinkled it when Ellie had seen her throughout the night.

"Is been a long time," Helen started.

"Has it? I just saw you by the Hippie Tree five minutes ago." Ellie responded.

She looked confused.

"You know, in the woods back there," she said, pointing. "When you helped with that monster attacking me."

Helen laughed, a deep chortle that rattled her chest.

"Hun, that wus over twenty years ago for me."

"You saved me. All night long, that monster was hunting me, playing with me, and you saved me. You gave me the courage, the friendship, and then really saved me in that tree. I am so thankful for you, Helen," Ellie said, tears filling her eyes.

"Is nuthin'" Helen said, waving her hand. "Besides, jus' like you's said all them years back. People was gettin' sick and I 'membered - dun't go near the sick people. I told myself that e'ery day that fall, and stayed safe until Christmas. I made it"

She beamed at Ellie.

"I'm-a done here now. I dun served my purpose, I think. That is my niece Sarah. My sister's daughter. She married her a nice man, and they have lotsa money. See that nice car there? BMW 335." The excitement in her voice was rising, the words drawn out.

"They's gonna take me to their place, and help me. I told them all about you. I think thas' why they cun see ya now."

"Oh, that's wonderful Helen, I am so happy for you"

"Yup, I even helped them get uh name for their daughter. Lil' one is just a month old now."

Ellie smiled at her, Helen's energy was so infectious.

"Yup, I gots them to name her after you. They named her Eleanor. They call 'er Nora, but I'll always call her Ellie."

Ellie felt a wave flow over her from head to toe, the joy from her pushed out of the way with the realization. They called her Nora.

She began to cry.

"Uh wuz wrong, hun?"

Ellie wanted to tell her that she knew Nora, that Nora saved her life multiple times just like Helen did, she wanted to tell her that she loved Nora. She wanted to tell her that just knowing that her story had been woven through time and Helen's family made her feel loved and that she mattered, her story mattered. And that feeling, after feeling like nothing, feeling like she didn't matter for so long, that she should just curl up on the floor and wait for life to pass, that feeling brought a warmth and joy to her like she had never experienced. It was a culmination of her life's transformation over the last three months, and the replaying of that transformation throughout the last twelve hours.

It brought an internal warmth that felt like a veil was lifted and God was right there smiling at her and telling her He had loved her all along, all she needed to do was uncover her eyes and look.

She reached out and hugged Helen, tears streaming down her face.

All she could say was "I love you. Thank you for everything."

Helen smiled back, and then it all melted away for the last time, the beauty of that world gone and the beauty of her world back.

The sun broke the horizon and the world lit up, a new day with a whole new chapter for her to write. The air filled with sirens as a crew of fire fighters pulled up on the scene, smoke billowing from the windows of the hospital where she had set the blaze earlier.

Anna was staring at Ellie, her mouth dropped agape when she saw her. Ellie had appeared out of nowhere as Anna had been looking at the burning asylum — one second not there, the next standing in front. Police sirens roared in the distance, closing in.

Ellie imagined what her battered body looked like to Anna, who was frozen with her mouth open.

She walked toward Anna and the firefighters, a smile on her face, blood dripping off her finger tips, her body beaten and bruised but her spirit light and joyful.

She didn't feel defeated, she saw the world for what it was.

She felt free, more than she ever had. She had faced the Devil in his own Hell, and won. She was strong, she believed she could do anything.

Her smile grew larger as she reached Anna, who looked at her horrified.

Nora would have been proud.

She smiled at Anna and said the first thing that came to her mind,

"Hey friend. I am starved, can we get some wings?"

Epilogue

Thanksgiving had lacked the joy at *Stronger Together* that it usually held, though Anna and Ellie had delivered on the menu. The loss of Carey and Ginny had cast a dismal air over the festivities. The story had broken out, perhaps some blamed Ellie, perhaps not. She had a few sideways glances from some that said they probably did whether they meant to or not. Ellie understood. Despite knowing that there was nothing more she could have done, she carried guilt at their circumstances.

The police had completed the investigation and found Zach's body. The asylum's outermost wing had burned significantly before the firefighters got it under control, but the rest of the building was unfettered. News had also broken that a development group was going to restore a lot of the buildings on the campus and turn it into a destination. Ellie didn't care for that idea, but she kept her opinions to herself.

She had sat with the police and told her story, leaving out all the supernatural events of the Hippie Tree, Helen, and flipping through time. There were times that she barely believed it herself. Anna had heard the altered version of the story and told her that she knew there was more to tell. Ellie had literally appeared out of thin air in front of the asylum while Anna was watching it burn, for crying out loud. Ellie told her she would tell her more over dinner one day, and Anna had immediately found a day. It was looming after this meeting with these estate lawyers that she was asked to attend.

The police had found all the evidence in the cottage of Zach. He had used wireless cameras and speakers, recovered all through the asylum. They found all the evidence of his stalking. Zach was obsessed with finding Ellie after she left. It was out of pure hatred at her standing up to him, and projection from the rest of his life falling apart. The police found that he had used his police friend in narcotics to run down leads he dredged up to find Ellie. They also connected him to the murder after his friend told him he couldn't do it anymore. He was under multiple investigations and he had to lay low if he wanted any shot of keeping his badge.

Zach had lost his temper and killed his friend. He had dug up enough to go on and felt like he had narrowed it down. After he killed his boss at the financial firm and he found out he was being left to swing in the wind for the SEC investigation, he had tried to get Joe to connect the final dots. Instead, he had killed Joe, ransacked the coffee shop and burned it.

The police were unclear as to whether he had figured out where Ellie was, visited multiple locations, or just gotten lucky, but a few days after the coffee shop fire, he had shown up in Traverse City. He had stalked Ellie for almost two weeks, setting up his labyrinth of horrors in the vacant asylum. They found two bums murdered and dumped out back, probably because they tried to seek shelter in the asylum and interrupted his work.

All in all, Zach had killed ten people before Ellie had taken him out. She was viewed as a hero, and the police closed the case.

Ellie, for her part, was recovering. Her spirit was fine, but her body still had some healing to do. She had multiple broken ribs and a concussion. The headaches were lessening in frequency and intensity, and her several different sets of stitches had been taken out. Honestly, the nail that was ripped off digging through the fallen tunnel was the worst part, still sensitive to the touch and she managed to catch it on damn near everything.

The door to the office opened and a kind lady beckoned her in from behind reading glasses on her narrow nose. Her hair was gray and up in a bun and Ellie immediately thought of her as a librarian. Entering the room, there was a lawyer sitting there along with the director of Bay View Independent Living Center. Nurse Emily was also there, and another attorney stood off in the corner, a silent witness to the proceedings.

"Are you Ellie Sloan?" the lawyer asked. He was a stout man with a bald head and bushy hair on the sides. He had a full but neatly trimmed beard that had more gray in it than brown.

She nodded, feeling out of place.

"As you may or may not know, Mrs. Nora Cahill was quite a successful lady. She came from a successful family and utilized her resources to create an empire. Her final net worth across all her assets as of this morning is just over two hundred million dollars. I will now read through her last will and testament."

Ellie was confused. First, she really wasn't sure why she was there, and second, she couldn't even understand that sum of money, let alone why a woman in Bay View would have that. She remembered Nora talking about her family being all gone. She remembered Nora saying she had plenty of money, and realizing the connection, that Helen's niece was very well off. Apparently Nora had used that to create her own success. And, as Nora had said, she was *loaded*.

Her mind swirled, missing her friend and wishing she could sink further into the chair. She heard bits and pieces such as:

"Bay View Independent Living Center will have a trust created with ten million dollars for the purpose of resident care, facilities, and events to bring joy to the residents as long as Mrs. Hall remains employed as the director or in some official leadership capacity, and will remain only after her willing departure, at which time five hundred thousand will be transferred to Mrs. Hall's next venture."

"Mrs. Hall will be the benefactor of the estate on Sutton's Bay and ..."

"Ms. Dalton will be the benefactor of ..."

Ellie raised her head at that one and saw Emily cover her mouth in shock.

"Ms. Winstadt will be the benefactor of fifteen thousand dollars in cash for use of a medical procedure to remove the stick from her ass – apologies, I have to read this verbatim – or for whatever purpose she deems fit."

Ellie chuckled, and felt close to Nora. She could just about hear that in Nora's voice. *Nurse Bitchy.*

Lost in thought, she realized everyone was looking at her. She panicked for a moment and realized that the lawyer had just said her name.

"I'm sorry, I was just lost in thought. What did you ask?"

"Young lady, I didn't ask anything. That last line was about you, and I wanted to make sure you heard me. 'The remaining assets, any and all and without restriction, are to be bestowed to Ellie Sloan, the closest thing to family I have,'" the lawyer looked up over the rims of his glasses. "As of this morning, the total value of all the assets amounts to one hundred and eighty nine million dollars."

Ellie looked around the room.

"I – I'm sorry, I don't really understand," she stammered.

"Mrs. Cahill, Nora, left you all of that. Her properties, her stocks, everything else in her portfolio, everything else she owned, she left to you," the lawyer said.

The room spun around and Ellie was speechless.

"I — I don't know what to do with all that," she managed to say. She felt her cheeks burning red. "I'd just rather have a cup of coffee with her instead." Tears began streaming down her cheeks, she wiped them quickly, but more followed.

A gentle hand rubbed her shoulder. She turned to see Emily there, ready to comfort her.

"Well, I believe she anticipated that as well," the lawyer said. "She left this for you too."

He stood and came around the desk, handing her a sealed envelope.

"We'll give you the office," he said, leading everyone outside the door.

She turned the envelope over in her hands. It was creamed colored and had a gold sticker sealing it. She peeled it open and unfolded the single page. The letter wasn't long, but it quickly brought tears to her eyes:

> *Ellie,*
>
> *Don't you dare shed a tear for me, I was blessed with a great life. Knowing you was a great part of it. I knew you from when I was just a child, my favorite aunt, Aunt Helen, used to talk about your great battles against the monster. These stories gave me strength as a child, and, you might say, were a major contributor to my success throughout my life. So before you take a moment to feel like what I have passed on to you is undeserved, it isn't.*
>
> *I felt a connection with you from the moment we met a few months ago, though it didn't even occur to me at the time that you were the Ellie from Aunt Helen's stories. In fact, I had discounted those as just great, heroic stories from a slightly crazy lady. Last*

week when you visited the tree, though, that's when I knew and it all came flooding back.

I should let you know that Aunt Helen thought highly of you, and told us how you saved her during the flu epidemic. She said you used to appear out of nowhere and disappear just the same. She thought you were a ghost at first, but then she realized you were her Angel. Aunt Helen lived a long life with our family.

You were my Angel as well, dear, and you lit up the last few months of my life in ways you cannot even imagine and, knowing your humility, you will not acknowledge.

As you now know, I have left you quite a sum of money. I have complete faith you will use this to continue to bless the world, to be a humble angel and servant of God. You may also realize now that Stronger Together is mine, Carey runs it beautifully but I started it and I fund it. I am not telling you this to tell you what to do, but knowing you the way I do, I am sure you will stay involved with the organization.

Finally, I will remind you that your battles on this earth aren't finished. More trials will inevitably come your way. Remain righteous, lead with love, but when you have to fight, fight like you're the third monkey on the ramp to Noah's ark..

... And baby, it's starting to rain.

Love,

Nora

Tears dropped to the letter, wetting the paper, and she cried. Trying to stifle the sounds, she rose and went to the door. Opening it, she saw the crowd from the will reading in the office had been joined by a series of people from *Stronger Together*, including Anna. They all had been very worried about what would come of the organization with Carey and Ginny gone. Ironically, it had been the newest member, Ellie, who they had all looked to for reassurance, some due to a respect for the strength it took to survive what she had been through and others perhaps because they saw it as her fault that the leadership void existed.

Everyone watched her with anticipation.

She cleared her throat.

"Umm, sorry, I am not very good at this, and I don't really know what to say. I guess all I can say is I love you all, you are my family, and Nora's generosity will continue. I guess I will be the benefactor of *Stronger Together* but we will all do it together. The legacy of Carey, Ginny, and Nora will live on."

Everyone cheered.

Ellie turned to Anna.

"I am going to need some serious help on all this," Ellie said, waving her arms.

"You always have," Anna replied with a grin.

Ellie smiled and thought, *serving and fulfilling my purpose. Here it is.*

"C'mon, let's get some wings," Anna said, patting her on the back.

"Always a good plan," Ellie smiled and followed her out.

Acknowledgements

First, I would like to thank my publisher, Facing Goliath Publishing. The team there was great through the process, not too mention their great coffee.

A special thank you to the people of *The Village at Grand Traverse Commons*, and our tour guide when we toured the Traverse City State Hospital, its history, and its tunnels. I took many liberties for the sake of this story, but tried to remain as accurate with the history as I could. Apologies for any errors. Also, the group restoring the facility that has made it into shops, restaurants, and condos. Ellie may not like that idea due to her connection, but it has been done beautifully.

I would also like to thank my daughter for inspiring me to pick up writing again. I wrote a lot when I was a kid, and gave it up to pursue other endeavors as I became older. Her fearlessness when it comes to putting herself out there, be it in her many sports, at school, or putting words on the page, has inspired me to not leave my words to myself, but publish them in hopes that others may enjoy a story as much as I do.

I would also like to acknowledge other authors who don't know how much they inspired me, but authors such as CJ Box, Brad Taylor, Vine Flynn, Mark Greaney, Stephen Hunter, Kyle Mills, Alexander Dumas, and Gregg Hurwitz have kept me entertained for years. Finally, Ryan Steck, a.k.a. The Real Book Spy, for simply interacting with me through my process on Twitter / X; I am certain he doesn't know how much his small interactions encouraged me to get over the finish line and start my next two novels. If you are not reading these author's stories, I strongly encourage you to do so.

I would like to thank my amazing wife, all my joy stems from the great family God has blessed me with, and she's the rock of it. She inspires me to be a better man every day.

I feel so incredibly blessed by God to have the opportunity to do all the things in my life I do, to share it with my family, and now to share my words with you, my readers (hopefully its plural...).

Thank you for sharing your mind, your couch, your evenings with me, Ellie, and the Minotaur.